A BEAUTIFUL FAMILY

Marilyn Cohen de Villiers

ISBN 978-0-620-59647-3
eISBN 978-0-620-59648-0

Published by Mapolaje Publishers

Edited by Vanessa Finaughty
Cover design by Francois Engelbrecht

Website: www.marilyncohendevilliers.com
Email: marilyncohendevilliers@mweb.co.za

'Do not go about spreading slander among your people'
Leviticus 19:16

PART 1
TRACY

CHAPTER 1
JOHANNESBURG, 2012

'Hey... T.T.'

Tracy looked across the newsroom at Tshepo Buthelezi, the burly political editor.

'Hey, T.T. Come here.'

She frowned. She hated her newsroom nickname. It had been bestowed on her – quite maliciously, she suspected – by the news editor, Prince Tshukudu, almost as soon as she'd introduced herself.

'So,' he'd sneered, staring at her chest before looking up at her face. 'They finally found someone to tick as many of our employment equity boxes as possible in one skinny package. Female, tick; white, tick; a religious minority – you're Jewish, aren't you?'

She'd nodded, startled at being so quickly, and easily, identified.

'So, Jewish, tick. Disabled, tick.' He'd giggled, indicating her glasses. 'You a lesbian?'

She'd gaped.

'Well, are you?' he'd demanded. 'If you are, we can tick

the sexual orientation box too... No? Too bad. Thought you'd be company for Thomas. Oh well, they haven't done too badly with their token appointment this time. Four out of five ticks should be great for our equity scorecard. Hey, everyone,' he'd yelled out to the newsroom, 'meet Tracy, our new token.'

That had been nearly four months ago and the stupid name had stuck. Token Tracy – T.T. for short. It didn't make it any better that most of her new colleagues also had nicknames. Prince – Mafuta to his subordinates – called Tshepo 'the Nigerian', either because of his dark complexion or to cast aspersions on his honesty; Tracy wasn't sure. His more respectful colleagues called him Kingmaker because of his reputed influence in the highest echelons in the ruling African National Congress.

Now Kingmaker asked her, 'You know a dude called Alan Silverman?'

She shook her head.

'You must know him – he's Jewish.'

'So are fifty thousand or so other people in Johannesburg.'

'Oh don't be such a smartarse.'

Tracy bristled, and then grinned at him. He was a good guy, Kingmaker, even if he teased her all the time. It was all good natured fun and, anyway, he was one of the few in the newsroom who bothered to speak to her, notwithstanding that she was, after all, just a novice.

'How come you don't know him? He's apparently a main man among your people,' Kingmaker said.

'They're not "my people". And I suppose you know every Zulu – or Nigerian – in Jo'burg too.'

'Sho – you are being cheeky today, aren't you?'

'Sorry. Okay, I know of him. Who doesn't? I went to school with his kids.'

'And?' Kingmaker waited.

'And nothing. All I know about him is that he's rich. They say he donates a whack of money – anonymously, of course – to the Chev every year.'

Kingmaker raised his eyebrows.

'The Chev. You know – the Chevrah Kadisha – the Jewish Helping Hand Society. It's the main Jewish charity organisation. For Jews, by Jews.'

'I didn't think you Jews needed charity.'

'Very funny.' Tracy sniffed, pretending to be annoyed.

'Silverman?' Kingmaker asked.

'I've never actually met him, not properly.'

'You sure? What about his wife?'

'Nah. Mrs Silverman was never around much at school. She certainly never stooped to help out in the tuck shop like the other moms. I saw her last week, though, at Moo-z bakery in the Sandringham strip, opposite Sandringham Gardens – the Jewish old age home. There's a whole bunch of kosher shops there and she was shopping for bagels and cheese cake. Not that she ever eats them, I shouldn't think – she's skinny as a rake. And dressed to kill. Anyway, why're you so interested? Jewish high society's hardly your beat. I'd have thought you'd

8

be more into Mrs Sexwale and Mrs Ramaphosa... and Mrs...
the one married to that mega rich *oke* – Patrick something...?'

'Patrice. Patrice Motsepe. Anyway, I can't tell you what's
going on, but something is. I'm hearing the name Alan
Silverman a lot lately. There's talk – totally off the record, of
course – that he's been spreading his generosity around a hell
of a lot more than before. They say he's trying to buy his way
back into ANC inner circles now that Thabo has gone... and
with the ANC's National Conference coming up in December.
Anyway, he needs watching. '

'*Ja*, of course he does.' Tracy dripped sarcasm. 'He's
Jewish; he's white; he's rich – he must be up to something.'
She widened her eyes, put her finger over her lips and
whispered, 'Shh. He's probably involved in a Zionist plot to
get all the Muslims out of government and replace them with
Jews. Think what that would do to our foreign policy towards
Israel.'

Kingmaker laughed. 'We're more likely to see Thabo back
on the throne.'

Tracy relented. 'Look, if you like, I'll ask my mom to keep an
eye out for any stories about the über-rich, gorgeous Silvermans
in the *Jewish Voice*. Okay? But it will probably only be society
stuff – although, if I remember correctly, Mr Silverman won the
Jewish Businessman of the Year Award a couple of years ago. I
think. I'm not really into that sort of thing.'

***

A few weeks later, Kingmaker waved at Tracy from Mpho, the crime reporter's, desk.

'I knew it. I knew it. I told you... I told you something was going to happen with your people,' Kingmaker said triumphantly as she made her way across the newsroom to the window behind the big TV stand. Mpho spent a lot of time gazing out at the brick wall of the neighbouring building as he chatted on the phone to his many and varied sources.

'I don't have any "people",' Tracy said.

'Tell her, Mpho.'

Mpho was irritated. 'It's just another dead body in Jozi. Even the gated, leafy suburbs get them occasionally. Anyway, you know you're not supposed to read my notes over my shoulder,' he whined at Kingmaker. 'This isn't a fucking story. Fourteen thousand people are murdered in South Africa every year. And they're not even sure this is a murder. It's just some dead white lady.'

'Not just any lady – one of the chosen,' Kingmaker said.

'Who's dead?'

'A Mrs Brenda Silverman,' Mpho said. 'Found dead in her bed this morning. No big deal….'

'Alan Silverman's wife? Shit! She wasn't very old. How did she die?' Tracy asked.

'No idea,' Mpho replied, and then looked down at his Rolex. 'Look, you're not busy with anything, are you? You can handle it. I've got a really important meeting across the road with a source about a big corruption story I'm working on.'

Tracy hesitated. She still had to finish the story Mafuta had gleefully assigned to her that morning – the outbreak of lice at a suburban nursery school. The white parents were blaming the black children while the black parents said… well, that was the problem; she hadn't managed to speak to any black parents.

She was also waiting for someone from the Health Department as well as the Education Department to get back to her with answers to her questions about the prevalence of lice in Johannesburg schools – but she wasn't holding her breath. She'd be lucky if they responded in the next month – probably with a comment that "this information is extremely sensitive and, therefore, cannot be made public". Translated, it meant they didn't have a clue. However, good journalist that she aspired to be, she was willing to go through the motions. Still, this could be her first big story. Brenda Silverman dead! Wow.

'Go, go, go,' Kingmaker said. 'I'll tell Mafuta and the editor I said you should go – the body being Jewish and everything.'

She weighed up her options. The bloody lice story would probably be spiked, but Mafuta would scream and yell if she failed to submit it. Or she could follow up on a possible murder of a relatively prominent person. She grabbed her bag and tatty shorthand notebook and loped down the corridor to the photographers' office. No one there. Typical.

She hurried to the pub in the local brothel across the road. Three of her reporter colleagues and a couple of photographers looked at her impassively, then turned their attention back to their beers and the replay of an old Kaiser Chiefs-Pirates game on the flickering TV in the corner.

'Got a possible murder – body's still at the scene,' Tracy announced. 'Who's coming with me?'

No one moved. Then Precious sighed, picked up her camera bag and followed her back across the road and into the car pool office.

After yet another altercation with the car pool manager over the correct documentation required to get a car – they had at least one run-in every day – Tracy took her beloved Buttercup that she'd bought just last month from Preloved Cars in Jules Street. Only 120,000 kilometres on the clock, just one old lady driver and an absolute bargain, the salesman – being a second-hand car salesman – had lied.

'Are we going to Jewish?' Precious asked as Buttercup crawled down Death Bend on Louis Botha Avenue.

Minibus taxis flew past, clearly not at all daunted by the name of that particular stretch of the notorious road, tearing through the traffic to get from Hillbrow to Alexandra Township as quickly as possible.

'Jewish?'

'You know. Jewish. My mother works in Jewish – at Mr Greenberg's house. I usually take the taxi to Alex to get there when I go visit her. I get off in Jewish.'

'There's no such place as Jewish,' Tracy snorted. 'Is that what you call this area? That's so funny. I grew up near here. We still live here – although obviously not in the same suburb as the Silvermans.'

CHAPTER 2

Tracy waited as the taxi that had cut her off at the traffic light trundled across the busy intersection. She followed it impatiently into Hathorn Avenue and slammed on brakes as the taxi stopped dead in its tracks to drop off a passenger. Fuming, she manhandled Buttercup around the minibus and headed towards Sandringham.

She pondered the angle to take on the story. Mpho had said that the cops had told him that they weren't sure if there had been any foul play. However, there had to have been. Brenda Silverman wasn't very old. She was probably younger than her mom, Maxine. The Silverman family had apparently first called Hatzollah, the Jewish paramedics, and the armed response – and only then did someone think to call the cops.

Tracy drove through high-walled, Jacaranda-lined streets and finally drew to a stop at a security boom where she had to argue with the guard about signing a register before being allowed through. Shit, he was stubborn. So she signed the book "Minnie Mouse, 011 555 6789". The guard studied her entry dubiously, then painstakingly copied her car registration number next to her scrawled signature.

She gunned Buttercup through the boom, bounced over the traffic calming bumps and wound her way through the quiet, shady streets, stopping outside an imposingly large house with a very high white wall.

She extricated herself from the car and strode towards a pair of high, intricately designed wrought iron gates. Precious scrambled after her. A uniformed man emerged from the guardhouse.

'You not allowed here. Go away.' He walked threateningly towards them.

Precious shrank back.

'This is a public pavement and a public street. I can be here. I want to speak to Mr Silverman.' Tracy heard her voice tremble. Just a little.

A big black 4x4 vehicle loomed up. Two large, black, heavily armed private security men emerged. 'You not allowed here.' They cradled their automatic rifles in their arms. 'Go.'

Precious turned, as if to run. Tracy grabbed her arm and stood her ground. 'I'm not going anywhere. I have as much right to be here as you do.'

One guard spoke into his radio and glared at her. Tracy glared back. The pedestrian gate at the side of the wrought iron driveway gates opened and a police officer approached them.

Tracy held out her press card for his inspection. 'Tracy

Jacobs. *Daily Express*. I'd like to go in and speak to Mr Silverman.'

'The family's traumatised enough. Leave them alone,' the officer said. 'All I can tell you at this stage is that Mrs Silverman was found this morning, in her bedroom. That's it. There'll be an autopsy and probably an inquest to determine the cause of death. You can stand out here if you must, but go through these gates, and I'll arrest you.'

***

Tracy looked down the long driveway to the white, double-storey Georgian house. It didn't look as if it had changed at all from the night of Yair's Barmitzvah party. Jeez, that was ten years ago already.

'Wonder what that house is like inside,' Precious said. 'It's much fancier than Mr Greenberg's.'

'It's huge, a bit like a hotel.'

'You been in there?' Precious' eyes were enormous. 'You didn't say you were friends with them.'

'I'm not. I just went there once, for Yair – the son's – Barmitzvah party. A long time ago.'

She had been surprised, and bloody thrilled, to receive her invitation, because she hadn't thought Yair Silverman knew she existed. She hadn't told her mom when she'd found out that the entire Grade 8 year – all two hundred kids – had also been invited. Maxine had been so excited that her daughter was going to be mixing in Silverman circles. She had dragged Tracy to the hairdresser that morning to try to get some of the frizz out of her hair, and had even let her wear some make-up to cover her freckles. But Tracy had drawn the line at the pretty pink dress Maxine had wanted to buy for her. Her mom was always trying to dress her in pink.

***

At the sound of the gates opening, Tracy looked up. A large black Mercedes, escorted by three police vehicles with flashing blue lights, shot out. The convoy turned right and wailed away.

'Hey, did you see who that was?'

Precious shook her braids.

'I swear that was that new MEC. What's his name again? Sipho something... Sipho Mphahlale. What the fuck was he doing here? Did you get a pic?'

'No, you locked my camera in the boot.'

'Jesus, Precious. Why's your camera still...? Here are the keys. Get the damn thing and do your job.'

The private security guard walked threateningly towards them. 'No photos,' he snarled.

Tracy looked appealingly at the police officer.

'You can take photographs outside the house. But nothing else.'

Everything looked very quiet down at the house. A couple

of police cars and a grey mortuary van stood in the driveway. As Precious snapped away, Tracy called Kingmaker and told him about her sighting.

'I'll check it out,' Kingmaker promised.

He called back fifteen minutes later. 'The MEC's office denies he's been at the Silverman house. Did you get a pic of him?'

Tracy glared at Precious. 'No.'

'You sure it was him? One darkie looks pretty much like another to you lot.'

'Don't be ridiculous. Anyway, I saw the MEC at a function last week. It was him. And, if it wasn't, then who was in that blue light brigade? I'm coming back to the office. There's not much to report here.'

Mpho was right. So far, it really wasn't much of a story at all.

***

The next morning, Tracy tottered into the kitchen, still pulling her dressing gown on over her shortie pyjamas. She was not a morning person. Her mom was. Despite her girls' night out last night, Maxine was already up, sitting at the table paging through the newspaper. The kettle was warm, but Tracy switched it on and added a heaped spoon of Ricoffy and two of sugar to her Barbie mug while it boiled again.

'Morning, Mom. What's the front page lead today?'

'I didn't read it. Something about some new ANC corruption thing again. I'll let you have the paper in a minute.'

The kettle clicked off and Tracy poured the bubbling water into the mug. She dunked a buttermilk rusk, impatient for the coffee to cool. Kingmaker hadn't told her he was working on anything big. Must be a bit of the same old, same old...

'Wow, Trace – listen to this!' Maxine was pointing at a story at the bottom of the page.

PROMINENT JOHANNESBURG SOCIALITE DIES

By Tracy Jacobs

The wife of Alan Silverman (50), one of Johannesburg's leading property tycoons, died at the family's palatial home in northern Johannesburg yesterday.

Police spokesperson, Captain Beauty Mogane, told the *Daily Express* that Mrs Brenda Silverman (44) was found in her bed by the domestic worker.

'There was no sign of a struggle or forced entry. We don't know what caused her death. It was a complete shock to the family, because she had been in excellent health.'

According to her family, Mrs Silverman went to bed at 10pm the previous night. Mr Silverman never noticed anything wrong when he left for the office in the morning, but the domestic worker was unable to wake her when she took her a cup of coffee at around 9am.

An autopsy is expected to be held as soon as possible to determine the cause of death.

Mr Silverman is believed to have close ties to the ruling ANC.

A prominent member of the Gauteng provincial legislature and MEC for Housing, Mr Sipho Mphahlale, was spotted leaving the Silverman home after paying his respects to the family yesterday.

After refusing to serve in the apartheid Defence Force, Mr Silverman fled the country in the 1980s. He is said to have met many of today's leading political figures while in exile.

He and Mrs Silverman, who had been married for more than 20 years, returned to South Africa before the first democratic elections in 1994.

He started his property development business, Silver Properties, soon thereafter. It has been billed as one of the country's largest listed property development and investment companies although its share price has been under pressure for the past few months and the company failed to declare a dividend at the close of its last financial year.

Mr Silverman, an active member of the Jewish community, was named as the South African Jewish Businessman of the Year some years ago.

Mrs Silverman was said to be involved in charity work for Johannesburg's underprivileged. Despite being an Orthodox Jewess, which required her to dress modestly and cover her hair, Mrs Silverman once featured in South African society's "Best Dressed" lists.

Mrs Silverman is survived by her husband and three children, twins Yair and Aviva (23), and Zivah (17).

Details of the funeral arrangements have not yet been made public, but Mrs Silverman is likely to be laid to rest at West Park Jewish Cemetery as soon as the autopsy is complete, in accordance with Jewish tradition.

Tracy sighed, not bothering to interrupt as her mother read her story to her. Maxine still didn't associate the "by Tracy Jacobs" by-line with her daughter.

'Heavens! Trace, did you know about this?'

'Mom, look at the by-line. It's my story.'

'So why didn't you tell me last night before I went out? The girls would have wanted to know.'

Tracy smiled to herself. Maxine would have loved to be able to break the news – and be the centre of attention, no doubt embellishing every little detail with her journalist daughter's "inside" information.

'I didn't think you'd be interested,' she teased.

'Of course I'm interested. She was so young. What happened?'

'I don't know.'

Maxine looked up from her third dissection of the story. 'Come on, sweetie, you can tell me. There must be more to it than what's in the paper. Surely.'

'Why? What have you heard?'

'Well, I didn't know her very well.'

'Oh, pu-leeze. You didn't know her at all.'

'Well, maybe we weren't close. Now that I think about it, there was something about her in the *Jewish Voice* a while back – some row or other at some function. I can't remember the details, but I remember thinking she'd behaved very stupidly and that she'd better be careful.'

'Really? You didn't tell me.'

'It was a while ago, sweetie. I think you were still at university. Anyway, you wouldn't have been interested in Brenda. I thought you were only interested in the son. Didn't he invite you out once?'

Tracy flushed, got up from the table and put Barbie in the

dishwasher.

'I've got to get to work early, Mom. I'll shower first, okay? But if you hear anything more, let me know.' Maxine had an amazing network of contacts across the community. If anything happened, she would know. She was an even better source of gossip than the Johannesburg Jewish Community Forum website.

CHAPTER 3

Tracy steered Buttercup through the stone gateway at West Park Jewish Cemetery and the little car laboured up the tree-lined road leading to the memorial hall.

She parked under one of the plane trees and climbed out. Buttercup's aircon was temperamental and the shade should help to ensure they didn't bake after the funeral. You couldn't drive in that part of Jo'burg with your windows open. You didn't drive in any part of Jo'burg with open windows.

'Take your cameras,' she told Precious and turned to Kingmaker, who was laughing, his merriment an affront to the regimented ranks of grey granite tombstones at attention behind a low diamond-wire fence.

'What's so funny?'

'Eish, T.T., I didn't know you had a skirt. I'd like to say it looks good on you, but, shit man, it's horrible.'

She flushed and yanked at the black garment, pulling it lower on her hips, where it was held in place by a red belt. Her legs glowed lily white in the gap between the tops of her ankle boots and the hem of the skirt. Maxine had only told her about Brenda Silverman's funeral late last night when she had got home from book club, so she hadn't had time to organise a decent skirt. She'd hauled one out of her mother's wardrobe this morning. She knew it looked ridiculous on her, but she wanted to speak to Alan Silverman – if possible – and he wouldn't be happy talking to a woman in pants. Not at his wife's funeral.

'Here, I've got my grandpa's old *yarmulke* for you. Put it on.'

She handed the blue skullcap to Kingmaker. The silver braid was coming loose, and it was quite grubby. Grandpa had worn it for as long as she could remember, keeping it in a tatty blue velvet bag along with his old fringed *tallis* and taking it out for *Shabbos* and holidays, weddings and funerals. 'It's the only one that stays on my head,' he'd always said when they tried to persuade him to get a new one. They'd bought him a new one for his funeral, and held it in place with his yellowing *tallis* prayer shawl.

She marched up the long, wide stairway to the open, tiled veranda and then into the empty memorial hall foyer. Precious scampered after her. Kingmaker strolled along behind. Their footsteps echoed on the highly polished parquet floor. Kingmaker examined the lists and lists of names etched in gold on the wooden boards that lined the walls.

'So now what?'

'Now we wait, here, where we can see everyone who arrives.' Tracy positioned herself at the top of the stairs. 'The

23

family should be here soon, if they aren't here already. I remember at my grandfather's funeral we had to come early to hand over the death certificate and his ID book. The body's probably already here – in that room over there.'

'What's that?' Precious pointed at a fenced off area with six white hands holding up six ram's horn *shofars* to form three archways.

'It's the memorial to the six million,' Tracy said.

'Six million what?'

'Jews. The Holocaust?'

Precious stared at her.

'Never mind.'

A large silver Bentley swept up the road, almost to the foot of the stairs. Alan Silverman, Yair and Zivah emerged. The men were wearing black suits, open-neck white shirts and wide-brimmed black hats. The older man was tall, good looking in a distinguished kind of way, with thick grey hair just visible under his hat. Little Zivah was in a long-sleeved white blouse, buttoned up to the neck and tucked into her long white skirt. A white Alice band held her long blonde hair back. She looked like a wraith, her unseeing dark eyes enormous in her pinched, deathly pale face. She looked a lot younger than seventeen – or was she eighteen now? Reports differed.

Yair's hair, dark like his late mother's, curled up at the collar. Like his father, he was unshaven. He looked briefly at Tracy's little team waiting silently at the top of the stairs, and then followed his father and sister into a room just off the foyer. Zivah was clinging to her father's hand.

Tracy's heart was thumping. Shit, she'd thought she was over her schoolgirl crush. But he'd always been pretty nice to her, not like the other boys… and certainly not like his snooty twin, Aviva. He'd even apologised at school that Monday after his Barmitzvah party, for the way the other kids had teased her.

***

'I thought you were going to speak to Silverman,' Kingmaker hissed at her.

'Not now,' Tracy hissed back. 'There'll be time later – or maybe at prayers tonight.'

More cars were driving up through the stone gateposts. A minibus taxi – as incongruous as Buttercup among the 4×4s and Mercs – snorted its way to the foot of the stairs and discharged a crowd of black women. They joined the throng climbing up to the hall.

'Look who's arrived,' said Kingmaker. 'That's the first ANC person I've seen so far.'

'Where?' Tracy looked around. 'I don't see anyone from the ANC.'

'That's because you're looking for darkies. There are also whites in the ANC – and that's one of them.' He indicated a bird-like woman dressed in a brown jacket, black slacks and sensible black shoes. Her grey hair, cropped off just below her chin, looked like an old warrior helmet. 'Mrs Annette Davies-Smedley. She must have come up from Cape Town especially because Parliament's in session.'

Tracy tugged at Kingmaker's sleeve. 'Let's get inside. I want to be as close as possible to the front so we can see who gets called as pallbearers.'

'The family, surely?'

'No, every man here can be a pallbearer. The family usually gives the Chevrah people a list of names to be called out – it's as bad as arranging the seating at a wedding. I've heard of family feuds resulting from that list if one person gets called out before another, or worse, gets left off. But, as your name isn't likely to be called out, you can always volunteer as a pallbearer at the end.'

'No thanks.' Kingmaker shivered.

A hush fell over the waiting crowd as a door opened and the three Silvermans emerged, the front of their shirts weeping around jagged rips. White undershirts preserved their modesty. The men looked grim. Zivah looked on the verge of collapse. Yair put his arm around her, but she shrugged it away and clung to her father.

'Shit, what happened to them?' Kingmaker muttered in her ear.

'They always tear the clothing of the chief mourners. My mom wore her oldest shirt to my grandpa's funeral. They ripped it so badly she couldn't even give it away afterwards.'

Suddenly, a pair of double doors banged open and a pale

wooden coffin draped in black cloth was wheeled into the foyer by six Chevrah men. Alan, his arm around Zivah, fell in behind. Yair followed, on Zivah's other side. The men hauled the coffin into the memorial hall. The crowd surged forward, filling the hall and overflowing back into the foyer. Sun poured through the high, arched windows and framed the coffin.

'That's a crappy coffin. You'd think the Silvermans could afford something better,' Kingmaker muttered.

Tracy grinned. 'We all get buried in the same pine box – rich and poor. Death is a great leveller.'

'You sure it's not just Jews being Jews?' Kingmaker asked.

She glared at him.

A tall, bearded rabbi began to chant.

'What's he saying?' Kingmaker whispered.

'Dunno. Shh.'

The rabbi fell silent and one of the Chevrah men stepped forward with a sheet of paper in his hand and called out, 'Gary James.'

An elderly man shuffled forward and moved to the front of the trolley. He looked like that big deal at the Zionist Federation, but she wasn't sure. She wrote down his name.

'Hedley Finkelstein, Lawrie Greenblatt, Arno van Zyl…'

As their names were called, men emerged from the crowd and took up a position around the coffin. Then the procession started moving, out of the far side of the hall and up a tarred pathway between row upon orderly row of closely packed tombstones, grim grey memorials to the departed. They had

27

gone no further than ten metres, or so it seemed, when the procession stopped and the eight pallbearers stepped aside. The man with the list called out more names and another eight men stepped forward. Again and again, the procession stopped, the rabbi chanted, names were called out and the pallbearers changed. Some of the names were familiar to her – pillars of the Jewish community, captains of industry.

'Who's he?' Tracy asked Kingmaker when a black man stepped forward to act as a pallbearer.

'Not sure – I think he's something at Luthuli House. He looks vaguely familiar,' Kingmaker whispered back. 'Odd that there are not more ANC luminaries here. I didn't expect the president, but some ministers or at least some of the Gauteng ANC elite. Very, very odd.'

'Maybe they got lost – or are just keeping African time,' she suggested.

It was Kingmaker's turn to glare.

'Or maybe the Jewish grapevine isn't in tune with yours and they don't know about it.'

The procession stopped again. The Chevrah men moved forward and manhandled the coffin trolley across a stretch of stony ground to an open grave. They lifted the coffin onto straps held in place across the grave by a rectangular frame, and, slowly, the grave swallowed the pale coffin. The men pulled up the straps and walked away. Alan and Zivah moved to the graveside, his arm around her. Yair stood, solitary and inscrutable, a little to the side. The crowd swirled forward.

The sun beat down and a young woman – her hair covered in a headscarf – opened an umbrella and held it up to shade the visibly shaking Zivah.

The rabbi chanted again. Alan and Yair stepped forward and, without looking at each other, quietly chanted, '*Yit'gadal v'yit'kadash sh'mei raba...*'

'What they saying?' Kingmaker muttered into her ear.

'It's the mourner's *kaddish* – the prayer for the dead.'

The rabbi picked up a spade, dug it into the red earth piled up next to the grave and threw it onto the coffin. *Thump.* The crowd shuddered. Zivah uttered a high, thin wail and stumbled forward. Yair grabbed her and pulled her into his side, his arm around her shaking shoulders. The rabbi thumped in two more loads, then planted the spade into the sand. Alan took it and gingerly trickled three shovels of the red earth down the side of the grave. He planted the spade in the pile of sand and Yair handed Zivah over to him, stepped forward and added three tiny shovel loads into the grave. One by one, men came forward, picked up the spade, added their three shovels and planted the spade. Slowly, the grave began to fill.

'Hope Precious is getting good shots of all these rich Jews doing manual labour. The gravedigger union should strike over this,' Kingmaker muttered.

'Shut up. You should do your bit too.'

'Not me – I didn't join the struggle to become a gravedigger for rich Jews.'

Tracy giggled, then snorted as a large woman in an

elaborate navy headscarf glared at her.

'Brenda Silverman was a good woman,' the rabbi said. 'Taken from us far too young. She was a loving mother to Yair, Aviva and Zivah; a faithful, supportive wife to Alan, standing with him through good times and bad, keeping a wonderful kosher home. Her *Shabbos* dinners were a marvel. A very, very good woman. She will be missed by us all.'

The Chevrah man stepped forward. 'Prayers every night this week, except for *Shabbos*, of course, are at 6:15 at the Silverman home. Donations to the Chevrah Kadisha in memory of the late Brenda Silverman can be made at the office on your way out.'

Tracy indicated to Kingmaker to join one of the two long lines that formed a guard of honour across the stony earth. Precious scrambled out of the way, trying to get a good angle as Alan, Yair and Zivah – who now clung to both her father and her brother – walked slowly through, their eyes fixed to the ground. As they passed the end of the lines, they stopped, and the crowd swirled around them.

Tracy hung back, waiting for the mob to thin. Alan walked off with Zivah. Yair returned to the grave and furiously began to shovel more earth onto it.

'Wait here,' she said to Kingmaker. 'Precious, don't do that.'

Precious dropped the stone she had picked up off a shiny granite tombstone.

'I'm just trying to clean this up a bit,' she said. 'Someone's gone and put these dirty stones all over this grave. That's so disrespectful.'

'That's because that's what Jews do when we visit someone's grave. Christians take flowers. We put a stone on the tombstone. No, don't ask me why,' she interrupted Kingmaker.

'Stones are cheaper,' Kingmaker muttered.

Tracy ignored him and walked towards Yair. He looked up as she approached. Tears were streaming down his face.

'Yair, I'm so sorry. I wish you long life.' She held out her hand, then dropped it to her side. Stupid. Stupid. Yair was ultra *frum* now, and strictly observant Jewish men like him didn't shake hands with women.

Yair leaned on the spade and smiled bleakly at her. 'Hello Red,' he said. 'Thought I recognised you. Long time, huh? Didn't expect to see you here, but thanks for coming. I appreciate the support.'

He remembered her!

'Yeah, long time.' She smiled back, her heart thumping. He was still absolutely gorgeous. 'You okay? It must have been a hell of a shock.'

'Yeah. It was. I still can't believe it, you know. She was so, so... before she died, you know? So together.' He wiped his eyes.

'How's your dad holding up? And Zivah?'

'Poor Zivah, she's taking it really hard, poor kid. I'm not sure she really understood, until today. She kept saying Mom would get better and come home.'

'And your dad?'

'He's fine – he's always fine. He's the great Alan Silverman.' He turned away and dug the spade viciously into the pile of soil.

'Where's Aviva?'

'She couldn't get on a flight. Rabbi Rosenberg wouldn't delay the funeral any more to wait for her.'

'But she had five days to get here. What did she say? Where is she?'

He shrugged and carried on shovelling earth into the grave.

'Listen, Yair, I'm really sorry to ask this, but I'm a reporter now, you know? With the *Daily Express*. Do you know what happened? I mean how your mother... I mean.' She didn't know what to say.

'*Ja*, I know.' Yair's blue eyes became grey flints and his jaw clenched. 'My father killed her.'

CHAPTER 4

'Are you fucking out of your mind?' Mafuta roared. 'Are you fucking crazy? You want the *Daily Express* to be sued? You'd want to get fired? You want to get *me* fired? That's Alan Silverman you're writing about, not some Booysens tow truck driver, you stupid, stupid…'

Tracy jumped up and glared down at the frothing news editor.

'Listen. I just wrote what Yair told me. He told me his dad killed his mother. No ands, ifs or maybes about it. He said quote, my father killed my mother, end quote. Those were his exact words. You heard him,' she appealed to Kingmaker.

'I heard him too,' Precious volunteered.

'I don't care what Mr Junior Silverman said. I'm not going to publish the accusations of a crazy, spoilt brat. You hear me, T.T.? For all I know, Junior was as high as a kite. When he says the same thing at the inquest, in open court, under oath – then you can write it. But for now, just give me a fucking straight story.'

Mafuta collapsed back into his chair, his shirt buttons

straining to contain his heaving belly.

She looked appealingly at Kingmaker, who shrugged.

'You heard the man,' Kingmaker said. 'Straight.'

'Yes,' said Precious. 'You heard. You gotta write it straight away.'

Tracy returned to her desk, slammed her fingers onto the keyboard, and typed:

[HEADLINE] BRENDA SILVERMAN BURIED

By *Daily Express* reporter

Mrs Brenda Silverman (44), wife of Johannesburg property tycoon, Alan Silverman, was laid to rest in a traditional service at Johannesburg's West Park Jewish Cemetery yesterday.

Mrs Silverman was found dead in her bedroom at the family's plush northern suburbs home five days ago. While foul play is not officially suspected, the results of an autopsy have not yet been made public.

Yesterday's funeral was one of the largest ever seen at West Park Cemetery, with many of the country's leading businessmen among the pallbearers. It was also attended by the cream of Johannesburg's Jewish community, including the Chief Rabbi, the head of the Beth Din – the Jewish Ecclesiastical Court – and the president of the South African Zionist Federation.

Mr Silverman was accompanied by his son, Yair (23), and younger daughter, Zivah, who turned 18 the day after her mother died. Aviva Silverman (23), Yair's twin, didn't attend. The Daily Express understands that she lives overseas and was unable to get on a flight to South Africa in time for the funeral.

Rabbi Jonathan Rosenberg, who led the service, said Mrs Silverman had been a loving wife and a good mother who was well respected in the community.

As is traditional in religious Jewish circles, prayers will be held every evening for a week at the Silverman home.

Ends.

She read over her story. There. Couldn't get blander or straighter than that. Mafuta couldn't complain now – but… She chewed some ragged cuticle skin as she walked over to Kingmaker's desk.

'Something's not kosher with this whole story.'

Kingmaker nodded. 'I've been trying to get comment from some of Silverman's *BEE* associates as well as some other ANC people and all I'm getting is crap – so sorry she died so young, heart-breaking for Silverman, an icon of the struggle who continues to make such a valuable contribution to the upliftment of the people, yadda, yadda, yadda. So why didn't any of them go to the funeral?'

'Yeah. And where's Aviva? Why didn't she come? Alan Silverman could have hired – no, he could have bought – a bloody airbus to bring her back from wherever she is. I wonder if they even know, because Yair didn't say when I asked him. I'm going to fish around a bit more. I'm going to prayers tonight. Wanna come?'

'Nah, I'd stick out like a bruised thumb. You go – see if you can get anything more from your old boyfriend – Red?' Kingmaker grinned as she flushed.

***

Just after six, Tracy turned Buttercup through the open security boom and rattled up the road towards the Silverman house. Cars lined the jacaranda-lined street, so she parked and walked the three long blocks to the white-walled mansion. Dozens of people walked up the road with her and turned in at the Silvermans' gate. This time, the guard didn't stop anyone, not even the group of black women whose taxi had dropped them right at the gate.

Inside the house, sheets had been draped over the gilt-framed mirrors and paintings. The huge room where Yair's Barmitzvah party had been held was devoid of furniture once again, except for a small table covered in a white cloth, bearing two gleaming silver candlesticks and a large, thick memorial candle, set against the far window. Alongside was a long, low bench on which Alan Silverman and Yair sat ramrod straight. Zivah wilted between them.

Tracy hung back in the double volume entrance hall, her eyes scanning the faces of new arrivals, storing away names of the rich, the famous and – in one or two instances – the infamous. She thought she saw that ANC MP woman with the fancy double-barrel surname, but she wasn't sure it was her. Apart from the women who had arrived in the taxi and were hanging around at the back of the crowd, there was just a sprinkling of black faces, but she didn't recognise any of them. Damn Kingmaker for not coming. He knew everyone.

'We are about to start. Will the men please come forward,' Rabbi Rosenberg called.

Alan and Yair stood and joined the throng of men. Zivah remained on the bench. Tracy moved back to join the crowd of women spilling out of the main room into the entrance hall. She watched as the men chanted together, occasionally taking a step or two forward, then back, then praying silently and, once or twice, thumping themselves on their chest over their hearts.

She didn't bother to follow the service in the slim little book she had been handed as she entered the house. She wasn't there to pray. Neither, it seemed, were many of the women who whispered quietly to each other. Two young women were complaining about the umpire in a school cricket game; an elderly woman, who leaned heavily on a stick, and her daughter – was it her daughter? – were arguing quietly about which delicatessen made the best chopped liver. She clearly preferred Feigel's, while her daughter was in favour of DJ's.

Tracy examined the room. Ten years ago, she'd stood in almost this exact spot for the most miserable few hours of her life.

It had taken all her courage to walk up the long driveway

alone. Sarah had gone away to Umhlanga with her family for the weekend. She had wanted a blow by blow account of the great event at school on Monday. It had been even worse than she had anticipated. She spent most of the night nursing her cream soda, slouched against the wall, hoping against hope that Yair would ask her to dance. She couldn't see him anywhere. She was too afraid to help herself to the schwamas and hamburgers in the dining room. No one spoke to her. Aviva barely acknowledged her when she handed her Yair's present to put somewhere safe. A lot of the kids were dancing to the disco in the big room on the right. No one asked her to dance. She hadn't really expected anyone to – she towered over all the boys, except Yair. Then she saw fat Joshua who was as much of a misfit as she was, making a bee-line for her, clearly intent on asking her to dance. And it was a slow dance too. She fled down the passage and scooted through a door, into the kitchen. Brenda Silverman was there, a wine glass in her hand. 'Toilet's that way, sweetie. Or you can use one of the bathrooms upstairs.' Upstairs seemed like a safer option. She bolted up the stairs and opened the first door. Yair and several boys and girls were lolling on the double bed, smoking. Empty bottles littered the thick grey carpet.

'Hey Carrots, join us,' one of the boys said. 'You can be our totem pole.' The other kids sniggered. They may as well have screamed with laughter. She turned and ran, down the stairs, across the enormous entrance hall, out the front door, pausing only to say 'Thank you for having me' to Mr Silverman who was standing on the front porch with Aviva.

She hid in the shadows next to the guard house, jealously watching Aviva and her father until Maxine came to fetch her at 11pm. Maxine had even thanked her for being punctual. If she had only known.

***

Tracy wondered what had happened to Joshua. She'd heard his family had emigrated to Australia.

One of the taxi women bumped into her and quickly apologised. 'Did you know Brenda Silverman well?' Tracy whispered.

'We are going to miss *Ma*Brenda.' Tears ran down her nutella cheeks. 'We don't know how we will keep the studio going. Eish, it's too sad.'

'Studio? Where?'

'Our studio, the best studio in Alex. Eish, eish, eish.'

'Here.' Tracy handed the woman a tissue and her card. 'Phone me. I'd like to come and see your studio. Maybe I can help.'

The woman tucked the card into her bra.

'Amen,' the rabbi sang.

Prayer books were closed and everyone filed past the Silvermans, who were once again ensconced on the bench. The taxi group left.

Tracy waited until the crowd thinned, then made her way

over to the family.

'I wish you long life, Mr Silverman,' she said. She remembered not to extend her hand.

He nodded, staring through her. Then he flushed as recognition dawned, and he stood up.

'You're that reporter. I saw you this morning at the cemetery.' His voice shook. 'Can't you vultures leave me and my family alone at a time like this?'

She stepped back as he raised his hand to wipe his eyes. 'I'm really sorry, Mr Silverman. Yes, I am a reporter, but I was at school with Yair and I just wanted to pay my respects.'

'Leave Red alone, Dad.' Yair looked exhausted. 'She's an old friend and...'

'She's a reporter. And being a friend of yours doesn't mean she's welcome in my house. You, Miss...'

'Jacobs. I'm Tracy Jacobs.'

'Well, Miss Jacobs. My family and I thank you for your concern. But please leave and I'd appreciate it if you don't come back.'

Shocked, she backed away, and looked helplessly at Yair. He shook his head at her and mouthed "I'll phone you" before slumping down on the bench. Zivah continued to stare sightlessly ahead. Tracy, her cheeks aflame, made her way out the front door and down the long drive to the street. She switched on her cell phone and called Kingmaker.

'Alan Silverman just threw me out. I couldn't get near Yair, but he said he'd call me. He doesn't have my cell number, so he'll probably phone the office in the morning.'

CHAPTER 5

By midday, Yair still hadn't called. Tracy took a deep breath, wiped her sweating palms on her jeans and phoned the Silverman house.

'Sorry, Yair's not here,' said the maid.

Tracy exhaled slowly. 'Please will you tell him that Red called?'

'Yes. But I not know when. The master say Mr Yair gone away. Hold on and I'll call the master – or Miss Zivah?'

'No, thank you.'

She replaced the receiver thoughtfully. What the hell was going on? You didn't only not go out in the week of *Shivah*, you certainly didn't travel.

Kingmaker was out, so she walked down the corridor to Thomas Gray's office and stuck her head around the door.

'You busy?'

'Never too busy for you, Tracy. Just trying to find something nice to say about "Mad Buddies" without being condescending. Inspire me, please.'

Tracy laughed. She dumped the pile of *Village Voices* and

Rolling Stones off the lumpy armchair onto the floor, and curled herself into it.

'So, you're a secret snob, Thomas.' She always called him Thomas, never Tom. Just as he never called her anything but Tracy. He had once asked her if Tracy was short for Theresa, as he felt that Theresa would be more appropriate for the future editor of *The Times* – London, not South Africa. She'd blushed, but he'd said he could see she had enormous potential and predicted a great journalistic future for her. It sustained her when Mafuta was being more of a bastard than usual.

'What can I do for you?' Thomas asked.

'I just wanted to bounce this story off you. There's something not right about it, but maybe it's all in my mind.'

Thomas listened attentively, as he always did when she invaded his space to pick his brain.

'So,' she concluded, 'he's a good-looking, ultra-smooth creep who probably inherited his daddy's millions and now thinks he's better than anyone else. Even his son hates him.'

'What's the problem, Tracy? Are you pissed because he threw you out of his house? I would have done exactly the same. The poor man has just lost his wife, for God's sake.'

'Well, he didn't have to be so damn rude, so bloody arrogant. I know his type. He's…'

'He's what? He's rich? He has it all – or had it all? He's Jewish? He could be your father?'

Her mouth opened in protest. 'That's not fair, Thomas. I told you about my dad in confidence.'

'And I haven't broken that confidence, my dear. But you can't hold your father against every rich, good-looking, Jewish middle-aged man.'

'Not every good-looking, middle-aged man. I like you.'

'I'm not Jewish. And I'm definitely not rich. And, of course, you don't really think of me as a man at all, do you? Not a man like Alan Silverman.'

She felt her face burn. 'I've never said you're gay.'

'No, you haven't – you're far too PC for that. But you think I'm gay, don't you?'

'Well, everyone says…'

'I know. I'm your stereotypical gay, right? I don't swear and fart, I'd rather savour a good Chardonnay than swill a beer, I like arty movies and the opera, I wear well-cut, good quality clothes and, oh my God, I actually have my nails manicured. I've even gone for a facial a few times – with my wife.'

'You're married?' She cringed at the surprise in her voice.

'For the past twenty years. You've sat in this office talking to me, how many times? Who did you think was in this photograph?'

She looked at the attractive blonde woman and two teenage boys in the silver frame and squirmed.

'I dunno. I always thought it was your sister, or something?'

'My wife, and our sons. You never asked, but don't feel bad. There are people here I've worked with for years and they've also never asked, because they just presume they know who and what I am.'

'I'm sorry,' Tracy said.

'I'm not blaming you, my dear. I'm just trying to make a point.'

'And that is?'

'Think very hard about what it is about the Silverman story that gets you so stirred up. I'm not saying Alan Silverman is innocent – I don't know the man at all. But don't let your prejudices shape the story.'

'I'm not prejudiced.'

'Are you sure? Prejudice can be a very dangerous thing – it can make you see things that are not there and blind you to what is. It can make you reduce people to stereotypes – me. Your father. Alan Silverman.' He paused and then added, 'Now go get the real story.'

She walked thoughtfully back to her desk. Maybe there was nothing there. But then why had Yair said what he had about his father? Where was he? Time to do some serious research into Mr Alan Silverman and his precious family.

CHAPTER 6

Tracy googled "Alan Silverman", sorted the references into date order and started trawling. The first articles she found were from around the mid to late 1990s. He had obviously employed a good PR person. Most of the early articles were about the imminent listing of Silver Properties. It was touted as the hottest new investment since sliced bread. Silver Properties seemed to be involved in all kinds of developments – residential, commercial and industrial – all over the country. A lot in Gauteng. She was bored. She had no idea what she was looking for, but this wasn't it. She ploughed on. A headline caught her eye: "Silverman Nominated". At last, some background on the man himself.

SILVERMAN NOMINATED

Silver Properties founder and CEO, Alan Silverman (38), has been nominated for the 1999 Jewish Businessman of the Year Award.

Silverman, who spent nearly 16 years in exile after refusing to serve in the South African Defence Force, founded Silver Properties in 1995. The company took the local property market by storm, revolutionising the way in which residential, commercial and industrial developments are planned and financed. Silver Properties is to be listed on the main board of the JSE later this year.

Bloody hell. It was a vacuous piece of PR puff that said absolutely nothing and didn't tell her anything new.

She carried on searching. It seemed the Silver Properties listing was a huge success – vastly oversubscribed and the share price rocketed, making the Silvermans rich. Tell her something she didn't know. Ah, there was an article about the Jewish Businessman of the Year Award. She clicked on the link: Alan Silverman was listed as one of the nominees. He hadn't won. Shame. She'd thought he had. She hoped Mafuta wouldn't find out that she'd got that fact wrong in her stories.

She found several photographs of Alan at functions and events – usually a group picture of him with some ANC luminaries. That skinny white ANC MP, Annette Davies-Smedley, was in quite a lot of them. Brenda Silverman was in a few of them too.

Tracy zoomed in and examined the couple closely. He really was a good-looking dude. Even in the early poor quality black and white newspaper shots, he looked good... Brenda also wasn't bad. In fact, she was very cute, with her long, dark curly hair and gorgeous figure. A good-looking couple. No wonder their kids were so gorgeous, especially Yair. From the way they were dressed, they couldn't have been ultra *frum* back then. She scrolled down the page. Silver Properties this,

Silver Properties that…

The headline jumped out at her. "Alan Silverman Wins Jewish Businessman of the Year Award". An article in the *Jewish Voice*, November 2010. So he had finally got it. Good for him. She examined the accompanying photograph closely. He was wearing a black suit, white shirt and a *yarmulke*, but he still looked really handsome. Brenda looked a bit frumpy in a black and white, high-necked, long-sleeved jacket; her hair was short and straight, in a sort of reddish colour. Obviously a *sheitel*. When exactly had the Silvermans become so religious that Brenda had to hide her curls under a wig? And that was a very young Aviva with them. No, it couldn't be. Avi and Yair would have been about twenty-one in 2010, the same as her. She checked the caption. It wasn't Aviva; it was Zivah Silverman, who must have been sixteen at the time. She looked about ten. In fact – Tracy searched back to the earlier photos of Brenda Silverman – Zivah was a little carbon copy of her mother, except she was much fairer, and she was also bloody pretty. You couldn't tell that she was – what was the PC word again? – intellectually challenged. If she remembered correctly, Zivah had been in the remedial class at school. Still, it wasn't fair how some kids got all their parents' good genes in the looks department, while she'd inherited only the worst.

There didn't seem to be much else on dear Mr Alan Silverman, apart from Silver Property financial reports – the company was obviously doing very well. Hang on, what was that?

She clicked on a headline "Silverman Insults Palestinians". It was an October 2011 story from the *Muslim Mirror*.

SILVERMAN INSULTS PALESTINIANS

Jewish property tycoon Alan Silverman snubbed a high-level Palestinian delegation at a function organised by the Support Free Palestine organisation in Sandton last night.

This was after his wife, Brenda Silverman, grabbed the microphone and unleashed a torrent of invective and curses after a man who had just asked guest speaker, former Minister Ronnie Kasrils, a question from the floor.

Silverman and his wife then stormed out of the function, which was attended by high profile members of the ANC, Cosatu and the South African Communist Party.

After the event, the Support Free Palestine committee issued a statement condemning Mr Silverman's actions.

A Cosatu spokesman said it was clear Silverman no longer supported the policies of the tripartite alliance.

'It's always sad when a struggle veteran loses his way like Alan Silverman has done,' he added.

Wow. That was hard to believe. Quiet, petite little Brenda Silverman cursing and spitting invective in public? Now she was getting somewhere. She changed her search to "Brenda Silverman 2011" and up came the same story, plus one from the *Jewish Voice*. The large dailies, like the *Daily Express*, had clearly ignored the story. The *Jewish Voice's* story was a lot longer.

BRENDA SILVERMAN TAKES ON HOLOCAUST DENIER

A Holocaust denier at a Support Free Palestine function held in Sandton last week got a lot more than he bargained for when Brenda Silverman, wife of property mogul Alan Silverman, took him to task.

A freelance journalist who was at the function, which was held to raise funds for the "oppressed Palestinians", has provided *Jewish Voice* with a recording and an account of the incident.

During question time, a member of the audience stated that Israel had been created on a lie. The speaker claimed that the "so-called Holocaust" never happened.

He said that there was documented proof that there weren't anywhere near six million Jews in Europe before the Second World War. He said the Holocaust was a giant propaganda exercise dreamed up by the Americans to suppress the Arabs and punish Germany.

Mrs Silverman then raised her hand and was handed a roving microphone. This is what she said:

'Do you know what the number 46664 is? That's Madiba's prison number. Do you know what the number 1643729 is? No? It's a number I saw every day, growing up. It was printed in blue on my mother's left forearm.'

The recording indicates that members of the audience started hissing at her, but she carried on, raising her voice to be heard above the noise.

'My mother survived Birkenau. For those of you who don't know, that was one of the Nazi death camps. Her little sister, my aunt, didn't. She was sent to the gas chambers when she got too sick to work. She was 16 years old.

'You say the Holocaust is a lie. If it is, then where is my aunt? Where is the rest of my mother's family? My mother was one of eight children. What happened to my aunts and uncles and my grandparents? Why did my mother have a number tattooed on her arm?'

The *Jewish Voice* understands that the microphone was then snatched out of Mrs Silverman's hand and she was instructed to sit down and be quiet. She left the room with her husband.

After the uproar died down, the master of ceremonies apologised to the "guests of honour" – a visiting Palestinian delegation – as well as to the Holocaust denier for Mrs Silverman's "unacceptable behaviour". He added that, in future, people "like them" would not be admitted to Support Free Palestine events.

It's understood the Silvermans were invited to the function by a prominent member of the ANC.

When asked why he and his wife had attended, Mr Silverman told *Jewish Voice*, 'I have an open mind. I wanted to hear what the Palestinian delegation had to say. Like many Jews, I yearn for peace in Israel.'

He added, 'My wife was understandably upset by the denial of the Holocaust and she challenged it, as was her right in a country that believes in free speech.'

The ANC declined to comment.

Tracy printed the articles and took them to Kingmaker.

'So that's why,' he said.

'Huh?'

'Why Alan Silverman has fallen out of favour with the powers that be. He's become too much of an embarrassment. The ANC loves Jewish money, as long as it's quiet and not too Jewish, if you catch my drift.'

She made herself comfortable on Kingmaker's desk. She knew that look in his eye. He was going to give her a lecture. He always did. His lectures always sounded plausible, but she knew that most of the time he was only speculating. However, she had to admit that, in the short time she'd known him, a lot of his speculation had turned out to be spot on.

'Alan has obviously become too Jewish and too noisy,' Kingmaker said. 'Jews like Ronnie Kasrils – the cheerleaders of the Israel bashing brigade – they're tolerated. They're useful. Whoever invited our friend Alan to the event was probably hoping he could take over from Kasrils. I mean, Ronnie boy isn't exactly ideal for his deployed role as ANC spokesman for the Jewish community, now is he? Especially as the Jewish community loathes him. Alan, on the other hand, flaunts his religion, so he would be absolutely perfect to use as the new pro-Palestinian poster boy. But poor Brenda put a spoke in that wheel. And embarrassed the ANC – and Cosatu – in front of their foreign guests. Bad move. Bad, bad move.'

'That couldn't be the only reason the ANC has cut him out.'

'Agreed. But it can't have helped his cause with them,' Kingmaker said.

'Do you think it had anything to do with her death?'

'Who knows? We'll find out at the inquest. Maybe.'

Her heart sank. She knew there was something more to this story. There had to be. However, so far, she'd come up with a big fat nothing.

'Why don't you contact Annette Davies-Smedley?' Kingmaker asked. 'She seems – or seemed – awfully cosy with our Mr Silverman. She probably knows a lot about him, and Brenda. They're in enough pics together. And she was at the funeral.' Kingmaker scrolled through his contact list and copied down a number. 'Here.' He gave her the scrap. 'I used her in a story I did last year, on overcrowding in the jails or something. She's quite outspoken about that, especially for an ANC MP. Call her.'

Tracy hurried back to her desk and dialled.

A woman answered and identified herself as Annette Davies-Smedley.

'Afternoon, Ms Smedley. Tracy Jacobs here from the *Daily Express*. I'm working on a story about Brenda Silverman and I was wondering if I could ask you a few questions.'

Tracy held her breath. The silence reverberated down the telephone line. Then she was told, 'I'm very sorry about Brenda Silverman's passing. I knew her, a long time ago. But I hadn't seen her for years, so I don't think I could help you in any way. I extend my sincere condolences to Mr Silverman and the family.' The phone went dead.

PART 2
ANNETTE

CHAPTER 1
LONDON, 1985

Annette fingered the brown envelope suspiciously. It was addressed to her.

Miss Annette Davies,
c/o WOAH/Anti Apartheid Movement,
Charlotte Street,
London

There was no return address. The post mark said Sydney, Australia. She didn't recognise the handwriting and she didn't know anyone in Australia.

'You sure this has been checked?' she asked.

'Of course. You know all our mail is checked,' Aunt Sally said.

Annette reached for the letter opener and slit the envelope at the bottom, just like the security men had shown them. If it was a bomb, the explosives would be at the top flap. Usually. She held her breath and exhaled with a wry laugh when nothing happened. Clearly the apartheid government's dirty tricks department had decided she wasn't worth the effort of a nasty little surprise. Still. One could never be too careful. The "Remember Ruth First" poster on the wall was testimony to that.

Another envelope and a piece of paper fell out. She read the note on the paper.

Dear Annette.

You don't know me, but I met your friend on my travels. He asked me to post this letter to you from my home in Australia "for security reasons". I don't know what that means and he didn't tell me. I hope this reaches you.

Yours sincerely,
Roger

She stared hard at the handwriting on the smaller, white envelope. Her heart thumped in her head. After all these years.

She ripped the envelop open and pulled out the letter inside. There was no address, but, turning to the last page, her eyes sought the signature at the bottom. "Rockspider". She grinned. Only he knew her pet name for him. She started reading.

Dear Annette.

'Who's it from, dear?' Aunt Sally asked.

'A friend.'

'Oh, I do hope it's not bad news. You've gone as white as a sheet, dear.'

'I don't know what it says. I haven't read it yet,' Annette snapped, and retreated to the small back room, flopping down onto the threadbare brown sofa to decipher his illegible scrawl undisturbed.

She felt immediate remorse. Aunt Sally was a nagging pain sometimes, but she meant well. She'd apologise to her after she'd found out what he wanted.

Dear Annette.

I hope you get this.

Typical. Why write that? If it didn't reach her, she wouldn't be reading it, now would she?

She forced herself to focus. Her heart returned to her chest.

Dear Annette.

I hope you get this. After you left South Africa, I completed my honours, but they wouldn't give me any more deferment and, when my call-up papers arrived, I just couldn't go. It seems you had a bigger influence on me than either of us suspected, so I managed to get out of the country just before

I had to report to Voortrekkerhoogte. My father told me the military police came looking for me soon after I left, but I don't know what's happened since. I haven't been in contact with my folks for about three years now because they say that I'm a coward, so I stopped phoning them and I've been hanging around overseas. Anyway, things have happened and I have to leave where I've been living for the last few years and I will be coming to England. I plan to travel by ferry from Belgium and I expect to arrive in Dover sometime in early July. When I have a better idea, I'll try to drop you a line or send a telegram or something.

I know it seems a hellava cheek asking you for help – but I'm asking. Sorry, but there's no one else I trust enough to ask. I remember you once said that your aunt was with this group and that they were connected in some way to the Anti Apartheid Movement? Do you think they would be able to get me refugee status in England? Based on the fact that, if I go back to SA, I'll be court martialled as a deserter and, as my pa was at great pains to tell me, deserters get shot. Well, maybe they do and maybe they don't, but whichever way you look at it, all that's waiting for me in apartheid land is a jail cell for a long, long time.

I look forward to seeing you soon. I've thought about you a lot over the years. Have you thought about me?

Much love,
Rockspider.

After all these years. He'd been thinking of her. Had she thought about him? Did it rain in London? He was all that had kept her sane – in solitary confinement and here. For months after she had first made it to England, she'd played their relationship over and over in her mind. Why had she been such a frigid fool to keep him at arm's length? He'd told her often enough that he wanted more from her than friendship. That one night when they had made love had been amazing – she hadn't been as drunk as she'd pretended. Now she only thought of him about once a day, maybe only every second day in a good week. She'd even learned to keep him out of her bed when Charles stayed over. Well, most of the time.

'Are you all right, dear?' Aunt Sally's voice floated anxiously through the closed door.

Plastering a smile on her face, she walked back into the front office.

'Good news, Aunt Sal. Sorry I snapped. It's from an old varsity friend. He's been on the run from the military police for the last few years and he's heading for England.'

'That's wonderful, Annette. Does he need our assistance? What can I do? Give me his name and I'll get right on to the Home Office. When is he arriving? Does he have any accommodation? Should…?'

She hugged Aunt Sally. 'You are an amazing lady. Just amazing. There's no ways PW and the apartheid government can last much longer with you on our side. His name is Alan Silverman.'

'Old boyfriend, is he? What's Charles going to say?'

'Old friend, just a friend. Look, I think I have a photograph of him somewhere.'

She paged through the pocket photograph album she kept in her bag. There were photos of her parents – Mom, looking remarkably like her older sister, her little brother, and her beloved Labradors, both long dead. She knew exactly where to find the photograph of Alan. The one she'd taken that magical day at a braai at someone's house. She couldn't remember whose. He was wearing old jeans and no shirt; his shoulder-length reddish blond hair was ruffled by the breeze. He was smiling at her with his perfect white teeth, his blue eyes crinkled at the corners.

Aunt Sally examined the photo closely. 'Mmmm. That's a very charming young man. Just friends, you say? Why? Is he queer? He doesn't look like a fairy – he looks like Paul Newman. What's he do? Is he a model?'

'Aunt Sal, you're brilliant. You know how hard it's been to find a South African guy to be the face of our next WOAH fund raiser – the one for the End Conscription Campaign? Most of the draft dodgers who come through here are bloody drips. But Alan – he's perfect. He's exactly what the South African Defence Force would use in one of their recruitment campaigns, except for the fact that he's as anti-Nat as I am. Well, almost.'

Aunt Sally frowned. 'Are you sure about that?'

'Absolutely. I got to know him really well at varsity. He

was a bit naive politically at first – but what would you expect from a *boertjie* – well, that's what he called himself – who was raised in some godforsaken, ultra-conservative Free State *dorpie*? I mean, he even called Blacks by the K word when we first met.'

Aunt Sally frowned and Annette quickly explained, 'He didn't mean it like that. It's just that, where he came from, everyone used that word. To him, it was just a word. But, when I explained that it wasn't right, he stopped.' Aunt Sally was still frowning so Annette hurried on: 'He covered for me quite a few times when the security police were after me. I'd trust him with my life.'

'Okay, if you're sure; I suppose WOAH could do worse.'

Annette hugged her aunt. She didn't know what she'd have done without dear Aunt Sally when she had first arrived in London, frightened and penniless – there hadn't been time for her father to get money to her before the bloody pigs had put her on a plane for England. She hadn't even been able to say goodbye to them. Or to him.

'You won't be sorry,' she assured her aunt. 'He's smart, articulate and – let's be honest – quite gorgeous. The ladies who ride and lunch are going to adore him.'

'You absolutely sure he's not queer or anything? The lords who hunt wouldn't give him snow in winter if he's a fairy. He wouldn't mind doing this for us?'

'Oh, Alan's as straight as they come – believe me. And yes, he'll do it if we ask him nicely. He's a great guy and I love him – in a purely platonic way, you understand. He's one of the brightest guys I've ever met, terribly ambitious and really great fun. You'll like him.'

CHAPTER 2

'There he is.' Annette left her aunt's side and ran towards him as he emerged through the doors into the arrivals hall at Dover port. It was hard to believe it had been more than three years since she'd seen him. He had barely changed. His reddish blond hair was pulled back into a ponytail; he had grown a beard, but he was still her Rock. She reached up and flung her arms around his neck; she couldn't help herself. He swung her around and smiled down at her, his blue eyes crinkling at the corners, his white teeth gleaming. Her legs felt like jelly.

'You made it; you made it.'

He beamed. 'Hi there, you wonderful, wonderful girl. You fixed it perfectly. I just gave them my name, waved my South African passport at them and they knew exactly who I was. Apparently I now have temporary political refugee status.'

'Oh Rock, it's so great to see you.' She hugged him and then stepped back to introduce him to Aunt Sally, who had followed her across the hall.

'Rock, this is my aunt, Sally McDonald, our miracle worker. I told you about her, remember? She's the one who arranged everything. Aunt Sally, this is Alan Silverman.'

He shook Aunt Sally's hand and then looked around.

'Hey, Brenda,' he called. 'They let me through, no problems, thanks to these wonderful ladies. Come here and meet Annette.'

A little girl with dark curly hair limped over, looking lost and frightened. Who on earth was this? Probably someone Alan had met on the ferry and taken under his wing. He was always taking care of strays, especially female strays.

'Brenda.' He held out his hand to the child. 'This is Annette – an old friend from South Africa. And Sally, is it?' He smiled at Aunt Sally, who beamed back at him.

'Annette, Sally, this is Brenda.'

They shook hands.

'So, ladies, what now?' he asked.

Aunt Sally took charge. 'My car is outside. We'll be heading back to London. You'll stay with me until we can find you something more permanent. I tried to get you a place at an ANC safe house in East Finchley. Lots of South African refugees like you stay there all the time. But they're overflowing. So I've got a spare room that I sometimes rent out, but you can use it until you get settled. What about you, dear?' she asked the waif gently. 'Where are you headed? Are your parents coming to meet you?'

The waif chewed her lip. She looked as if she was about to cry.

Alan put his arm around the girl's shoulders. 'Brenda's

with me,' he said.

The floor tilted. The room spun. Annette's heart shifted into her stomach. What did that mean? Travelling with him? She couldn't be with him, with him. Not like that.

'That isn't going to be a problem, is it, Sally? It's really kind of you to offer to put me – us – up, but if you can't, we'll understand,' Alan said.

What about me? Annette's silent scream echoed in her head. Why don't you ask me if it's a problem for me? It is a problem. I was expecting, hoping... after your letter, I thought you'd missed me, wanted to be with me. However, she didn't say any of it. She'd had plenty of experience hiding her hurt back at Wits when he had screwed around and then introduced her to his many and varied girlfriends. Well, it had probably been her own stupid fault for being so bloody influenced by those radical women's libbers who said sex objectified women and allowed men to dominate them.

Now he'd arrived with another little tart in tow. So much for the happy fantasies that had dominated her every thought since his letter had arrived. About how he'd tell her he'd always loved her; how he'd missed her; how he'd make slow, passionate love to her. She'd already decided not to even pretend to want to fight him off. She'd rehearsed her "dear John" speech for poor Charles over and over again. Now it looked as if she'd just have to be satisfied with being his friend. She'd done it before; she'd do it again. However, once she reminded him of how close they used to be, how much he enjoyed her company, perhaps he'd come to realise that they were meant to be together. Properly together.

'So you're also a South African,' Aunt Sally was saying to the waif, who was hanging onto his hand.

Christ, how old was she? Even Alan couldn't be so stupid, surely, to run away with a child. That couldn't be why he'd had to leave wherever he had been for the past few years, could it?

'Of course you can stay with me. The more the merrier, I always say. It will be lovely to have you. Now let's go find the car.' Aunt Sally chattered on cheerfully as she led them to her tiny caramel car. 'Just as well you're such a little thing, or it would be a very tight squeeze. We were only expecting Alan, but aren't you a nice surprise.'

Some bloody surprise, indeed. Annette didn't say a thing. She couldn't. She'd cry if she opened her mouth.

'Alan, you'd best sit in front, with me,' Aunt Sally went on. 'Annette, you and Brenda should be comfortable enough in the back. Is that all the luggage you have? Right, then. Let's put it in the boot. And off we go.'

The little car lurched out of the parking lot. Annette stared intently out of the window at the passing countryside. She didn't see a thing. She didn't look at the waif. She just couldn't.

In the front, Alan turned on his charm full bloody blast and Aunt Sally was obviously lapping it up. She was laughing and more animated than Annette had ever seen her.

'As you know – or maybe you don't,' Aunt Sally was saying to Alan, 'Annette and I work for WOAH – that's Women Opposed to Apartheid. We try to raise money to assist with the struggle in any way we can. The Anti Apartheid Movement is big in the cities and they help us with offices and things like that. We focus more on the country areas and also areas where the people tend to be a little more conservative. And rich. There's lots and lots of money among the landed gentry, I can tell you. They're going to love you.'

'They are?'

'Oh, of course, Annette hasn't had a chance to ask you yet. She had this brilliant idea, Annette did. She's such a clever girl, our Annette.'

He nodded. 'Mmm, I know.'

Not clever enough, Annette thought. In fact, bloody stupid to love a guy who obviously still chases anything in a skirt. Anything.

'Well, I may as well ask you now,' Aunt Sally was still burbling. It was funny how older women also fancied him. Even that speech and drama professor – the one everyone thought was butch – had fallen for him. It had been the joke of the arts department, especially the whole elocution excuse bit.

'We're going to be running a campaign to raise money for the End Conscription Campaign.'

'What's that? I'm very out of touch with what's been happening back home, I'm afraid. South Africa's not exactly big news in Israel.'

'Of course, you must have left South Africa before the ECC was formed. It's an organisation in South Africa that campaigns against national service conscription and, where possible, tries to help boys like you who are not prepared to serve in the apartheid army.'

'Sounds like my kind of organisation. Bloody dangerous, though.'

'It is, indeed it is. But if they can persuade more and more boys like you not to go to the army, if enough of them refuse, the South African Government would be in real trouble. They're having to use the conscripts in the townships now, you know, and a lot of national servicemen don't like that. The ones who come through our offices say that fighting communists on the border is one thing, but fighting your own citizens in townships right where you live, that's something different. It's civil war in South Africa now. It's terrible. It has to stop. Botha and his Nazis have to go.'

'So where do I figure in all this?'

Annette smiled to herself. He was going to do it. He liked to be needed, and he loved being the centre of attention. If he came to work for WOAH, they'd be spending a lot of time together. Perfect.

'Well, we need someone to be the face of our campaign,' Aunt Sally explained. 'The problem is that most of the "draft dodgers" we see here are not exactly going to encourage the mink and manure set to sign a cheque, now are they? The husbands are highly suspicious of anyone who looks – dare one say it, a bit… um… effeminate?'

Alan laughed. 'I can imagine. And so you want me to… what? Charm them out of their daddy's and mummy's millions, huh?'

Aunt Sally laughed softly. 'That's right. Would you do it? Unfortunately, we couldn't pay you, but it's for the cause, isn't it?'

'Why not? Sounds easy enough.'

Yes. Yes. Yeesss. He was going to do it!

'I was wondering, though, Alan. It would sound so much more convincing if you spoke a bit more like an Afrikaner. So they realise that there are lots of Afrikaners who are opposed to apartheid and that there's a good chance that, with their help, things really could change for the better. Do you think you could do that?'

He threw back his head and roared with laughter. 'Sally, if you only knew what I had to do to lose my Driespruitfontein accent. You've just paid me the biggest compliment of my life. *Ja*-well-no-fine.' He dropped back into the thick, guttural tones he had been so mocked about at Wits when she had first met him. 'Ah kin do it. Howzat?'

CHAPTER 3

For the first time since she'd started working for WOAH, Annette got to the office before Aunt Sally. It was Alan's first day and she wanted to impress him. Aunt Sally had agreed to let her show him around. She caught her breath as he filled the doorway leading to the little kitchen where she was preparing tea. He was magnificent, his tan making his eyes even bluer and his teeth even whiter. He'd filled out since varsity – must have been all that manual labour in Israel. It made sense that he'd gone there first after fleeing South Africa, she supposed, being Jewish and all. Funny how she'd never really thought of him as being Jewish. He certainly wasn't like all the *bagels* who flocked to Wits to study B.Com IDB – In Daddy's Business – or law. He didn't look Jewish and he certainly didn't sound Jewish. Aunt Sally had been shocked when she had realised. Well, not really shocked – more surprised than anything.

'We'll just have to fudge his ethnic origins with the landed gentry if we want them to donate to our cause,' Aunt Sally said. 'They may not like the *boers* much, but I suspect – no, I know – they like Jews even less.'

'So, what's the programme for today?' Alan asked as he took the cup of tea she offered from her. His fingers brushed hers. Deliberately? She couldn't tell. At least he'd left the waif back at Aunt Sally's flat, so she'd have him to herself.

'First, you have to have a haircut, Aunt Sally said. And the beard has to go. You have to look like a clean cut Afrikaans boy, not a hippy refugee from Woodstock. So you'll need some new clothes too. She said I could take you shopping. Nothing fancy, mind. We're on a tight budget here.'

***

When they got back to the office, Aunt Sally was delighted with Alan's transformation. He really did look amazing. His hair was short – shorter even than it had been the first time Annette had laid eyes on him in the Wits cafeteria. She'd never forget that day. Ever.

'Is anyone sitting here?' he'd asked, indicating the empty chair opposite her.

She had shaken her head and he had sat down and smiled at her, and her heart had lurched. He was the most gorgeous guy she had ever laid eyes on.

'I'm Alan,' he said.

They spoke. They always had so much to talk about. He was so smart, so witty. They laughed at the same jokes. They both loved *Blondie* and *The Rolling Stones*; he went with her to see *Saturday Night Fever* – twice, and she suffered through *Star Wars* and *The Exorcist* with him. And they argued. About everything. He loved to play devil's advocate, to pretend he was a *verkrampte* right-wing racist. He loved to call black people *kaffirs* just to get her back up. She knew he didn't mean it. He laughed at her when she got angry with him. He made her think about her beliefs. He challenged her assertions, pounced on any contradictions in her statements, helped her to sharpen her mind. After years of his probing questions, interrogation by those security police oafs, even Rooi Rus, had been – well, not a breeze exactly, but manageable.

He posed patiently for the photographs for the WOAH campaign posters and brochures. The photographer had been in a state of rapture from the time he laid eyes on Alan. She agreed. He really should be a model – except he was far too bright. Now, they were arguing again. About his fund raising presentation. He was as bloody stubborn as ever. He wanted to tear into Afrikaners and the National Party government, let the audience know just what bigoted idiots they all were. He'd lived with them all his life, he said, so he should know.

'No, we can't do that,' she explained. 'If they think Botha and his bullies are just stupid thugs, they'll think we are even bigger idiots for taking so long to overthrow them. And we have to make them sympathise with white Afrikaners – like you. They need to see that whites in South Africa also want change.'

Finally, they crafted a draft both of them could live with.

***

Friday was Alan's first presentation. They drove to the little village outside London in Aunt Sally's car, Alan folded into the front passenger seat again; she and the waif chilly in the back. The hall, next to a pretty stone church with roses lining the path, was already set up for the WOAH meeting. There were rows of chairs, and a table at the front for Aunt Sally and Alan. She went to the back to help set up for tea. The waif, too precious to get her hands dirty – she'd probably never done a hard day's work in her life – sat down at the end of one row near the front.

Annette could see Alan was nervous, but he winked at her as she took up a seat in the front row on the other side of the hall.

'This is a really important meeting,' Aunt Sally had said in the car. 'Our audience tonight has oodles of money and a very keen interest in South Africa. Some of their forebears probably fought in the South African War and might even have died there. So, while they think the world of Maggie Thatcher, they're not as supportive as she is of Mr Botha and his henchmen.'

Alan had looked over his shoulder and smiled at the waif. 'That's good to know, isn't it, sweetheart?' he'd said.

Annette's stomach had knotted. She hated it when he looked at Brenda like that. 'They find PW uncouth and they don't like the way he treats the "natives",' she'd blurted out.

'It makes them feel guilty about colonialism when they see white cops shooting black children.'

Alan had laughed. 'Don't worry, Annette. I'll show them that not all *boers* are thugs.'

***

The hall was filling up. That was a good sign. Aunt Sally would be pleased. As usual, the women were mostly well preserved, middle aged and neatly groomed. They wore slacks and jackets and sensible shoes. Their husbands tended to have the ruddy complexions one associates with people who spend a lot of time outdoors – golfing or riding or some other pursuit of the leisured class.

Annette crossed her fingers. She was sure Alan would be wonderful, but still…

Aunt Sally blew into the microphone. She looked like a little grey dove on the stage, in her pale grey twinset and her grey tailored slacks. Then she drew herself up to her full five feet one and commanded the hall like the headmistress she used to be before she'd decided to do something "useful" with her life.

'Testing, testing. Please will everyone be seated. Thank you.' The hall quietened down. 'Ladies and gentlemen, thank you for accepting our invitation to this meeting of Women Opposed to Apartheid. Vicar, thank you for your generous hospitality. As you know, things in South Africa are deteriorating daily. Troops are being sent into the townships to ruthlessly squash the legitimate protests of the native black population – people who are not even treated like second class citizens. They are not regarded as citizens at all. Or even as human beings.'

Aunt Sally paused and looked around. 'How do you think young white South African boys feel about being used to suppress other South Africans? Many of them don't want to do it – but most have no choice. Tonight, we are privileged to have a one of those young South Africans with us. He has been forced to leave the country he loves, his home, his family, everything he holds dear, because he won't take up arms against his fellow citizens. Ladies and gentlemen, please give a warm welcome to our brave young guest.'

Alan smiled and walked to the microphone as the polite applause faded. Annette's heart fluttered. He looked so gorgeous in his new cargo pants and blue shirt. His arms and face were still tanned from Israel, contrasting with his fair hair. The woman in front of her leaned forward. Annette smiled. She had no doubt he'd have the women eating out of his hand before long. The men might prove a bit more of a challenge.

'*Dankie*, Miss McDonald,' he said. 'Good evening, vicar, ladies and gentlemen.'

She smiled. Alan had broadened his accent slightly. He didn't sound quite as guttural as PW, but there was no mistaking his origins.

'My name is Alan and I am an Afrikaner.'

A titter of amusement rippled through the hall, which – on other nights – was used for Alcoholics Anonymous meetings, according to the notice on the board in the foyer.

'I am an Afrikaner,' Alan continued. 'I support the Springboks. I love to braai – barbecue.'

Annette smiled. She'd warned him not to use too many Afrikaans phrases. 'They won't understand and we'd hate them to feel stupid.' Alan had listened, for once.

'I love my country and my language. But I am not a proud Afrikaner.' He paused and Annette could see that the big man sitting next to her was watching him intently, weighing him up, judging him.

'Before I tell you why I am not a proud Afrikaner, let me tell you a little about myself. I come from a little *dorp* – a village – you've probably never heard of. Driespruitfontein. It's in the Orange Free State.'

She'd lost that battle. She'd told him they wouldn't know where the Orange Free State was, but he said there were so many British graves all over the province from the Boer War, there was a chance someone in the audience had family buried there.

'Driespruitfontein means Three Stream Fountain, but I have no idea where that name came from because we only had one little stream and not a single fountain. Anyway, there's one main street and one set of traffic lights – we call them robots.' He waited for the laughter to fade. 'There's a police station, a bank that opens three days a week, my parents' general dealer store, the tote, the church, the bottle store, the farmers' co-op, the Royal Hotel – isn't it odd that every *dorp* in our proud republic has a Royal Hotel? – and a couple of other shops. It's a farming town, a little like this, but not nearly as pretty.'

The audience laughed. Annette began to relax. Alan was starting to win them over. She knew he could do it.

'Most of the farmers in the district send their kids to the boarding school there,' Alan said. 'I did all my schooling at Driespruitfontein Laerskool and Hoërskool. We had a great rugby team. My best friend, Thys van Zyl, played prop for Free State schools. I think he'll be a Springbok one day.' He paused. 'If Peter Hain will let him.'

Laughter and applause. Annette began to enjoy herself.

'I had an older brother, David. He was killed on the border during his national service.'

There was a collective gasp around the hall. This had surprised her too. Alan had hardly ever mentioned his brother to her before. It was only when they were working on his presentation that he had told her how close he and David had been, even if David had been three years older.

'But that isn't why I refused to do my national service when they called me up.'

The big man next to her leaned forward. Annette held her breath. Alan was about to come to the crux of his presentation. If the big man bought it, if the audience accepted Alan's explanation for his refusal to do his duty to his country, the money would come flooding in. If not...

'I'm not afraid of fighting for my country,' Alan said. 'I'm not a conscientious objector or a pacifist. My *pa* was in the South African Army in the Second World War. He fought in Egypt and Italy. It couldn't have been easy for him. Many Afrikaners supported Hitler and refused to support Jan Smuts. To be honest, Smuts probably had more support in England than at home – even today. I've seen his statue next to Churchill's in the square near your Parliament. I can't recall seeing a statue of Smuts at home, although there might be one in the airport – but I didn't stop to look for it when I left. Anyway, my *pa* went against most of his friends and volunteered to fight the Nazis. I'm proud of my *pa*.'

Alan waited until the smattering of applause faded.

'My *boet* – my brother, David – he went because he thought it was his duty to defend his country against the communist onslaught. That's what the National Party government told him, and boys like him. He stepped on a landmine and there wasn't even enough of him left to send home in a box. It nearly killed my *ma*, to lose her oldest boy. But, when the time came for me to go, she said I must go. That's what good, patriotic Afrikaner boys are supposed to do. English boys too. A lot of my mates from Wits University, good guys I graduated with, they felt they had to go. I hurt my *ma* and *pa* by refusing and I'm sorry about that. But I had no choice.'

The big man sat back and folded his arms again, shaking his head slightly. Annette hoped he was sympathising with

Alan's dilemma, rather than disagreeing with him.

'I had no choice because my government lied to David.'

Annette held her breath. The silence in the hall was tangible.

'I believe my government lied to my *ma* and *pa*. David didn't die to save our country from communists. He died to keep our black people in their place, to keep PW Botha and the National Party in power.'

Alan paused and looked around. The hall was expectant. No one moved.

'Let me tell you what would have happened if I had obeyed my call-up. Just outside Driespruitfontein – the white town of Driespruitfontein where I lived with *ma* and *pa* and David – is a township, a *lokshin*, where the black workers live. They live in shacks with no electricity or running water. There is no school for them. If they get sick, they have to go to the witchdoctor because the white doctor in town won't treat them and it's too far for them to get to the black hospital in Bloemfontein. I have good friends who live in that township. Pretty – that was her name, but she was also very pretty…' There was some laughter in the hall, quickly muffled. 'Pretty was one of my closest friends growing up. I adored her. We used to play together. She was Johanna's daughter. Johanna was my nanny.'

Alan had got a bit emotional and sentimental when he had told her about Johanna and Pretty.

Now he was telling the audience about how, when he was

little, Johanna had carried him on her back. 'I loved her,' he said. 'She played a huge role in making me into the man I am today.' He drew in a deep, slow breath as if to bring his emotions under control.

Annette felt tears prick her eyes, even though she'd rehearsed the speech with Alan at least a dozen times. In all their years at Wits, Alan had never told her about Johanna. Or Pretty. 'You know how it was, back then,' he'd explained when she'd asked why he had never mentioned them. 'Black employees – black people in general – were kind of invisible. It's really only now, when I look back, that I see what an influence they had on me. And how lucky I was to have had them in my life.'

She admired him for his honesty. It showed just how far he had travelled from Driespruitfontein. She'd told him they could ask the ANC to track down Johanna and Pretty and maybe even get them out of South Africa. He'd refused. It would be too dangerous for them, he'd argued. He'd won that argument. He obviously loved Johanna and Pretty, and she couldn't risk their lives because she wanted to make him happy.

***

The audience was dead quiet as Alan went on. 'How could I ride through Driespruitfontein Township on a Ratel armoured vehicle and point an R-5 rifle at the woman who virtually raised me? How could I bash down Pretty's door, supposedly looking for terrorists – but really only doing it to frighten her and my other black friends in the township? Just to keep them in their place? I couldn't do it. I wouldn't do it. My parents didn't understand and they won't speak to me anymore, and that hurts. Thys doesn't speak to me either. But Johanna understood. She gave me her life's savings so that I could leave the country. So that her *kleinboetie*, her *kleinbasie* – that's what she called me when I was younger – wouldn't have to go to jail. One day, I hope to be able to pay Johanna back.'

The big man next to her twirled his moustache. His wife wiped her eyes. Annette swallowed hard. She looked across at the waif – she was also crying. So Alan hadn't told her the story before either. Good.

'When I left South Africa, I was on my own,' Alan said. 'But now there's a fantastic, brave organisation, the End Conscription Campaign, which is trying to help guys like me. So we won't have to take the life savings of people like Johanna to avoid going into the army or to jail. So we won't have to shoot the people we love. Please support them. Thank you.'

***

The church hall rose to its feet. The applause rattled the windows. Annette felt as if her heart would burst. She was so proud.

Aunt Sally stepped forward. 'Thank you, Alan.'

The applause rose again. Aunt Sally held up her hand for silence. The hall sat down.

'If more young men like Alan, good, loyal, Afrikaner boys, refuse to go to the army, the apartheid government would not be able to survive. We need to make it easier for them to refuse. We need to show them that there are people out there who support them, who understand. Ladies and gentleman, if you would like to help young men like Alan and play a small part in destroying the evil of apartheid, please give generously to WOAH. Every penny we collect tonight will be sent to the End Conscription Campaign in South Africa. Thank you'.

***

Later, in the car driving back to London, Aunt Sally was jubilant.

'We've never raised so much money in one night before,' she said. 'Alan, you were wonderful, quite marvellous.'

Annette was so proud. She beamed at Alan and smiled inwardly as the waif glared at her and chewed at her lip.

But then Aunt Sally dropped her off at her flat, where Charles was waiting for her, and Alan and the waif went home together.

CHAPTER 4
LONDON, 1988

Alan was late. It was probably Brenda's fault. She spent an inordinate amount of time primping herself up – and she still looked like Orphan Annie. However, Alan was clearly still infatuated with her. It didn't make sense. What did he see in her? The only thing Annette could think of was that little Brenda was a dynamo in bed, because she had the personality – and brain – of a flea.

Thank heavens she'd had the sense to hang onto Charles after Alan's letter had come. Her every instinct had been to break it off. But then Alan had arrived with the waif in tow and, three years on, she was still around. It had been fine, at first, when Alan was working fulltime at WOAH and they could spend a lot of time together. Now, however, she didn't see nearly enough of him, not since he had started working for Ben Shapiro and had moved out of Aunt Sally's into a bedsit near his job in North London. Ironic, really, that it had been Alan's performance at a WOAH meeting that had landed him the job at Shapiro and Son.

'There they are,' said Charles, waving regally at the festive hordes of people moving towards Wembley Stadium. She could see Alan, towering over most of the crowd, his fair hair glinting in the sunlight. And, there was the waif, skipping along at his side like a flipping child. She was twenty-one, now, for heaven's sake. Would she never grow up?

Annette stretched up and kissed Alan on the cheek, and the two men shook hands. She ignored Brenda.

'Rock, let's go in. I want to get as close to the stage as possible.'

Annette grabbed Alan's arm and led the way, leaving Charles and the waif to follow. It irritated her to see Charles and Alan together. The contrast between them became so glaringly obvious she wanted to weep. She knew it was unfair of her to compare. Charles was a good man. He loved her. He was comfortable, a bit like an old slipper. But she was too young for slippers. She wanted excitement; she wanted romance; she wanted a man to look at her the way Alan looked at Brenda. She wanted a man who looked like Alan. She wanted Alan.

'Doesn't Brenda look fantastic,' said Alan, looking back at the girl, who was skipping along holding onto Charles' hand. Alan frowned, shrugged off Annette's hand and put his arm around the waif. Brenda smiled triumphantly at her.

'Mrs Shapiro gave me this jacket for my twenty-first. It's gorgeous, isn't it? I was keeping it to wear somewhere special and I think my first real concert is very special,' Brenda flirted with Alan, who looked down at her adoringly.

Annette felt bile rise in her throat. Grabbing Charles, she marched into the stadium. She was really looking forward to seeing Whitney Houston and George Michael. Alan loved *Dire Straits*. He had all their albums.

Charles, she knew, didn't particularly want to see anyone. He didn't even want to be here. He hated crowds and noise. He was already looking miserable, but determined to do his bit to support her and WOAH and, of course, the Anti Apartheid Movement, even if he was a dyed-in-the-wool Tory and everything. Poor Charles. He tried so hard to please her. She really should love him more. She could sense him, standing stiffly behind her. He put his hand tentatively on her shoulder. No wonder Alan called him "Fog". 'Wet and dense,' he'd explained when the waif hadn't caught the joke. That was a little cruel – and unoriginal – but spot on, even she had to admit.

'I can't believe so many people have actually come out to support the Mandela Freedom at 70 concert. It's wonderful, isn't it, Rock? Gives us hope, doesn't it?' Annette said, managing to manoeuvre herself next to him. That left Charles on his own again, but so what? He'd survive and he was too much of a gentleman to make a scene.

'Actually, I'm pretty certain most of these people – well, a lot of them, anyway – don't give a hoot about Nelson Mandela. They just want to go to the concert,' Alan said.

He was such a cynic sometimes, but he was probably right. If it wasn't for her, Charles would have nothing to do with the

Free Mandela Campaign and the waif probably didn't even know who Mandela was.

But Alan cared. She knew he did. He still did quite a lot for WOAH, which was fantastic now that they really had to step up their efforts after Dr Ivor Toms was sentenced to jail, the poor man. South African jails were no picnic, as she well knew. Fortunately, Alan had been spared that by getting out of the country in time. However, it wasn't always easy for him to keep doing his bit for the struggle, because Mr Shapiro, kind as Alan said he was, expected him to put in his eight hours every day – and then some. He still addressed fundraising meetings when he could, and helped out in the office. But then he'd rush off, anxious to get back to the waif. It wasn't fair. They still got on so well, her and Alan. She knew he enjoyed her company. It was just that he made it so bloody obvious that he preferred being with Brenda. And when that little twit was around, he could barely keep his hands off her. It was quite sickening.

The crowd roared as *Sting* came on stage. She let the music wash over her. She wasn't going to let the waif, or Charles, ruin her day with Alan.

***

Annette was freezing. This was hardly the weather for a protest, but, because the ECC had been banned back in August, it was essential that WOAH show solidarity with the oppressed of South Africa at all times. So it was good that Alan had come along too. She hadn't expected the waif to tag along as well, but Alan said she also wanted to be part of history in the making. Yeah, right. Brenda probably just didn't want Alan to be alone with her.

They marched down The Mall together, Alan sandwiched between them, Charles bringing up the rear, as usual. They had to try to get as close as possible to Nelson's column. Brenda sneezed. She clearly wasn't feeling well. She was always sick in winter, and always moaning about the weather and the fact that it never stopped raining. This was London – what did she think the weather would be like? If she hated it so much – she kept on and on about how much nicer winters were in Jo'burg – why didn't she just bugger off back to South Africa? It wasn't as if she would be arrested once she got there, unlike them – Alan and her. However, Alan said she had no family there – and no friends. She didn't seem to have any friends in London either. Aunt Sally said she liked her. But Aunt Sally liked everyone.

Brenda sneezed again. Why didn't she just go home?

'Charles, poor Brenda's sick. You don't need to be here. Why don't you take her home?' Annette suggested.

'No, I'm fine. Really. Alan said this protest is really important. We'll go after the main speaker, won't we, Alan?' Brenda sniffled.

Alan put his arm around her and she gave him one of her really pathetic little girl smiles.

Annette turned away, disgusted. Charles put his arm around her. She wanted to shrug him off, but she couldn't hurt him like that, and it would show Alan that she didn't need him. She had to make a decision soon about Charles. She couldn't keep him dangling forever. He'd asked her again, last night, to marry him. Her plea for more time was starting to wear a little thin. They'd been together for four years, for heaven's sake. Charles had all but moved into her nice new flat in Chiswick. He wasn't such a bad catch, as Aunt Sally kept telling her. She agreed. The only problem with him was that he wasn't Alan.

***

The waif was tugging at Alan's sleeve. 'Alan, how much longer is this going on? I'm really not feeling well.'

It was starting to get dark and even colder. Annette felt a tiny frisson of pity for her.

'Not much longer. I heard someone say he was on his way. Then we'll just listen to his speech and leave.' Suddenly, Alan waved at someone in the crowd. 'Come on, there's one of the guys I met at the ANC offices last week. Let's just go over and say hello. We want to team up with them for our next fundraiser, so be nice to him, okay?'

He guided Brenda through the throng of people; she followed with Charles. They stopped at a group of young black men.

'Hi, fancy meeting you here,' Alan said.

The men looked at him blankly.

'Alan Silverman. We met last week, you know, from WOAH.'

'Yeah, right. Sorry. Didn't recognise you. One *mlungu* looks pretty much like another,' one of the men said.

Alan laughed. 'Well, good to see you again. Just wanted to say hi and I'll see you next week.'

She didn't hear their response because the crowd was starting to chant. A tall black man was making his way onto the platform. The crowd fell silent. The man started talking. Brenda sneezed again.

***

Annette held out her cracker so that Alan could pull it with her. It snapped loudly and a ring fell out. If only. Brenda pulled her cracker with Charles, and sneezed. She obviously hadn't managed to get rid of the cold she'd picked up at the Trafalgar Square demonstration, and that had been weeks ago. Alan looked concerned.

'Sweetheart, you must go back to the doctor after Christmas. Those antibiotics he gave you clearly aren't working,' Alan said.

'I'm so sorry. I'll get over it eventually. It's just that I'm always cold and it's so damp in London. I wish it would snow. That would at least make the cold worthwhile.'

Charles looked up from carving the turkey and smiled at

her sympathetically. His nose was also red and chapped.

After lunch, they opened their presents. Alan seemed delighted with the book she'd chosen for him – *Biko,* by Donald Woods – and Brenda thanked her nicely for the bath salts. Alan's present to her – well, the present from Alan and Brenda – Johnny Clegg and Savuka's *Third World Child,* was exactly what she wanted. Charles wrapped the warm scarf they'd given him around his neck and planted a kiss on Brenda's forehead. They settled down to listen to her new album and the waif climbed onto Alan's lap. She always did that. Like she was a child, or something. Alan didn't seem to mind, though.

'You should have seen Brenda's end of year concert,' he said. 'How she got all those kids to dance together was bloody amazing.'

'They're sweet children,' Brenda said. 'They learn fast. I'm so lucky to have got the job with Patricia. And now that I can exercise regularly at the community centre, my knee is getting so much stronger. Perhaps, one day, I'll get to dance at Covent Garden.'

Yeah, right, who did she think she was? Fonteyn?

'You should have seen the dance she put on with some of the older kids,' Alan went on. 'She was brilliant. Even the Shapiros were impressed. What was it, sweetheart? Something from *Swan Lake*, right?'

'Yes, we did the dance of the cygnets. It isn't a particularly difficult dance, but it looks lovely. I taught it to some of the *ulpan* guys back on the kibbutz. We were going to call it *Duck Pond*, but...' She flushed and looked quickly at Alan. 'Anyway, it was a great achievement for the girls, because it was their first performance on points. Their parents loved it.'

'We all did. And you were brilliant. You should have seen her. I had no idea my girl was so talented.' Alan kissed her.

Annette went into the kitchen to make coffee. She couldn't bear watching the two of them. They were like bloody adolescents with their hormones in overdrive. She was pretty sure Brenda knew how she felt about Alan. She could see the pity in her eyes when she looked at her. She hated it – she didn't need, or want, the waif's pity. She had so much to be thankful for – a meaningful job with WOAH, a beautiful – if tiny – flat, a good man who loved her, and a great family; even if her parents did live thousands of miles away, their unwavering support sustained her. They'd always supported her, even when they disagreed with her tactics. It couldn't have been easy for them, having a political activist for a daughter.

They'd pretended not to notice the clicks and buzzes when the security police bugged their home telephone. Mom even joked and said she was relieved her daughter was being followed by the cops, because then she knew she'd be safe when she went out at night. Plus, they'd been there, waiting for her, each time she'd been released from jail. She couldn't wait to see them again when they came to visit in May. She was sure they'd like Charles. She wondered what they'd make of Alan. And Brenda.

PART 3
BRENDA

CHAPTER 1
ISRAEL, 1985

Brenda jumped. Who on earth was that? She'd been on the kibbutz for a week and no one had come near her.

She hauled herself off her bed, clumped across the concrete floor in her over-sized work boots and scraped the door open. It was him – the guy from the dining room. The one she'd seen the very first day when Noni had instructed Linda – American Linda, not London Lynda – to show her around. You couldn't miss him, not with his blond hair – or the crowd around him. Usually girls, but guys seemed to like him too.

'Down, girl,' Linda had muttered. 'That's Alan – the *ulpan* gigolo. I think he's one of yours. African.'

Now here he was. In her doorway.

'Hi. Have you got any cotton wool?' he asked.

Why, oh why, hadn't she showered and changed out of her work clothes when she had finished her shift in the laundry? However, after five hours of feeding sheets through the giant ironing machine, it was just too much effort to change. She tried to brush back her hair with her fingers, but she could feel that it was all curly and wild from the steamy humidity. Her rolled up workpants were dragging on the floor and the army jacket Noni had found for her reached almost to her knees. Noni had hacked about a foot off the sleeves for her, but she still looked like Sad Sack.

She stared at him. Had he really asked for cotton wool?

'You know. The white, fluffy stuff you girls use for whatever. You are South African, aren't you? You do know what cotton wool is?' he asked.

'Yes, *ja*, of course.' She scampered across the room, ignoring the pain in her knee, and tore a large piece of her precious supply of Johnson's from the roll, then handed it to him with shaking hands. She tried to focus on what he was saying, but she could barely hear him over the thumping of her heart. She chewed her lip.

'Hey, aren't you a little young to be doing *ulpan*?' he asked.

Everyone always thought she was younger than she actually was. She hated it.

'I'm eighteen.' Well, it wasn't exactly a lie. She'd be eighteen next month.

'Sorry, I'm being rude. I'm Alan, from South Africa.'

As he grasped her hand, the big blister from the ironing machine popped. She didn't flinch.

'I'm Brenda. From Jo'burg.'

'Hello, Brenda from Jo'burg. Nice to meet you. Thanks for the cotton wool. See you around.'

She couldn't let him leave, not yet! 'What class are you in?' she blurted. She knew exactly which class he was in.

American Linda was quite a font of information when she wanted to be. So she knew that he had been on the kibbutz for a few years, first as a volunteer and then he had joined the *ulpan*, although apparently he was already almost fluent in Hebrew. She didn't need Linda to tell her that he was the most popular guy on the kibbutz – any idiot could see that. Apparently some of the younger women kibbutz members thought highly of him too, Linda said. Also, he didn't have a specific girlfriend – at least not for long.

'He doesn't want to deprive any of us of his many charms,' Linda had explained. She'd probably been one of his girls, but Linda denied it vehemently. 'Not my type,' she'd insisted. 'Too pretty for me.'

'I'm in *Kitah Gimmel*. You?' he asked.

'*Kitah Aleph* – I… I've never learned Hebrew before, you see.'

'Well, if you need any help, you know where to find me.' He waved vaguely in the direction of what was probably his room.

'*Ja*, okay, thanks.'

She dragged the door closed and collapsed onto her bed. Oh God. He probably thought she was an idiot. He must know she knew he was in *Kitah Gimmel*. Oh God, he'd probably never speak to her again.

He was the most gorgeous man in the world. Nothing like the boys from school. He was so tall, over six-foot for sure. His hair was amazing, not really blond-blond – more reddish blond. Her mother would freak at his ponytail, but it looked fantastic, not at all girly. And his eyes. Oh God, his eyes! Up close, they were even more, more… wow! Paul Newman eyes. Better than Paul Newman's – deeper blue. And those lashes. Those long dark lashes! On any other man, they'd look queer, but he was definitely not queer. After five years at the Johannesburg School of Performing Arts, she had a built-in queer-alarm.

***

Brenda limped across the muddy pathway between the *ulpan* prefab houses to the communal bathroom. If she hurried, she might just get to see Alan in the dining room – and he might just smile at her, or at least acknowledge her existence.

The water in the shower was freezing – again. Noni said the solar geyser – sorry, the "water heater" – worked really well in summer. However, it certainly didn't do well when it rained, and rained, and rained. She shivered through her drip shower – there was no water pressure in the girls' bathroom. The boys' was apparently better and she'd seen that some girls used it, but what if she went in and some guys came in while she was undressed? It was bad enough when girls saw her showering. Yesterday, big Australian Emily had shouted to her friends, 'There's a boy in our showers. Oh, no, my mistake, it's a girl!'

Brenda wrapped her threadbare towel around her. Her

mama hadn't let her pack any of the huge, fluffy towels she'd always used before. 'You'll forget to bring it home again and I can't afford to lose a good towel.' *Mama* had never complained before, not even when she'd left towels in backstage dressing rooms all over South Africa.

She put on her work jacket and boots and hurried back through the rain to her room. Quickly pulling on her jeans and T-shirt, she added her only cardigan and slipped her feet into her sandals. She wished she'd thought to bring her winter clothes with her. They were hanging safely in her cupboard in summertime Jo'burg. Who knew Israel would be so wet and cold in January? She'd have to ask for permission to go into Jerusalem to buy a jersey and some closed shoes. Her mother would never pay to send her warm things over. It had been okay, so far, if she wore her work jacket and boots to class and the dining room, but now that Alan knew who she was... she'd rather freeze than let him see her masquerading as Sad Sack outside of working hours. She tried to dry her hair with the damp towel in front of the weak flame of the *neft* heater, and then squelched to the dining room, her hair dripping in rat's tails down her back.

Drawing a deep breath, Brenda pushed through the big glass doors into the huge room, big enough to seat all one thousand kibbutz members at long Formica tables. She glanced up and there he was, sitting with his fan club at a table right at the door. Usually, they sat at a table near the back.

'Hey, Belinda,' he called.

So much for her making an impression. Brenda lifted her chin, walked briskly to the serving cabinets and helped herself to salad and juice. Coffee would have been nice. South African coffee, not the disgusting stuff that left you with a mouthful of black mud if you forgot and drained your cup, as she always did. Gross. She found an empty table and sat down, peeking towards Alan's table, but dropping her eyes when she saw American Linda glaring at her.

'Hey, *wat's fout*? *Hoekom groet jy my nie*?' Alan was standing in front of her.

'Sorry. My Afrikaans isn't very good. What did you say?'

'*Ja*, you're a Jo'burg girl, all right. Why can't Jo'burg girls speak Afrikaans? I asked you why you didn't say hello to me when I called you just now.'

'Oh, were you speaking to me? I thought Belinda was one of your girlfriends. I'm Brenda.' Brenda surprised herself with her sharp response.

He turned a chair around and straddled it, supporting his chin on his crossed arms, and watched her. She put down her fork before she choked. She could feel American Linda and her gang's eyes boring into her. She didn't care. Alan, the most gorgeous guy on the kibbutz, had not only greeted her; he had actually come over to sit with her! Until now, all her meals had been solitary affairs. The *ulpan* girls obviously didn't like her. Girls never liked her. Boys also didn't. However, Alan wasn't a boy. He was a man, and he seemed to like her. At least a little.

'So,' Alan said. 'Brenda who's from Jo'burg and is eighteen. Where'd you go to school?'

'JSPA. The performing arts school in Jo'burg. And I'm not really eighteen. I will be, next month. And you? You're not from Jo'burg – or Cape Town – are you?'

Alan frowned. 'I didn't realise I still sounded like such a rock.'

She was horrified. She hadn't meant to offend him.

'I never said that. I just thought you didn't sound, well, like the boys I grew up with. Are you Afrikaans? I didn't know Jews were Afrikaans. Anyway, you don't really sound Afrikaans.'

'Actually, I'm a Free State boy. From a *dorp* called Driespruitfontein. And I used to sound a hellava lot more like a rock than I do now. I had intensive elocution lessons at varsity. But let's talk about you, seventeen-year-old Brenda. You're an actress?'

'No, a dancer. But I don't dance anymore.' Tears welled up in her eyes.

'Hey!' Alan reached over and squeezed her hand. 'I didn't mean to upset you. Why don't you dance anymore?'

'Sorry.' She gulped. 'I don't know why I still cry about it. I should be used to it by now. But you're being so kind and, and…' She burst into tears, pulled her hand free and ran out of the dining room, back to her solitary *ulpan* room.

***

Noni had said someone would be put in to share with her. 'This isn't a holiday resort,' she'd told her. 'Everyone has to share.'

She wasn't sure whether she would like a roommate or not. She'd never shared a room. Not even with *Mama*, and *Mama* always insisted that she have her own room when the school company travelled out of town for competitions or performances. 'Brenda needs her sleep,' *Mama* had told the teachers. 'She's a light sleeper and must have her own room.' Brenda was pretty sure *Mama* had had to pay extra for the privilege, but – back then – *Mama* had never begrudged her anything, never refused her anything.

Except that once. When the school had chosen her to go on tour to France and Germany to compete against other junior companies from all over the world. They had had a grant from the City Council and everything. It wouldn't cost her mother a cent, the principal had said.

But her mother had gone ballistic. 'No daughter of mine, no family of mine is ever, ever going to set foot there. Never again. My daughter is never going to perform for those people! Never again! You hear me?'

Brenda had stayed home and practised harder than ever.

***

Brenda was lying on her bed sobbing when Alan walked in and insisted that she tell him the whole stupid story about how she'd hurt her knee in rehearsals and how they'd operated, but it couldn't be fixed properly and that she'd never be able to dance again. Not at a professional level.

'There. That's it. Now you know. Not much of a story, is it?' she said.

But she didn't tell him everything. She couldn't tell him how her collapsing world had crushed her mother. About how *Mama* had dragged her from one specialist to the next, one physiotherapist to another, had tried every useless, painful treatment she could think of, had rubbed in gooey ointments and bound heated pads around her knee and leg, even burning her skin a few times. How *Mama*, face grim and accusing, had forced her to exercise her leg until she'd wept in pain, and how *Mama* grew colder and angrier and more remote until she wasn't there anymore.

One day, if she got to know him a lot better, she might tell him the whole story, but not now. Not yet. He'd think she was a drama queen, and she couldn't bear that.

'Shame, you poor little thing. Is it sore? I noticed you limping just now.'

'No, it's okay most of the time. Just if I turn suddenly. But the doctor gave me something for pain, so it's fine.'

He looked at his watch and stood up. 'We'd better get to class,' he said.

They walked together up to the *ulpan*, her heart singing.

'I'll see you later, okay?' he said at the door of her classroom.

More than okay. Much, much more.

CHAPTER 2

Alan swung Brenda up into his arms and carried her into his room. She was sure he could feel her heart thumping. She couldn't believe it was happening – she'd fantasised about this since she'd fallen in love with Mikhail Baryshnikov when *Mama* had hired *The Turning Point* and they'd watched it together, flickering on the lounge wall. Alan was a thousand times more handsome than Baryshnikov. She shivered.

The first time Alan had kissed her and put his tongue in her mouth, she had got such a shock. So this was French kissing. She didn't know what to do. Should she also put her tongue in his mouth? It was all so strange. In her Mills and Boon novels, the girls usually swooned or something when the man French kissed them, but no book she'd ever read explained what else the girl was supposed to do. She'd never even held hands with a boy, except as part of a dance routine, and most of those boys had been queer. However, Alan was so gentle. It was as if he knew how ignorant she was. He'd held her in his arms and looked at her with those incredible blue eyes, before lowering his head and putting his lips so softly over hers. 'A birthday kiss for a beautiful young woman,' he'd said.

His kisses had become more... different, sort of harder after that. It was so exciting. Boy, had she changed! She wasn't the same, frightened little girl who had fled Johannesburg and her mother's hatred. She was a woman, desired by the most incredible man in the world.

'You okay?' Alan asked. 'We don't have to do this, you know. I want you so much, but if you're not sure...'

'Please yes. I'm sure. I've never been more sure of anything in my life,' she lied. She buried her face in his neck. She was terrified. She had a pretty good idea how it all worked; of course she did, from her biology text book and the *Everywoman* book she'd flipped through quickly in CNA while *Mama* had been looking at the ballet books on the next shelf. It sounded awful. What if she couldn't do it? What if it hurt? What if he laughed at her because she was so bad at it? He could have any girl he wanted; she had to get it right or he'd never love her like she loved him.

He started to lift her T-shirt. She quickly crossed her arms over her chest.

'Put the light out. Please,' she whispered. She hated her double A-cup breasts and he would too, particularly after girls like American Linda.

'No,' he said. 'You're beautiful. I want to see you.'

He loosened her arms and pulled her T-shirt over her head, quickly undoing her bra – thank heavens she'd put on the pretty one – and then unzipping her jeans. She couldn't stop trembling. She couldn't breathe.

He started to pull off his jeans and she squeezed her eyes closed. She couldn't bring herself to look at him. She couldn't. She'd blush.

He picked her up and put her gently on the narrow bed. She could sense him bending over her; she felt his hands wandered slowly over her body, giving her goose flesh. Her eyes flew open as he cupped her stupid little breasts, so gently, as if he really did like them. She shivered. Then he was touching her down there and oh God, she didn't know what to do...

'Sweetheart,' he said. 'You are on something, aren't you?'

'What? I'm not sure what…'

'The pill, Brenda. Are you on the pill? Or something? Otherwise, I'll have to borrow one of Javier's condoms. I don't want kids, not now, not ever.'

She giggled. 'Oh gosh, I never thought. It's okay. *Mama* put me on the pill when I was fourteen. It was easier to control my periods, you see. So I didn't have a bad one during a competition, or something.'

'Thank you, *Mama*,' he murmured.

It didn't hurt. Only a little. Then he gave a shudder and rolled off her. It was over. She'd done it! She hoped she'd been okay. He seemed to have enjoyed it, but what did she know?

'I love you, Alan,' she said.

'Me too, sweetheart. You're beautiful.' After a while, he proceeded to show her just how beautiful, all over again.

***

Alan was just starting to make love to her once more when Javier, Alan's roommate, walked in, his shift in the chicken houses apparently having finished early.

'Shalom Brenda,' Javier said. He marched around collecting this and that, chattering away like Speedy Gonzales before heading off to the showers. She wanted to die. She just knew that the news about her and Alan would be all over the kibbutz within hours. She wasn't sure how she felt about that. Proud that Alan wanted her, of course, but she didn't want everyone to think she was easy, or cheap. She'd only known him for a couple of months. It was all happening so fast.

As soon as Javier closed the door behind him, she scrambled out of the bed, pulled on her clothes and fled, Alan's chuckles echoing in her ears.

CHAPTER 3

'What are you doing? Lie still,' Alan said.

They had just returned to their room after the movie in the kibbutz theatre. Alan had moved in with her a week after the first time they had made love, because Javier had complained about always being locked out of his room when she was there. Which was often. Brenda hadn't enjoyed the movie. She had found it difficult to follow the story, because, although it was an English movie, the *kibbutzniks* had continued chatting loudly, content to read the Hebrew subtitles. She couldn't read Hebrew, but it wouldn't have helped if she could, because she had her eyes shut a lot of the time. In South Africa, that movie would have had a four to twenty-one age restriction – if it hadn't been banned. She forced herself to watch some of the rude bits. Alan had put her on his lap and had his hand up her shirt, teasing her nipples. She had been so scared someone would see, but Alan didn't care and it had been quite nice, really.

When the movie had finished, they hadn't hung around for coffee and cake with the others. Alan had grabbed her hand

and they had raced back to their room. He slammed the door, undressed her quickly and tore off his clothes. Brenda smiled. Making love was actually quite nice now that she wasn't so scared, and Alan certainly seemed to enjoy it. She could even look at him a little without blushing now. Even when he had his pants off. Even when he was all hard.

She moved under him, thrusting her hips in what she hoped was a good imitation of what those women had been doing in the movie.

He stopped abruptly. 'Don't do that.'

'I thought you'd like it if I was more like... like the movie,' she whispered. 'I want to please you.'

'Those girls were sluts.'She wanted to die.

'You please me, just as you are,' he said. 'You don't have to pretend and fake things. Just lie still and enjoy it, okay?'

'Okay, if you're sure that's what you want?'

'I said so, didn't I? Look, Brenda, when I want you to do something different, I'll tell you.'

She blinked hard, but the tears still spilled down her face. 'Sorry.'

She lay stiffly on her back, terrified. She wished she knew what to do. He must hate her. He'd virtually called her a whore. What would she do if he threw her out? If he didn't love her anymore? He'd had so many women, beautiful, experienced women, who knew what they were doing, and she was so stupid and clumsy. And now he thought she was a slut. She tried to muffle her sobs.

Alan gave a little sigh and rolled off her. He gathered her in his arms.

'Oh don't cry, sweetheart. It's okay. You were great. You couldn't have known what I want, what turns me on. But now you do, so it's all okay again, all right? We won't have to talk about this ever again.'

She nodded, relieved. He still loved her. Later, she lay as still as she could as he showed her again just how much he loved her.

***

The *ulpan* farewell concert was coming up and Brenda had a brainwave. She approached Javier, Australian Jim and American Robbie, three of the biggest men in the *ulpan*, to do the act with her. She didn't tell Alan. It was to be her surprise. The guys were sworn to secrecy.

'We're going to do the dance of the cygnets, from *Swan Lake*. Except we'll call it *Duck Pond*,' she said. 'Usually, the four cygnets are the same size, but you will be dancing with me, so that will be really funny. And, you guys will wear your work boots and funny skirts. I've spoken to Noni and she's found me a leotard, tights, and a short net thing I can tie around my waist as a tutu. And even toe shoes, so I'll be a proper ballerina, which will make the whole thing even funnier.' And she'd be able to show Alan just how talented she was.

She put on the *Tchaikovsky* LP she'd borrowed from the kibbutz music library, positioned herself between Javier and Robbie, and showed them how to link their arms.

'Okay, first we go to the left. Let your right leg cross behind the left. One, two and three, four, five six. Stop, stop, stop!' She laughed as the boys tripped themselves up. 'It's easy, look. Watch me.'

The three men watched as she floated through the steps, first to the left, then to the right.

'Now the next bit is a bit more complicated, so watch carefully,' she said, going up on points. 'You just stand on your toes, if you can, then bring your feet in together. Like this.'

The four "cygnets" fell about laughing as they stood on each other's toes, but, by the end of the first rehearsal, Brenda was confident they'd be able to get it together in time for the concert.

'Rehearsals again tomorrow, okay guys?' Her three oversized cygnets agreed. What a pity, she heard Jim say, that it had taken them to right near to end of the six-month *ulpan* to find out what a good sport little Brenda was.

Javier agreed. 'Alan, he never tell me she so funny,' he said to Robbie. 'He selfish, that one.'

Brenda hugged herself in delight. It was so nice to be liked.

Two days before the concert, the four cygnets were rehearsing as usual in the theatre when Alan burst in.

'What the hell do you think you are doing?' he shouted.

'Oh, Alan.' Brenda was so disappointed. 'This was supposed to be a surprise.'

'It's a surprise, all right,' he said. He looked furious. 'I couldn't believe it when Linda told me you were screwing around half naked with these guys. Shit, Javier, I thought you were my friend.' Alan marched onto the stage and grabbed her hand. 'Come on, we're leaving.'

She pulled back. 'No, Alan, what's the matter with you? We're not doing anything wrong. We're just rehearsing for the concert; it's really funny and…'

'It's not bloody funny. It's sick. I'm not going to let you flaunt yourself in front of the entire kibbutz dressed in that. It leaves absolutely nothing to the imagination. Been enjoying yourself, have you, Javier, feeling up my girl?'

Javier's olive skin darkened and he walked threateningly towards Alan. Brenda scurried between them. 'No, Javier. It's okay. I should have asked Alan if it was okay for me to dance with you.'

She turned to Alan. 'Please, we've worked so hard. Just watch, you'll see.'

'I don't want to see and you're not going to dance at the concert.' He grabbed her hand and pulled her off the stage.

'Alan! I wasn't doing anything wrong. I thought you'd enjoy it.' She stumbled along behind him. She was frightened. She didn't understand. What had she done to make him so angry?

He pushed her into their room and slammed the door.

The bang seemed to rouse him, because he pulled her into his arms and made love to her – so passionately, she gasped. Afterwards, she clung to him, tears of relief streaming down her face. He still loved her.

'Oh, sweetheart. I didn't mean to go off at you like that. But when I saw you up on your toes in those stupid shoes, I was so frightened you'd hurt yourself. You know your knee isn't right. You shouldn't be dancing,' he said.

'My knee is fine. Really. I've been really careful, and the dance isn't difficult. I've hardly had to take any pain tablets since we started rehearsing. Please let me dance in the concert.'

'No. We're leaving tomorrow. I have to get out of Israel. If you love me, you'll come with me. Otherwise, you can stay and dance with Javier in your stupid concert,' he said.

'Alan, I love you. You know I do. But I can't just leave tomorrow. Where would we go? I don't have any money. I have to ask *Mama*...' Her voice trailed away.

'You haven't spoken to your mother once since we've been together,' he said. 'You haven't received a single letter from her in six months? You said yourself, she doesn't give a damn about you. Well, I love you. I really do love you, sweetheart. Come with me. I'll take care of you. I promise.'

***

The next morning, early, they left the kibbutz, all their stuff packed in Alan's old rucksack.

They caught the bus to Haifa and took a ferry to Greece. For three nights, they slept with dozens of other young people on the deck, sweltering under an airless canvass awning. They hadn't had time to get food from the kibbutz dining room, so they ate the stale baklava that was all that was available for the deck passengers, after the curly ham and cheese sandwiches ran out. In Athens, Alan used most of his remaining dollars to buy two Eurorail tickets.

'We take another ferry to Brindisi in Italy,' he said, pouring over the map he'd taken from the Eurorail ticket office. 'Then we get a train to Milan. From there, we travel through Switzerland to Frankfurt, and then get a ferry train to Ostend. That'll get us to Dover. It shouldn't take us more than a couple of days.'

'Do we have to go to Germany? *Mama* will be really upset if I go there.'

'So I won't tell her if you don't,' Alan said.

'What will we do when we get there? To England? We don't have money and my father's family disowned him when he married *Mama*. I don't know where they live or anything.'

Alan put her on his lap and rocked her. 'Shh, don't worry. Things will work out. You'll see. I'll take care of you, sweetheart. I'll always take care of you.'

It was dark when they travelled through Germany, so all they saw of the country that had shaped her childhood was railway stations.

'I suppose we shouldn't complain,' she said, as they lay in

each other's arms on the platform at Frankfurt station waiting for the ferry train that would take them to England. '*Mama* must have had it far, far worse when she travelled across Europe. She was about my age then, I suppose. She must have been so frightened.'

They clung together miserably as the steel grey Channel heaved and tried to push them back to Europe. She tried to sleep, but it was no good. She was too cold and hungry. Alan couldn't sleep either. They chatted about nothing, anything to forget their misery. The sight of the famous white cliffs looming up out of the mist sent them into a pensive, worried silence. What would she do if they wouldn't let Alan in? What if they sent him back to South Africa? To jail. She'd die; she'd just die without him.

CHAPTER 4
LONDON, 1985

'Why did you lie to me?' Brenda gazed up at Alan. She felt as if the bottom had dropped out of her world. She was so frightened. They'd had a much needed bath and an even more welcome meal soon after arriving at Sally's little flat on the High Street upstairs from a Chinese takeaway. Sally, that awful Annette's aunt, had apologised for their spartan accommodation, but it was warm, dry and spotlessly clean.

'It's wonderful, thank you,' Alan said. Brenda hoped Sally put her silence down to tiredness.

After supper – "tea", Sally called it – they walked slowly down the road, exploring the neighbourhood. She was seething with rage and jealousy, and yes, terror too. Finally, she burst.

'You lied to me, Alan. You lied to me about everything.'

'What the hell did I lie about?'

'Everything. You didn't tell me about Annette – that she'd be waiting to fall into your arms as soon as you arrived in England. You didn't tell me anything about her! Ever. How do you think I felt when I saw her all over you?'

'You're being ridiculous.' Alan chuckled.

Brenda clenched her hands.

'I wasn't sure she would be at the port. I didn't even know if she got my letter telling her I was coming to England. I hadn't seen or spoken to her for years. And I didn't tell you about her because there's nothing to tell. That's not a lie.'

'But she was your girlfriend, back in South Africa. And you never even mentioned her to me!'

'We were friends. That's all. I hadn't heard from her in years.'

'Then how did you know where to find her? How did she know when and where to meet us – you, I mean. She obviously wasn't expecting me.'

'I wrote a letter to her care of the Anti Apartheid Movement. I thought she'd probably be working for them, or an organisation like them, and hoped they would pass on the letter. I never told her about you because, when I wrote to her, I didn't know I'd fall in love with you and want you to be with me, always.'

She melted. 'Oh Alan, I love you too. But please, let's not have any secrets from each other in future. Even if we're worried they will make us cross or hurt or whatever. Promise?'

'Promise.' He picked her up and sealed his promise with a deep kiss.

'Let's go back,' he said when he finally released her. 'I need to sleep – with you!'

Brenda giggled. It was okay. She was just being stupid. Alan loved her. They were together, in London. They had a nice place to stay. Sally was great. She still wasn't sure about Annette. She seemed like a bit of a snob. However, life was good. Perhaps it was time to make up with her mother too. She surely couldn't still be angry with her. She'd write to her tomorrow.

***

Sally gave Brenda some airmail paper, an airmail envelope and a stamp.

'Is it safe to give my *mama* my new address?' she asked.

Sally laughed. 'If the South African security police want to find out where you are, they'll know soon enough once we get young Alan going on our campaign. I wouldn't worry too much about it, dear. We take what precautions we can and then we just get on with what we have to do, don't we?'

The next morning, while Alan was at the WOAH office working on the new fund raising campaign with Sally and Annette, Brenda settled down to write to *Mama*. It took her five attempts, but, finally, she was as satisfied as she could be with it. It wasn't perfect, but it was an olive branch and that's what counted.

Dear Mama. I'm so sorry not to have written before. I am well. I'm in London with a wonderful man, who loves me. He's South African too. I met him on the kibbutz and we travelled here by train. We had to go via Germany. I'm sorry about that, but we didn't get off the train, not once. His name is Alan Silverman. He has a degree from Wits in accounting. He has applied for political asylum in England because the security police at home are after him because he is opposed to apartheid. Luckily, I have my British passport, so I'm okay. Please God, one day, you'll meet him. I love you, Mama. I look forward to hearing from you. Your loving daughter, Brenda.

Sticking the stamp on the letter, she walked down the road to the red post box and pushed the letter through the slit. There. She'd done it. Then she explored the shops and the side streets, killing time until Alan came home.

She couldn't believe she was finally in England, in London. She and *Mama* had spoken about travelling to England since she was little. One day, *Mama* had said, one day you will dance at Covent Garden for Anna. Maybe Alan would take her to see a ballet at Covent Garden, and maybe she could ask Sally where the Royal Academy of Ballet was and go and watch a class or two, if they'd let her. She could have been in those classes. She was supposed to have auditioned for them, but then that clumsy twit, Ronald du Toit, had dropped her during rehearsals for *Swan Lake*. Suzette had got to dance Odette – but Suzette hadn't been invited to London to audition.

She sniffed and sat down at a bus stop. Her knee hurt. She would have to find a doctor soon. She was running out of pain pills. Should she try to find her father's family? Daddy might have told her where they lived, but she couldn't remember.

Perhaps she could ask *Mama*. Although *Mama* had never wanted anything to do with them, just as they'd wanted nothing to do with her. A Jewish refugee, a concentration camp nobody, wasn't good enough for their son and heir, *Mama* had told her when she asked about them after Daddy had died. They probably didn't even know she existed. After all, Daddy and *Mama* had been married for almost twenty years before she'd been born, and her passport said just that she was plain Brenda Anna Jones. Not Brenda Anna Armsford-Jones. She put the Armsford-Joneses out of her mind and limped back to the flat.

She was sitting in Sally's little lounge watching *The Two Ronnies* when Alan walked in with some chop suey for supper.

He was really excited. His blue eyes were sparkling… and his hair! He'd had a haircut. The ponytail was gone and he looked so distinguished.

'They said I had to look less like a hippy and more like a good, clean living *boereseun*.' Alan smiled at her, his white teeth gleaming.

Her insides turned to jelly. She'd never understand what this beautiful, clever, gorgeous man saw in her. Never.

He sat down on the couch and she snuggled onto his lap while he told her about his day. The haircut and the shopping for new clothes and the photographs for the posters and pamphlets, and how he and Annette had worked on his speech. She let his voice drift over her. She didn't want to know the details. She didn't want to hear about Annette. She just wanted to be close to him.

By the time Alan had finished telling her everything, the chop suey was cold. Sally only had a little two-plate stove and they didn't know how to work the microwave oven thingy. Neither of them had ever seen a microwave before. So they ate the chop suey quickly and tumbled into bed. Apparently, Annette popped in later, to visit Sally. They hadn't heard a thing.

***

A few weeks later, a letter plopped through the letterbox for Brenda. The post mark said Hillbrow, South Africa. The return address was a P O Box. She didn't recognise the handwriting. Her heart sank. Still nothing from her mother.

She was alone in the flat. Sally and Alan were at the office with Annette. She'd washed her hair, because Alan had told her that the meeting tonight was really important, and very different to what they had done before. It was in London this time, at the Golders Green *Shul* Hall. 'These people usually give lots of money to Israel, but we're not sure how they will respond to an Afrikaner from South Africa,' Sally told them. 'So we're really going to have to charm them.'

With her hair wrapped into a towel turban, Brenda carefully slit open the envelope with one of Sally's kitchen knives.

Dear Brenda,

I don't know if you remember me. I live in the flat three doors down from yours. I regret to tell you this, but your mother died tragically in a car accident soon after you left. I told the police that I thought it was very strange, because she was always such a careful driver. But the police think she fell asleep and drove off the road into a tree. Anyway, the car was a write-off. She never told me where you'd gone and you never wrote or phoned, so I didn't know where to get hold of you until now. She was buried in West Park Cemetery. The Chevrah Kadisha took care of everything. They took her clothes and furniture – to cover the cost of the funeral and pay the rent on the flat. The flat has now been let to a lovely young couple. I wish you a long life. Sincerely, Myrah Finkelstein.

Alan came in. Brenda was still sitting on the bed in her underwear with a towel around her head.

'Brenda, for God's sake. Why aren't you ready? I told you to be ready by the time I got home. Get a move on.'

She held out the letter. She was trying not to cry. She didn't want to upset him, because he was always nervous and tense before a big presentation, but this was important.

'Alan, read this. It's from South Africa.'

'I'll read it later, okay? But now we're going to be late. Get dressed. Christ, you haven't even done your hair. What have you been doing all day?'

'Alan, please read it, please!' Tears rolled down her cheeks.

'Oh for heaven's sake. Here. Give it to me.'

He glanced at the letter, and then read it again. Then he took her in his arms and she sobbed. She just couldn't help it.

'Oh my poor sweetheart,' he said. 'My poor baby. Look, should I phone Sally and cancel tonight?'

She shook her head. She knew this meeting was important. Alan had to go. And she would go with him. He needed her. Staying home and moping wouldn't bring her mother back, and, if Alan went alone, Annette would be thrilled.

She pulled her pale blue dress over her head. Alan liked that dress best. He said it made her look like one of those porcelain dolls she liked so much. She quickly zipped it up and slipped on some flat white shoes. Alan didn't like her to wear high heels. He said it could make her knee worse. She ran her fingers through the tangles of her hair and examined her reflection in the mirror. Not too bad. By the time they got to Golders Green, her eyes should be less puffy. She put on some pale pink lipstick – Alan didn't like her to wear too much make-up – grabbed her bag and walked to the door.

'Let's go.'

They walked in silence to the tube station. On the train, Alan held her hand, but she couldn't bring herself to look at him. If she did, and saw the loving sympathy in his eyes, she'd just start bawling again. Then there was a mad dash to change lines at Embankment and they just made it in time onto the Edgeware train. The journey to Golders Green continued in silence, but she noticed Alan looking at her with concern from time to time. She wanted to tell him not to worry, that she was a trouper and wouldn't fall apart. She kept silent.

They walked towards the *shul*. On North End Road, Alan pointed to a beautiful old house. 'Look, that's Ivy House. I heard that's where Anna Pavlova used to live.'

She lost it. Tears streamed down her face. He stared at her in bewilderment. 'You're so into ballet, I thought you'd find it interesting that she lived there. Annette told me to point it out to you. I thought you'd be pleased.'

Annette! Always Annette. She hurried on. The *shul* hall should be on the left. There it was. She turned in at the gate, stopped, drew in a breath and smiled radiantly at Annette and Sally, who were waiting at the door for them. Showtime, folks!

As usual, Annette ignored her, her eyes only on Alan, but Sally looked at her curiously. 'Are you all right, dear? You haven't been crying, have you?'

'I'm fine. Thanks,' Brenda answered crisply. She saw Sally was taken aback at her abruptness, but she couldn't bear her warm sympathy. Not now. Not if she was to hold it together, and Alan needed her.

She watched as Annette linked her arm in Alan's and they walked into the hall together. She followed with Sally.

The audience was not all that different to what she was used to. Except a lot of the women wore floral skirts and dresses, rather than slacks, and a lot had scarves or hats on their heads.

Some even wore what looked like wigs. Brenda was glad she'd worn a dress too. A lot of the men wore *yarmulkes*, and several had beards.

Sally did her introductions and then Alan look over. Brenda tried to concentrate.

'Thank you, Miss McDonald,' Alan said. 'Good evening, rabbi, ladies and gentlemen. *Shalom.*' There was very little sign of Alan's distinctive Driespruitfontein accent tonight. Instead, his speech was sprinkled with Yiddish and Hebrew. 'My name is Alan Silverman and I am a South African. A Jewish South African, although I am quite a rare Jewish South African.'

Brenda stopped listening. She'd heard it all before anyway.

Suddenly, she realised everyone was looking at her. Alan was pointing at her.

'That's my Brenda,' he said. 'Stand up, sweetheart. Let them see just how beautiful you are.'

Brenda cringed. However, Alan needed her, so she fixed a smile on her face, stood and graciously, gracefully bowed her head – Pavlova's dying swan.

She fell back into her chair as Alan continued. 'My Brenda's mum was in Birkenau.' This was too much. Tears flowed down her face again. The fat little woman sitting next to her squeezed her hand, the pain from the rings on her dumpy fingers a welcome release from her internal agony. Her husband, a bald man with a *yarmulke*, leaned over his wife and offered her his handkerchief. Brenda gulped down her sobs as Alan continued. The silence in the hall roared in her head.

The fat little woman turned to her and smiled warmly. 'You poor dear, It's hard, isn't it, when the Holocaust is so close.'

She nodded, then added, 'It's not that, really. It just that *Mama* died... um... recently.'

'Oh you poor, poor child. I wish you long life. How sad, how very sad. What about your father?'

'He died years ago.'

'Brothers? Sisters?'

Brenda shook her head.

'So you're all alone?'

'I have Alan. I'm so lucky to have Alan,' Brenda said.

The little woman chuckled. 'Indeed, you are, dear. Very lucky indeed. Come along, let's have a nice cup of tea and you can tell me all about yourself. You're also South African? I'm Ruth Shapiro, by the way. And this,' she said, 'is my husband, Ben.'

CHAPTER 5
LONDON, 1989

Brenda was tired. So tired. She wasn't sleeping well. She kept having that awful nightmare, the one where her mother drove her car into a tree, over and over again. After four years, it was still as vivid as ever. And the cold she'd picked up at the Trafalgar Square demonstration just wouldn't go away. She always got sick in winter. She'd never get used to winter in London. She would rather have slept than schlep all the way with Alan to Annette and Charles' flat in Chiswick for Christmas lunch, although it had been wonderful to see Sally again. Albeit very briefly. She didn't see Sally from one month to the next, now that they lived so far away, but their bedsit was closer for Alan to get to work and it was nice and close to the Shapiros' beautiful Golders Green house. Actually, Brenda would rather have spent Christmas with the Shapiros, except they didn't celebrate Christmas. They had given her and Alan a lovely little *Chanukah* present for their bedsit – a pretty gold *menorah* that she had put on the chest of drawers.

She felt sick and wobbly. If she didn't feel right soon, she'd have to go back to the clinic to get more antibiotics. She also needed more pain pills for her knee anyway, so she could kill two birds with one stone. Meanwhile, she had a class to get through. She only got paid per lesson and they needed every penny she earned. London was so expensive.

The music stopped and her little puddings stood patiently, waiting for her to give them their next exercise. They were so cute, especially the littlest one, Bridgette. She was only four, but already there were signs of true talent emerging. The others were sweet and tried hard. Their Christmas/Chanukah/ end-of-year concert had been adorable. All their mummies and daddies had crowded into the community centre hall to watch their budding Fonteyns (never Pavlovas) dance the ballet she had choreographed especially for them. *The Little Milkmaid*. Patricia's older girls had also put on a great performance. And then, to the absolute delight of all their young students, she and Patricia danced for them. Grown up ballet. Alan hadn't objected, even though she had to dance on points. Hiring a real tutu had been so worth the expense when she saw the absolute delight on her kids' faces. She was no longer their teacher; she was a real ballerina, like the one in their music boxes. Alan had stood proudly at her side when she chatted to the parents over refreshments after the concert, his arm around her shoulders. It had made her so proud to see the mummies' reaction when she introduced them to Alan. They'd patted their hair and pulled at their jackets and smiled brightly at him, telling him how wonderful she was with their angels. The dads had also been very kind to her.

She'd found dancing with Patricia quite easy. She had been doing her ballet warm-up and exercises regularly, ever since Patricia had invited her to join the little community centre ballet school. So perhaps her knee was getting stronger and the pain was manageable, most of the time. The pain pills were pure magic. Perhaps she could still be a ballerina, one day – if Alan agreed. Now, however, she had to get through today's class.

Brenda fell into bed when she got home. She hoped Alan would let her sleep tonight, but that was unlikely. He loved her so much and she loved him. But she was so tired; she was terrified she'd fall asleep and snore while he made love to her. She really should consider herself lucky that he still wanted her so much and wasn't like Patricia's husband. Patricia had confided that her husband, Bill, only made love to her once a week. On Saturdays. If Arsenal won. Brenda had squirmed with embarrassment.

***

'Jesus, Brenda, are you still sick?' Brenda could hear the concern in Alan's voice as she emerged from the toilet. 'I think you need to see another doctor. You can't possibly have flu again, surely.'

She sniffed miserably. 'I'm so sorry about this. I don't know what's wrong. I've been fine, for ages. You know that. It's only been the last couple of weeks. I think it must be some kind of tummy bug. I just can't keep anything down.'

'Shame. My poor little angel.'

Brenda looked at him miserably and sat on the bed.

'Do you mind if I don't go? Really, I just want to sleep. I'm exhausted. And I think I have a bladder infection too because I spent half the night going to the loo. Please. Annette won't mind, I'm sure. Please go without me.'

She tried to smile. She knew she was no fun when she was sick. She'd been like a wet blanket at the New Year party. All those interesting people from the Anti Apartheid Movement and a lot of South Africans from the ANC, and she'd barely had enough energy to mope in the corner all night.

She couldn't eat and she was still getting fat. Only last night, Alan had teased her that she'd better watch herself or she'd turn into one of those floppy, wobbly women he loathed.

'Okay, sweetheart. You stay home and get better. Don't worry about making supper for me. I'll eat with Annette and Charles at a pub somewhere.'

As the door closed behind him, she dissolved. This was more than a tummy bug, she was absolutely certain. She hoped it wasn't cancer.

CHAPTER 6

The next Friday morning – she didn't have any classes on Fridays – Brenda made her way to the hospital. She followed the signs to the emergency room and slipped into a chair close to the door. What was she doing here? This was a nightmare. She was still feeling awful and she was terrified that Alan would lose patience with her. She could have gone to the clinic where she got her pills and pain tablets. But they knew Alan there and she couldn't risk that flirty nurse comforting him when they told him how sick she really was.

A nurse took her into a private cubicle and waited for her to speak.

'I feel sick all the time and sometimes I vomit. And I need to pee all the time and I'm so tired,' Brenda said.

'Oh my goodness! Is it possible you could be pregnant? How old are you, dear?' The nurse looked really concerned.

'I'm twenty-two and I'm not pregnant.'

'Goodness! That's okay then.' The nurse laughed. 'You don't look a day older than fifteen. I was worried I'd have to call Social Services. Get undressed and put this on so the doctor can examine you. Opening at the front. I just need to ask you a few questions.'

Brenda took the proffered white cotton gown.

'Are you married?'

Brenda shook her head sadly.

'Steady boyfriend? Good. That's good. Do you live with your boyfriend? Lovely.'

While Brenda changed, the nurse prattled on.

'You might be pregnant, you know, but that shouldn't be a problem then, should it?'

'I'm can't be,' Brenda said. 'I'm on the pill.'

'Good girl. We have so many little girls like you coming in here, too scared to ask their mothers about contraception; too embarrassed to ask us for it. And then they fall pregnant and it's so sad for everyone. Of course, it's worse when the girls have been raped, especially by their fathers…'

'You're kidding. Fathers actually rape their daughters?' Brenda couldn't believe it.

'It happens. Not often – as far as we can tell – but often enough.'

'But I thought this was a nice neighbourhood.'

'Indeed it is. But unfortunately, money in the bank is money in the bank. And what goes on behind closed doors, goes on, doesn't it? I apologise. I didn't mean to upset you. Your situation is nothing like that, is it? You have a lovely boyfriend and you are a grown up young woman, quite capable of making your own decisions, if you are pregnant.'

'I'm not. Really, I'm sure it's some kind of tummy bug or something,' Brenda insisted.

The nurse smiled at her and then stepped aside as the doctor, a tall blonde woman, came in.

'When did your last period start?' the doctor asked.

'A couple of weeks ago. On my birthday. When it was supposed to.' She wouldn't forget that. Alan had been a little upset. It had messed up his birthday plans for her.

'And your next period is due... when?'

'I've about six of the while pills left before the red pills start.'

The doctor raised her eyebrows. 'So you're on the pill and you haven't missed a period?'

'That's right.'

'And you've been feeling nauseous. Are your breasts tender?'

Brenda nodded.

'Need to urinate frequently – go to the loo a lot?'

She nodded again.

'Well, it sounds like you might be pregnant, but let's take a look, shall we? Just to rule that out before we start investigating what else it could be. Raise your knees and open your legs. Good girl. You've given nurse a little urine sample, yes?'

The doctor examined her and Brenda gazed up at the ceiling, willing herself elsewhere. This was so gross and embarrassing.

Then the doctor spoke. 'Well, my dear. There's no doubt about it. You are pregnant, and quite far along too. '

Brenda burst into tears. 'I can't be. It's just not possible! I take the pill every single day. I've never missed. Not once. My boyfriend even checks. You're wrong. You must be!'

'Have you been ill at all recently?'

Brenda shook her head.

'You're sure? No antibiotics by any chance?'

'Yes, just before Christmas. I had a cold and it wouldn't get better.'

'Well, sometimes antibiotics and the pill don't agree. Your doctor should have told you to take additional precautions. Didn't he warn you?'

Brenda bit her lip. He had, but she hadn't paid too much attention. Anyway, Alan hated condoms. They'd had to use them once when she had a thrush infection and he'd complained and she hadn't wanted to upset him, especially as they were spending so much time with Annette over Christmas and everything... and now look. Now he would hate her and it was all her fault for being so stupid. He was always telling her that he didn't want kids.

'But I haven't missed a period!' she insisted. This wasn't happening to her. This was a huge, gigantic joke and she'd wake up and find she was still in bed, with Alan beside her.

'I'm afraid the pill can do that sometimes. Make it seem like you're having a period when you aren't,' the doctor said.

'What do I do now? My boyfriend doesn't want children.'

'He may change his mind. The dads often do once they've faced with the facts. You can discuss it with him and see...'

'No! I can't tell him. I just can't. I can't lose him. He's all I've got.' She could hear her voice rising in hysteria.

The doctor patted her arm sympathetically. 'You still have a little time to decide what you want to do. I can do an ultrasound now and that will give us a better idea of your options.'

'You mean how long I have before I have to decide whether to keep the... this...'

'Whether or not to take the pregnancy to term? Yes.' The doctor waited.

Brenda closed her eyes, but the tears squeezed through. How had it come to this? This morning, she'd come to the hospital to get something for a tummy bug. Maybe cancer. Now they were talking about abortion. As if from a distance, she heard the doctor's voice asking if she'd like the ultrasound. She shook her head. She didn't want to see it, if there really was anything there.

The doctor pressed on her tummy again.

'Yes, there it is,' the doctor murmured. 'No question, my dear. You are pregnant. About ten weeks along, I'd say.'

***

Brenda flung the door open and hurtled into the bedsit's tiny bathroom, just in time. She wasn't sure if this was her normal mid-afternoon morning sickness – at least she now knew what her nausea was – or whether this nausea had a different source altogether: sheer terror. She couldn't remember leaving the hospital; she had no idea how she had got home. Two weeks. She had two weeks to decide whether to tell Alan. Or not. The good news was that, after two weeks, the nausea would probably end – whatever she decided.

Well, she wasn't going to think about it now. They were going to the Shapiros for *Shabbos* dinner tonight and she only had a couple of hours to pull herself together. Then, later tonight, after they'd made love, she'd find a way to tell Alan. Or maybe it would be better to wait for tomorrow. Or next week. She hoped Alan wouldn't insist on an abortion.

PART 4
BEN

CHAPTER 1
LONDON, 2012

Ben started awake. Miss Patel was standing by his side, a document in her hand. Must have dozed off again. What an old fart, *alter kocker* he was. Put his *tuches* in a chair and he was lights out in two minutes.

'I thought this might interest you,' his secretary/companion said. 'I found it on the internet. It's from a South African newspaper, the *Daily Express*. It's about that little ballet school the Foundation got involved with last year. Looks like they may need our help again. I've printed it out for you.' She knew how he hated reading anything on the computer, and why should he? She handed him his specs and the document. He was pleased to note that it was in large type. The old eyes weren't as young as they used to be. Now what was this all about?

FINDING FREEDOM –
BRENDA SILVERMAN'S SECRET LIFE

By Tracy Jacobs

Photographs: Precious Motholo

Alexandra Township, on the outskirts of one of South Africa's most affluent areas, is not a pretty place to visit.

Across the highway in the west lies Sandton. Its mansions, set in luxuriously rolling emerald lawns, cower behind high walls. But the streets are largely un-potholed and many are shaded by large plane and jacaranda trees. Brenda Silverman lived in a suburb just like that.

The streets of Alex are rutted. Raw sewage spills out of an open manhole and runs down the tar. What passes for a gutter is clogged with rubbish. Manoeuvring a car through the narrow streets, avoiding strolling pedestrians, squeezing past minibus taxis, requires nerves of steel.

Cheek-by-jowl shacks fester like pimples on the faded faces of the few solid brick houses still standing. There isn't a tree to be seen. Not a blade of grass.

The assembly area at Alexandra Junior School is a whirlwind of dust, kicked up by the children playing there. They are dressed in an odd assortment of uniforms. Many are barefoot.

Several classrooms sport broken windows. From one of these comes the sound of music. Inside, 20 little girls, dressed in pink tights and leotards, are holding onto the backs of a line of chairs with their left hands, while their right foot snaps sharply to the front, to the side, to the front, and back together.

A heap of desks is piled in the corner.

The little girls stand on their toes, turn around and hold the chair with their right hands. The exercise is repeated with their little left legs.

Miriam Mazebuko (21) calls instructions to the children. Florence Sibiya (19) works the tape recorder.

'*Ma*Brenda started teaching us ballet here in Alex many years ago,' Ms Mazebuko says.

*Ma*Brenda. That's what they call Brenda Silverman in Alex. To most readers of the *Daily Express*, she is – was – Mrs Alan Silverman, wife of the property magnate.

The late Mrs Silverman.

But in Alex, on a hot Wednesday afternoon, Brenda Silverman's legacy lives on.

Miriam was one of her first pupils in the township. Now she is teaching the skills she learned from Brenda to another generation of potential ballerinas.

'When she first started her studio here, we thought she was crazy. We didn't know what ballet was,' she recalls.

'But she brought us a movie – *The Turning Point* – and that was it for me. I wanted to be like that girl in the movie. We show that video to the kids every year. They love it.'

'I wanted to be like *Ma*Brenda,' Florence interrupts. 'Sometimes she would dance for us – right here in this classroom. She'd take off that stupid wig she always wore and she'd go into the toilet and change into her leotard and tights. I'd take them home and wash them for her. I looked after her ballet shoes too.' She holds out a pair of worn toe shoes.

'She said she found freedom here, with us,' Miriam adds. 'She said she wasn't allowed to dance where she lived; that's why we looked after her things. She was so sad sometimes, and then she'd dance and be happy. And the little girls would dance with her, like I used to. They loved her. We all did.'

They open a photograph album and sadly page through it. Joy radiates from the pictures, some faded, some blurry, but each one a symphony of love and dedication and… freedom.

'That's my favourite,' Miriam says, pointing to one dog-eared picture. Florence agrees. It's a classical ballet pose (see left): Brenda Silverman on points, her arms reaching out gracefully. But what makes the photograph so compelling is the adoration on the faces of the children seated on the floor in front of her.

Brenda Silverman didn't only teach the budding ballerinas. She kitted each of "her girls" with tights, leotards and shoes. She arranged for two of her pupils to attend Johannesburg School of Performing Arts on full scholarships.

Another of her young stars, Lindiwe Zulu, is currently in London, with the Royal Ballet Company.

'We don't know if we can carry on with the studio,' Miriam says. '*Ma*Brenda promised us she would send us money every month when she went away. She was so happy that day. But now there is no more money.'

That was the last time they saw her. The next day, 6 February this year, Brenda Silverman was found by her domestic worker, dead in her bed.

According to the police, she hadn't been ill. She had gone to bed as usual. There was no sign of forced entry or any kind of violence. An inquest is to be held next month in the Johannesburg Magistrate's Court to determine the cause of death.

But in Alex, as the music drifts across the playground and 20 little girls in a makeshift studio dream of a famous future, Brenda Silverman lives – for now.

Anyone wishing to find out more about the Alex Ballet School can call Miriam Mazebuko on 072 345 6789.

Ben took off his glasses and wiped his eyes. Tears rolled down his cheeks, got caught in the furrows alongside his mouth and dripped off his chin. Brenda was dead. He wished he'd known. He would have made an effort to get to the funeral, but it was too late now. The funeral was months ago. He would like to have gone and paid his respects. He couldn't believe she was dead. He put his glasses back on and studied the photographs Miss Patel had thoughtfully attached. She had barely changed, after all these years. It was so long ago. He remembered the first time they met as if it was yesterday.

CHAPTER 2
LONDON, 1985

Ben shifted and tried to make himself comfortable on the hard chair. He'd have to try harder to persuade the *shul* committee that they needed padded chairs in the hall, for meetings like this. Not that he intended coming to any more events like this one. He didn't even want to be at this one. He had no interest in horses. He didn't like any animals, for that matter. He wanted to be at home, with his feet up, watching *MasterMind*, but Ruth had insisted… and when Ruth insisted, well, it wasn't worth arguing. He smiled at his wife. She was looking lovely, as always. A little plump, maybe, but what could you expect for a woman of what? Over fifty. He shook his head – where had the years gone? He straightened his *yarmulke*, folded his arms over his stomach and let the buzz in the hall flow over him.

The buzz subsided as a small grey woman walked towards the microphone. She looked like, what was her name again? The English teacher at Jeremy's old school, the one who told the little *pisher* he could act. If he ever met her again, he'd have a serious bone to pick with her.

'Thank you, rabbi, ladies and gentlemen,' the grey woman said. 'I'm Sally McDonald and I work for WOAH – Women Opposed to Apartheid.'

'You didn't tell me WOAH had anything to do with apartheid,' he hissed at Ruth.

She beamed back at him. 'What did you think WOAH was about?'

'*Ver vaist*? Who knows? I thought it was about horses. I don't give a damn about apartheid. Fought with some South Africans in the war and fine fellows they were. Wouldn't have come if I'd known...'

'Shh.' She nudged him with her elbow.

The grey woman stepped away from the podium and a strapping young man took her place. Good-looking youngster. Clean cut. Fair hair. Looked like he knew what a hard day's work entailed. Not like Jeremy.

'Thank you, Miss McDonald,' the young man said. 'Good evening, rabbi, ladies and gentlemen. *Shalom*.'

Well, that was nice. The boy had made an effort to learn a little Hebrew.

'My name is Alan Silverman and I am a South African, although I am quite a rare South African. You see, I'm what's known as a *boerejood* – an Afrikaner Jew.'

Ben smiled. He'd met Afrikaners during the war, and a few *Yiddisher* South Africans too, but he'd never realised there were *Yiddisher* Afrikaners. This should be interesting.

The youngster continued, 'Let me tell you what that means.

I grew up in a little *dorp* – a village – you've probably never heard of. Driespruitfontein. It's in the Orange Free State. There's one main street and one set of robots – traffic lights.'

That brought back memories. How he and his mates had all laughed that day in Rome when the South African corporal had told them they had to cross the road at the robot.

'... The farmers' co-op, the tote, the church, the bottle store, the Royal Hotel and a couple of shops. My parents own the general dealer store. That's what we Jews do in Afrikaner communities. We run the shop. I used to work in the shop with them after school and in the school holidays. And, I'm afraid to say, on *Shabbos*.'

Not all that different to him. He'd helped his parents with their stall in Spitalfields Market. A lifetime ago, that was.

'My parents weren't *frum*, which was just as well, really. There wasn't a *shul* in Driespruitfontein – we were the only *Yidden* in the entire district and the travelling rabbi only came once or twice a year just to visit.'

Nothing like Spitalfields back then, where, if you sneezed, you'd have infected a dozen Jews. He listened closely. This youngster sounded like he had a good story to tell.

'But my parents made sure I was Barmitzvah – my *ma* schlepped me to Bloemfontein once a week for *cheder* to prepare for my Barmitzvah. That's about a two- to three-hour drive away.'

And Jeremy had moaned about walking two blocks to the *shul* for his Barmitzvah classes. No wonder his son had turned out to be a bit of a *schmuck*, even if he did say so himself – but not to Ruth. She'd murder him.

'I did all my schooling at Driespruitfontein *Laerskool* and *Hoërskool*,' Alan continued. 'My brother, Dovvie, and I, we were the Jew boys. It wasn't easy, but I had a great friend. Thys van Zyl. He played prop for Free State schools and protected me as much as he could. I think he'll be Springbok, one day, if Peter Hain lets him.'

Ben frowned. He didn't like that Hain chappie. Politics and sport should not mix. Look at Munich. It was the mixing of politics and sport that got those Israeli athletes murdered in the middle of the Olympics – while the world just stood by and let it happen. Terrible. Terrible. But what was so new? The world always stood by when Jews were getting killed. He listened more attentively.

'Anyway, Dovvie was killed on the border during his national service. But that isn't why I refused to do my national service when they called me up.'

Ben's heart sank. 'You didn't tell me we were coming to listen to a coward. You know how I feel about *feiglings*,' he muttered in Ruth's ear.

'Shh.' She patted his knee.

He frowned and focused his attention on the speaker.

'I'm not afraid of fighting for my country. I'm not a conscientious objector or a pacifist. My *pa* was in the South African Army in the Second World War. He fought in Egypt and Italy.'

Good heavens, perhaps he'd met the youngster's father? Silverman? Silverman? He couldn't recall meeting a Silverman...

'Many Afrikaners supported Hitler and refused to support Jan Smuts. But my *pa* was Jewish, even though he'd grown up surrounded by Afrikaners, speaking Afrikaans a hell of a lot better than he spoke English. So he volunteered to fight the Nazis even though he knew he would be beaten up by the local Afrikaner thugs if they'd caught him alone when he went home on leave. I'm proud of my *pa*.'

Ben joined in the applause. So did Ruth, who was smiling at him now.

'I'm proud of my *pa* and I'm proud and thankful for those of you here tonight who also fought the Nazis even though it's never easy for Jews in the army, is it? That's what my *pa* and Dovvie told me. Or is it only in the South African Army that Jews are given a really hard time by the corporals and sergeants?'

Ben nodded. It hadn't been easy being Jewish in the British Army either. Unless you were good at soccer, which he wasn't.

'I'm grateful to those of you who fought Hitler,' young Silverman said, 'because, if you hadn't, my beautiful Brenda might never have been born.'

The youngster was pointing at Ruth. No, at the pretty girl next to Ruth. Ben hadn't noticed her before.

'That's my Brenda. Stand up, sweetheart. Let them see just

how beautiful you are.'

The young girl stood. She was obviously painfully shy, but she smiled and sat down again quickly.

'My Brenda's mum was in Birkenau.'

Ben stared at her. Tears were flowing down her face, poor little thing. Ruth squeezed her hand. He leaned over and offered her his handkerchief. The girl wiped her eyes and tried to hand it back. He waved it away. Let the pretty child keep it. It was the least he could do.

Her husband was still speaking. 'Her beloved aunt, Anna, died in the gas chambers in Auschwitz. If brave people like you hadn't had the courage to fight Hitler, chances are Brenda's mum would have followed her sister into the ovens, if disease hadn't killed her first. So I'm not opposed to war. How could I be? The war you fought against Hitler, that's a war I would happily have fought too, and from the bottom of my heart, I thank you all.'

Ben felt his heart swell with pride, and gratitude – that this charming young girl – he supposed she was a young woman, really, being married and all – was alive today because of the tiny part he'd played in the war.

'But let's look at the situation in South Africa today. Dovvie, my brother, went to the army because he thought it was his duty to defend his country against the communist onslaught.'

Ben listened attentively. He wasn't sure he agreed with everything young Silverman was saying, about the communists and the National Party government, but what did he know? He wasn't a South African. He certainly didn't like that Botha fellow. A most unpleasant *schmuck* with his fleshy lips and wagging finger. He wasn't particularly comfortable with young Silverman's attachment to his *shvartze* black nanny, but then that's what happened in the colonies. He'd never had a nanny, so he couldn't really understand, and they hadn't been able to afford a nanny when Jeremy was small – not that Ruth would have had one, even if they could. Might have been better for the boy if they had – might not have been so much of a mamma's boy. Might have turned out a bit more like young Silverman up there, a *mensch*, a decent man's man with good, strong, old-fashioned principles.

The youngster finished his speech, appealing to the audience to give generously to WOAH. Ben decided to consider it.

The grey woman thanked everyone for their generosity, and invited them to have a cup of tea and some cake – kindly prepared by the Shul Women's Committee – in the foyer.

Ruth turned to the pretty young woman and smiled warmly, her special Ruth smile. She introduced herself, and him.

Ben smiled at the girl. She reminded him of Ruth when he had first fallen in love with her – pretty, with dark curls. Ruth was never as skinny, though, despite all her dieting. He hoped young Silverman loved this sweet, delicate young woman like he loved Ruthie.

They wandered together over to the tea tables. Young

Silverman was surrounded by a throng of well-wishers. He saw him look over at the girl and give her a warm smile. Good. The boy was obviously a loving husband.

'So, young lady. How are you and your young man managing in London? Do you have jobs?' he asked.

'No, it's difficult. I'm not trained for anything. I only finished school last year, you see, and then I went to Israel. That's where…' She stopped.

'And your young man, what does he do?'

'He's working really hard helping WOAH, but they can't afford to pay him much. He has an accounting degree from Wits University, but…'

Bashert! Fate! 'An accountant! Wonderful.' He turned to Ruth. 'You see? I knew there was a reason we had to come tonight. We weren't going to, you know,' he told Brenda. 'We give plenty to Israel and lots of English charities. South Africa? Not really our problem, is it? Although I didn't realise there were smart Jewish boys like your Alan who need our help, did I? So now I need to speak to your young man.'

He pushed through the throng around Alan, grabbed him by the arm and shouted at him to come over to join him and his wife as soon as he could. Then he returned to the women. He was delighted. He'd liked young Silverman on sight. A *mensch*. He could tell. A real gentleman, even if he wasn't English.

CHAPTER 3
LONDON, 1988/89

Ben folded his arms over his stomach and tried to make himself comfortable on the hard little chair. He really, really didn't want to be here, but Ruth had insisted.

'It's for Brenda,' she'd said. 'It's her first end-of-year concert. She needs our support.'

His insistence that she had Alan, and that was more than enough support, had fallen on deaf ears. He pulled his jacket closer and turned up the collar. Didn't they have central heating in the community centre? Those little kids in their silly little pink leotards must be freezing, but they looked happy enough. Brenda appeared on the stage with a string of toddlers in tow.

'Good morning, ladies and gentlemen, moms and dads, children. I'm Brenda Jones and I'm delighted to present our beginners' class in their first public performance of *The Little Milkmaid.*'

He kept his hands in his pockets while the audience applauded enthusiastically.

'Don't expect too much,' Alan whispered in his ear.

'Brenda calls them her little puddings.'

He smiled. That was so like Brenda, to have an affectionate name for a bunch of brats. In all the years he'd known her – what was it now? Two? Three? – he'd never heard her say a nasty word about anyone.

Actually, it wasn't too bad. The kids seemed to know what they were doing. Not one of them cried or fell off the stage. Ruth was beaming with pride; anyone would think one of those kids was hers. A curdle of anger rose in his throat. How could Jeremy deny his mother the chance of being a *bobba*? Then came the familiar guilt because he had only been able to give Ruth one child. He looked at the delighted doting faces of the parents around them. He hoped none of them would feel disillusion and disappointment in thirty or so years. He honestly did.

He squirmed. The chair was really too small for him. He'd been here long enough. 'Ruth,' he hissed, 'let's go. *Genug es genug.* Enough is enough.'

She ignored him. The music changed. He recognised it. From the time Ruth had dragged him to see Fonteyn and that Commie Russian – Nureyev, was it? – in *Swan Lake* at Covent Garden. He'd actually quite enjoyed it, not that he would ever tell her that.

He blinked. What on earth was Margot Fonteyn doing on the stage at the Hendon Community Centre?

'Ladies and gentleman, boys and girls,' said Patricia, the head teacher. 'Hendon Community Ballet School is proud to present our very own Brenda Jones and three of our senior pupils – Hayley Maizels, Catherine Fortesque and Zara Steiner – in the *Dance of the Cygnets* from *Swan Lake.*'

He applauded loudly. Ruth's eyes were sparkling. Alan was beaming with pride. Brenda was magnificent. Quite magnificent. Even he could see how talented she was. She floated across the stage, a beautiful, beautiful girl. Alan was a lucky young man. He just wished he'd marry her. It still made him uncomfortable that these two beautiful young people insisted on living in sin. He'd asked Alan one day when did he intend making an honest woman of Brenda? Alan said they didn't believe in marriage. And what about children? 'We don't want children,' Alan said. So they lived together and Ruth said it was none of their business and, when he thought about it, it really didn't make all that much difference. In fact, he'd be delighted if Jeremy told him he was living in sin with a beautiful *Yiddisher* girl like Brenda. Actually, any girl. Even a *shiksa* – God forbid!

***

'Please. No business talk at the table tonight,' Ruth said as Ben came in from the evening service and took off his coat. It was still bitterly cold, but, fortunately, the *shul* wasn't far away. That was one of the reasons he had bought this house – and, of course, because it was the house Ruthie wanted. It was much too big for just him and Ruth now that Jeremy had moved out, but they wouldn't leave. Never. There were far too many good memories in these walls.

Ruth put the gold embroidered *challah* cover over the plaited bread and stood back, examining her table critically. As she did every week. The table looked beautiful, as it always did: the starched white tablecloth, the crystal wine glasses, the best cutlery, the Royal Albert dinner service, and the silver candlesticks with the lighted candles. Ruth lit them, just before he left for *shul*, the same ritual he'd seen her do countless times, the same ritual he'd watched his mother do: closing her eyes, circling her hands three times above the flame, then holding her hands over her eyes and murmuring the *brocha*: *Baruch a-ta A-do-nay Elo-hei-nu me-lech ha-o-lam a-sher ki-dee-sha-nu bi-mitz-vo-tav vi-tzi-va-noo li-had-leek ner shel Sha-bbat.* Blessed are you, Lord our God, King of the universe, who has sanctified us with His commandments, and commanded us to kindle the light of the Holy Sabbath.

Shabbos was special to Ruth. To him again now, as well – ever since Alan and Brenda had started joining them every Friday night. It was like having a real family. And with Jeremy living so far away... He must ask Alan if he and Brenda couldn't come earlier – before *Shabbos* came in – so that Brenda could join Ruth in lighting the candles. That would make her so happy.

He looked at Ruth fondly and prepared for their weekly argument.

'I have things to discuss with Alan, important things,' he

said. 'He's been working on that deal with O'Brian Properties and he told me he hoped to be able to close it while we were in LA.'

It was a big deal. It would transform the Shapiro and Son's portfolio if Alan pulled it off. Ben was pretty confident Alan would. Young Alan seemed to have an incredible gut instinct for the property market. Employing that boy had been the best thing he'd ever done – apart from marrying Ruth, of course. The second best was moving Alan out of the group's accounting department into the fledgling property division. Now property was well on its way to overtaking the retail division in turnover. It would, if the O'Brian deal came through. Which would mean a generous bonus for Alan and a promotion. Perhaps a share in the company. But not yet. Not while there was still a chance – an ever receding chance, he'd had to accept on this latest trip to LA – that Jeremy would ever give up his dream of being a movie star, come home and fill the "and Son" role he'd always planned for him. He'd have to get well first, though. Poor Ruthie was so worried about the boy. Some boy. Jeremy was thirty-two already. More than enough time to grow up.

***

Amen. Ben broke the *challah*, salted the pieces, handed one each to Alan, Brenda and Ruth and popped one into his mouth. Ruth and Brenda went to the kitchen to fetch the food. Brenda didn't look well. She surely still couldn't have that dreadful cold, poor child.

'What's the latest on O'Brian?' he asked as soon as Ruth disappeared through the door.

'Mrs Shapiro said we're not to talk business tonight.' Alan grinned at him, the impudent young bastard. 'So I'm not going to say a word.' Then his smile broadened and he stuck both thumbs in the air.

Ben exhaled happily. That Alan. Without breaking his word to Ruth, he'd told him all he needed to know.

'I've tried something a little different with the chicken tonight,' Ruth said, carrying a large platter heaped with food into the dining room.

Brenda followed with the vegetables. Ben hoped there were lots of potatoes. Ruthie loved cooking. She was always trying something new for *Shabbos* dinner.

'I added some dried apricot slices. It's not a *tzimmis* – you need brisket, not chicken, for that – but it will be sweeter than usual. Tell me what you think.'

Ruth dished up an enormous plate of chicken, potatoes and vegetables and put it in front of him. No wonder his girth kept spreading. It smelled and looked wonderful. She dished up a similar sized serving for Alan. Brenda's serving was only slightly smaller. They all waited politely while Ruth helped herself and sat down. He was concentrating on slicing his chicken breast so the thud when Brenda's chair fell over made him jump. She fled from the room and he heard the guest bathroom door slam.

'Oh dear,' Ruth said. 'I do hope it wasn't my food that did that?'

'No, I'm sure it wasn't,' Alan said. 'Brenda has some kind a tummy bug. I told her weeks ago to go to the doctor for some medicine, and she said she would. He gave her some antibiotics, I think. But clearly it hasn't helped. I do apologise.'

'Nonsense, dear. There's nothing to apologise for. I thought she was looking a little peaky, poor child. How long has she been like this?'

Ruth was clearly worried. So was he. There was enough sickness in this family already, with Jeremy.

'Oh, since long before her birthday, I think. And she's always tired. I'm really starting to get quite worried about her.'

Ben looked at Ruth anxiously. He hoped this wouldn't upset her. She was so fond of young Brenda.

Brenda quietly slipped back into her chair. 'I'm so sorry,' she said. She looked as if she had been crying. 'Would you mind if I didn't eat this? I'm sure it's delicious, but…'

'It's the smell of the cooked chicken, isn't it?' Ruth asked.

Brenda nodded. Ruth was smiling at her. What was she so happy about? Couldn't she see the child was ill?

'It's not a tummy bug, is it, my dear?'

So now Ruthie was a doctor? Brenda stared at her, her eyes enormous. She had gone even whiter. Ben hoped she wouldn't faint. She looked terrible. It was obviously a tummy bug. Even Alan was staring at Ruth as if she'd gone crazy, *meshugga*.

'I couldn't bear the smell of chicken either. With Jeremy. Remember?' Ruth said.

What on earth? 'Oh. Yes. Right,' he said.

He didn't have a clue what she was talking about, but, with Ruth, you agreed first and asked questions later.

Ruth clapped. 'So, when were you planning to tell us? How far are you? This is so exciting.'

Brenda chewed her lip. She looked at Alan. Alan was frowning. He was staring at Brenda, at Ruth, back at Brenda. Ruth rushed over to Brenda and hugged her.

'*Mazeltov. Mazeltov*. Congratulations. This is wonderful. Wonderful.' She turned to Alan. '*Mazeltov*, Alan.'

No. Brenda couldn't be. Ben pushed back his chair and got up. He walked around the table and shook Alan's hand. It was limp. The poor boy was the colour of the table cloth.

'I only found out today,' Brenda whispered. 'I haven't had a chance to tell Alan yet.'

'And now I've ruined the surprise. I do apologise. But honestly, Alan, it was as plain as plain could be. Even Ben here could see.' Ruth beamed at them.

Alan went red. Sweat beaded his forehead, poor chap. What a way to find out – in front of your boss and his wife. All he probably wanted to do was hug and kiss his little wife like he'd hugged and kissed Ruthie when she'd told him about Jeremy. He'd burst into tears – he'd all but given up hope of being a father.

Ruth was gushing like a fountain, she was so excited. He went to his liquor cabinet and took out that bottle of schnapps he'd been saving for Jeremy's engagement. Well, this was also excellent news, so why not open it now? Alan looked like he needed it. He handed Alan a glass.

'To celebrate,' he said. 'At last, some good news in this family. *Le chaim*. To life – to the new little life that is coming to enrich ours.'

The boy gulped his schnapps down. Brenda still didn't say a word.

'*Le chaim*,' Alan said. He sounded odd. Well, he'd just had an enormous shock.

Ruth kissed him and hugged Brenda.

Ben gave Alan money for a taxi home that night. He couldn't expect them to go on the bus, not on a night like tonight. A baby. What a blessing. What a wonderful couple. Oh dear, he remembered, Brenda and Alan weren't married. So now they'd get married. They had to.

CHAPTER 4

'What are you doing?' Ben asked Ruth.

She'd gone out early, while he was shaving. Now she appeared to be writing lists. There were papers all over the sitting room, and magazines all over the coffee table and the sofa. He picked one up. *Today's Bride.*

'Don't touch that,' she said. 'I like the flower arrangements on that page.'

'Ruthie, *neshomeleh* – what are you doing?'

'Planning the wedding. There's so much to do. It's going to be beautiful. I never realised there were so many bridal magazines. I went down to Brent Cross this morning and got them.'

His heart sank. She was setting herself up for disappointment, he just knew it. 'Ruthie, they might not be getting married. Alan told me they didn't believe in marriage. And it's not our place to arrange their wedding even if they do decide to get married.'

She smiled at him. 'Of course they're getting married. They can't have that baby growing up a *momzer*. And Brenda has no family, so we're her *mishpocheh*. Alan's too, as far as I can make out. I don't think he's had any contact with them, not since they threw him out. How can parents do that to their children? Even if they don't agree with him. Especially a *sheine* boy like that?'

He knew she was thinking of Jeremy. She picked up another magazine and leafed through it, sticking in bits of paper to mark pages. He went off to his study to read the *Sunday Times* in peace. He'd speak to Alan in the office tomorrow. Maybe. It really wasn't his business.

Ruth walked in and plonked herself down on his sofa. He turned the page and kept reading. He had no idea what he was reading. He waited for her to speak. Her silence was ominous. Ruthie was never silent for this long. He looked up at her.

'What?'

'I agree with you,' she said.

'About what?'

'About having the wedding here.'

'I never said anything about having the wedding here. We don't even know if there's going to be a wedding. I told you...'

'It will be in the garden. If we open the patio doors from the sitting room, and if we move the dining room table back against the wall, there'll be enough space, even if it rains. But the weather should be fine by then. I was thinking, April the second. That will give us enough time to plan everything and she still shouldn't be showing. The *chupah* will be in the *shul*, of course. I'll give Elizabeth Emanuel a ring tomorrow for an appointment. We obviously don't want a puff pastry *shmattah* like Lady Di wore when she married Prince Charles – something soft and pretty and elegant I think, in a cream rather than pure white – so draining, I always think...'

He shook his head. Ruthie never ceased to amaze him. 'Don't you think you should discuss this with Brenda first – we don't know if there's even going to be a wedding. Ruth, please.'

'Of course I'll discuss it with her. It's her wedding. I'll phone her now and invite her to tea.'

'Ruthie, stop! Stop right now. Wait until I've spoken to Alan. Can you do that?'

Ruth folded her arms. Oh dear. He knew that look. She wasn't going to listen to him. She never did.

The phone rang. Ruth picked it up.

'Brenda, *bubbeleh*. We were just talking... What? No. No, I don't... When? No, Ben hasn't... Yes... Yes, I will.... Let me know the minute... Goodbye, dear.' She put down the phone.

'That was Brenda. Alan's missing. He went out after they got home from *Shabbos* on Friday – and he hasn't been home since. That's nearly thirty hours, Ben. I'm worried.'

***

Ruth's instructions were still ringing in Ben's ears when he walked through the Shapiro and Son foyer. He didn't even stop to admire the new brass "Shapiro & Son" sign behind the reception desk. He barely acknowledged the receptionist's cheery "morning, Mr Shapiro". 'Find that boy and give him a piece of your mind,' Ruth had told him. 'Tell him he has to face up to his responsibilities towards Brenda and his baby. How can he worry us all like this? Ask him where he's been.'

He walked down the corridor, past his office, directly to the property department. The door to Alan's office was closed. He knocked. Silence. His heart sank. He turned the handle and pushed the door open. Alan was sitting behind the desk, the telephone receiver pressed to his ear. He stood up and indicated to Ben to come in and sit.

'Fine. Yes, okay,' Alan said. 'Bring the papers around now. Mr Shapiro has just walked in. We'll go over them together and hopefully have the whole deal wrapped up by close of business today.'

Ben examined Alan's face. The boy looked pleased, excited even. No sign of any of the tension and upset that had plagued him and Ruth since Brenda's phone call yesterday, and her call early this morning to say that he'd arrived home.

'Morning, Mr Shapiro. Well, that's it. O'Brian deal sealed, except for the signing, but we can do that later. *Mazeltov*.' They shook hands.

'Everything all right?' Ben asked.

Alan beamed. 'It's perfect. We got exactly the terms we'd been hoping for. O'Brian whined a bit, but in the end he was only too happy to-'

Ben's anger erupted. 'Bugger O'Brian. Where the hell

were you? We were worried sick, Ruth and I. How can you just disappear like that?'

Alan frowned. 'How did you know? Did Brenda tell you? I told her I just needed time to think. She shouldn't have worried you. I apologise. I'll speak to her about it.'

'Where were you?'

'I needed to be alone. I needed... Look, I'd never thought about having a child. I never wanted a child. Ever. Brenda and I had always agreed we'd never have children. It was a shock. We were so careful. I had to decide...'

'What's to decide?' Ben found he was shaking. He and Ruth had tried so hard for children. They'd been disappointed so often... and then, finally, Jeremy had come along.

'You're having a baby. It's wonderful. A miracle. A blessing. Look, I know this is none of my business, but Ruth is very fond of you both. She's come to regard Brenda as the daughter she never had. So, I ask – and you can tell me to mind my own business – do you love her?'

'Of course I love her. I adore her. You know that. I fell in love with her the moment I saw her. I knew the moment I laid eyes on her that we belonged together.'

Relief surged through Ben. 'So, that's settled then. You will marry her and you will have a baby. It's *beshert*. It's wonderful, wonderful news. *Mazeltov, mazeltov*. Miss Smith,' he yelled at the closed door to the adjoining office. It opened and Josephine Smith, Alan's new secretary recently promoted from the typing pool, appeared, shorthand notebook and pencil in hand.

'Yes, Mr Shapiro, Mr Silverman?'

Alan cut him off. 'When the O'Brian deal papers get here, bring them straight in,' he said.

Josephine Smith retreated.

'With all due respect, Mr Shapiro, don't you think Brenda and I should discuss it? Before you announce my impending marriage to the world? I haven't even asked her yet what she wants to do.'

Ben flushed. Who did this boy think he was? He sat down. Alan was glaring at him. Oh dear, he was turning into Ruthie. Getting ahead of himself. Being pushy.

'My apologies, my boy. It's your life, yours and Brenda's. We won't interfere. I promise.'

'I'll speak to Brenda this evening. After work. We have to complete everything on the O'Brian deal today.'

'Good lad. And tell her we'd be honoured to host your wedding – and pay for everything, of course. Ruth will call her tomorrow about the arrangements. No time to waste, none at all.'

Ben smiled as he left Alan's office. It was all going to be fine. The boy clearly loved Brenda. It was written all over his face.

PART 5
ALAN

CHAPTER 1
ISRAEL, 1985

Alan knocked at the door and waited. He could hear scuffling inside. The door scraped open and a vision appeared in the doorway. Her rolled up work pants dragged on the floor, virtually covering her army boots; the hacked off sleeves of her old army jacket still needed to be turned back. Long, dark curls cascaded over her shoulders and she peeped at him shyly with huge brown eyes from under her fringe. A flush rose in her cheeks. His heart turned over.

'Hi,' he said. 'Have you got any cotton wool?' *Oh brilliant, Alan. What a way to impress this girl.*

She looked confused. No wonder. Any girl would be confused if a great big idiot of a man she had never spoken to before appeared at her door asking for cotton wool... but he was stunned. She was beautiful. Incredible. The girl he'd dreamed about since he'd started fantasising about girls. The girl he'd never been able to put a face to. The girl he'd never expected to find... and here she was. He wanted to enchant her, to impress her, to make her swoon at his wit and charm.

'You know. The white, fluffy stuff you girls use for

whatever,' he said. He couldn't stop himself. The banal words just flowed. 'You are South African, aren't you? You do know what cotton wool is?' He wanted to kick himself. He sounded so aggressive. He didn't mean to. It was just that she had taken him so much by surprise. Why hadn't he noticed her before?

'Yes, *ja*, of course,' she said, her voice breathless and husky, just as he knew it would be. She floated across the room and tore a large piece from a roll she took out of her suitcase. She handed it to him and chewed on her beautiful bottom lip.

He had to keep the conversation going. 'Hey, aren't you a little young to be doing an *ulpan*?' he asked. She looked about twelve, maybe thirteen.

'I'm eighteen. Nearly. I'll be eighteen next month.'

'Sorry, I'm being rude. I'm Alan, from South Africa.'

Her little hand disappeared into his. He held onto it, a lifeline for a drowning man.

'I'm Brenda. From Jo'burg,' she said.

'Hello Brenda from Jo'burg. Nice to meet you. Thanks for the cotton wool.' He gazed at her. He didn't know what to say. 'See you around,' he said. What was wrong with him? For Christ's sake, he was twenty-four years old and he was behaving like a tongue-tied teenager. He'd chatted up more girls – and women – than he cared to remember. The words would flow and they would simper and get all blushy and he'd have them in his bed – or somewhere similar – without too much persuasion… but not this girl. He wanted to woo her like they did in those old fashioned movies. He wanted her to fall into his arms and gaze up at him adoringly. He wanted to be Rhett Butler to her Scarlett, Danny to her Sandy, Archie to her Veronica. He turned to go.

'What class are you in?' she asked.

He swung back, his heart soaring. That was one of the lamest lines he'd ever heard. 'I'm in *Kitah Gimmel*. You?' he asked.

'*Kitah Aleph* – I… I've never learned Hebrew before, you see.'

'Well, if you need any help, you know where to find me.' He waved vaguely in the direction of his room.

'*Ja*, okay, thanks.'

He stared at her, trying desperately to think of something else to say before she closed the door.

She closed the door.

He leaned against the wall and exhaled. He hadn't been aware that he'd been holding his breath. He felt weird. He tried to replay every word of their conversation, to savour it. He couldn't remember any of it. He remembered having to stop himself from reaching out and twisting her curls around his fingers. He must be going nuts. No girl had ever, ever, got to him like that. Not even that little Pinky, Pretty, Portia – whatever her name was. Johanna's niece or sister or something. She'd been young too, and shy – just a kid, really. Like this girl. Pinky had been fantastic, easily the best of the lot. Funny, he hadn't really thought of her for years, but this little South African girl brought the memory of all those amazing times and incredible feelings flooding back. This little girl had something of little Pinky – or was it Pretty? – about her. Sort of. Even Annette hadn't done it for him like this girl. Breathe, man. Breathe.

***

He hurried back to his room. Bloody hell, American Linda and her gang were still there waiting for him and chatting to Javier.

'Did you get it?' Linda asked.

'What? Oh *ja*. This is cotton wool.' He held up the little wad of white fluff he had forgotten he had in his hand.

'That's cotton, not cotton wool. I thought you Africans spoke English,' American Linda said scornfully.

He wasn't in the mood to argue. Idiots like American Linda would never get it through their thick skulls that South Africa was a country, not a continent. She irritated him. She was loud and fat and poked her boobs at him whenever she got close. He just didn't get it – why she was so bloody proud of her floppy boobs. She displayed them all the time, even in the coldest weather, and she didn't wear a bra, so they bounced and wobbled when she walked or laughed. It was revolting. She was revolting. He must have been crazy to let her climb into his bed after the wild party at the end of the last *ulpan*. Crazy or drunk. Linda had generously shared her bottle of arak with him and, if there was one thing about American Linda, she was bloody persistent. Now she thought she owned him.

'Okay, *windgat*.' He loved insulting her in Afrikaans. She thought he was being affectionate. 'So if this…' he held up the white wad, 'is cotton, what do you use to sew on buttons and things?'

'Thread!' Linda shouted, as if she'd won a bloody jackpot.

'Well, where I come from, we sew buttons and things with cotton, and this…' he waved the wad at her, 'is cotton wool. Now *voetsek*. I'm going to lunch.'

CHAPTER 2

It was raining. Again. Alan splashed through the mud to the dining room, the gaggle of girls – Linda wobbling in the lead as usual – trailing behind. For his first six months on the kibbutz, his job had been to work in the dining room, cleaning the tables, over and over again. Kibbutz members were expected to load their own plates into the giant dishwasher that adjoined the dining room, but the dining room team had to unload it. It was the pits, almost as bad as having to work in the laundry. He preferred working in the kitchen, even if it meant having to clean out the huge industrial pots and scrub the floor all the time. He'd become a whiz at slicing tomatoes and peeling potatoes. In summer, kitchen duty was nice, because you could go and cool off in the cold room all the time. Now, after three years of proving his worth to the kibbutz members, he'd been promoted to work in the cow shed.

He grabbed a tray and helped himself to a couple of turkey schnitzels, finely diced salad, some hummus, fresh bread and juice. Nothing original about kibbutz food. The menu hadn't changed at all over the years. Then he sat down at a table near the door, so he would be sure to see her when she came in. American Linda plumped herself down next to him, her boobs jiggling. He ignored her and started eating, his eyes glued to the door.

Linda yakked away. He tried to tune her out, but it was difficult. She had a voice like a chainsaw that just went on and on and on, even as she chewed and swallowed her way through a heaped plate of schnitzels and anything else she'd been able to lay her hands on.

Big Australian Emily was telling a story about the boy who'd mistakenly used the girls' communal shower the day before.

'But then I took a closer look and do you know what? It wasn't a boy at all. It was a girl.'

Linda's chainsaw transformed into an asthmatic buffalo as her gang cackled and hissed in amusement.

'Bet it was the new South African girl,' London Lynda said. 'Oh shit, there she is.'

They fell about laughing as his fairy princess squelched into the dining room. She looked at them, flushed, looked away and made her way quickly past his table to the serving cabinets.

'Hey, Belinda,' he called.

She ignored him. The bitches at his table snickered. He wanted to kill them. He watched as she helped herself to a dainty portion of salad and juice and made her way to an empty table on the far side of the room.

It was too much. He couldn't bear to see her so vulnerable

and alone. So ostracised. He knew all about being an outcast. He picked up his tray and walked over to her. He could hear the silence from his table following him.

'Hey, *wat's fout? Hoekom groet jy my nie*?' he asked.

'Sorry. My Afrikaans isn't very good. What did you say?'

'*Ja*, you're a Jo'burg girl, all right. Why can't Jo'burg girls speak Afrikaans? I asked you why you didn't say hello to me when I called you just now.'

'Oh, were you speaking to me? I thought Belinda was one of your girlfriends. I'm Brenda.'

He wanted to kick himself. Talk about foot-in-mouth disease, but he'd always been useless with names.

'Oops, sorry,' he said, and gave her the rueful smile that usually melted the coldest female heart.

She didn't smile back. She carefully pierced a tomato slice and put it into her mouth.

He sat down and watched her eat. She put down her fork and looked at him with her velvet eyes, then she looked down at the table, her thick dark lashes fluttering. She was perfection. He devoured her with his eyes as he spoke about this and that, anything that came into his head. She answered. They were chatting; they were connecting. He could feel it. He touched her hand. She pulled away, jumped up and ran. He was stunned. He went over their conversation in his head. What on earth had just happened?

***

Brenda was lying on her bed, sobbing, when Alan walked in. He sat down on the bed, resisting the urge to pull her onto his lap and fold her in his arms. He wanted her to bury her face in his chest. He wanted to rock her and tell it would all be okay. He wanted to tear off her clothes and make mad, passionate love to her.

'I don't know what got into me. I've never cried about it, not once. I'm so sorry,' she said.

'What is it? What happened?' He handed her a tissue from the box on the upturned cardboard carton she was using as a bedside table.

'It's not important. It doesn't matter.'

'It's obviously important if it made you cry. So tell me. Please.'

She sat up, just far enough away from him to ensure they didn't touch. He made himself clasp his hands together.

'I was a ballet dancer. I hurt my knee in rehearsals,' she said in a curiously flat voice. 'They operated, but it couldn't be fixed properly. I can walk and I'm happy about that, but I will never be able to dance again. Not at a professional level. There. That's it. Now you know. Not much of a story, is it?' She chewed her bottom lip.

He didn't know what to say, so he just said anything, anything to keep her looking at him. She kept looking at him. She smiled.

They walked up to the *ulpan* together. He felt bereft as she disappeared into the *Kitah Aleph* classroom.

CHAPTER 3

In class, Alan couldn't concentrate. It didn't matter. He was only going through the motions of the *ulpan* anyway. He watched the rain pouring down, overflowing the gutters and splashing against the windows. *Morah* Rivkah's droning voice faded to a background hum.

It never rained like this in Driespruitfontein. On and on and on. And Israel was supposed to be hot and dry. Driespruitfontein was hot and dry, especially in summer. With dramatic, short electrical storms that came up so suddenly, emptied their fury quickly and violently, and moved on. Like the one that he and Annamari had been caught in down by the dam that time. They hadn't noticed the sky darkening, and then, suddenly, a huge clap of thunder had made her squeal even louder. Lightning lashed out and the heavens opened. It was almost biblical in its fury. She was so frightened.

'*Jislaaik*, Alan, what am I going to tell them when I get back to the hostel? *Mevrou* Beneke will want to know what I was doing that I got caught in the storm.'

They pulled on their pants and ran through the pelting rain.

They parted at the school gates. She went in and he continued to his house along Kerkstraat. He never had found out what she had told the hostel matron, but it must have been good, because she hadn't got detention.

Annamari. He didn't think of her much anymore – unless he saw some pink and white marshmallows. Or he was with a new girl for the first time. He wondered how she was getting on. And Thys. It was sad about Thys after being *chommies* since they were *laaities* and everything. The only kid in Driespruitfontein who'd be his friend. Probably because he was *Dominee* van Zyl's kid and no one messed with the *dominee*. Or Thys either. He was strong, that *ou*... and fit. When they had run down past the dam and around by *Meneer* Groenewald's milking sheds and then up around the *koppie* before heading home, Thys had hardly broken a sweat. Sometimes they'd run past the township and some of the *kaffir* girls would come out to smile and wave. Thys had always ignored them: Thys had had no time for girls, except Annamari. *Ja*, Thys was really a good *ou*. He always said his *pa* said Jews were the Chosen People and he should be honoured to be Alan's friend. But Thys hadn't spoken to him in years.

***

'Mr Silverman, Mr Silverman, my apologies to disturb your contemplations.' *Morah* Rivkah glared down at him. 'Would you be so kind as to translate the passage into Hebrew, so the class can learn from your great wisdom, Mr Silverman?'

Morah Rivkah made no effort to hide the fact that she didn't like him. Well, the feeling was mutual. She looked like his ma. She had *Ma's* moustache. She even smelled like *Ma* when she leaned over him to check his work. It made him want to puke. She always accused him of talking unfair advantage of the good intentions of the young Zionist state by – as she put it – "hiding out" on the kibbutz year after year while young Israeli *Sabra* boys and girls, and a growing number of new immigrant *olim*, were dying to keep diaspora parasite Jews like him safe.

'You young, healthy and Jewish. It is your duty go to army and protect Israel,' she'd told him when he had first walked into her *Kitah Bet* class. Now she was his teacher again, in *Kitah Gimmel*. 'You speak Hebrew good. I can teach you no more. You'd learn much better in army. That's the way of all new *olim*. Why you not go to army? You lazy, or you scared?'

Shit, he hated her. Like he hated his *pa* when *Pa* had called him a coward just because he refused to go to the army. 'I'm not fighting for the Nats and their illegitimate apartheid regime,' he'd said. That's what Annette had always about the Nats, and the army, the police and the South African Government.

CHAPTER 4

'Are you okay, sweetheart?' Alan asked. 'You're limping.'

'I'm fine. Just my knee. I must have twisted it a bit.' Brenda slipped her little hand into his and smiled up at him.

His heart turned over, as it did every time she looked at him like that. So loving and trusting; it made him feel like Danny in *Grease*, after he'd got Sandy sorted. They strolled up the road, past the hothouses where the *moshavim* were growing carnations. Summer was still a way off, but it was getting warmer. Soon, it would be too bloody hot to walk anywhere, and anyway, he wanted Brenda to himself for a while. Without everyone watching and *skinnering* and wondering and listening... and it was time to move their relationship along a bit. He couldn't believe how patient he had been with her. Usually, after all this time, he'd have had her and moved on to the next girl. But she was not like any other girl. Except for Pretty – Pinky – what the hell was her name again?

They reached the town, a *dorp* really, even smaller than Driespruitfontein. The only reason to come here – rather than catch the bus to Jerusalem – was for Yaron's ice cream. It was the best in the world. Brenda had loved it the first time they'd gone for a walk together.

'*Shalom*, Alan,' Yaron said. 'What's this – the same girl again? You're losing your touch, my friend.'

Alan glared at the little Israeli – a Yemenite, dark as the coloureds back home – thankful that Brenda couldn't understand Hebrew.

'Yaron, you remember Brenda? We'll have one chocolate and one strawberry, in a cup.'

They sat at the rickety wooden table and slowly licked at their spoons.

'Here, try mine,' she said and fed him a little.

He caught her hand and gazed deeply into her eyes as she put the spoon to his mouth. She blushed.

He reached over and gently massaged her knee. 'You poor thing. Will it always hurt?'

'No, I don't think so. It seems to be getting stronger and the tablets help. It's nice when you do that,' she said as he stroked her knee, her leg. He moved his hand a little higher.

She scraped the last bit of ice cream into her mouth. He put his arm around her and she snuggled against him. He tipped her face up and kissed her. He felt her lips open and the kiss deepened. He stood up.

'We'd better get back. It's nearly time for supper.' If he didn't move, he'd rip her clothes off and take her right there.

They walked back to the kibbutz in silence. They couldn't carry on like this for much longer. He'd go crazy.

'I'm so sorry, sweetheart,' he said. 'I don't want to rush you into anything, but I'm finding it really hard to keep my hands off you, so maybe it's better if we don't go out alone anymore.'

She stared at him and then, so softly that he could hardly hear, she said, 'Don't you like kissing me? I like it when you kiss me.'

He folded her in his arms. 'I love kissing you. The thing is, I want to do more than kiss, but I don't know... I'm not sure... I'd hate to...' Shit. What was wrong with him? He'd never been this scared of making a move on a woman in his life.

'Alan,' she whispered. 'I know girls aren't supposed to say this first, but I can't help it. I love you.'

He glowed. His heart soared. She was going to be his. He just had to coax her along for a few more days – he mustn't frighten her off; he had to remember she was probably still a virgin.

Pretty had been a virgin. So had Annamari – although she had denied it that first time, when he had been helping her with her maths after June prelims up in his room when *Ma* and *Pa* were at the shop. All she wanted, Annamari said, was to see what a Jew *dingus* looked like. And then she said she'd been doing it with Thys for ages. He didn't believe her – not Thys. However, she obviously wanted to do it with him, so they did it and afterwards she said he was much better than Thys. He knew she was still lying. Anyway, she definitely wasn't a virgin after that. It wasn't his fault that Thys went away on so many rugby tours and Annamari's maths was really putrid. It had been a hellava lot of fun. He just knew that little Brenda was going to be even better. Much, much better.

***

Alan could feel Brenda trembling as he carried her into his room. This was it. This was what he'd been waiting for, hoping for since that first day she'd given him the cotton wool, since the first time he'd kissed her, a birthday kiss on her eighteenth birthday – and realised she didn't have the first idea of how to French kiss. It was hard to believe – this was the eighties, for Christ's sake. But then all the boys she knew were queer. Well, she hadn't exactly said that, but what else could you expect from the bunch of boy ballerinas she went to school with? She was so innocent… and shy… and was trying so hard to be grown up and sophisticated for him.

Her inexperience really excited him. He couldn't wait to train her to do things the way he wanted. He just had to remember to be very gentle.

'You okay?' he asked. 'We don't have to do this, you know. I want you so much, but if you're not sure…' Shit, if she chickened out now, he didn't know what he'd do.

'Please, yes. I'm sure. I've never been more sure of anything in my life,' she said.

He locked the door and slowly unbuttoned her cardigan.

'Put the light out. Please,' she whispered, crossing her

arms across her chest.

'No,' he said, her obvious distress sending his pulse racing. He fought to control his excitement. This was even more incredible than he'd anticipated. 'I want to see you, sweetheart. You're beautiful.'

He loosened her arms and pulled her T-shirt over her head, quickly unhooked her bra and gazed at her perfect little ballerina tits. He gently stroked them and her nipples popped up.

'My God,' he said 'You are stunning.'

He unzipped her jeans and pulled them down. Her tiny bikini panties followed. He feasted his eyes. He felt like a starving man led to a groaning buffet table. He could barely wait. He pulled off his clothes. She shut her eyes, so shy, so afraid to look at him. God, he was ready to burst. Slowly now. Slowly.

He picked her up and put her softly on the narrow bed. Her beautiful little tits fitted perfectly into his palm. He moved his other hand between her legs. She gasped. Then he remembered. Annamari.

'Sweetheart.' He nuzzled her neck. 'You are on something, aren't you?'

'What? I'm not sure what…'

'The pill, Brenda. Are you on the pill? Otherwise, I'll have to get one of Javier's condoms. I don't want any accidents, not now, not ever.' He held his breath. He hated condoms.

Relief surged when she confirmed that it was safe for him

to proceed. Forcing himself to keep calm, he slowly, gently, set about showing her what being a woman was all about, trying his best not to hurt her. He was amazed at his self-control. It was only when he was sure she was ready that he finally allowed himself to let go. He soared. *Fuuuuuckkkk.* It was amazing!

'I love you,' she said when he was finished.

'Me too, sweetheart. You're beautiful.'

CHAPTER 5

Alan woke and looked at the angel sleeping so peacefully in his arms. He'd never dreamed she'd be so incredibly perfect. Beautiful and pure and so, so… tiny and fragile. He swallowed the lump in his throat. He'd never, ever felt like this. Never. It was hard to believe she was eighteen. Most of the eighteen-year-olds he'd had were more like Annamari, sort of soft and squashy. Except Annette. She was neat and trim, with nice flat little tits. But she'd never looked at him like Brenda did, so trusting and adoring. It was incredible. He wanted her again. Jesus, did he want her! But not just yet. He had to control himself; he had to savour each moment with her. The anticipation of what was to come was exquisite. She slept on, a little smile on her lips. He was pleased that he'd made her first time so special. First times should be special. He still remembered his proper first time, when he had become a real man.

***

In *shul* that morning, during his Barmitzvah service, the rabbi had told Alan that he had become a man that day, but he wasn't so sure. After his *brocha* lunch in the hall next to the *shul,* his *ma* kept watching him in the rear-view mirror as she drove them home from Bloemfontein, and his heart dropped. He knew that, as far as *Ma* was concerned, he'd always be her baby. At home, he and David helped *Ma* to get *Pa* to his bed to sleep off the bottle of whisky he'd shared with the rabbi. Then David went out, like he always did.

Alone in his room, Alan tried to quell the familiar sick feeling of helpless anticipation that always paralysed him. He wanted to cry. This was supposed to be his big day. His Barmitzvah. It was supposed to be a celebration; the rabbi had said so. Alan fought the temptation to crawl under his bed and hide. He'd tried it before and it didn't do any good. He wondered what was taking so long. He couldn't bear it. He wasn't a baby, not anymore. He thought about the rabbi's words, about becoming a man and everything, and he made his decision. He had to move quickly. He tiptoed down the stairs, through the kitchen and sneaked across the yard. Swallowing his terror, he pushed open the *khaya* door.

'*Kleinboetie*, what do you want? Where's your pa?' Johanna asked, clutching her unbuttoned overall. She'd taken her *doek* off too and Alan was surprised to see a sprinkling of grey in her peppercorn hair.

Then he'd taken charge and he felt so grown up… and, when he bounced away between her wobbly Royal Instant

Chocolate Pudding thighs and she called him *kleinbaas*, he knew he really had become a man, just like the rabbi said. It made him feel so powerful, being on top. Johanna smelled so nice, like Lifebouy. When he was a baby and Johanna had strapped him on her back with a towel in summer and a big warm blanket in winter, he'd loved the warm, clean, comforting smell of her. Nothing like *Ma*, who always smelled so sweaty and sour when *she* babied him.

***

Alan let his hand drift up Brenda's firm tummy, up, up to her tiny, neat little tits. He gently massaged one. She stirred, but slept on. God, her tits were incredible. The best. Johanna's boobs were big and brown and smooth, a bit soft and droopy, but not floppy, not like *Ma's*. *Ma's* were huge, pasty white with long, black, tickly hairs around the dark part and sometimes, if he opened his eyes, he could make out the blue veins beneath the skin. He shuddered and pushed the nightmare vision out of his mind. He focussed on the good times with Johanna. It had been good fun until that night when he had pushed open the door of Johanna's *khaya* and found that his *pa* had got there first.

Pa had picked up his belt off the floor and beat him, and then Johanna wouldn't do it with him anymore, not even when *Pa* was away in Lesotho. She had said she was scared *Pa* would find out and beat her too, but by then it was okay, because the *kaffir* girls in the township were more than happy to do it, often for free – and they were much younger. Especially little Pretty. Pretty had stopped being so shy after a while.

He wondered if Brenda would also stop being shy and become just like all the other girls. He wouldn't let her. Girls, women – they were all the same, but Brenda was different; he just knew it. The girls back at Driespruitfontein Hoërskool were the worst. They would fall over themselves to be chosen to meet him after church on Sunday down at the dam. The storeroom under the stage in the school hall was better in winter. It was his eyes, the girls said. It was like making love with Paul Newman. He knew they were lying – he didn't look like Paul Newman at all. They only wanted to do it with him because he was sort of forbidden fruit or something, and because they wanted to see what it was like with a Jew penis. That's all they cared about, because, except for Annamari and a couple of the fat, ugly ones, after they'd done it with him once, they wouldn't do it again… and they'd just look through him in school or when he went to the Wimpy for a milkshake. He still couldn't believe how stupid he had been to ask Sunette, then Esme and then, in desperation, even that fat, stupid cow Mina, to go to the Matric dance with him. He should have known they'd all say their fathers wouldn't let them. So then he hadn't asked anyone else. He hid behind the pillar outside his *ma's* shop and watched his classmates trooping into the Royal Hotel in their Matric dance finery. He didn't care. He didn't need them. He didn't need any of them. He left them to it and had his own dance in the shack with a couple of the *kaffir* girls. They were always available, especially if he managed to sneak extra sweets and stuff past *Ma* out of the shop. One time, Pretty had even had the cheek to ask him to pinch one of those shiny plastic toy handbags *Ma* had ordered all the way from Johannesburg for the Christmas sale. Pretty was damn lucky he hadn't given her a fat *klap* for that, but he never hit girls. *Pa* told him only sissies hit girls.

***

Alan woke and kissed Brenda softly on her nose. She lifted her hand as if brushing away a fly. He smiled. He still couldn't believe that this beautiful girl was his, all his. He'd never let her go. He silently vowed to protect her, to take care for her, forever. He swore to himself that he'd never let anyone hurt her. Annette had got herself badly hurt, but then she'd never let him protect her. Not like he wanted to. She could take care of herself, she said.

Annette had been so bloody surprised that an Afrikaner had come to Wits. She'd thought he was a spy for BOSS that first time he'd gone up to her in the canteen. She'd caught his eye the minute he walked in – a cute little thing in her red vest with the black clenched fist and no bra. Not that she needed one. It had taken a long time and he had had to work really hard, but, eventually, she trusted him... but it was easier to convince her that the Bureau for State Security didn't recruit

Jews than it had been to get her into bed. She honestly seemed to believe that sex was a male chauvinist plot to oppress women. So was shaving under her arms, so she didn't do that either. She always moaned at him about the way he, as she put it, "used women", but at least she didn't call him a rock, crunchie or hairyback. Well, not as an insult, not like the other girls, especially the Jewish *kugels*. They treated him like a leper. Worse than a leper. An Afrikaner. Annette, on the other hand, really seemed to like him. She was happy to be with him, and to be seen with him. She just wouldn't sleep with him. Except that once when he finally managed to get her drunk on vintage Tassies.

However, butch Prof. Jackie from the speech and drama department was willing. With her fat white boobs thankfully pinned in place by her sensible cross-your-heart bra, she made him practise his pronunciation. Poor Prof. Jackie. She was so bloody grateful… and it was a fair exchange. She got sex and he eventually sounded northern suburbs Jo'burg enough for the stuck-up *kugels* to let him into their pants. Not that he wanted them. Not really. They were too prescriptive and demanding… and fat. He'd really only wanted Annette. He didn't have to pretend with her and, best of all, although it was also bloody frustrating, she sort of looked a little like Pretty, only whiter, cleaner and considerably more intelligent. She'd taught him a lot, had Annette. And David.

What happened to them proved – as if he really needed proof – that the only cause worth fighting for was Alan

Silverman. *Morah* Rivkah had two chances if she thought that, when his current tourist visa expired, he'd take up Israeli citizenship and go to the army. He'd rather leave Israel… but not yet. Not when he'd just found his soul mate, and she was right here, in his narrow kibbutz bed.

He couldn't help himself. He kissed her. Brenda opened her eyes and smiled. He kissed her again and slipped his hand between her legs. She gasped. He was just moving over her when the door was flung open and Javier marched in. Brenda cowered under the blankets. Poor little thing looked so embarrassed. She wasn't the first girl Javier had seen in his bed, but he couldn't tell her that or that he'd also walked in on Javier and some or other girl. It wasn't any big deal.

Javier went off to shower and get the chicken shit off him. Brenda scrambled off the bed. He wanted to stop her, but she pulled on her clothes and fled. Poor kid. She still had so much to learn.

CHAPTER 6

'What you see in that little girl?' Javier asked as they ran down along the path by the cotton fields before turning up the track towards the grapefruit and orange orchards. They ran together at least twice a week, which was crazy, really.

'We work all day like fucking kaffirs, and then we still run. We must be *meshugga*,' Alan said.

'What this word, kaffir? I no heard that before.'

'It's what we call *shvartzes* in South Africa. You know, the black unskilled workers and farm labourers. If you ever go there, remember to call the *shvartze* hotel cleaner or the porter at the airport "kaffir". It's polite.' He smothered his laugh.

Javier shook his head. 'I no go there. I applied for South African visa, but they no want Mexican engineers in your country.'

'Not my country anymore, *bru*.'

They ran on in silence for a while and then Javier asked, 'Why you like Brenda so much? I hear you even like her more than Gabriella. You crazy, man. Leetle Brenda, she good in bed, huh? Me, I want my woman must be woman, not leetle girl. So.' He waved his hand through the air, indicating generous curves. 'Your Brenda, she fssst.' He flicked his fingers dismissively.

'That's the point, *bru*.'

They ran on in silence. He wasn't going to make the mistake of telling Javier why he liked Brenda so much. He'd never forget David's reaction when he'd told him, after he'd got back from Pretty... and David was his brother.

David had been examining one of the *Penthouse* magazines *Pa* had smuggled in from Lesotho and hidden on the top of his cupboard. David started shoving the magazine under the bed and then realised it was only his little brother. David patted the bed and they sat together, slowly turning the pages while their prized *Sugarman* Rodriguez LP spun at thirty-three and a third on the portable record player, quietly, so that *Ma* didn't hear Rodriguez wondering how many times they'd had sex. *Ma* didn't like any sex talk in the house.

'I had a girl just like that up in Pretoria,' David said, jabbing a finger at the centrefold. 'Shit, I thought I was drowning in those jugs. Now that would be the way to die. Made the border seem a million miles away.'

'Nah,' Alan said. 'I like little baby tits. Like Pretty's. Big ones like that – it'd be like fucking *Ma*.'

He had been shocked when David called him a "fucking pervert" and hit him so hard he fell off the bed and banged his head against the bedside table. He looked up "pervert" in his Afrikaans-English dictionary. He was so ashamed. He wanted to tell David that he wasn't. He hadn't… and he certainly didn't enjoy it, not all of it. None of it! It made him feel funny – sick, but also sort of nice sometimes, all at the same time. He couldn't be a fucking pervert. He wasn't a pervert. David was so wrong.

He'd lost count of the number of *Penthouse Pet* types he'd fucked since then, to prove to David, to himself, that he could fuck girls like that, like the best of them… but not anymore. Not since Brenda. He hadn't fucked that South American whore.

Alan had been stunned when he had found her in his bed after his shift in the cow sheds. She obviously knew Brenda was working the supper shift in the kitchen. He'd never said more than two words to her. Her English wasn't great, not that that had stopped him chatting up other non-Anglo-Saxons before, and anyway, sex was a universal language.

Gabriella/Antoinella/Whatever threw back the sheet, stretched her toned and tanned body and purred. Literally. Like she was a fucking lioness or something. She was stark naked, with hard, milky Nesquik boobs and pink nipples, highlighted by the paler triangles that her tiny bikini top covered – when she wore one… and she had nothing down there. Like a kid. Shit. He was hardening. He was only human.

'Get out of here. Are you nuts?'

The cow smiled at him and held out her arms. 'Come here, lover boy. Come to a real woman.' She sounded like a bad B-grade movie.

'Fuck off, you bitch. Get the fuck out of my room and don't ever, ever try anything like that again. And tell your bitch friends as well.'

Before Brenda, he'd have taken her without a second thought. She probably wouldn't have even had to go this far to seduce him... but, if he gave her what she wanted, she'd make bloody sure Brenda would be the first to know about it. In detail. And it would upset Brenda, possibly even turn her against him... and he wanted Brenda, not this over-endowed tramp, shaved pussy or not.

'Keep away from Brenda – you hear me?' he yelled after her as she scurried from the room.

***

'If you want that South American bitch,' Alan told Javier. 'I'm sure you can have her. But be careful, she's as loose as a rusty door hinge. God knows what horrible diseases she'd give you. But I suppose, being a Mexican, you're immune? Still, you'd better use two condoms with that one.' He laughed as Javier punched him on his arm.

'You one crazy African,' he said.

They ran on in silence. Javier could have Gabriella, Linda, Lynda, Emily – all of them. The *ulpan* was one big orgy of bed hopping and partner swapping... but it wasn't for him. Not anymore. He'd found the girl of his wildest fantasies. The girl he had been waiting for all his life, ever since Pretty.

The first time he had seen Pretty, he had known, for sure, he'd found his dream girl. Well, not her, obviously. She was just a kaffir girl. It was supposed to be Katie's turn, but he was short of cash and had forgotten to bring the bag of toffees she'd asked for the last time. So she walked out, all huffy – the cheeky bitch – and then the door opened and Pretty was shoved in. He heard the other kaffir girls laughing outside. She stumbled to the far side of the shack and stood there in her dirty T-shirt and torn, faded skirt, pressed up against the corrugated iron wall. She stared at the red clay floor, and rubbed one dusty foot up and down her leg.

'Come here,' he said.

She peeped up at him with huge, glistening eyes, then looked down again and giggled.

'Come here.'

She walked slowly towards him.

'Take off your clothes.'

He had to see what was under that shirt. She stood still.

'Take off your clothes, damn it.'

She pulled her T-shirt over her head. He stared. His mouth went dry. They stood out on her skinny brown body like little chocolate-covered strawberries. His ears roared. He pushed up her skirt. She wasn't wearing anything underneath. She was all ready, just waiting for him.

He was bursting... He pulled her down onto the faded mattress. Oh God. Oh Gooodddd. He heard someone yell, 'Fuuuuuuckkkkk.'

'*Baas* Alan, you want me now?' Katie swung through the door, her bare boobs drooping.

'Fuck... off.' He was sprawled out, catching his breath, massaging a sweet little mulberry boob.

The girl made little snuffling noises, like girls do when they've been well and truly satisfied. She started to get up. He pulled her back. It was even better the second time... and the next time, and the next and the next... She was his. Every time he visited the shack, she was waiting for him. All ready on the mattress. She was perfect.

But then she got herself pregnant and it was never the same, because, when she came back to the township afterwards, she was totally ruined, all soft and fat and floppy just like all the other kaffir girls, and it broke his heart. He just couldn't do it with her again. It didn't matter so much with the others, but Pretty had been absolutely perfect. It was like that time *Pa* had driven over his precious tractor – the first brand new toy he'd ever had. *Ma* had given it to him, all shiny and new in its dented, slightly torn cardboard box, for being such good boy. David had tried to fix it for him, but it wasn't the same. He couldn't bear to part with it, but he had never played with it again.

CHAPTER 7

The siren started wailing as they ate breakfast together in the dining room after their early work shifts. Brenda choked on her juice. Alan patted her on the back.

'Get up,' he said.

She scrambled to her feet. Everyone in the dining room was standing too. People who had been carrying trays of food to their tables stopped dead in their tracks. No one said a word. A couple of the older *kibbutzniks* were crying. Everyone looked like statues. The siren wailed and wept… and then it stopped, and the room came to life. People sat down and resumed eating. Those carrying their food to their tables resumed walking.

'What on earth was that?' Brenda asked.

'It's *Yom HaShoah* today,' he said. 'The sirens go off all over Israel. A couple of years ago, I was on a bus in Tel Aviv when it happened. It was weird. The bus just stopped dead in the middle of the street and everyone stood up. Cars were stopped all over the place and the people got out and stood to attention. And when the sirens stopped, everyone just got back in the cars and carried on. It was the strangest thing I'd ever seen.'

'Why?'

'To remember the six million who died in the Holocaust, apparently. Me, I think it's time to move on from all that. It was nearly forty years ago.'

'Alan, how can you say that? My aunt died in Auschwitz.'

Shit, he hadn't known that. 'Really?'

'*Ja, Mama* told me. *Mama* was in Birkenau too, but she survived – obviously. Aunt Anna was only sixteen when she was sent to the Auschwitz gas chambers. Before the war, *Mama* said, she was the Pavlova of Rotterdam. The Nazis made her dance for them, but then she got sick and they sent her to the showers. *Mama* couldn't stop them. I was named after her, you know. I'm Brenda Anna Jones.'

He drew a deep breath. This obviously meant a lot to her and he didn't want to upset her, but really, she should get over it.

'I'm sorry about your aunt. But you never knew her. She's gone. Oh, I know it was terrible and millions died. But there no point in having sirens wailing and holding huge memorial services and building museums like *Yad Vashem*.'

She looked horrified and upset. She looked as if she was about to cry. He had to try harder to make her understand.

'Look, Brenda. Nothing's changed. There's still anti-Semitism all over the world. Including in South Africa. I should know. I grew up in Driespruitfontein where Jews were only slightly more tolerated than the k- blacks. And we Silvermans were the only Jews in that godforsaken *dorp*.'

'I never experienced any anti-Semitism in Jo'burg. What did they do to you?'

'They called us names, like Jew boy and other things I won't repeat to you. They beat us up. I didn't get selected for the Free State cross country team even though I was the fastest. The kids at school – they wouldn't be friends with me. Not in public. Except for Thys. It was like being a leper, you know? And David told me how bad it was for him in the army just because he was Jewish. I still don't believe he stepped on a landmine as they say. I think he was murdered. That's why they never sent his body home.'

'You're kidding. Really?'

Alan nodded.

'But still, that's different. You can't possibly think anti-Semitism in South Africa is like the Holocaust,' she said.

'It all starts somewhere, Brenda. Hitler didn't invent anti-Semitism and it didn't end when the Nazis lost the war. Sirens and standing and remembering and honouring the six million isn't going to change a damn thing.'

'So why did you stand when the siren went off?'

'Because everyone is really emotional about it and it's a waste of energy getting into an argument you can't win. Look, I'm sorry; I didn't mean to upset you.' He took her hand and kissed it. 'I think all this remembering and honouring is a big bloody waste of time. But I love you and I'll respect your feelings and I'll stand up with you, always.' He tilted up her chin and gazed into her eyes.

He could see her start to melt, but then she said, 'I'm so sorry about your brother and everything. I'm really sorry. I never knew. But you're wrong about the Holocaust. And you're wrong to say I didn't know my aunt. I did know her.'

'Brenda, you couldn't have known her. She died long before you were even born.'

'Okay, I never met her, but she was always part of my life. *Mama* said we were going to beat the Nazis, me and her, through my dancing. It was all for Anna. One day, I would dance at Covent Garden or Carnegie Hall, and the audience would applaud for me – Brenda Anna Jones – but they would also be applauding for Anna, you see? The Nazis had stopped her from living her dreams as a ballerina, but I would be there doing it for her.'

'That's crazy, Brenda. You aren't your aunt.'

'To *Mama*, I almost was.' She wiped her eyes. 'When I hurt my knee, I could see that it was as if Anna was dying all over again – and she still couldn't do anything about it. She could hardly bear it. That's why I left. So she didn't have to suffer through Anna's death all over again. Anyway, she never loved me. She never loved anyone. Only Anna.'

'My poor sweetheart.' He pulled her onto his lap and murmured into her hair, 'It doesn't matter about your mother. It doesn't matter about your dead aunt. And it certainly doesn't matter about those bastards in Driespruitfontein or the

Holocaust or anything. We have each other now.'

'Was it really that bad for you, Alan, growing up there?'

'Nah, you got used to it,' he lied. He'd never got used to it. He hated being an outcast. Although once or twice, being Jewish in Driespruitfontein had had its advantages.

Like that time with Annamari.

***

Her face was all white and pinched, her eyes puffy and red. He felt sick. This was some kind of bad, bad joke. A fucking nightmare.

'Fuck, Annamari – I thought you were taking something.'

'I was. I don't know how it happened.'

'Of course you know. You're a farm girl.'

'No man.' She giggled. 'I mean I don't know why it didn't work.'

'So, what are you going to do about it? Will your *pa* send you to England to get it fixed?'

'Abortion?' She whispered the word as if afraid the cops would hear and arrest her for even mentioning it. 'I can't do that. It's illegal. And it's a sin.'

'Well, I'm not going to marry you.'

She looked so horrified he almost laughed out loud.

'*Nee* man. Are you crazy? *Pa* would kill me if he thought I'd been sleeping with a Jew boy. No, I've told them it's Thys'. Well, maybe it is. It could be. You can't really think you were anything special to me.'

Tears stained her white school shirt.

'Thys is happy about it. *Pa* and *Dominee* van Zyl have discussed it and we're getting married next month, in Bloemfontein. That's where Thys' *ouma* lives. I'm going to stay with his *ouma* there until, well, until…' She faltered. 'I just wanted to let you know that I can't meet you on Saturday. That's all.'

'What about your maths lesson? And Matric? Aren't you going to finish school? I thought you wanted to be a nurse.'

'I'm going to be a *ma*. You don't need Matric for that, *Pa* said. Anyway, *Meneer* Joubert expelled me. And he took away Thys' prefect badge. *Totsiens*, Alan.'

She touched his hair, then turned and walked away. He never saw her again… and things were never quite the same between him and Thys either, because, even though they'd been friends for years and years, Thys still hadn't been able to bring himself to invite a Jew to his wedding.

CHAPTER 8

With the *ulpan* drawing to a close, Alan had to make a decision. What to do? He could stay in Israel, but then he'd have to go to the army. Not a fucking chance in hell would he do that. He couldn't go back to South Africa. Not that he wanted to – he didn't even know if his parents were still in Driespruitfontein, or if they were alive or dead. He certainly didn't care, and anyway, from what he'd seen on CNN, there was a fucking civil war going on there. Anyway, he'd probably be arrested the moment he set foot on sacred apartheid soil.

Then there was Brenda. He couldn't leave her. He'd think of something. Where the hell was she, anyway? She was taking volunteering in the children's houses too far. He wanted her with him when she wasn't in class or working in the kitchen, but she said she enjoyed helping out with the children. She was so sweet. She felt so sorry for the kids, because they didn't live with their parents.

'How can they take those babies away from their mothers? It's mean,' she said.

'The moms have to work, Brenda. Everyone on a kibbutz

has to work and it makes sense to put all the kids together, have a few women looking after them and the moms doing their fair share of real work.'

He actually thought it was a brilliant idea, if you were stupid enough to have kids. The parents only had to put up with their kids for a couple of hours a day. That was more than enough. However, even that was more than he'd spent with *Pa* growing up. Which had been just fine, because *Pa* had always found an excuse to *klap* him and it was hard, sometimes, to hide the bruises, not that anyone ever asked – not even the cross country coach. And he would love to have seen a hell of a lot less of *Ma*, because, even after that last time, after he'd pushed her out of his room and told her that if she came near him again he'd kill her, she'd still come to his room, especially when she'd had too much to drink, and she'd beg. It made him feel physically sick. Anyway, not sleeping in the same house as your parents was no different to going to boarding school. He wished he'd been able to go to boarding school, but not in Driespruitfontein. He'd have loved to have gone to a boarding school where he wasn't the only Jew.

***

'Alan, what's up with Brenda and Javier?'

Linda's question startled him. 'What do you mean?'

'I saw them sneaking into the theatre together.' Linda's little piggy eyes gleamed. 'And Emily saw them going in there yesterday. Is Brenda getting some from Javier now?'

He was furious. 'You fucking lying bitch. Brenda's working in the children's houses.'

Linda snorted. 'That's what you think. If you don't believe me, why don't you go check it out?' She shoved her boobs at him, squeezed his hand, snorted again and waddled off, laughing.

He couldn't remember running all the way from the *ulpan* houses, past the dining room to the theatre, but then he was outside the door. He could hear her inside. She was laughing. He could hear Javier laughing. He tore the door open. They were on the stage... and there were two other guys with them. They were all laughing. Javier had his arm around her. She was naked – no, not naked, but she might as well have been. He'd kill Javier. How could they do this to him?

She was saying something. Javier was talking to him. He couldn't hear them over the roaring in his ears. He grabbed her hand and dragged her off the stage, out through the door and back to their room. He was raging inside. He was dying inside. How could she betray him like this? He slammed the door and swung her around to face him.

At the sight of her tear-stained, frightened little face, he felt himself harden. Oh God, he'd never wanted her so much. He pulled off her stupid leotard and tights. He crushed her on the bed. She lay nice and still, just like he'd told her to. When he was finished, he rolled off her. She clung to him, tears streaming down her face, begging his forgiveness. She promised she'd never look at another man again. She agreed that it was best if they left the kibbutz. She told him she loved him when he promised her he'd always take care of her – even if she didn't deserve it. He meant it too. He couldn't imagine life without her. In England, it would just be the two of them. Always. The way it was meant to be.

PART 6
ANNETTE

CHAPTER 1
LONDON, 1989

Annette tentatively turned the key and pushed the door open. She was certain she'd switched the lights off when she had locked up the offices for the weekend, but maybe she hadn't. It was just as well, then, that she'd forgotten to take home the papers she needed to work on tomorrow to prepare for her meeting with the Anti Apartheid Movement on Monday. It was the first time Aunt Sally was letting her handle a meeting like that on her own and she had to do a good job.

She walked into the little back office… and screamed. There was someone lying on the old brown sofa, huddled under her tartan blanket. The figure threw off the blanket and stood up. Her heart was thudding.

'Rock! What the hell are you doing here? It's late.'

'I know. I hope you don't mind. I didn't know where else to go.'

'What's happened? You look awful.' He really did. He was pale and crumpled. 'How long have you been here?'

'Since last night. I'll leave tomorrow if it's a problem for you.'

She shook her head. What was wrong? 'Where's Brenda?' she asked.

'I don't know. At home, I suppose. I left her there last night, after we got home from *Shabbos* supper at the Shapiros. I needed to be alone. To think.'

'Why, what's happened? Did Ben Shapiro fire you?'

'No, nothing like that. Look, I don't want to talk about it.'

'Okay. Do you want some coffee?'

'*Ja*. Thanks.'

She went into the little kitchenette and put on the kettle. Her mind was racing. Had Alan and Brenda broken up? She said a silent prayer and carried the two steaming mugs back to the office. Alan was sitting on the sofa, his head in his hands.

'There's no milk,' she said.

'I know. I finished it just now.' He took a sip of the coffee and grimaced. 'Shit, I hate black coffee.' He put down the mug and turned to her, despair etched on his face. 'Oh God, Annette. I don't know what to do. I just don't know.'

Her heart broke for him. She put her arms around him. He clung to her. She looked into his eyes. He stared back and then he kissed her. It was like nothing she had ever experienced before. She kissed him back. She put her hands under his shirt. He felt so good. They kissed again… and then he was touching her and she was kissing him and touching him. They rolled onto the floor. She pulled the blanket over them. It was cold without clothes. When had they taken their clothes off? They crawled back onto the sofa. He was in her.

She was on him. She couldn't get enough of him. She clawed at him, kissed him, held him. Eventually, he fell asleep. She lay awake, curled up next to him, reliving every sensation. She slept.

***

'Isn't it brilliant?' Aunt Sally asked Annette when she floated through the WOAH office door on Monday afternoon. It was late. The meeting with the Anti Apartheid Movement and ANC people had gone on for ages, but it had gone well. Better than well, actually. They had been really impressed with her proposals. Well, she had been impressive, even if she had to say so herself. When she had put her presentation together yesterday, after that amazing night with Alan, the ideas had just flowed. She'd been inspired. She'd been able to see solutions to problems that had seemed insurmountable just the day before. Everything was sharper, clearer, more focussed. The cold February air was crisper; London was shining; every sound had a clarity she'd never heard before. It was as if the world had been honed from some pristine Waterford crystal. Alan loved her. Alan loved her. Alan loved her. She'd smiled at the ANC cadres around the table, and they'd smiled back. Her joy was clearly infectious.

'Yes, it's wonderful,' she said. 'Who called you? I was hoping to tell you all about it myself.'

Aunt Sally looked puzzled, then laughed. 'I wasn't talking

about your meeting, but it obviously went well. I've never seen you look so happy. You're positively glowing. What did they say?'

'That they'd support us and endorse our next campaign. They might even ask Oliver Tambo to attend. Isn't that amazing?'

Aunt Sally clapped and then flung her arms around her niece. 'You're brilliant, Annette. I know you are family, but I truly admire and respect you. I've never been able to get that kind of endorsement before. I salute you, my dear.'

Annette rushed to the phone. 'I must phone Rock, I mean Alan, and tell him. They want him to speak at the function – in fact, they insisted on it.'

'Oh, I don't think Alan will be at home now.'

'Why not? Don't tell me he has to work late again. Honestly, Ben Shapiro takes such advantage of him.'

'No. They're going out with the Shapiros. To celebrate. That's my news. Brenda phoned me just before you got in. She was so excited. She and Alan are getting married.'

***

'I do,' Annette said.

She was pleased to hear her voice was clear and firm, with absolutely no indication of the turmoil inside her. She'd done it. She was now officially Mrs Charles Smedley. Charles, looking spiffy in a grey suit, white shirt and navy tie, beamed at her.

'You may kiss the bride,' said the registrar.

Charles pecked her lips. She glanced across at Alan. He was sitting behind Mom and Dad, next to Aunt Sally. He was smiling at her. Brenda was hanging onto his hand, as usual. She wondered if Brenda was comparing this wedding to her own, just six weeks before. Even she had to admit, the contrast couldn't be greater, although the Rosetti Room in the Chelsea Old Town Hall was very pleasant. Not like a registry office at all, really. It was small and intimate, only for their very closest nearest and dearest. Now that the ceremony was over, they were going to have morning tea at the Savoy. Brenda's wedding had been ostentatious, totally over the top. She and Charles only had their families – the Smedleys had travelled down from Birmingham; her mom and dad had arrived from South Africa two days ago – and their closest friends, like Alan.

Her mom and dad's trip was the reason she and Charles were getting married now. That's what she had told Charles when she'd proposed to him that dreadful night. 'Let's get married in May, when my parents come,' she'd said. She'd gone home in a daze, silently screaming denial at Aunt Sally's "wonderful news". Aunt Sally had looked at her in concern. She knew Aunt Sally had always suspected how she felt about Alan – but at least she didn't know about their little tryst on the brown sofa. She'd just die if anyone ever found out. The bastard. The bloody, effing bastard. The fucking bastard... and then he'd pretended it had never happened. When he'd breezed into the office later that week, and accepted everyone's congratulations, he'd kissed her cheek, took her hand and examined her ring, and then he'd bloody said Charles was a lucky man. If that was how he wanted to play it, so be it. They'd be "just" friends. It was better than nothing.

Alan kissed her cheek and shook hands with Charles. 'You look beautiful,' he said.

Her heart leaped even though she knew he was just going through the motions. Everyone told a bride she looked beautiful… but, actually, she knew that she *did* look wonderful – just like a modern, 1989 liberated bride should. Her knee-length pale green dress and jacket were elegant and sensible. She'd be able to wear the outfit again. Her mother was horrified that she'd chosen to wear green. 'It's unlucky,' she'd said. Mom was also upset that she refused to wear anything on her head, but she was too short to wear a hat – she'd look like a squashed toad. Anyway, it was bad enough having to promise to "obey" any man, even if she had absolutely no intention of "obeying" Charles. She wouldn't even "obey" Alan... well, maybe she would agree to be a little less assertive with him, if that was what he wanted – but that was only because he was so, so... She shook her head. She mustn't go there. Not on her wedding day. Her very modern, liberated wedding day.

There was no way she would have submitted to the antiquated rituals of a traditional "white" wedding. Not even for Alan. How hypocritical would that have been, seeing as she and Charles had been living together for ages? Brenda, obviously, didn't mind hypocrisy. She'd floated down the aisle at the Golders Green synagogue on Ben Shapiro's arm dressed in an obscenely expensive, virginal floaty white designer creation to join Alan, incredibly handsome in his grey morning suit, under the canopy.

'Isn't she quite, quite beautiful,' Aunt Sally had said, as they helped themselves to the buffet luncheon served on the patio at the Shapiro's magnificent Georgian house and looked across at Alan and Brenda strolling hand-in-hand around the lawn, greeting their guests. Even the bloody sun had played along. 'She looks like a little porcelain doll. She and Alan make the most beautiful couple, don't you agree, Annette?'

'I suppose their children will be beautiful too,' she had snapped back. She was pretty sure Brenda was pregnant – she was starting to look a little chubby. Why else would Alan have married her so suddenly?

CHAPTER 2
LONDON, 1990

Annette stamped her feet in an effort to warm them. She'd been stupid to arrange to meet Alan outside Camden Station in this weather. It was freezing… but it was convenient. They were going to the Anti Apartheid Movement offices. There was a rumour that FW de Klerk was going to be making some important announcement in the South African Parliament.

Finally, Alan emerged from the station, looking flustered. She tucked her arm through his.

'It's going to be really crowded at the AAM office, Rock. Let's watch at WOAH. There's a bottle of champers in the fridge, I think. If it's good news, we can celebrate,' she said, and mentally crossed her fingers. She saw so little of him lately. In fact, she'd hardly seen him at all since the twins had been born. She wanted some time alone with him.

'It better be good. Otherwise, I'll have to write to FW and complain that he made us waste a perfectly good bottle of bubbly,' he said.

They settled down companionably on the sofa.

'How's Brenda? And the babies?'

'Fine.'

He didn't add anything, and she wasn't going to ask. He looked exhausted, poor man. Who would have thought that tiny little Brenda could produce twins? One baby would have been bad enough, but two… Poor Alan. Brenda was so selfish, expecting Alan to get up at night to see to the babies when he had to work so hard.

Alan settled back on the sofa and seemed to relax. She couldn't. She was too excited. She pushed the memory of their last time on the sofa to the back of her mind. It was so long ago, yet every second of it was deeply etched into her mind. She tried to concentrate on the TV. The light in South Africa's House of Assembly reflected off the South African President's shiny head. FW was saying something about the end of communism; something about human and individual rights – yeah right, human rights in South Africa – and about no more hanging. That was good.

Alan put his arm around her. That startled her, but she snuggled closer. He didn't move. FW was talking on and on about the economy. Alan slipped his hand up under her shirt, pushed aside her bra and massaged her breasts. She held her breath. What was he doing? It felt so good...

She tried hard to concentrate. 'The prohibition of the African National Congress, the Pan Africanist Congress, the South African Communist Party and a number of subsidiary organisations is being rescinded,' FW said. No. It couldn't be. She tried to focus, but Alan's hand was so distracting. She wanted to push it away. She wanted him to keep touching her.

FW went on – lifting restrictions on this, unbanning that... it was quite incredible. That bottle of bubbly was definitely going to be opened. FW mentioned Nelson Mandela. She sat up.

'The government,' FW said, 'has noted that he has declared himself to be willing to make a constructive contribution to the peaceful political process in South Africa.'

She held Alan's hand still.

'… The government has taken a firm decision to release Mr. Mandela unconditionally.'

She shrieked. 'I don't believe it. I don't believe it.' She jumped up.

'What?' Alan looked dazed.

'He's done it. He's actually done it. Did you hear? Mandela is going to be freed. Oh my God. Oh my God. I never, ever thought I'd see the day. Oh my God.'

She flung herself at him and kissed him. They rolled onto the floor.

It was later, much later, that they remembered to open the champagne. He smiled at her. They made love again. Eventually, they made their way to Trafalgar Square to join the party outside South Africa House.

***

Ten days later, Annette and Alan snuggled down on their sofa again to watch Nelson Mandela's release. It took forever and they got bored waiting. So she ended up trying to see the big moment when the cameras first caught sight of Mandela from over Alan's shoulder as he worked his way to his climax. Well, Alan was right about one thing. She'd certainly always remember exactly where she was, who she was with and what she was doing when Mandela walked out of Victor Verster prison. Not that she'd ever tell anyone. He rolled off her and she had a clear view of her idol and his wife walking slowly towards the crowd, hand in hand. Winnie gave a clenched fist salute. Annette saluted back. This was the best, the very best day of her entire life.

***

'Brenda wanted to come with, but I told her it was by invitation only,' Alan said while they waited outside the hotel with a large group of people from the Anti Apartheid Movement. 'She'd have to leave the twins with Ruth and that wouldn't be fair. And anyway, it's raining.'

Annette didn't care what he'd told Brenda. Just as long as she stayed away. She was apparently finding it really hard to cope with the twins, Aunt Sally said.

'You wouldn't recognise her, Annette, the poor little thing. She looks too terrible and she's obviously having a real problem losing the weight she put on during the pregnancy. It's difficult enough having to cope with one baby on your own, with no support. But two. Poor child. I wish I could do more.'

Now that Mandela was free, WOAH's work was just about finished, with just Annette holding the fort. Aunt Sally had taken up with another good cause and was busier than ever.

'She has Ruth Shapiro,' Annette said. 'Poor Rock, I mean Alan. It's not fair that he has to keep getting up at night for them when he has a full-time job and a lot more responsibility.'

Alan confided in her a lot lately. The old brown sofa in the WOAH offices was their secret refuge. No one ever disturbed them there.

It was such an exciting day that she couldn't resist hugging him as they joined the queue in the foyer. She spotted several ANC people they knew and they smiled at them. She saw that Susan woman Alan had introduced her to outside Harrods a few weeks ago. Her father was something big in the ANC, or was it her husband? They all shook hands in the glare of the huge chandelier. With the changes that were coming in South Africa, Alan said the ANC guys could be really useful to know. So she watched, amused, as he was especially charming to them. They mocked him about his WOAH poster boy contribution to the struggle, but it was good-natured teasing, not at all malicious. They knew he had been disowned by his family and his community. They said they didn't know how they would cope if they were exiled, not only from their beloved country, but also their people. She knew exactly how they felt – although she had never lacked for support from her family. Alan had no one. However, he said that, while it was hard, he had role models like Beyers Naude to inspire him. She was so proud of him, of how much he had matured politically.

The doors of the meeting room opened and they all filed in. She could feel the tension and excitement in the room. Alan gazed down at her. He loved her; she could see it in his eyes. He just had to stay with Brenda because of the babies, but if he ever gave the word, she'd leave Charles in a flash. Poor Charles.

'I really don't get all the excitement about what is really just one old guy, who spent a long time in jail,' Alan had teased her when she'd told him they were going to finally meet him – in person. 'He speaks like my old garden boy.'

'That's a terrible thing to say. Just wait till you see him in the flesh. I've been told he's mesmerising.'

'Well, I wouldn't know about that. But I must say that the best part of this whole thing is that it must be killing those fucking racists in Driespruitfontein. They must all think they've died and gone to hell. Or that hell has come to South Africa. And for that alone, I'm prepared to like your Nelson Mandela.'

She'd laughed. Alan was so funny.

Mandela walked into the crowded room. He was taller than she had expected. The silence was deafening. It was as if everyone held their collective breath. She found herself crying. So were Susan and a lot of the other women in the ballroom. She gripped Alan's hand. He pulled away – he was always worried that someone who knew Brenda might see. She wondered if Susan had met Brenda. Mandela was thanking them for their support. People were clapping and cheering and singing. And then it was over.

'That was incredible. He's incredible,' Annette said.

'Hey, you'll make me jealous. He's an old man.'

'Very funny. I can't believe I've just been in the same room as Nelson Mandela. I mean, when other girls would dream of John Travolta or Robert Redford, I'd dream of Mandela. I even put up a poster of him on my wall – it was banned, of course, but Aunt Sally sent it to me. My parents took it down. They were scared someone would report us to the cops. For having a bloody poster. When I was in solitary, I'd imagine what it must have been like for him to be locked up for so long. It made it easier for me, you know? And Winnie – isn't she just incredible? She's gone through so much.'

'I wonder if she'll be at the concert too.'

'Of course she will. Gosh, isn't it strange? The last time we went to a concert at Wembley, it was to protest at Mr Mandela's imprisonment. And now he's here. And he's going to be at the concert himself. Will Brenda be coming?'

'No, of course not. Will Charles?'

'Oh God, no. He hated every minute of the last one. So it will be just the two of us.' She stood on tip-toe and kissed him on the lips. He slipped his arms around her and then pulled away. Susan was watching them. She came over and smiled at Annette.

'Hello, Brenda,' Susan said. 'Isn't he just too marvellous?'

She put her smooth brown hand on Alan's arm and smiled up at him. Annette wasn't sure who she was referring to – Alan or Mandela – but at least Susan had acknowledged her prior claim, even if she did think she was Alan's wife.

***

Annette and Alan returned to WOAH's offices after leaving the hotel. Alan seemed distracted.

'Are you sleeping with her?' Annette asked him later, her head resting on his bare chest.

Alan pushed her away so forcefully that she almost tumbled off the sofa. He sat up, his eyes flashing with a fury she'd never seen before.

'Don't you dare ask me about Brenda. I've told you before. My relationship with my wife has absolutely nothing to do with you.'

She was stunned. 'I didn't mean Brenda. I meant that other woman. Susan, I think her name is.'

'That's none of your business,' he snapped. Then he smiled, his blue eyes twinkling: 'Oh come on, Annette. You're not jealous, are you? I met her at a WOAH meeting, in York. She's a fascinating woman. Clever too, but not as clever as you.'

He pushed her back on the sofa and kissed her. He hadn't answered her question, but she knew that, if she nagged him, they'd end up arguing again. She didn't really want him to answer, anyway, because then... and she didn't want to waste any of her precious time with him arguing over something that she was sure didn't mean anything to him. She just hoped they wouldn't bump into Susan at the concert.

CHAPTER 3
LONDON, 1992

Annette snuggled up to Alan, tucked her legs under her and put her head on Alan's chest. It would be their last time here. The WOAH offices were closing tomorrow. It was silly to keep the organisation going. South Africa was going to change. Everything they'd fought for was coming to fruition. Even the whites were changing – or at least were willing to accept change. Last week's referendum confirmed that.

Alan's hand was under her jumper, lazily teasing her nipples like he always did. She never wore a bra when she was with him anymore. He told her how well things were going at Shapiro and Son. Since Jeremy's death, Ben was taking less and less interest in the business.

Annette listened as Alan told her how much he liked the property investment and development side of Shapiro and Sons, far more than the retail interests. Retail reminded him too much of Driespruitfontein General Dealer – although Shapiro's Deli chain bore little resemblance to his mother's shop. Property was totally different, he said. It was exciting to spot an opportunity and then go after it. There was something immensely satisfying about closing a deal, particularly when he got exactly what he wanted despite opposition from whomever.

'It gives me a rush, you know. Kind of like when I first used to make love to... um... well, anyway. It's a good feeling, like having the audience stand and applaud me at a WOAH meeting,' he said.

She let him speak. She loved just listening to his voice; they had been together like this for more than two years now, and she still loved the feel of his hands on her body. She'd always love the feel of his hands when he touched her; she'd always love the way he'd...

The South Africa-Australia game would be starting soon. She'd told Charles she was going with Aunt Sally to Bath. She didn't know what Alan had told Brenda, and she didn't care. They had the whole night. They seldom managed to spend an entire night together, but this was a special occasion. She loved cricket. He was more of a rugby man.

'It's amazing that South Africa is playing,' she said. 'It's absolutely incredible, really.'

'Uh huh.' He pulled her shirt and jumper over her head and resumed playing with her breasts. She kept talking.

'I mean, I can still vaguely remember that Springbok rugby tour of New Zealand. When they flour-bombed the field. I was just a kid then. My dad was furious about it all. And now the Springbok cricket team is playing in the World Cup. I wonder what Peter Hain is thinking.' She tried to focus on the television set.

'*Ja*, well, they're probably going to get slaughtered,' Alan said.

'Doesn't matter. Just the fact that they are there shows you how much things are changing back home.'

'I don't know. Probably the same old, same old there.'

'I disagree. Look at the huge majority the "yes" vote had in the referendum. We're going to have a democracy, a real democracy. You'll see.'

Alan snorted in derision. 'Yeah, right!'

Bowled. Alan Border out for a duck. She sat up and cheered. Alan smiled at her.

'Maybe South Africa has a chance, after all,' she said.

He unzipped her jeans.

Afterwards, she held him close as they spooned on the couch, savouring the feel of his strong, lean back against her breasts. She swallowed. She mustn't cry; he hated it when she cried. He dozed off.

She shook him awake.

'You have to see this. South Africa's going to win,' she said. She was bursting with excitement.

He propped himself up on one elbow to watch.

'Kepler Wessels went back home and look what he did to Australia. South Africa couldn't have done it without him,' she said as the South African captain walked off the field, a huge smile on his normally taciturn face.

'He's a fool. No one should go back,' Alan said.

She sat up. 'I'm going back.'

'*Ja*, right.'

'I am. We are. Charles and I. We're going back to South Africa. Or rather, I'm going back. Charles is coming with me.'

She was babbling. She only babbled when she was nervous. He was shocked, she could see.

'When did you decide this?'

'Charles and I have been talking about it for ages. But, after the referendum, I just have to go. I never wanted to leave in the first place. I'm South African. Not British, never mind what my passport says. We've made enquiries at the South African Embassy and it's okay for me to go. They've forgotten, or are prepared to ignore, my deportation order. A lot of exiles are going home. Your friend, Susan, has gone.'

'Why? I don't get it. South Africa treated you like shit. Now you want to go back so that they can treat you like shit all over again?'

'The Nats treated me like shit, not South Africa. The new South Africa will need people like us. And my family is there. Everything I love is there…'

'And me? I thought you loved me.'

'Oh, Rock, I do love you; you know that.'

'So you're just going to walk out on me, on us?' He gestured angrily at the room, the sofa, the pile of clothes lying in a heap in the corner where they'd thrown them.

'Tell me you love me, Rock.'

He stared at her.

'Leave Brenda. Marry me.'

'Are you crazy? Whatever gave you that idea?'

'Precisely. Well, I'm tired of being your, your – bit of fluff or whatever the hell I am. I want children and I can't have them while I'm with you. Charles also wants children and I'm running out of excuses.'

'Jesus, Annette. Kids? You don't know what you're asking for.'

'Maybe not, but I do know I can't keep on sneaking around to be with you.'

'But if you go to South Africa, you realise we'll probably never see each other again? Is that really what you want?'

'If I stay, I'll never make my marriage work. And I'll never have a baby. I'm thirty-two years old. So I'm going home, with my husband, and I'm going to complete what I started here. I'm going to make a difference in this world, Rock. Even if it kills me. Even if I never see you again. I'm married to Charles. He loves me. And I'm going to make it work. And you can play happily ever after with your precious Brenda.'

Tears streamed down her face as she pulled on her clothes, silently berating herself for thinking, for hoping that he'd ever choose her over Brenda. She just wished he'd explain why nothing she did to please him, why none of the other women she knew he messed around with, could prise him away from Brenda. He watched her in silence. She pulled on her coat and kissed him, a soft, lingering kiss. And then she turned and walked to the door.

She pulled it open, stopped and looked back at the man she had loved for fourteen years. He was sitting on the sofa, staring at the wall.

'Tell me something. What is it about Brenda? Why does she have such a hold on you? It can't be because of the children. You never wanted them.'

'I love her,' he said. He didn't look at her.

'Don't forget to lock up when you leave,' she said, and shut the door quietly behind her. Then she ran, before she changed her mind.

PART 7
BEN

CHAPTER 1
LONDON, 1989

Ben rushed down the corridor to the pay phone. He was running out of change. He dialled. 'Miss Smith, anything yet?'

She was still waiting at the office.

He could hear Josephine Smith's anxiety as she confirmed, yet again, that Alan still hadn't reported in. Where was the boy? According to the secretary, he'd gone to a meeting in York, but that had been on Wednesday. He'd stayed over because he was scheduled to speak at a WOAH meeting in Leeds. Then, yesterday morning, he'd phoned to say his car had broken down, and that was the last they'd heard. According to Miss Smith, he'd checked out of his hotel, so he could be anywhere. Anywhere. Maybe he'd had an accident, but they would have heard if he had, surely? Perhaps he should call Miss Smith back and get her to call around hospitals and, please God, no, mortuaries. He phoned her and told her to go home. It was after ten. Alan wouldn't phone the office this late.

He walked back to the waiting room. Ruth came in. 'Where's Alan?' she demanded. If she'd asked him once, she'd asked him a thousand times since she'd phoned him, frantic with worry, to say she was calling an ambulance to take Brenda to hospital. That had been – he looked at his watch – nearly twelve hours ago.

'Ruthie, I told you. When I hear anything, I'll let you know. How's Brenda doing?'

'How do you think she's doing? She's in pain. She's worried sick about her husband. How could you send him away on a business trip at a time like this with no way to contact him? Brenda needs him.'

She turned on her heel and disappeared back through the double doors. He thought he heard Brenda screaming. He had to do something. Perhaps Alan had gone straight to the flat. Perhaps he was phoning the Golders Green house and there was no one there. He walked down to the hospital entrance and hailed a taxi.

He hurried up the stairs to Alan and Brenda's little flat, too anxious to wait for the lift. He hammered at the door. He rang the bell. He shouted. Alan wasn't home. He tore a page from his diary and scrawled a note: "Brenda's in labour. Go to the hospital immediately". He pushed the note under the door.

Why on earth had Brenda gone into labour early? He'd never hear the last of it from Ruth. He waited for the lift. It creaked and groaned its way to the second floor. He'd ask maintenance to look at it in the morning. One had to take care of one's buildings, or they'd go to wrack and ruin in the blink of an eye. This was a very nice building, an excellent investment. Alan had found it and persuaded him to buy it. There was huge demand for the flats in this area. Good rentals. Of course, he couldn't charge Alan and Brenda full rental on their flat. Ruthie and Brenda had decorated it so prettily – he should look at possibly investing in that Laura Ashley woman's business. She was very popular.

He made his way back to the waiting room. Ruth was there, weeping. His heart stopped.

'They've taken Brenda to theatre. They're doing an emergency caesarean section. She can't... She isn't... Oh Ben, that poor child.'

He put his arm around her. He didn't know what to say. He prayed.

A doctor approached them. 'Mr and Mrs Silverman?'

Ben didn't bother to correct him.

'Your daughter is fine. She's in the recovery room. They'll be moving her back to her ward soon, so you can go and wait for her there. Oh, and congratulations. You have a beautiful grandson, and a very feisty little granddaughter. We've put them in premmie intensive care, but that's just a precaution. They're perfect. Surprisingly big too, especially as your daughter is such a tiny little thing.'

Ruth burst into tears. He felt tears rolling down his face too. '*Baruch Ha'shem*. Thank God.'

They stood and looked at Brenda sleeping, her dark curls spread over the pillow. Ruth took his hand. 'Go home,' she whispered. 'You have to go to the office tomorrow – today, rather. I'll stay. She'll need someone here when she wakes up.'

He kissed her. He'd kill Alan when he saw him. How could he do this to his little wife? Ruth settled herself down in the chair next to Brenda's bed and took her hand. He looked at the two most important women in his life. He couldn't believe how much Brenda had come to mean to him and Ruth, in just a few years. It was like she really was their daughter... and Alan... Where was the boy? He prayed nothing had happened to him. He'd grown to love that boy, almost as much as he loved Jeremy. He was smart and hard-working, and charming and polite. Even to the secretaries. A bit too opinionated at times, but he was never afraid to admit his mistakes. Ben went back to his house and checked the answering machine. Nothing.

***

Ruth looked haggard. She hadn't been home at all since she'd followed the ambulance to the hospital – was it only yesterday? She was telling Brenda about the babies, but Ben could see Brenda wasn't listening. She grimaced every time she moved. Surely the doctor could give her something a little stronger for the pain. She was so worried. They all were. Where was Alan?

'Alan,' Brenda said.

Ben turned. Alan stood in the doorway, a bunch of drooping flowers in his arms. Where had he found that *drek*? He couldn't afford a decent bouquet, for his wife who'd just given him two beautiful babies?

'Where the hell have you been?' He'd never been so angry in his life. Or so relieved. 'How can you go away for three days and leave your pregnant wife with no way to contact you? I honestly never thought you'd be so thoughtless.'

'Shh, Ben,' Ruth said. 'He's here now. That all that matters. Let's leave the children alone. We're not needed here now and we have to go and get ready for *Shabbos*.' Ruth kissed Brenda on the forehead and led him from the room. 'Oh, *mazeltov*, Daddy,' she said as she closed the door.

Ben couldn't say anything. He wanted to wipe that cocky smile off that *shmo's* face. He wanted to hug him.

***

Ruth knocked gently at the door before pushing it open. Alan was sitting next to Brenda, holding her hand. Brenda was glowing. It was incredible, the effect having Alan at her side had on her. He'd never seen two people so much in love – apart from him and Ruthie, of course. It was wonderful.

'So, Daddy Silverman, what do you think of your angels?' Ruth asked.

'They're just perfect. Like their mother,' Alan said.

'Mmm. They're dark like Brenda, but I think the boy is like you. What are you going to call them?'

'You know they can't tell us the names until the *bris*,' Ben chided Ruth gently.

Ruth counted on her fingers. 'That'll be on Friday. Would you allow us to host it at our house?'

Brenda looked at Alan, who nodded.

'It's wonderful, all the *simchas* we're having at the house. It hasn't been such a happy place since… Anyway, Jeremy says *mazeltov* and sends his love. He wants us to send photos of his adopted niece and nephew as soon as possible.'

'Thank you, Mrs Shapiro, Mr Shapiro – for everything,' Brenda said.

Ben beamed at her. 'Don't you think it's about time you started calling us Ben and Ruth? I mean, if we are to be the twins' *bobba* and *zaidah*. You too, Alan.'

'Even at the office?' Alan asked.

'Why not? It seems to be the growing trend nowadays anyway. It's all first names and buddy-buddy before you've even shaken hands. And – as I said before – you are like family to us now.'

They chatted. Then he remembered. 'By the way, Alan, what was wrong with the car?'

'The car? Oh, the car. It wasn't serious. It's all fixed now.'

'How much did it cost?'

'What? The repair? It wasn't too bad.'

'Well, don't forget to claim back from accounting – you did get an invoice, didn't you? And also for the hotel. Where did you stay over, by the way?'

'It's fine, Mr Shapiro – I mean, Ben, really. Ruth, I saw the cutest twin pram at that baby shop near here. We'd really appreciate it if you'd have a look at it for us. Brenda and I are clueless about what to buy. I mean, with the babies arriving early, there's still so much we need.'

Ruth sparkled. Ben groaned. He could just see the excitement written all over her. He hoped the best and most expensive London baby shops were equipped to withstand the coming Ruthie tsunami as all her pent-up *bobba* emotions were unleashed.

'Ben, I think it's time to go. Brenda needs her rest. And I want to stop at the nursery to look at our babies.'

'Ruth,' he said as he turned the Daimler out of the hospital parking, 'tell me I'm being stupid, but...'

'All right. You're stupid.'

He laughed, but something was niggling. Something wasn't quite right.

'Ruth, did you notice that Alan didn't answer my questions? About where he'd stayed or what was wrong with the car?'

She shook her head and looked away. She didn't answer. So she'd noticed too. It began to rain. Drops plopped and slid like big fat tears down the windscreen. He put on the wipers and brushed them away. The traffic light was taking ages to change. A car hooted loudly. He turned his head and saw Alan – was that Alan? – hurrying into the tube station. Why had he left Brenda alone? Why was he catching the tube? Where was he going in such a rush on a Saturday afternoon?

***

They'd pushed the dining room table to one side, where it groaned under the weight of the food Ruthie, bless her, had organised. The *mohel* had handled the snip very neatly, but it still wasn't pleasant. Ben had hung on to the boykie's ankles so hard the poor *babbela* had screamed even before the *mohel* did his thing, but rather a screaming baby than a mutilated little pecker. A *bris* was really quite brutal, but at least the baby wouldn't remember anything, not like those poor African tribes, which circumcised youngsters in their teens. That really was primitive.

Then Alan announced the babies' names. Ben almost burst with pride. Yair Benjamin Silverman, and the little princess – Aviva Ruth Silverman. Such *naches* Alan and Brenda were bringing them. Such joy.

He took Alan aside and handed him an envelope. Alan looked surprised.

'Ben, you shouldn't have. You and Ruth have done so much for us. We're so grateful.'

Alan opened it and took out the cheque. He went red, then white. His eyes filled with tears. Ben felt his eyes well up too. This was marvellous. Wonderful to be able to do something that would make a real difference to these beautiful babies, the only grandchildren he was ever likely to have. Now they could have the best education money could buy, if Alan invested the money wisely. He'd already spoken to Saul Mendelsohn at Barclays to ensure that Alan got the best advice possible.

'Ben, you are crazy. You and Ruth are quite crazy. I don't

know what to say. Fifty thousand pounds. My God, this is unbelievable. Unbelievable. Thank you.'

He watched Alan walk away, clearly dazed. He smiled across at Ruth. She beamed back at him. Brenda came over and put her arms around him.

'Thank you, Ben,' she said. 'I couldn't ask for better grandparents for my children. I love you. I hardly remember my own father, but I know he must be so grateful that I have found a new father like you. I am blessed. Truly blessed.'

His heart was so full, it overflowed.

CHAPTER 2

Ruth looked up from her book. She hadn't been reading, Ben could tell. After forty-odd years together, he could sense her moods even before she was aware of them herself. Anyway, she hadn't turned a page for at least the last ten minutes.

'What's wrong, *neshomeleh*?' Ben asked.

She carefully put her bookmark between the pages, closed the book and put it down. This was clearly very serious. She sat back in her favourite armchair and clasped her hands.

'I'm worried about Brenda,' she said. 'She's not coping. She looks like hell. I was over there today and there were nappies piled in the bathroom – the place stank. I don't think she is bathing either; her hair was filthy. And God forgive me, she smelled terrible. I don't know what to do.'

He put down the newspaper. He suspected something was up with Alan too. He was as conscientious as ever, working as hard as ever. But he was spending hours in the office when he could have been home with his wife. And he was taking a lot of out-of-town trips as well… but maybe he and Ruth were overreacting.

'It can't be easy with twins, Ruthie. Perhaps we should offer to pay for a char or something, to help her.'

'I offered. She said no. Then she started crying. I asked if everything was okay between her and Alan, and she just cried more. I hate to say it, but I think Alan is having an affair.'

He suspected as much as well... and the babies not even six months old. Shocking. Shocking. He'd bumped into Alan and a *shvartze* woman in the ladies' cocktail bar at the Ritz last week. Pretty little thing too, if you liked that exotic look. Alan had looked terribly embarrassed, but introduced them. Susan, he said her name was. She was something in the ANC or Anti Apartheid Movement, or WOAH or something like that. Also a South African, although she sounded Cockney. She said she'd met Alan at a WOAH meeting in Leeds a few months before. Alan changed the subject, but Ben put two and two together and he hadn't liked the total. If he remembered correctly, Alan had been in York or Leeds or somewhere when Brenda had gone into labour. When his car had broken down.

'Nice to meet you,' Ben said. The *shvartze* put out her hand to shake his. Her hand was tiny, almost as small as Brenda's.

'How's Brenda doing? And my grandchildren? You know Alan and his wife have twins?' Ben asked her.

She nodded and lifted her cocktail glass as if to toast them. He wanted to knock it out of her hand. Don't do this, he wanted to beg Alan. Don't mess up a perfectly good marriage because of this black tart. Instead, he'd smiled at them – more of a grimace, really – and walked out. He hadn't had the courage to raise the subject with Alan since. In fact, he'd tried to put it out of his mind.

'What makes you think he's having an affair?' Ben asked Ruth.

'Just some of the things Brenda said – or didn't say. I mean, I couldn't really ask, but, from what she said, I'd swear Alan doesn't make love to her anymore.'

'What on earth gave you that idea?' Ben was shocked. Surely women didn't discuss that kind of thing?

'I asked her if she was on the pill, because that can make you depressed and she really is very down. She cries at the drop of a hat. The pill can also make you gain weight and, in case you haven't noticed, Brenda has put on a lot of weight.'

'Well, she's just had twins. Of course she's put on weight.'

'She should have started losing some of it by now. I know I did. Well, anyway, she said there wasn't any point in being on the pill. That it wasn't necessary. So I said she had to be careful or she'd fall pregnant again and she mumbled something about there not being any chance of that. The way she said it, I got the feeling that he doesn't... that they don't... you know. That they don't make love anymore.'

'Ruth! They love each other. Anyone can see that.'

'I'm sorry. I don't know what I was thinking. They're probably just going through a bad patch. All young married couples do. I'll go over every day and help her with the babies. I'll take Mrs Naidoo with tomorrow to help clean that flat.'

'You do that. And put those terrible ideas right out of your head. There's nothing wrong with Alan and Brenda. I'm sure of it.'

Ruth picked up her book, but he could see she still wasn't reading. He stared sightlessly at his newspaper. This was terrible… and it wasn't true. Not Alan and Brenda. They were a beautiful couple. He wondered whether or not he should speak to Alan, just to check that everything was all right. No, he couldn't do that. He wasn't Alan's father, and, even if he was, the young couple should be left to sort out their problems without interference. There was nothing worse than having someone meddle in your marriage. He should know. Ruthie's mother had interfered all the time and it had nearly destroyed them.

***

Ben looked over at Brenda and Ruthie, sitting on the patio. Brenda looked almost back to her old self again. So delicate and beautiful. And Ruthie was smiling. It was so good to see Ruthie smile again. Jeremy's death had been hard on her. So hard. If it hadn't been for Brenda and Alan and the twins, Ruthie would not have made it. No mother should ever have to watch her child die. Not like that. So terrible, terrible.

'Kick ball, *Zaidah*. Kick,' Yair shouted.

Ben kicked the ball softly to the little boy, who missed and scampered after it. Aviva ran past her twin and picked up the ball. She threw it to Alan. Yair howled. Alan frowned at him.

'Big boys don't cry, Yair. You should have beaten Avi to the ball. She's only a girl.'

Aviva's face crumpled.

'Oh, for heaven's sake,' Alan said. 'Ben, Ruth – please excuse me if I don't stay for tea. I have a pile of papers to go over before my trip up to Birmingham. I think I'll leave this evening so I'm fresh for the meeting tomorrow. So I'll see you on Wednesday,' he said to Brenda, who nodded and looked away to where Yair was howling. Alan shook Ben's hand, kissed Ruth on the cheek and walked out. He didn't even glance at his beautiful children, who were now both crying.

Brenda got up. 'Excuse me, please. I need the bathroom.'

The tension was palpable. Ben had hoped, after that skinny women's libber – Annette something or other – and her *nebbish* husband had gone back to South Africa, that things would improve between Brenda and Alan, but clearly they hadn't. Perhaps it was time to speak to Alan. Things hadn't been right between him and Brenda for far too long.

'Let's have something cool to drink,' Ruth said. Bless Ruthie, she always knew exactly when and how to diffuse a situation. A wonderful mother she had always been to Jeremy. A wonderful *bobba* to these two precious angels. Angels they were, Yair and Avi. Angels. Ruth poured some orange juice into the two Winnie the Pooh mugs and put them on the little red plastic table.

'My chair,' said Aviva, pulling the little green chair away

from Yair just as he was about to sit down.

The poor little chappie howled again. Avi put the green chair down next to the yellow chair, and sat on the yellow chair.

'My chair,' she said again as Yair tried to take the green chair back.

Ruth gently removed the green chair from the little girl's grasp and placed it back on the opposite side of the table. 'No, Avi, this is Yair's chair. The green chair is Yair's chair. You have a yellow chair. What colour is Avi's chair?'

'Green,' said the little girl. 'Want that chair.' She pointed her pudgy finger at the green chair.

Ben could feel laughter bubbling up, but he smothered it until he had walked back through the patio doors into the sitting room. He knew better than to let the twins – especially that little Avi – see his mirth. She was such a bright little thing, *kaynahora*. She'd play up to him and make Yair cry even more, and he wasn't in the mood for another lecture from Ruth on the intricacies of child rearing in 1992. She really did take her *bobba* role extremely seriously. Her bookshelf was laden with child-rearing books. Dr Spock was clearly out of favour, although he didn't understand why. It had been good enough for Jeremy... On second thought, perhaps Dr Spock hadn't known everything.

He immediately felt the familiar guilt and remorse flood through him. He wiped away the tears that rolled unbidden down his cheeks. He really was turning into an *alter kocker*, getting old and sentimental. It had been months since they'd buried their boy. Surely he should be over it by now. He needed to pull himself together, get on with it. He couldn't let Ruthie see how much he still hurt. She had enough to cope with.

'Ben?' He swung around. He hadn't heard Brenda come back into the sitting room. She looked pale and desperately tired. She put her arms around him and just held him, not saying a thing.

He tried, so hard, to stop the tears, but they just kept falling.

'I loved Jeremy,' he heard himself saying. 'I loved him and I never told him. I should have told him instead of making him feel inadequate and useless and a failure. And now I can't even go to his grave and tell him how sorry I am.'

He should never have allowed Mark – Jeremy's "dear friend" – to persuade them to let Jeremy be buried in San Francisco so he could always be among friends. Literally. He and Ruth had been horrified at how many of Jeremy's and Mark's friends were buried in the cemetery. All young Jewish boys too. Who would have believed so many Jewish boys were queer – he'd never call them "gay"; there was nothing "gay" about it. He didn't know of a single queer British *Yiddisher* man. Apart from Jeremy, but that was only because he'd wanted to be an actor and had moved to California and got in with the wrong crowd. That's what had killed him… and it was all his fault.

'Jeremy knew you loved him,' Brenda said. 'I'm sure of it.'

'He never wanted anything to do with the business. I should have accepted that. I should have accepted him. I drove him away and Ruth will never forgive me.'

'Ruth loves you, Ben. But it must be hard for a mother to lose her child.' She looked through the patio doors at Yair and Avi, who were sitting still, for once, frowns of concentration on their little faces as they coloured in with their new wax crayons. Ruthie really was a marvel.

'I know. Thank God for you and your children. And Alan; he's been like a son to me, you know. I just don't know how I would have coped without him at the office. Without all of you.'

'Thank you, Ben. I love you and Ruth too. I don't know what I'd do without you.'

Ruth bustled in. 'What's this, the two of you so serious. It's a beautiful day. Come outside. Brenda, you and Alan and the *kinderlach* will be joining us for *Shabbos* this Friday, yes?'

'Thank you, yes. We'll come. I'm not sure about Alan, though. But just one thing, Ruth – please, no chicken.'

Ben looked at Ruth. She looked back at him, and the smile she gave him was radiant. He felt joy – and relief. Brenda was pregnant again, so things must be fine between her and Alan again. Thank God. *Baruch Ha'shem*. He must have been imagining the tension between them. Ruth always said he had an overactive imagination.

CHAPTER 3
LONDON, 1994

'Alan, I had a call from the auditors this morning. They want to set up a meeting for next week to go over the figures,' Ben said as Alan walked into his office.

'Is there a problem?'

'No, they just have a couple of queries before they sign off the books. They asked me, but I told them that's your department.'

Sometimes he found it hard to believe how little he knew about the actual running of the business these days. Since Jeremy... and anyway, he was almost seventy years old now – sixty-nine on his next birthday, actually. He had every right to take things a little easier now. Thank God for Alan. Without him, he would have had to bring in a stranger to run the place. Now Shapiro and Son would always be a family-run business.

'I'm quite hectic at the moment, Ben. And I have to go out of town for a couple of days next week. But I think I'm free next Thursday afternoon. What about three-ish?'

'Good. I'll tell them. You'll all be joining us for *Shabbos* this week?'

He hoped so. They hadn't come for *Shabbos* for months, not since the baby had been born and she must be ... what? Almost a year now. He wanted to break the news to them as soon as possible, but he wanted to tell them together – away from the office – because it was for both of them, not just Alan. And it involved more than the business.

'I'll have to ask Brenda,' Alan said. 'It's so difficult with the baby, you know? Tell you what, Ben. Let's make it for *Shabbos* next week. That will give Brenda a chance to sort herself out a bit more. I tell you, Zivah is really a difficult baby, so we might have to arrange a sitter for her and just bring the twins.'

'I understand. It will be wonderful to see them. They are growing up so fast. They are such little people now. That Yair – he looks more and more like you every time I see him. And Avi is going to be exactly like her mother.' He beamed at the framed photograph of Aviva in her little pink ballet outfit that had pride of place on his desk, next to a photograph of Yair in his karate kit.

***

Ben was worried about Ruth's reaction to his decision. They were in the formal drawing room, which was where they always went when they had something important to discuss. There was something about the deep red furnishings, the brocade wallpaper and the marble fireplace that gave the room an authority, a gravitas that was missing in the rest of the house.

Ruth clasped her hands in her lap. She looked worried, the poor darling.

'Ben, you're not ill, are you?'

'Of course not. What on earth gave you that idea? I've never been better.'

'Then why are we in here? We never come in here alone unless you have something serious to tell me.'

He handed her the papers his lawyers had drawn up. She sat down in the wing-backed chair and switched on the lamp – the Pollyanna lamp, she always called it. The rainbows danced on the ceiling as she perched her glasses on her nose and read. She didn't say a word. She turned the page. Her expression remained neutral, bland. If it hadn't been Ruthie – who was as sharp as a button, *kaynahora* – he'd have thought she didn't understand the opaque legalise lawyers always use when they want to charge you more just to explain what they'd written... but Ruthie would understand. Whether or not she would understand *why* he was doing this remained to be seen. She read the last page and put the document down on the Italian inlaid coffee table, the one they'd bought in Florence. It had been their fifth wedding anniversary gift to themselves and it had always taken pride of place in their home.

'Nu?' He couldn't bear her silence.

'Nu – what took you so long?' Ruth asked.

'I wasn't sure – you know. Jeremy...'

'Ben, my darling, Jeremy has been gone for years and nothing will bring him back. Alan and Brenda are here. They are our family now. And the *babbelehs*. They have made it possible for us to be grandparents. They have taken us into their hearts just as we have taken them into ours. We are lucky, so lucky to have family we can pass everything on to.'

He pulled her to her feet and took her in his arms.

'We'll tell them on *Shabbos*. Alan is out of town this week, but he'll be back on Thursday – we have a meeting – and he said they'd come for *Shabbos*.'

Ruth smiled. 'Good. I can't wait to see the children. I tried to phone Brenda today. It's hard for her to be on her own so much, but their phone must be out of order. It just rings and rings.'

Business over, they strolled, arm in arm, back into the sitting room. They settled down to watch the show with the fat psychiatrist, Cracker. Clever chap. Always got the crook. Great new series, even if some of the crimes were a little unrealistic. He and Ruth were thoroughly enjoying it.

***

Ben looked at his watch. Four o'clock. Max Lieberthal shifted in his chair.

'Mr Shapiro, it's getting late. Please can we start without him?'

He picked up the phone and dialled Alan's extension.

'Mr Silverman's office. Josephine Smith speaking.' Damn. Alan still hadn't returned, she told him. She was getting a little concerned, because he had been scheduled to return to the office that morning. Dear God, he sincerely hoped this wasn't going to be a repeat of that episode when the twins had been born. In fact, if Alan had found a *shiksa* to delay him on this trip, he'd disown him. He smiled grimly. He hadn't even told him about his inheritance yet, and already he was disowning him.

'Look here, Max. It seems Alan has been unavoidably delayed. Leave the documents with me – with your list of queries – and I'll go over them with him this evening. Then we can meet again tomorrow when I'm sure he'll have the answers you require.'

Max Lieberthal hauled himself out of the chair and rocked back on his little feet. So little, Ben always expected him to topple over, like the Wobbly Man in Noddy. He really didn't understand why Noddy was out of favour in schools nowadays. He enjoyed reading Jeremy's old books to the twins, and they clearly loved Noddy and Big Ears. Children were children; he didn't care what the experts said.

'Mr Shapiro, I'd really rather go through the numbers with you. It gets quite complicated and...'

'I'm not in my dotage yet, young man. I can still read a set of financials. Leave them with me, as I said, and I'll see you back here tomorrow, at ten.'

Max Lieberthal nodded glumly and waddled out of the office.

Ben dialled Alan and Brenda's flat, but, again, it just rang. Damn. He'd go around there and see what was going on.

Harcourt dropped him at the front entrance. He took the lift to the second floor and walked down to their front door. He was pleased to see that the paint work on the balustrade looked fresh and clean. He knocked at the door. Silence. He tried the handle – now why did he do that? If they weren't there, the door would be locked. The handle turned. He could feel the hair rise on his neck. Something was wrong. Very wrong. He pushed the door open and walked in... and stopped... and stared. The flat looked like it had been hit by a bomb. They'd been burgled. He rushed out and banged on the door of the adjacent flat. A young woman answered.

'Do you have a phone? Please. You must call the police.'

'Why? What's wrong?'

'Alan and Brenda, next door, they've been burgled.'

'No, they haven't. They've gone.'

'Gone? Gone where?'

'They've gone. Left. Last Sunday, I think it was. Are you Ben Shapiro?'

He nodded. She disappeared into the flat and returned with an envelope. It was addressed to Mr Ben Shapiro.

'Brenda gave me this. Asked me to post it, but I haven't had a chance. Anyway, now you're here, so I don't have to. Awful upset she was, when she gave it to me. Crying like anything. When they left too – with all their luggage and the baby's pram and car seat and everything, even the twins' teddies. She didn't even say goodbye, and he just ignored me, and him usually such a friendly man too, I always thought. I would say to Joe, "Joe. That Alan Silverman next door, such a nice friendly bloke". Always so polite and his little missus, such a sweet person. Reserved, though. Never came around for a natter; kept herself to herself...'

'Thank you.' His voice wasn't his. He walked down the stairs and out the back of the building to where the Bentley was waiting. He opened the door before Harcourt could open it for him, and collapsed onto the back seat. He opened the envelope. He read:

Dearest Ben and Ruth,

This is the hardest letter I've ever had to write in my entire life. I don't know what to say or how to say this, so I'm just going to say it. We are leaving London and going back to South Africa. Alan says it's so we can participate in the first democratic election in April and help the new democracy to flourish. We have to get back to the country before the end of next week in order to register, Alan says. Now that national service has been abolished, he no longer has to worry about being arrested. I wanted to tell you, in person, but Alan says that saying goodbye will only make it more difficult for all of us. Perhaps he's right. I cannot bear the thought of saying goodbye to you both. I love you. If people could choose their parents, I would have chosen you. You are wonderful,

wonderful people and we are so lucky to have you. Perhaps this isn't really goodbye. Perhaps you'll forgive us and, once we've settled in South Africa, you'll come and visit us. Yair, Avi and Zivah need their zaidah and bobba.

Please forgive us for leaving like this. I'll send you our address as soon as we have one.

We love you.
Brenda, Alan, Yair, Aviva and Zivah.

He put his head in his hands and wept. He knew he'd never see Alan or Brenda or his grandchildren again. He knew it. He didn't know why they'd left so suddenly, but he was sure he'd find the answer in Max Lieberthal's report. He hoped he was wrong. He knew he wasn't.

He blew his nose. Ruthie. What was he going to tell Ruthie? To lose one child was tragic. To lose five – in one fell swoop – was beyond human endurance. He found himself muttering a prayer: *Yit'gadal v'yit'kadash sh'mei raba...* the mourner's *kaddish*.

PART 8
TRACY

CHAPTER 1
Johannesburg, 2012

Tracy paged through the paper, searching for her article. There it was. Page Fourteen – and Page Fifteen. Great. "Finding Freedom – Brenda Silverman's Secret Life." Nice headline. They've given her a double page spread and a picture by-line – her first. Her first feature article too. Even Precious had a by-line for her photographs. They'd used five of Precious' photos, and the beautiful one she'd borrowed from Miriam. This was fantastic. Mafuta hadn't been happy about it, but she'd gone to Alex on her off day, so he couldn't complain. She read the article avidly – just to check how much the subs had messed it up.

***

'T.T. Get your arse over here.'

Tracy walked over to Mafuta's desk.

'I've just had Alan Silverman on the phone. He's fucking furious about your story.'

'Why? What's wrong with it?'

'He said you made the whole thing up. He said his wife could never have gone into Alex on her own – she apparently couldn't drive – and that she would never, and I quote – "dance half naked" – unquote or uncover her hair in public. Seems that's a big no-no in your culture.'

'So who does he think is in the photograph?'

'He says we photoshopped it. He says we've insulted his wife, his religion and culture and he's going to get the chief rabbi to complain to the editor. He wants a correction and an apology.'

She was stunned. Okay, maybe the freedom bit was a bit much, but it was a fantastic story. It would probably earn him back some brownie points with his ANC buddies, what with the wife doing her unheralded upliftment thing.

'Oh, and he says that you are not to go near the inquest and that, if he sees you there, he'll have you thrown out.'

She wanted to cry. This was her story. Surely he couldn't get her barred from the court?

'But if that arrogant prick thinks he can tell me how to run my news desk, and which fucking reporter I send where, he's got another thing coming. And if he wants a fucking apology, he can sue us.'

For the first time since joining the *Daily Express*, Tracy almost liked Mafuta.

***

Tracy curled her legs under her and leaned back in the once-green armchair. She loved Saturday afternoons. No deadlines. No pressure. Just a peaceful few hours at home, drinking proper coffee – not the instant stuff at the *Daily Express* – and eating *melktert* and rusks, or yummy Moo-z cheesecake for a treat – catching up on the week that was. Mom was cosy in her favourite chair, perfectly groomed as always.

Maxine could be a pain, sometimes, but, now that Tracy was older, they got on remarkably well – especially since her mother had appeared to have resigned herself to the fact that her darling daughter was unlikely to snag a nice rich Jewish doctor or lawyer. In fact, her mother would probably be prepared to settle for a plumber or tow truck driver – as long as he was Jewish and put a ring on her finger. She wondered what her mother would say if she brought home an Ethiopian Jew. Then maybe the Jewish bit wouldn't be so important.

'So what did you think of my story about Brenda Silverman? The ballet one. Did you know she'd been a dancer?'

'Oh dear, Tracy. Everyone was talking about it at book club.'

'Did they like it?'

'Well, it was a shock, you know. Who would have thought Brenda Silverman had a secret life? Everyone was stunned about that. It made things very awkward for me.'

'Well, it is strange. It's really a very odd situation.'

'I'm sure there's a perfectly logical explanation. There must be.'

'Why?'

'Because it's the Silvermans we're talking about here. Not some trash from Booysens or Brixton. Alan Silverman is one of Jo'burg's most respected businessmen. He's a good man, Tracy. He gives a fortune to the Chevrah and lots of other charities. And you're saying that Brenda sneaked around behind his back.'

Tracy was startled. She was so proud of her story. She'd thought Maxine would also be proud. Instead, she was upset about it. It was as if she agreed with Alan Silverman, that it was somehow offensive.

When the letter had arrived from Alan Silverman's attorneys demanding a retraction and apology, the *Daily Express* lawyers had laughed it off. Her story was factual. She had the photographs to prove it. End of story. So why was Mr Bigshot Silverman so upset? Why was – from the sound of it – the whole Jewish community upset? Even some big deal *macher* from the *Beth Din* had apparently phoned Mr February, the editor, but she didn't know what had been said... and no correction or retraction was printed.

CHAPTER 2

'My name is Ben Shapiro,' said the voice. 'I've been reading your articles about Alan Silverman and I wondered if we could meet. I might have some information that would be of interest to you.'

'Sure, why not? What about this afternoon?'

The voice chuckled. 'I don't think so, my dear. I'm in London. But I'm planning to come to South Africa next week.'

They made arrangements to meet at the Michelangelo Hotel.

Tracy googled Ben Shapiro. Judging by his voice, he wasn't a young man, and he was definitely a Brit, but there were dozens of Ben Shapiros who could fit that description. Bloody hell. She should have asked him for more information. She tried googling "Ben Shapiro and Alan Silverman". Nothing. She hoped this meeting wasn't going to be a waste of time.

'At least you'll get a decent cup of coffee out of it,' Kingmaker said.

Mafuta was less supportive. 'You think you're a hotshot reporter now you getting all those by-lines, don't you? Well, you can go to your meeting with your mystery man, but don't think that means you don't have to finish the stories I've put on the diary for you.'

The receptionist at the Michelangelo seemed to be expecting her, because she was immediately directed to a suite on the twentieth floor. She knocked and waited. The door opened. The little old man was dressed in a dark grey suit, white shirt and pale blue tie. His black shoes gleamed. His fringe of white hair was neatly trimmed and a white *yarmulke* was perched on his bald patch. He shook her hand with gnarled fingers and led her briskly into the lounge. She put his age at around seventy, possibly eighty. Older than Grandpa. He indicated to her to sit, but she moved to the windows.

'Wow. This is an incredible view. I've never seen Sandton from up this high before.' She gazed out at the city she had grown up in, trying to identify landmarks. It was difficult. It all looked so different from up here. Another world. It was really impressive. Beautiful. You could really see why Jo'burg claimed to be the largest man-made urban forest in the world. From up here, you'd never think that down there was crime and litter and potholes and robots that didn't work.

Mr Shapiro sat on the couch, waiting patiently for her to stop gaping out of the window. She moved away reluctantly and sat opposite him on a high-backed chair. She put her voice recorder on the coffee table, opened her notebook and waited while he poured tea from a silver pot into two delicate white cups.

He began to speak. He spoke fluently. His story was sprinkled with Yiddish expressions. 'You are Jewish, aren't you? You understand a little Yiddish?'

She started writing notes – but then she had to stop. This was unbelievable.

'Mr Shapiro, I'm sorry to interrupt. Do you have any proof of all this?'

He indicated a folder on the table. She opened it. There were pages of documents, letters and spreadsheets.

'As you can see, all the documents are certified copies of originals. There's also an affidavit from my solicitor that all the information in these documents is a true and accurate reflection of the events I've outlined to you,' he said.

She was worried. This story was too big for her. How did she know this old guy was for real and that it wasn't some kind of a set-up to get her into real trouble? How could she trust this man? She wouldn't put it past Alan Silverman to get back at her by feeding her false information. She didn't know the first thing about this old *toppie*. For all she knew, all these documents could be fakes. She put the folder carefully back on the coffee table.

'Mr Shapiro, why are you telling me all this stuff? I don't know you. I don't know anything about you. And this is all ancient history now, anyway.'

He stared at her, tears welling up in his eyes. She squirmed.

'It's ancient history to you, my dear. But to me, it's like yesterday. And it destroyed my wife. She never got over what

Alan did to us. And now it seems he has destroyed Brenda too. He has to be stopped.'

She gaped at him. 'That's what Yair said. Yair told me his father killed his mother. Do you have proof of this?'

'No, of course not. I can't prove that he killed Brenda. And much as I loathe him, I don't believe he would actually murder anyone. But I strongly suspect that his actions led to her death. Like they did to Ruthie's. He broke her heart and she never recovered. I tried so hard to help her get over it, but I couldn't. It was as if a light had gone out in her. Alan hurt so many people. His secretary, Josephine Smith, she resigned from Shapiro and Son, after nearly thirty years of dedicated service to the company. Quite unnecessary, but she felt somehow responsible, poor woman. She was duped – like the rest of us.' He paused and gazed out of the window. She waited. Just when she thought he'd fallen asleep, he continued.

'Brenda wrote to us at first, you know. After they ran away. But then she stopped. She contacted me again, a few months before she died – she needed some assistance for a young dancer, which I was fortunate enough to be able to provide. But that's not part of this story.'

He picked up the folder and leafed through it, muttering to himself, 'I should have made all this public when he ran away, but the scandal would have hurt Ruthie even more. And Brenda and the children. What was the point?' He looked fiercely at her. 'It was only money. And the shame was too great. But now Ruthie and Brenda can't be hurt anymore, and the children are all grown up. And that man deserves to be exposed for hurting them.'

He stopped. Tracy waited for him to speak again. He picked up the folder and handed it to her. 'Do whatever you like with these, my child. It all happened too long ago for any legal action to be taken against him. But it's a story that needs to be told. People need to know what a *gonif*, a crook, Alan Silverman is. However, I'm an old man, so perhaps it's me just trying to deal with my conscience before I die.'

'Oh, you're not that old.' She didn't know what else to say.

'I'm eighty-seven. My Ruthie was only seventy-five when I buried her – but she died a long time before that.'

***

Tracy read through the documents. She took them over to Kingmaker. He looked through them and picked up the phone on his desk, checked his cell phone contacts for a number and dialled. It appeared to be a long, international number.

'Hey, Gary, Tshepo Buthelezi here... Cool man... Long time. Listen, have you heard of a company – Shapiro and Son? Yes... What do you know about Ben Shapiro? Uh huh. Really? When was that? No, that's okay. Thanks. *Ja* – email it to me. Appreciate it. Later.'

Kingmaker read from his notes. 'That was Gary Sullivan from the *London Telegraph*. You're onto something, T.T. This old dude is legit. More than legit. Seems he's a Sir.

Sir Benjamin Shapiro – knighted for services to the arts or something. Also incredibly wealthy. Shapiro and Son was one of the largest privately owned conglomerates in the UK before the old man retired and sold it. That was years ago. Company doesn't exist anymore. Now he's involved in something called the Ruth and Jeremy Shapiro Foundation – Gary's going to email me something about that. Fuck, Silverman really is a piece of shit, isn't he?'

Tracy googled "Sir Benjamin Shapiro". She found a photograph. It was him. The old man. She wrote her story. Mafuta grilled her. Then Mr February called her in and questioned her. She handed over the documents Sir Ben had given her, and her voice recorder. The *Daily Express* lawyers grilled her and Kingmaker. She didn't know who else they spoke to, but, two days later, her story was published. The subs – or the lawyers – had walked on eggs with it. Huge chunks of her original copy had been cut... but they hadn't buried it. It was on Page Three.

'ALAN SILVERMAN STOLE FROM ME' – BRITISH BUSINESSMAN

By Tracy Jacobs

A respected British businessman and philanthropist, Sir Benjamin Shapiro OBE, has alleged to the *Daily Express* that he was swindled out of hundreds of thousands of pounds by Johannesburg property tycoon, Alan Silverman, in the early

1990s while Mr Silverman was living in exile.

According to Sir Benjamin (87), Mr Silverman was employed by his company, Shapiro and Son, as head of the property division. He left the company – and the country – quite suddenly in February 1994.

'One day he was there and the next he and his family were gone. They left all their furniture, some clothing, the children's toys – everything. It was clear they had left in a fearful hurry,' Sir Benjamin stated.

Documents in possession of the *Daily Express* indicate that Shapiro and Son paid large bonuses and commissions – all authorised by Mr Silverman – to a host of fictitious individuals over a period of about four years.

However, a trail uncovered by a team of forensic auditors revealed that all these payments allegedly eventually found their way into a single private bank account at the Cayman National Bank and Trust Company (Isle of Man).

An affidavit from his then-secretary, Ms Josephine Smith, claims that Mr Silverman had frequent telephone conversations with a Mr Jenkins at Cayman National Bank.

Like Swiss banks, banks located in the Cayman Islands and the Isle of Man maintain strict security around the identity of their clients.

Mr Silverman has emphatically denied all allegations contained in this article. He accused the *Daily Express* of using "a senile old man" to further its "vicious vendetta" against him.

Mr Silverman (50) returned to South Africa from exile just before the first democratic elections in 1994. He founded Silver Properties soon thereafter, and the company was listed on the Johannesburg Stock Exchange in 1999. The share price has been under pressure for some years and has fallen by a further 10 percent since the sudden, mysterious death of his wife, Brenda Silverman at the family's palatial home in Johannesburg in February this year. An inquest into Mrs Silverman's death is expected to get underway next month.

***

Tracy walked into the kitchen. Maxine was sitting at the table, the *Daily Express* open on Page Three. She could see that even from the doorway.

'What a day,' she said. 'Alan Silverman's threatening to sue us. Again.'

Maxine glared at her. Tracy waited. Here it came. The lecture.

Maxine unclenched her hand and stabbed the page with a long, red acrylic nail.

'And just what,' her mother said, 'do you have to say about this? This rubbish, this absolute *bobbemyseh* crap. I sent you to university to learn to be a journalist, not a trashy sensationalist shit stirrer.'

Maxine was really, really angry. She never swore.

'It's true, Mom. All of it. And that's only a teeny bit of what Sir Benjamin told me. You won't believe what a crook Alan Silverman is. He's lied about everything. He wasn't some big political *macher* in the ANC in exile – he was a little *pisher* fund raiser for some little...'

'Be quiet.'

She kept quiet.

'Tracy, I'm telling you for the last time. Stop this, this thing you have about Alan Silverman. He is a respectable... a respected member of our community. He wouldn't steal or cheat or lie or anything else you've accused him of doing.

And even if he did – and he didn't – you should not be writing about it. It makes us all look bad. It makes us all vulnerable. Jews don't – we do not accuse other Jews of such terrible things, not like this. Not in the newspaper. If Alan Silverman has broken any laws – and he hasn't – let the authorities deal with him. But you, my girl... you should not be spreading such terrible rumours about him. You've given the anti-Semites exactly what they want.'

'But Sir Benjamin is a Jew. And he's making the accusations – with piles of documented proof to back him up, I might add. I'm just reporting what he...'

'He's not a member of our community. I don't know why you trust this... this, this foreign shit stirrer. I'm ashamed of you, Tracy. You are going to find yourself without a single friend if you're not careful, while this trouble maker buggers off back to wherever he came from.'

Tracy retreated to her room, her mother's shrill voice following her down the passage. She crawled under her duvet with its faded pink ballerinas and pulled it over her head. She really should buy herself a new duvet cover, but she felt about ten years old again. She didn't know how she was going to get through the inquest, because she knew, she just knew, that Alan Silverman had murdered his wife... and then what would her mother, and the community, say when she reported it?

CHAPTER 3

As Tracy was leaving the newsroom – a new notebook and four pens in her bag all ready for the inquest on Monday – Mr February called her in.

'Be damn careful about how you cover the inquest, Tracy. Silverman and his lawyers will be itching to have a go at us. If you're not sure about anything – anything at all – check it out with the prosecutor who leads the evidence. And if he can't help, then leave it out. Understood?'

She'd nodded, absolutely terrified. The editor never spoke to her.

'And report only what's said in court. I don't want any bits of gossip or "off the record" stuff in this story. You hear me? Absolutely by the book.'

***

Maxine continued with the warnings at home. All weekend.

'Listen, Trace. Alan Silverman is a powerful man. He's a big deal in this community. He might not be able to sue you, but he can make your life hell and your newspaper won't be able to help you then.'

'You mean your life, Mom. I don't give a hoot about him – or the community.' That wasn't quite true. Of course she gave a damn, especially about her mother. She didn't really want to make life difficult for her, but she was a journalist. She had a job to do.

'Okay, it's my life and you're making it difficult. You can do what you like, but I have to live here,' Maxine said. 'But besides that. What I really don't understand is why you are picking on him. For heaven's sake, look at him. He's rich. He's respectable; he's generous; he's a good father...'

'And don't forget the Jewish, Mom. He's Jewish.'

'Yes, well, that too. What I don't understand is why you are doing this. Why you are printing these terrible stories all the time. Why don't you just leave it alone? You know Alan Silverman couldn't have done all these terrible things. And Jewish wives like Brenda don't do things behind their husband's back; I don't care what those *shvartzes* in Alex told you. They just don't. Especially if they're *frum*. Although...' Mom's voice dropped as if she was afraid someone would overhear her revelation. 'Sylvia told me she heard that Brenda Silverman wasn't really Jewish. Her father was a *yok*, apparently.'

Tracy held back her laugh. So now the community was starting to look for ways to disown Brenda? Why? Because her father wasn't Jewish? Because she taught kids in Alex to dance? For dying? For daring to bring the wonderful Silverman family into disrepute?

'Mom, Brenda's mother was a Holocaust survivor. You don't get better Jewish credentials than that. Anyway, how can you say Jewish men don't lie and cheat when Dad did – big time? He screwed anything with big boobs and two legs. And then he walked out and married the bitch.'

Maxine went red. Then white.

'Leave your father out of this. He's no Alan Silverman. He's a *schmuk*. I hear he's still cheating on his wife – thank God that's not me anymore. But look at the Silvermans. They were married for years and years – and it was obviously a good marriage. I certainly never heard anything different, and you know what this community is like. How the hell do you think I found out about your father and his floozies? And the day after I finally chucked the bastard out, everyone was talking.'

That wasn't quite how Tracy remembered it. She'd never forget the humiliation – the sly looks from the boys at school, the giggling of the girls, the sudden silences when she walked past a crowd of kids. Except for Sarah, but Sarah was her best friend, after all. And Yair. Yair had even come over to her as they were lining up outside history class.

'I'm sorry about your mom and dad,' he'd said. 'It must be hard for you.'

'No, it's fine. I'm okay with it, really.' She had blinked back tears.

'Listen, Red. If you want to talk...'

But she knew he didn't mean it, because just then Tiffany had come over and asked him if he was going to Sandton Square on Saturday night, and he had turned away and never mentioned it again. Tiffany had just ignored her, like all the popular girls and boys did. Except Yair when the others weren't with him.

However, it was the sympathetic understanding from the teachers that had really got to her, and the awkward pats on the shoulder from the other mothers, and it wasn't even as if divorce was all that unusual. In fact, most of her classmates were divorced. Okay, not most, but a hell of a lot of them.

'And they had three beautiful children.' Maxine was on a roll. 'Beautiful children, all of them. Especially that boy you had such a crush on, although I heard he wasn't such a good boy, not clever like his sister. But boys will be boys, I suppose. Anyway, they were a perfect family. May you also be blessed with such a family one day, my girl.'

'Mom, you don't know what the truth is. Yair said something to me at the funeral, and I just can't get it out of my mind. Then he disappeared off the face of the earth. I've been trying to get hold of him.'

'You have? I didn't know the two of you were still such good friends?'

'We're not. We weren't. We never were. I just saw him at the funeral and he remembered me from school – sort of – and he said at prayers that he'd phone me. But he didn't.'

'Well, lots of boys don't phone you back. You should be used to it by now.'

Sometimes, her mother had the tact and delicacy of a rabid rhino. Should she tell Maxine that Yair didn't want a date, that all he wanted was to talk to her about his mother? Nah, her mother would simply have something sarcastic to say about it. But it was his disappearance more than anything that made her so suspicious. Leaving the day after the funeral, without sitting *Shivah* with the family and them being so *frum* and everything. It didn't make sense. There might be a perfectly logical explanation, but she couldn't think what it could be. Perhaps her mother was right. Perhaps she was taking what Maxine called "this bloody journalism thing" a bit too seriously and looking for a story when there really wasn't one? She might have thought so before, but, since Ben Shapiro...

Maxine was still going on about Alan Silverman's many and obvious virtues. Tracy sighed. There was no arguing with her mother when it came to good-looking, rich, community conscious Jews like Alan Silverman. A man "like that" could do no wrong, as far as Maxine was concerned. Unless he happened to be her father.

CHAPTER 4

'All rise.'

Tracy scrambled to her feet. So did everyone else in Court 33. The magistrate, her black gown billowing behind her, strode in. She nodded, and everyone sat down again.

The orderly called the case. 'Inquest into the death of Mrs Brenda Anna Silverman nee Armsford-Jones. Magistrate Patricia Ngubane presiding. Leading evidence for the state, Ms Marie du Toit. Representing the Silverman family, Mr Gideon Feinberg of Jacobs, Jafta and Khumalo. This court is now in session.'

Tracy glared at Gideon Feinberg, a tall, smooth-looking man in a R10,000, impeccably tailored suit and a matching *yarmulke*. Tracy disliked him instantly. One of her father's slimy minions, obviously. She hadn't realised her father's firm represented Alan Silverman, but it was to be expected. They were two of a kind… and Feinberg made three. Why did Alan Silverman need a high-powered, bloody expensive lawyer at his wife's inquest if he had nothing to hide?

Alan Silverman wasn't in the court. None of the Silvermans

were. Pity. Tracy had been hoping to see Yair. They were probably going to give evidence later. There weren't many people in the court at all, which was just as well, because there wasn't much room. Tucked away on the top floor of the imposing Johannesburg Magistrate's Court building, the inquest court wasn't much of a court at all, really. There was no dock or anything. Just a creaky room with unmatched tables and chairs for the officials, and a few rickety chairs for spectators. She was perched along the wall at the side of the court with the other members of the media – a reporter from *The Citizen* and another from the *Sunday Times*. They'd all met at the enquiries counter when they were trying to find out which court to go to. The counter was unattended, and remained so until well after nine o'clock when they had decided to try to find the inquest court on their own. A helpful prosecutor had told them where to go. 'It's not far from the registrar's office – you know, where you go to get married. Just follow the confetti,' he'd said.

***

The orderly called the first witness. Dr Servaas Schneider, from the state pathologist's office. Tracy poised her yellow Bic over her notepad, ready to take fast, accurate notes as instructed by Mr February. Mafuta's parting words had been a little less encouraging.

'Fuck this up, T.T.,' Mafuta had said, 'and you'll be on

permanent night shift until... until...'

She hadn't waited to find out.

After going through a number of routine questions – his name, qualifications, place of work, years of experience and so on – Ms du Toit got down to the nitty gritty.

'In your examination of the deceased, were you able to ascertain the cause of death?'

'Yes.'

There was a pregnant pause. Tracy had never heard a pregnant pause before, but this was clearly one.

'Well, could you share your findings with the court?' Ms du Toit was obviously unimpressed with the good doctor.

The witness was not to be hurried. He opened a brown file and began reading.

'I examined the deceased, a white female, aged forty-four years and three hundred and fifty-eight days, on 7 February 2012. Initial examination of the body revealed a woman who had been in good physical condition. There was no bruising noted or other unusual marks that would indicate any signs of a struggle. She had a ten-point-five centimetre scar on her stomach congruent with a previous caesarean section – and another five centimetre scar on her left knee.'

Oh boy. This was going to take a while. She put her pen down.

'Anything else?' Ms du Toit asked. 'What did she die of?'

'I'm getting to it.' Dr Schneider found his place in his notes and continued, 'There were numerous needle marks on the deceased's stomach above the scar, as well as on the tops of her thighs.'

Tracy wrote in capital letters: "NEEDLE MARKS".

'Were you able to ascertain what caused those marks?'

'The deceased was an insulin-dependent diabetic. The marks were consistent with injections with an insulin pen.'

'So nothing unusual about those marks, then?'

'No, not the marks.'

Tracy scratched out "needle marks" and put down her pen again.

'What then?' Ms du Toit asked.

Dr Schneider searched through his notes.

'As I said, there was nothing in the initial external examination of the deceased to indicate anything that might have resulted in or contributed to her death. An examination of her internal organs also revealed nothing unusual, except there were indications that the deceased had suffered from heart failure.'

'She had no history of a heart condition?'

'None that I could detect or ascertain from her medical records, which I obtained from Dr Irwin Schwartz, the family physician.'

'But heart failure's what caused her death?'

'Probably.'

'Thank you, Dr Schneider.'

Tracy closed her notebook. Heart failure. How bloody boring.

'I'm not finished yet,' Dr Schneider said. 'You should have asked me what caused the heart to fail.'

Ms du Toit flushed. Gideon Feinberg smirked. Tracy opened her notebook and held her pen at the ready. Dr Schneider took off his glasses, carefully wiped them and perched them back on his bulbous nose. He resumed reading.

'I tested the deceased's blood for a variety of substances to see if any could have contributed to her death.'

'And found what, Dr Schneider? Please don't leave us in suspense.'

'I found unusually high levels of Benzodiazepines. Specifically Lorazepam.'

'English, please, Dr Schneider. What's that?'

'The core ingredients of a type of tranquiliser or sleeping tablet.'

'Like Valium?'

'Yes.'

'As far as you know, was any Valium found in the deceased's home?'

'No.'

'So there was no indication of how the Valium got into her blood or where it came from.'

'She didn't have Valium in her blood.'

Ms du Toit's face went red. 'But you said she had Valium...'

'My dear young lady. What I said was that she had Lorazepam, a Benzodiazepine in her blood. *You* said Valium.'

Ms du Toit sighed, visibly frustrated. 'Dr Schneider,

please. What exactly was in her blood?'

'Well, the police found ninety-seven yellow 2.5 milligram Ativan tablets, and about six 1mg white Ativan tablets in her medicine cabinet. Ativan is a Benzodiazepine. That's how I knew to test for Benzodiazepine.'

'Okay, so it wasn't Valium, but Ativan. Right?'

'Correct.' Dr Schneider folded his arms and rocked back on his heels.

'And the quantity of tablets found in the deceased's medicine cabinet. Can you comment on that?'

'Well, I don't think many doctors would prescribe that many Ativan tablets at once, especially not at the higher dosage.'

'Is Ativan dangerous?'

'It's highly addictive.'

'Could an overdose be fatal?'

'Possibly.'

Tracy felt sorry for the poor prosecutor. Dr Schneider seemed to be determined to make things as difficult as possible for her.

'Did Mrs Silverman die of an overdose of Ativan?'

'No.'

Tracy giggled. She couldn't help it. The magistrate glared at her. She put her notebook over her face and tried to compose herself.

'No? But you said she high levels of...'

'Indeed. But not enough to lead to the respiratory

depression that would cause death.

The prosecutor tried again. 'Dr Schneider, please. You can hand in your very thorough and comprehensive report to the court to form part of the record later. For the sake of brevity, and our lack of medical knowledge, would you please tell us, as simply as possible, what caused Mrs Silverman's death? If you know.'

'Of course I know. Insulin. She had an extremely high level of insulin in her body tissues, even many hours after death.'

'She overdosed on insulin? Surely insulin isn't dangerous? Diabetics take it all the time and you just said that she was a diabetic.'

'Too much insulin causes hypoglycaemia.'

Ms du Toit glared at him.

Dr Schneider smirked. 'My apologies. Low blood sugar. If the blood sugar level goes too low, it can induce coma. If it isn't treated, it can – and does – cause death.'

'So why don't we have diabetics dying of this hypo – um, low blood sugar – all the time?'

'Most diabetics will recognise the symptoms of hypoglycaemia and take measures to counter it.'

'Like what?'

'Often, a few glucose sweets, a handful of sugar, even a glass of Coke will do the trick and push the blood sugar up to relatively safe levels, with no harm done.'

'That's all? So why couldn't Mrs Silverman have done that?'

'I suspect that she wasn't aware that she was experiencing a hypoglycaemic episode.'

'Why not?'

'Well, this is pure speculation, but I suspect it's because she was already in a drugged state from the Ativan.'

Tracy exhaled slowly. Jeez. This was getting very interesting.

Ms du Toit leaned forward, her fingertips pressing down so hard on the desk in front of her that her knuckles were white. 'Dr Schneider, would it be possible for someone to accidentally take too many Ativans, and then accidentally overdose on insulin?'

'It's possible.'

'Could someone do this deliberately if he or she wanted to die?'

'It's also possible.'

'Think carefully before you answer this next question, Dr Schneider. Is it possible that a third party could have maliciously given an innocent party an overdose of either Ativan or insulin – or both?'

Mr Ginsberg jumped up. 'Objection, Your Honour. Calls for speculation on the part of the witness. He's a pathologist, not a detective.'

The magistrate frowned. 'Mr Ginsberg, this is an inquest, not a murder trial. We do allow a little extra latitude here and I am perfectly capable of evaluating whether or not a witness is speculating. Carry on, Dr Schneider.'

'It's possible that Mrs Silverman – or if we are going to

continue with our hypothetical someone – that someone could be given the medication without their consent, although we must consider the fact that, in Mrs Silverman's case, she did not have any bruising on her body to indicate that she was forced to ingest anything against her will.'

'If she had already taken the Ativan, is it possible that a third party could then have given her the insulin without her knowledge?'

'I suppose that's possible.' Dr Schneider looked troubled.

'So she could have been murdered?' Ms du Toit's voice had soared an octave, at least.

'It's possible. Yes.'

As Mr Ginsberg rose to object, Tracy charged out of the courtroom – the magistrate was likely to adjourn for lunch anyway – and tweeted:

> Brenda Silverman inquest told she may have been murdered #silvermaninquest

***

After lunch, three more reporters joined the media contingent against the wall.

'Someone re-tweeted your tweet to my news editor and she sent me here pronto. What's going on?' the *Beeld* reporter asked.

'Tell you later,' Tracy whispered as the next witness, a Captain Bhulu Matabane of the Sandringham Police Station, swore to tell whole truth.

No, he said, there was no sign of forced entry; no sign of a struggle; no sign of assault or anything suspicious. The domestic helper had discovered the body; the young daughter was in the garden at the time and had run into the room; her brother was taking care of her when the police arrived. She was quite hysterical and they only managed to speak to her a few days later. She couldn't tell them much.

'She's a little, um, you know, not quite, um…' he said, looking embarrassed.

Ms du Toit moved on.

Mr Silverman had clearly been very shocked, but was co-operative. The son had been extremely emotional and it had been difficult to get much sense out of him either.

'He kept saying his father had killed his mother. But he couldn't explain what he meant,' Captain Matabane said.

There. She had it. As the captain continued with his testimony, she tweeted:

> Son told cops Alan Silverman killed Brenda #silvermaninquest

CHAPTER 5

The next morning, Tracy scanned the paper for her story. She found it on page five:

STARTLING EVIDENCE AT SILVERMAN INQUEST – ALAN SILVERMAN ACCUSED OF MURDER

By Tracy Jacobs

Was Brenda Silverman (44), the late wife of property mogul Alan Silverman, murdered? Did she commit suicide? Or was her death the result of an accidental overdose of prescription drugs?

Those are the questions Magistrate Patricia Ngubane will have to ponder as the inquest into the death of the Johannesburg socialite and philanthropist unfolds in the Johannesburg Magistrate's Court this week.

There was consternation in the court on the first day of the inquest yesterday when Captain Bhulu Matabane, who is heading the police investigation into the death, testified that Yair – the Silverman's 23-year-old son – told him that Alan Silverman had killed his wife.

Neither Yair Silverman nor Alan Silverman, a prominent member of Johannesburg's

Jewish community, was in court yesterday. Instead, they were represented by high-powered lawyer Gideon Feinberg of Jacobs, Jafta and Khumalo.

Mrs Silverman was found dead in her bed on the morning of 7 February.

State pathologist Dr Servaas Schneider testified that Mrs Silverman had significant quantities of Lorazepam, the core ingredient of the popular tranquilliser, Ativan, in her blood at the time of her death.

Nearly 100 high dose Ativan tablets were found in Mrs Silverman's bathroom cabinet. No Ativan tablets or containers were found in her bedroom.

However, Dr Schneider said that the actual cause of death was heart failure resulting from an insulin overdose. Mrs Silverman was an insulin-dependent diabetic.

Two empty insulin pens – one containing a long-acting and the other a fast-acting insulin – were found next to her bed. According to Captain Matabane, there were no useable fingerprints on the pens. 'But they didn't look as if an attempt had been made to wipe them clean,' he said.

The police found six unused insulin pens in the fridge in the kitchen.

It had also not been possible to identify any fingerprints on the bottles of Ativan, or on the other prescription medicines, including Ritalin and Adaphen – popular stimulants – that were also found in the bathroom cabinet.

Captain Matabane said there was no sign of any struggle or violence in Mrs Silverman's bedroom, while Dr Schneider testified that she did not appear to have been physically abused.

The inquest continues today.

Good, the subs had hardly changed anything except to add that bit about him being a "prominent member of the Jewish community". She wished they hadn't done that. It really wasn't relevant. It would just piss off her mother.

Tracy quickly checked her emails. Nothing important. Time to head to court.

***

A large crowd was milling around in the corridor outside Court 33. Tracy pushed through the people, holding up her shorthand notebook like a shield. Inside, the courtroom was packed. The media contingent seemed to have swelled to around twenty reporters, but she couldn't be sure. There were dozens of people crammed into every possible space. A very fat woman in a floral dress was sitting in Mr Ginsberg's chair, shaking her head and refusing to move despite his seemingly eloquent pleas. Tracy couldn't hear what he was saying.

'Quiet in court,' the orderly yelled. 'Quiet!'

It didn't help. The magistrate pushed through the throng and made her way to her desk. The banging of her gravel finally penetrated the din. The court fell silent.

'What on earth is going on?' the magistrate asked.

'Members of the public and the media, Your Honour. They all want to get inside, but there isn't enough room.'

'Well, they have a right to stay, but this court is obviously too small. Orderly, find out if we can transfer to one of the district courts downstairs.' She banged the gravel again. 'Court adjourned until we find a new venue.'

Tracy tweeted:

> Huge interest in Silverman inquest. Larger courtroom required #silvermaninquest

***

After the tea break, they all filed into Court 15. Tracy was squashed between the *Daily Times* and SABC radio news on the media bench along the wall. She considered moving to the large public gallery at the back, but that was pretty full too. Alan Silverman sat next to Gideon Feinberg. No, wait, that wasn't Alan Silverman. He was too young – in his late twenties or early thirties.

'Who's that?' she asked the *Daily Times* reporter. He shook his head.

Magistrate Patricia Ngubane took her seat up on the podium. 'Before we commence,' she said, 'I wish to remind you all that this is an inquest, not a circus. I appeal to the media to respect the emotions of the loved ones of the deceased. Right. Let's get on with it.'

The court orderly called Thembi Dlamini. The domestic worker wiped her hands down her black skirt as she answered the prosecutor's questions with a quiet determination, even when Gideon Feinberg objected to several of her replies, particularly those that related to Brenda's relationship with Alan Silverman. His cross examination of her was, Tracy thought, unnecessarily aggressive.

'Did you know Mrs Silverman had large quantities of sleeping pills and other medicines in her bathroom cabinet?'

'Yes.'

'Did you ever see her take these medicines?'

'No.'

'No? Are you sure?'

'I never saw her take the pills. I just knew that she did.'

'When did she take them?'

'I don't know.'

'Were you worried about the pills?'

She shrugged. 'She was the madam.'

'Did you see her take her insulin?'

'Sometimes. Sometimes if she didn't have her eyes in she would ask me to check that the pen was on the right number.'

'I presume you mean her contact lenses. Didn't she wear glasses?'

'No, I never saw her wear glasses.'

'So she couldn't always see how much insulin she was injecting herself with? Did she sometimes make a mistake with how much she was giving herself?'

Another shrug. 'Yes.'

'Was her behaviour erratic?'

A blank stare, followed by a shrug.

'Was she moody? Did she sleep a lot during the day?'

'She was the madam.'

The court adjourned for lunch.

***

'I want to talk to you.'

Tracy looked up, surprised. Alan Lookalike was glaring

288

down at her with the brightest blue eyes she had ever seen. 'Outside. Now,' he said.

'But court is about to start.'

'It will be a while. Mr Feinberg and the prosecutor are meeting with the magistrate about this bloody circus you've created.'

Tracy asked the *Beeld* reporter to keep her seat and followed Alan Lookalike out onto the balcony.

'What the fuck do you think you are doing?' He was standing so close to her she had to pull her head back slightly to look into his face. For the first time in her life, she was pleased she was so tall; his height wasn't nearly as intimidating as she had no doubt he would have liked.

'I'm sorry,' she said. 'We haven't been introduced. I'm Tracy Jacobs.'

'I know exactly who you are, Ms Jacobs. What I want to know is why you are gunning for Alan Silverman.'

'And you are?'

'Arno van Zyl. Executive director of marketing at Silver Properties.'

'Nice you meet you, Mr van Zyl. As a marketing man, I assume you have lots of experience in how to treat the media?'

'This isn't a Silver Properties thing. This is me, in my personal capacity. And it's off the record.'

He glared at her. She glared back. She put her hands in her pockets to hide their trembling.

'I'm waiting, Ms Jacobs. I want to know why you have it

in for Alan Silverman. Why are you trying to crucify him? He lost the love of his life, damn it, and you're trying to make out that he's a murderer or something. Are you anti-Semitic or something? It's because he's Jewish, isn't it?'

'First, Mr van Zyl, I don't do "off the record" with people I don't know – or like. Second, not that it's any of your business, I'm also Jewish. And I've reported nothing but facts and what's been said in this court. If you don't like what I've written, sue us. You have some pretty high-powered lawyers. Let them earn their retainer.'

'I'm warning you…'

'Are you threatening me? Should I call the court orderly – or one of my media colleagues – to witness this?' She pulled her cell phone out of her bag and switched on the recorder. 'Okay, Mr van Zyl. Let's continue this conversation on the record.'

He glared at her.

'I'm curious, Mr van Zyl. Why are you doing this? What's Mr Silverman to you, besides being your employer? How much does he pay you to be his bully-boy messenger?'

'Alan Silverman knows nothing about this. I respect and admire him. I cannot just stand by and watch little nobodies like you try to destroy a good, decent man.'

He stormed back into the court. She hurried to her seat. She opened her notebook, surprised to find that her hands were still shaking.

***

'Call Stembiso Tshabalala,' said the orderly.

A rake of a man, dressed in a too-big grey suit, white shirt and old fashioned wide tie with blue and red stripes, made his way slowly to the witness stand.

It was difficult to follow his testimony, because he had a Shangaan interpreter who was not translating in a way that satisfied him. Tracy suspected that Mr Tshabalala's English was better than the interpreter's.

Mr Tshabalala had been Mrs Silverman's driver for almost eighteen years. Now he was retired. Mr Silverman had fired him, he said.

He'd taken Mrs Silverman everywhere and played taxi driver for the children too. Mrs Silverman had been very good to him. He wiped his eyes. She had given him money for his children's school fees, and when he had needed a deposit to buy an RDP house. She had told him not to tell Mr Silverman about that. She had also told him not to tell Mr Silverman about some of the places he took her to. Like Alex Township.

'What about doctors? Did you take her to doctors?' Gideon Feinberg asked during cross examination.

'Yes. She wasn't a strong woman. She was sick a lot. She had lots of headaches.'

'And did you take her to the pharmacy to get medicine?'

'Sometimes. Sometimes I would go and get her medicine

for her. She would give me the money and I would get it for her.'

'Didn't she have an account at the pharmacy?'

'Not all of them. Most of them, they only wanted cash.'

Gideon Feinberg smirked knowingly, and continued. 'Where else did you take her? Did you take her to visit friends?'

'No, I would take Avi and Yair to friends and to training and competitions when they were still at school. And I would take Zivah to her doctors and classes.'

'What about Mrs Silverman's friends?'

'I don't know about her friends. She didn't have a lot of friends.'

'You mean she didn't have any?'

'She was a kind, good lady. She had friends.' The old man fluttered his hands and then gripped the bar at the front of the witness stand.

'Can you tell us their names?'

He shook his head. 'She told me not to tell anyone.'

'Why? Because she had a boyfriend?'

'No!' he shouted. 'She was a good, kind person. No boyfriend. An old lady. Carol. I took her to visit Carol at the Jewish old age home, there by Sandringham Gardens.'

CHAPTER 6

Well, well, well – Tracy was moving up in the world. There was her story, in prime position on Page Three. Tracy read it avidly. This time, the subs hadn't changed anything. She wondered if any of the other reporters had taken the same angle.

BRENDA, ALAN SILVERMAN ARGUED BEFORE HER DEATH

By Tracy Jacobs

Property mogul Alan Silverman and his wife, Brenda, had a furious argument two nights before her death on 7 February from a deadly cocktail of tranquilisers and insulin, the Johannesburg inquest court heard yesterday.

The couple's domestic worker, Ms Thembi Dlamini (48), testified that she had overhead the couple shouting at each other, but she was unable to make out what the argument was about. She said the Silvermans hardly ever argued, but also claimed that they spent very little time together as a family.

'They didn't even have supper together, except on Friday nights when they had a lot of visitors,' she said.

Questions about how Mrs Silverman came to have a large quantity of prescription drugs in her bathroom cupboard at the time of her death were partially answered when her driver, Mr Stembiso Tshabalala (54), testified that she was treated by several different doctors, as she suffered from frequent headaches. He would also collect medicine for her from a variety of different pharmacies.

Mr Tshabalala, who was fired by Mr Silverman after Mrs Silverman's death, despite his nearly 18 years of service to the family, told the court that Mrs Silverman was a "kind, generous lady" who paid for his children's education and helped him to purchase a house, all without Mr Silverman's knowledge.

Frequently breaking down in tears while testifying, his portrayal of Mrs Silverman was of a sad, lonely woman with very few friends. Her life appeared to be devoted to her children, her husband and her ballet school in Alexandra Township.

Silver Properties continued to lose ground on the JSE yesterday, closing some 75 cents down in quiet trading.

The inquest continues today.

***

Tracy hurried through the side door of Court 15 and claimed her space on the media bench. Alan Silverman was scheduled to testify today and she wanted a good view of his face. Alan Lookalike – Arno van Zyl – was already in his place next to Gideon Feinberg. Marie du Toit was seated at her table, reading through some papers. A low-level hum of expectation hung over the packed public gallery. Every seat was filled and, still, people were pushing in through the doors at the back and arranging themselves along the walls. Several "black hats" –

men in the traditional garb of ultra-religious Jews – many of them bearded, had claimed the front row on the left. On the right sat their wives or daughters in their long sleeves and *sheitels* or headscarves.

The court orderly's "all rise" shut down the buzz as effectively as flipping a switch. The magistrate emerged from her private entrance behind her seat on the podium. Her eyes widened slightly, then she sat slowly and lifted her gravel.

Alan Silverman walked briskly to the witness stand. Dressed in a black suit that seemed to hang on his tall frame, white shirt, white *yarmulke* and with the fringes of his *tzitzit* hanging down beneath his jacket, his blue eyes gleamed brightly in his ashen face. Tracy was shocked to see his handsome features were now partly obscured by a bushy grey beard. He looked every one of his fifty years, and then some. A niggle of sympathy was quickly suppressed.

Raising his right hand, he solemnly affirmed that the evidence he would give would be the truth, the whole truth and nothing but the truth.

'Brenda and I were more than husband and wife. We were soul mates,' he said. 'She was the only woman I ever loved, truly loved.' His voice broke and he cleared his throat. 'I believe she felt the same about me. We met and fell in love when she was just seventeen – eighteen nearly. I was twenty-three or four and I knew the first time I laid eyes on her that she was the woman I would spend the rest of my life with.' He stopped and shook his head.

Tracy looked at him in surprise as he cleared his throat again.

'I'm so sorry,' he said. 'I get quite emotional when I think of her. She was so perfect, just the most beautiful, perfect human being I've ever met. Inside and out, she was good and kind and gentle.'

Ms du Toit examined her nails, waiting for him to compose himself, then she said, 'But you were aware that your wife was a drug addict.'

Tracy flinched. That was harsh.

'She wasn't a drug addict,' Alan said and paused. 'But I suspected that she sometimes did take too many pills.'

'How could you not know? The bathroom cabinet looked like a pharmacy.'

'That was her bathroom. We each had our own.'

'What did you do about helping her with her addiction?'

'I told you. She wasn't a drug addict. She was perfectly okay. She was a fabulous hostess; an excellent mother, always there for our children.'

'But even though you suspected she took too many pills, and there were times when she wasn't okay, you made no effort to get her some help, some treatment. Why?'

'Look, you can't help anyone with a drug problem if they don't want to be helped. But, as I said, she didn't have a problem. I mean, it wasn't as if she was a crack addict or anything. And she didn't – you know – she just took a few too many perfectly legal pills occasionally. That's all. Why are you making it out to be more than it was? The media is already doing that.'

Tracy felt his eyes boring into her. Alan Lookalike turned in his chair and glared at her. Her last vestige of sympathy for Mr Bigshot Alan Silverman evaporated.

'So the deceased's excessive use of prescription medication never embarrassed you in public?'

'Of course not.'

'Not even when she passed out at the function where you won the Jewish Businessman of the Year award?'

Gideon Feinberg was on his feet, objecting. A buzz rose from the gallery. Some of the *frum* women had their hands over their open mouths; several of the black-hatted men were staring at their feet.

'She was ill that night. It was her diabetes. She didn't pass out.'

'So you didn't – and I quote here from "Shulah's Blog" – "drag her from the hall so forcefully that her *sheitel* fell off"?'

Tracy stared at Ms du Toit in admiration. She'd never heard of Shulah's Blog and her Google search had missed this bit of gossip. She wondered who Shulah was and where she got her information from.

Gideon Feinberg was on his feet objecting. The magistrate banged her gravel. The objection was sustained.

Ms du Toit continued, 'All right. Let's talk about the Support Free Palestine function. That was just four months before her death, correct?'

Gideon Feinberg was on his feet again. 'Relevance, Your Honour.'

'Mr Silverman has testified that his wife never embarrassed him. I'm trying to show that this isn't the full truth, that his wife's erratic behaviour was having a profoundly negative impact on his business,' Ms du Toit said.

'I'll allow it. Proceed.'

Tracy smiled to herself as Alan squirmed and insisted that the condemnation from his political – and business – associates was not important. Yeah right.

Ms du Toit looked as if she was about to wind up her cross examination. She looked down at her notes, turned a couple of pages and then asked, 'Were you always faithful to your wife? Your – what did you call her? Your soul mate?'

The black hats in the public gallery exploded. Gideon Feinberg objected. It didn't help. The magistrate told the public gallery to be quiet. Alan Silverman had to answer the question.

Alan Silverman glared at her. He ranted that she was trying to destroy his reputation. When he finished, Ms du Toit said, quite calmly and coldly, Tracy thought, 'I have a signed affidavit from a Ms Ingrid Lamont that you had an affair with her over a period of several years.'

The proverbial pin would have shattered the stillness in the court.

'During this same time,' Ms du Toit went on, 'she claims you were also being unfaithful to your wife with several other women. She has provided us with – let me see – eight names in her signed, sworn affidavit. Can you confirm her allegation? She said she is willing to come to court to testify to this allegation under oath and we could also subpoena some of the other women named, if you prefer.'

Silence. Alan Silverman just stood in the witness box, expressionless. A noise from the public gallery made Tracy turn. A woman was pushing her way through the crowd to the door. It looked like that ANC MP, Annette Davies-Smedley. Tracy hadn't noticed her before. Could she be one of the women on the list? Tracy wanted to go after her, but she wanted to hear the rest of Alan Silverman's testimony too. She wanted to see how Gideon smarmy Feinberg was going to get the creep out of this.

Gideon Feinberg did his best to re-establish Alan and Brenda as a latter day Romeo and Juliet. He tried to paint Ingrid Lamont as a bitter old woman who'd had bad business dealings with Silver Properties and was trying to get her revenge... but somehow it didn't quite ring true. Not to her... and – Tracy hoped – not to the magistrate either. Or to the black hats.

Tracy tweeted:

> Alan Silverman had numerous adulterous affairs – ex-lover #silvermaninquest

CHAPTER 7

Yair Silverman was back. Tracy hoped she'd be able to ask him where he'd been. He looked dreadful when he took the witness stand after lunch. Very thin and pale. Like his father, he was dressed in a black suit, white shirt, black hat and *tzitzit*. He glanced at her and winked. She swallowed. She wanted to put her arms around him and tell him it would all be okay. Like that time, in Grade 10, when he'd been so upset. She'd gone up to him where he was waiting outside the hall and told him he'd better hurry up and get backstage, because he still had to get his make-up done.

'I'm waiting for my parents,' he'd said. 'I've kept them seats in the second row.'

From the wings, from where she had been prompting the actors, she could see the two empty seats. They remained empty throughout the musical. Back stage later, while the cast whooped and shouted about the standing ovation they'd received, she saw Yair standing alone, although the loudest applause had undoubtedly been for him.

'I'm so sorry, Yair,' Tracy said. 'You were brilliant. It's

their loss, you know.'

'*Ja*, sure. I don't know why I expected them to come.' He turned away, but not before Tracy had seen the tears in his eyes. She didn't know what to do. So she went over and joined the celebrations. He had followed a few moments later, laughing and joking, the life and soul of the party as usual.

***

Prompted by Ms du Toit, Yair described that dreadful morning. He avoided looking at his father, who had taken the seat between Gideon Feinberg and Arno van Zyl.

Yair said he had been in his room when he heard Zivah screaming. He had tried to calm her. He'd called the paramedics. They'd called the police. His father had come home later.

Marie du Toit then got down to business. 'Mr Silverman, you told the police that your father had killed your mother. What did you mean?'

'Exactly that. He killed her.' Yair stood up straight and tall in the witness box, and glared at his father.

Tracy felt her heart swell. He'd be okay.

'How?'

The court held its breath.

'He abused her. All the time.'

Tracy dropped her pen. The court gasped.

Alan Silverman jumped to his feet. 'That's a lie. That's a

damn lie.'

Tracy smothered a grin as the magistrate warned him to sit down and shut up.

Ms du Toit continued, 'What do you mean, abused her? Did he beat her?'

'No, I don't think so. But he abused her. I could hear her crying when he was in her room.' Yair paused, then muttered, 'He made her do disgusting things.'

'What do you mean? How do you know? Did your mother tell you?'

'Of course not. She would never say a thing against him, even when he treated her like shit. Sorry. When he treated her badly. I saw him.'

The magistrate pounded her gravel. The court quieted. Tracy couldn't believe this. Never, in her wildest moments of speculation, had she suspected anything like this. Affairs – yes, why not? All men had affairs. Her father was a prime example. But abuse? That was incredible. Unbelievable. Impossible. Wasn't it?

'What did you see?' Ms du Toit asked.

Yair flushed. 'I can't... It was too horrible.'

Gideon Feinberg was gripping Alan Silverman's arm, restraining him in his seat. Alan Silverman looked odd, sort of white and red and sweaty and sick and angry all at the same time. If looks could kill, Yair Silverman was about to die.

'Mr Silverman,' the magistrate said. 'You must answer the questions put to you by Ms du Toit.'

Yair exhaled loudly, then drew in a deep breath. 'One night, I heard him go into her room and I could hear her crying. I wanted to stop him hurting her. He was always making her cry. The door wasn't closed properly. I could see…' He stopped.

'Yes, Mr Silverman? What exactly could you see?'

'His trousers were down, sort of like around his knees, you know? He was yanking her hair, pulling her down… and she was crying, on her knees… and he was forcing her, you know. He was making her… She was crying. And I was frozen. I couldn't do anything. I ran back to my room. I ran away. I let him…' He hunched over in the witness stand, his shoulders heaving.

The magistrate adjourned the hearing. Tracy tweeted:

Alan Silverman sexually abused his wife, says son
#silvermaninquest

CHAPTER 8

Tracy lifted her hands off her keyboard and looked at her story with satisfaction. If this didn't get her a front page lead, nothing would. Kingmaker had given her some juicy additional information as well. He apparently had a pretty good idea who the women on Ingrid Lamont's list were. Annette Davies-Smedley's name was there and Kingmaker had confirmed with her office that Ms Smedley was in Johannesburg at present.

Tracy wondered what her mother would say when she read her story tomorrow. What would Alan Silverman say? He was obviously following her articles – his arse-licking little shadow had made that clear enough, as had the constant barrage of demands for retractions from his lawyers.

She checked her copy for typos.

ALAN SILVERMAN – ADULTERER AND WIFE ABUSER?

By Tracy Jacobs

Johannesburg Magistrate Court 15, where the inquest into the death of socialite and philanthropist Brenda Silverman (44), wife of property mogul Alan Silverman (50), is taking place, yesterday heard shocking allegations of abuse and betrayal in what had previously been perceived as the couple's "perfect marriage".

Despite his testimony that he and his wife had been "soul mates", Ms Marie du Toit, who is leading evidence in the inquest, quoted from a sworn affidavit from a former business associate of Mr Silverman's, Ms Ingrid Lamont, that they had had an affair.

In later testimony, the Silvermans' son, Yair, testified that he had witnessed his father sexually abusing his mother by forcing her to perform oral sex. This allegation was vehemently denied by Mr Alan Silverman and his lawyer, Mr Gideon Feinberg.

Mr Yair Silverman will continue testifying when the inquest resumes today. The inquest was adjourned late yesterday afternoon after Mr Silverman Jnr broke down in the witness stand.

Mr Alan Silverman also strongly denied the allegations in Ms Lamont's affidavit. In it, the so-called "queen" of

*Johannesburg's public relations practitioners in the 1990s
and early 2000s claimed she had had an affair with Mr
Silverman over a period of around four and a half years.*

*She also alleged that, while he has having the affair with
her, he had numerous affairs with a variety of women. The
Daily Express is aware of the names of at least six, four of
whom are married and two of whom are also prominent in
ANC circles.*

*(**Note to subs**: we have a copy of the affidavit with eight
names. We think two of them are a bit iffy as they must have
still been in high school at the time Silverman was supposed
to have been screwing them – one is the older sister of a guy a
couple of years ahead of me at school – so we're discounting
them. They are both quite prominent socialites in JHB today.
We're trying to track them down for their comment.)*

She had been shocked to read the names. Especially the
woman who sat in the same row as Maxine and her in *shul* on
Rosh Hashanah and Yom Kippur. That woman was married to
one of the richest guys in Jo'burg. Tracy had gone to school
with her kids. Shit – so had Yair and Aviva, of course. In fact,
if she remembered correctly, Aviva had been quite friendly
with her daughter. Should she tell her mother? Nah, Maxine
would never believe her. Anyway, they were only allegations
and, from what Thomas had told her, Ingrid Lamont was
known to have offered her clients more than PR back in the
day. 'Some called her the queen of public relations, but it was

more like pubic relations,' he said. Thomas really could be quite bitchy at times.

Tracy finished checking the copy and submitted it. She decided she wouldn't tell her mother anything. It would be bad enough tomorrow when she read the paper – and even worse if she managed to carry out Mafuta's instructions before the paper went to bed.

'T.T.,' Mafuta had said, 'get hold of these women and make them say something on the record. Anything. Even a denial will do. Then we can publish their denial – with their name.'

Tracy felt sick. She couldn't phone these women and say, 'Can you confirm that you had an affair with Alan Silverman?'

So she googled "domestic violence in Jewish community" instead, because she really couldn't bring herself to believe Yair's unbelievable allegation. There was no way Alan Silverman had really sexually abused Brenda. Yair must have got it wrong. That kind of thing only happened in the townships and really poor suburbs. Otherwise, why did all the activities during the annual Sixteen Days of Activism against Gender Violence only take place there? The domestic violence experts knew it never happened in the suburbs. Not to middle-class, educated people like... like her... and certainly not within the Jewish community. The Silvermans had had a... a good marriage. Okay, it obviously wasn't perfect – no marriage was. Lots of men had affairs. But sexual abuse? That was impossible.

PART 9
BRENDA

CHAPTER 1
LONDON, 1989

Brenda couldn't believe it was finally happening. Alan was carrying her over the threshold for their first night in their new two-bedroom flat... and her first night as Mrs Alan Silverman. It was all going to be okay. Alan hadn't been exactly happy about the baby, but he wasn't nearly as angry as she'd thought he would be.

'I need to think about this,' he'd said when they got home from the Shapiros after Ruth guessed about the pregnancy. It had been such fun riding in a taxi, even if Alan hadn't said anything the whole way.

'You know this isn't what I wanted,' he said as he unlocked the door of their bedsit. Then he just turned and walked away. As late as it was, he just left her. It was the worst night of her life. And the next one. And the next. She even phoned the Shapiros in panic. She wept with relief when he reappeared on Monday morning early. She didn't dare ask him where he'd been. He didn't speak to her, but at least he'd come back.

When he got home from work that evening, he announced, 'We're getting married. Mrs Shapiro will be in touch with you about the arrangements.'

Brenda couldn't believe it. She was so excited she had to tell someone. She phoned Sally, who was delighted and so happy for them.

It had got even better when they went out to celebrate and Mr Shapiro said that he would pay for the wedding, and Mrs Shapiro said they should go and choose the dress as soon as possible. And Mr Shapiro was going to let them rent a flat in one of his buildings at a very reasonable rate. When she tried to thank Mrs Shapiro for all her kindness, the little woman smiled at her. 'I've always wanted a daughter, or at least a daughter-in-law. God has chosen to give me neither. But He brought you and Alan into our lives. You don't have a mother, or a family. So would you do me the honour of becoming my – what should I call you? – my adopted daughter?'

Mrs Shapiro's rings cut into her fingers as they clasped hands.

They spent the next few days happily planning the wedding. There wasn't much time. They were getting married on Sunday the second of April.

'At least it's not April Fool's Day,' Ruth joked.

The ceremony would be in Golders Green Shul and the reception – a finger luncheon by the best kosher caterers in London – would be at the Shapiro house, which could accommodate about a hundred guests if they pushed the dining room table to the wall and moved some of the formal sitting room furniture into the spare room. They could spill out onto the patio and into the garden if the weather was kind.

Brenda didn't think there would be that many people at the wedding. She couldn't think of anyone to invite besides Patricia and Bill... and Sally. Alan would no doubt want to invite Annette, and Charles and some of the other WOAH people, and, of course, there were his colleagues from Shapiro & Son. He hadn't mentioned his family in South Africa.

So she was very surprised to see quite a crowd in the *shul* as Mr Shapiro led her proudly down the aisle to the *chupah* where Alan waited for her. He looked so handsome in his three-piece suit and Ruth said she looked lovely. The Elizabeth Emanuel dress Ruth had helped her choose was beautiful: a pale ivory satin and lace confection with an empire waist that showed off her developing cleavage and cleverly disguised the first signs of her little bump. A lacy bolero preserved her modesty in *shul*. Her veil was held in place with little pink rosebuds and flowed down over her long dark curls. Ruth had agreed that she should not put her hair up. 'I want to look like me, even if it is my wedding day,' she'd told Ruth.

After Alan had crushed the glass under his foot and lifted her veil, she had seen the love and admiration in his glittering eyes. She thought her heart would burst.

The reception passed in a blur of faces and names and congratulations from people she'd never met. Friends of Alan's from WOAH and the Anti Apartheid Movement, and even some people from the ANC. Ben and Ruth had also invited their friends and important people from the community, to celebrate the marriage of their "adopted children". Alan never left her side. His speech was so warm and loving, tears had pricked her eyes. He said how happy he was to be married to the most beautiful woman in the world. They drank toast after toast, Alan and the guests with fancy French champagne, she with sparkling grape juice.

Ben had also been generous with the whisky. She hated the stuff, but Alan enjoyed it. The only sadness that day was that Jeremy had been too ill to make the trip from California. He'd phoned the week before and said he was looking forward to meeting his new adopted siblings.

It had all been absolutely perfect, the best day of her life. Now, as Alan carried her into their beautiful Laura Ashley flat – again thanks to Ruth, who wanted only the best for her new family – Brenda knew that it was about to get even better.

CHAPTER 2

Alan closed the door behind them and dropped Brenda on the floor. He pushed her into the bedroom. Brenda giggled, relieved. The only blight on her happiness – the only thing that really troubled her in the frantic rush to get everything ready for today – was that Alan hadn't made love to her. Not once. Not since he'd found out about the baby. But now they were married and he had told everyone at the wedding how much he loved her. Perhaps he was just frightened of hurting the baby. She'd heard that some men were.

'Take off that ridiculous dress,' he said.

'What?' He sounded strange, not like Alan at all.

'You heard me, get it off. It makes you look like a fat cream puff.'

Her hands were shaking so much she couldn't undo the tiny pearl buttons that that ran from her neck to the small of her back. It had taken Ruth nearly twenty minutes to fasten them all.

'Please, help me. I can't reach,' she said.

Alan turned her around, placed his hands on her shoulders…

and ripped. The buttons flew off and buried themselves in the thick cream carpet. Then he spun her back to face him. He glued his eyes to hers, and tore at the delicate fabric.

'Wait, don't. I'll get out of it. Don't...'

Too late. He tore it again. The ivory lace wept onto the floor and piled up around her feet.

He yanked off her beautiful lacy bra, and it joined the devastation on the floor. Her pretty panties, with the sweet little daisies on the left by the elastic, which fitted so snugly just below her little bump, followed. She stood trembling in the middle of their cosy bedroom, frozen as her new husband appraised her nakedness with the curiosity of a biologist examining a new species of insect. Her hands edged over her bump.

Alan didn't move. For what seemed like hours, he just looked at her. Then, silently, he unbuckled his belt.

'Come here,' he said.

She hesitated, her mind frozen in shock.

'Come here.' Softer this time. Yet infinitely more menacing.

She stepped closer. He pushed his hands into her hair and forced her head back. He smiled into her eyes. Then he pushed her down, down. She was on her knees now, in front of him, tears streaming down her face. What was he doing? He was hurting her.

'Time to consummate our marriage, Mrs Silverman,' he said.

***

It was over. Finally. Brenda had gagged and struggled, but he was relentless. He climaxed and she heaved, choking. He pushed her away and she sprawled on the carpet. He stood and looked down at her for a minute and then went into the bathroom. She dragged herself up onto the bed and sobbed quietly into the crisp, new lavender and blue floral duvet. She spat into a tissue, trying to get the taste of him out of her mouth. The bathroom door opened. She held her breath. He came out, neatly dressed in jeans and a T-shirt. He grabbed a jacket and walked out. Without saying a word.

She forced herself off the bed. She picked up her ruined wedding garments and stuffed them into the bottom of the cupboard. She crawled across the carpet, rescuing the little pearl buttons one by one. She felt drained. Empty. Stunned.

Then she felt the baby kick, as delicate as a butterfly fluttering inside her. It was a sign. She knew it. Alan loved her. The baby was proof of that. Plus, he'd called her Mrs Silverman. That showed he was proud to be married to her. She pulled on the sheer, floaty honey coloured chiffon honeymoon nightgown that she and Ruth, giggling like schoolgirls, had bought for her "first night", and settled down on the bed to wait for her husband to come home and make love to her properly.

She didn't hear when Alan returned, much, much later.

CHAPTER 3

Brenda was being torn in half. Breath. Breath. Blow. Blow. Blow. Breath. Where was Alan? Where was he? The contraction passed. Ruth flexed her fingers and smiled at her.

'You're a strong little thing, aren't you?' Ruth said.

'Sorry. I'm so sorry. Where's Alan? Have you heard from him yet?'

'Ben's trying to track him down, but we're not sure where he is. He checked out of his hotel in York yesterday and there was a message from him at the office that he had car trouble. But we've heard nothing since. He's probably on his way home.'

'But he won't know where I am. And I left the flat in such a mess!'

When her water had broken, she hadn't understood what was happening. She'd felt something warm running down her legs as she stood in the kitchen making herself a cup of coffee. In her panic, she knocked over the tin of instant coffee. She'd waddled to the bathroom, leaving a dripping trail down the passage, and wadded a towel between her legs. It was too early. The babies weren't due for another four weeks. A contraction had stopped her in her tracks on her way to the phone to call Ruth. Then she'd doubled over on the bedroom carpet and wept.

The hammering at the front door had roused her. Alan. He was home. He must have forgotten his keys. Relief had given her strength. Hugging the wall, she had made her way to the door and pulled it open. Ruth. She had sunk to the floor and howled as another contraction took hold.

'Hold on, dear. I've called an ambulance.'

'Call Alan. Please call Alan'

'We're trying. We don't know where he is, but I'm sure he'll be here soon.'

The ambulance had wailed her to the hospital and she had been wheeled into the labour ward. A doctor had examined her, patted her on her shoulder and told her she still had a long way to go. 'You're doing well. Just relax and go with the pain. Don't fight it,' he said.

'He's obviously never had a baby,' she hissed at Ruth when the next contraction passed.

It had been hours and hours. Days maybe? They'd given her something for the pain, but it hadn't helped. It just made her want to throw up. Ruth drifted in and out of the room. Ruth held her hand. Alan held her hand. But when she opened her eyes, Alan was gone. Ruth was holding her hand again. The doctor drifted in and out of the room. A nurse. Another nurse. The doctor again.

'Mrs Silverman. I think we're going to have to do a caesarean section. You're fully dilated, but nothing's happening. You're so tiny, I don't think you'll be able to deliver both babies naturally. And they are becoming very stressed. We're going to take you to theatre. We have to get those babies out now.'

'Alan. I won't go without Alan. Please, find Alan. I'm so scared. What's the time?'

Ruth wiped her forehead with a cold, damp cloth. 'It's about two o'clock.'

'Is that all? I thought I'd been here longer.'

'In the morning. It's two o'clock on Friday morning.'

'Where's Alan? He's had an accident, hasn't he? And you're not telling me. Don't lie to me. He's dead, isn't he? Alan's dead!'

Another contraction cut her hysteria short.

Ruth was deathly pale. 'Shh. Shh. Alan's fine. We haven't heard from him yet, but, if he'd had an accident, we would have been informed. Shh. He's probably staying overnight somewhere while the car is fixed. He'll be here in the morning. You'll see.'

They wheeled her into the theatre. A masked man held her hand and told her to count backwards from a hundred.

***

'Mrs Silverman. Mrs Silverman.'

Brenda's eyes flew open. Alan. Where was he? She wanted to see him before the babies were born. She needed to see him.

'Mrs Silverman. You have two beautiful babies. A boy and a girl. Can you hear me, dear?'

'My husband,' she croaked. Her throat hurt. She could barely swallow. 'Is my husband here yet?'

'We're going to take you back to the ward now, dear. Your babies are in the paediatric intensive care. Just a precaution. For premmies, they're nice and big. Strong too. We'll bring them to you once we're sure everything is fine. You sleep now.'

She drifted. Ruth was holding her hand again.

'*Mazeltov. Mazeltov.* The babies are beautiful. I just saw them.' Ruth smiled at her.

'Where's Alan? Has he come yet?'

Ruth looked away. 'It's still very early. Only six o'clock. He'll be along later.'

'Have you heard from him? Have you told him?'

Ruth shook her head. She looked exhausted.

'Oh Ruth. Have you been here all night? You poor thing. Go home now. Ben must be worried.'

'I'm perfectly all right, child. I'll go when Alan gets here.'

They brought her some ice to suck. It helped to soothe her parched throat. It felt as if someone had taken a blowtorch to her stomach. They gave her an injection for the pain and it helped a little, if she didn't move.

'What's the time?'

Ruth started out of her doze and looked at her watch. 'Eight o'clock. They should be bringing you some breakfast soon. I think I'll go see where it is.'

Tears slid down Brenda's face. She couldn't help it. Where was Alan? Why didn't he come?

***

Alan arrived. He gave Brenda some flowers… and then he was gone. Just like that. He'd hardly said two words to her. He didn't even see the babies. She hadn't seen them yet, either. She supposed she should make an effort. She forced herself to sit on the side of the bed and then slowly lowered her feet to the floor. Holding her flabby stomach with one hand, pushing the drip stand in the other and hunched over like an old woman, she hobbled down the corridor to the nursery. She knocked on the nursery window. A nurse came over and opened the door.

'Mrs Silverman, go back to bed. Your babies are fine. We've been giving them some formula, but, if you're feeling strong enough, I'll bring them to you and you can try to feed them. Now get along with you.'

Brenda hobbled back to her bed and sank into it gratefully. She raised her knees. It eased the pain a little. Tears began to slide down her cheeks again. She was so lonely. So alone. So frightened. What if Alan didn't come back? What if he never came back? She'd die. She'd just die.

The nurse walked in pushing a little basket on wheels. There were two tiny bundles inside. She looked at them dully. They were too small to be babies. The nurse took one bundle and placed it on her lap. She flinched. That was sore!

'Oops. Sorry, dear. Here, bend your arm like so... now, here's your little princess. Isn't she beautiful?' the nurse asked.

The little eyes fluttered open and looked directly at Brenda. The little mouth opened and a blood-curdling howl emerged.

'She hates me,' Brenda wailed.

'Nonsense. She's just hungry. Would you like to try to feed her? Here. I'll show you.' The nurse opened the front of her nightie and grabbed one of her breasts. Taking the breast in one hand, she pushed the baby's face towards her nipple. The baby screamed. Brenda looked at the nurse in horror. 'Shh, Shh, Shh,' the nurse said and rubbed the nipple across the baby's cheek. The baby opened its mouth and bit.

'Ow. Ow, ow, that hurts!'

'She just hasn't latched on properly. Let's try again.'

The baby shrieked.

'Take it away. Take it away. I can't do this. I just can't.' Brenda sobbed.

The nurse put the baby back in the basket.

'I think this little one is too hungry to wait for her mummy to learn to feed her. I'll give her some formula, and we'll try again at the next feed. Should we try your little man now?'

The other baby didn't open its eyes when the nurse pushed its face towards her nipple. It just opened its mouth and attached itself. It felt funny. Like a little leech or something.

'Well now, he seems happy enough. I'll just leave him with you while I take little madam here back to the nursery for a bottle.' The nurse disappeared out the door with the screaming basket before Brenda could protest.

She looked down at the baby. Her son. She waited for a wave of maternal love to wash over her. Nothing. She pushed the blanket back from its head. Dark hair. Her nipple dropped out of its mouth. She waited for the howl. Silence. Then the baby gave a tiny snore. She examined it curiously. It – he – he didn't look like her. He didn't look like Alan. He looked like… nothing. A stranger. A stranger who had disrupted her life and made Alan hate her. She tucked her breast back into her nightie and waited for the nurse to come and take it away.

CHAPTER 4

Brenda was too tired to cry. She was too tired to sleep. She was too tired to breathe. At least Alan had said she didn't have to breastfeed them. She had tried, but it had been horrible and Alan had agreed with her. But making bottles, washing bottles, dozens and dozens of them, all the time, was exhausting. A baby screamed. Aviva. Always Aviva. Yair ate and slept and ate and slept some more. He only cried when his nappy was dirty or he was really hungry. Aviva cried all the time. She cried when she was being fed. She cried even more when Yair was being fed. She cried when Brenda picked her up… and when she was put down, or bathed, or changed. She cried and cried and cried. And Brenda cried with her, feeling utterly helpless. The doctor said there was nothing wrong. A wind, perhaps.

The doctor prescribed her a mild tranquilliser. 'Babies can tell when their mothers are tense. You need to relax and you'll see, the baby will relax too,' he said.

Guilt wracked her. She was a bad mother. She'd always known she'd be a bad mother. She hadn't wanted them and they knew it. At least, Aviva knew it. She was clever, that child. She knew exactly when her mother was about to doze off. Then she'd scream. She knew when her *bobba* came to visit. Then she'd be as good as gold... and then Ruth would look at her as if to say "you're imagining it. There's nothing wrong with this beautiful baby. You're just being hysterical".

She was a bad wife. Alan hardly came home. He hated her and he hated her even more when the babies cried. 'Can't you shut that brat up? What kind of mother are you?' he said. He complained about the dirty flat, but she had no energy to clean. He hated the pile of dirty nappies that seemed to grow of its own accord, but they couldn't afford disposables, Alan said. She could barely get up the strength to bath herself. Alan hated her lank, dirty hair... and her fat, flabby tummy... and her fat, flabby boobs. He couldn't bear to look at her. Or to touch her. Except when he grabbed her hair and pushed her head down and made her do... that thing that he seemed to enjoy so much. She tried to enjoy it, but it was horrible. Disgusting. That's the only time she welcomed Aviva's screaming, but then Alan would walk out. She hated it when he left. She felt so alone. She hated it when he was there, when he looked at her as if she was something the cat had dragged in. She hated it.

She took two more tranquillisers and a couple of her pain pills – her knee hurt and her Caesar scar was still tender. The doctor said it would get better, but it had already been nearly four months. She lay down. She'd rest a bit. Aviva started screaming. She screamed, and screamed.

CHAPTER 5
LONDON, 1993

Brenda lifted her head out of the toilet bowl and wiped her face on a towel. Aviva was standing at the bathroom door regarding her with enormous brown eyes.

'It's okay, Avi. Mommy is fine. Really.'

Aviva shrugged and walked off.

Yair was crying. She was late with his breakfast. As always, Aviva just sat patiently at the table, waiting, as if she knew her mother would eventually get herself together and shake the cobwebs out of her head. She had never been a morning person, but Yair didn't take that into account, did he? Aviva hardly ever cried or complained, and she had the most disconcerting way of looking at you in a way that indicated she knew exactly when you were – not lying exactly – but not quite telling the truth. Like now.

Yair was pulling at her nightie. 'Hungry, Mommy. I hungry.' He started crying.

She picked him up and he put his little arms around her neck. He smelled awful. His nappy was full. Why were boys so much slower than girls at potty training? Aviva had all but trained herself. Yair was getting there, during the day, but he still needed a nappy at night. She'd tried him without one a few weeks ago, but he'd messed in his pyjamas.

'I called you, Mommy. I called and called, but you didn't come,' he'd said.

'I'm so sorry, baby. Mommy's so sorry. I didn't hear you.'

'I shook you, Mommy. But you wouldn't wake up. Avi also tried. And then the poo just came.' His little face had crumpled. His blue eyes, so like Alan's, had filled with tears. Her heart had broken. He deserved a better mother. If she had known Alan wouldn't be coming home that night, she wouldn't have taken her sleeping pills and then she'd have heard Yair. She really was going to try to cut down on them. Alan hated the fact that they made her sleep when he wanted to make love to her, but that was the point, really. She wished he didn't want to make love to her. Not the way it was now. Not the way he did it… and not all the time.

Soon, thank God, he wouldn't want to, because she knew she was pregnant.. Why was she surprised? She hadn't resumed taking the pill after the twins were born. What had been the point? Alan wouldn't touch her. Correction. Alan wouldn't make love to her. Not properly.

He didn't seem to have a problem with that other thing. Even though she'd tried to tell him that she hated it. He had been furious. He'd nearly ripped her hair out of her head when he forced her down to her knees that time. He'd said she was frigid. He'd said it was time she grew up and acted like a woman. He'd said that, if she loved him, she'd make him happy. She did love him. She really did. Who wouldn't? He was the most gorgeous man in the world, and he was hers. Even if he messed around with Annette, he always came home to her. He still loved her, she knew he did, even though she'd been so stupid and had fallen pregnant with the twins, messing everything up and now was all fat and flabby and revolting. So no wonder he was sometimes cross with her. Perhaps she should get the boob job he'd suggested, and perhaps they could do something about her Caesar scar and tummy petticoat, which Alan said was so hideous he couldn't bear to see it. Then maybe he'd make love to her again, properly… but not while she was fat and flabby and ugly. How could she possibly have thought things were going to be back to normal after Annette and Charles left for South Africa?

She gave the twins their cornflakes, helped them dress and then quickly got ready. She was running late again. She still had to drop off Yair at the playgroup and then get to the community centre for the babies' class. Avi had joined the class and was doing nicely, although she was careful not to show her daughter any favouritism. Alan refused to allow Yair to do ballet. It was odd, really, because he didn't seem to care about anything else either of the twins did. As long as they didn't make a noise, or leave their toys lying around. It was as if he didn't want to know they were there. Except when they went to the Shapiro's. Then he and Ben would spend hours teaching Yair to kick a ball. Avi tried to join in too, sometimes, and Ben didn't mind. Even Alan was sweet to her then.

She and Ruth would sit on the patio and watch them play. It always made Ruth smile. It was so good to see her smile. She hardly ever did anymore, not since Jeremy had died. He'd been sick for ages. Ruth said it had been cancer. Brenda was just sorry she'd never met him. She would have liked a brother. Or a sister. Someone to talk to. Especially now. Sometimes she felt so alone.

***

The twins were bathed, fed and in bed. Asleep, Brenda hoped. Alan was late. He was working so hard. Ben said he really didn't know how he would have managed without him.

She heard Alan's key in the door and tensed. She hadn't taken her sleeping pills. She dreaded telling him that she thought she might be pregnant. His shadow loomed through the door. She clenched her hands.

'Alan?'

'You awake? Good. That makes a change.' He sat down on the bed and took off his shoes. Then he stood, unbuttoned his shirt and dropped it on the floor.

'Alan, we need to talk.'

'Later. I've been looking forward to this all day.' He unbuckled his belt and pulled off his trousers.

'No. Not tonight. Please. I need…'

The mattress sagged as he climbed in beside her and

reached for her.

'Alan, please. No. Please don't… not like that…' Her words were smothered by the pillow as he flipped her over.

She felt him tugging down her panties. She felt his hands on her shoulders, holding her down. She felt his knee forcing her legs apart. Oh God, would she ever get used to this? She felt him pushing himself into her, into her vagina. Thank God. That didn't hurt as much. She couldn't breathe. She prayed that would be all he wanted tonight.

It wasn't. She clenched her jaw as he drove into her again. The other way. She knew better than to struggle, but, sometimes, it was just so painful. That first time, a few days after Annette and Charles had left, he'd almost broken her nose pushing her face down so hard into the mattress when she'd cried and tried to get him off her. It had hurt so badly she'd screamed into the pillow. It hadn't helped. Then he'd taken her again, and again. Both ways. Then, for the first time in months, no, years, he'd said "I love you, sweetheart. That was great".

She lay still and he rolled off her, allowing her to turn over. She could breathe at last. She held her breath. He was propped up on one elbow, examining her face, her breasts. He squeezed one, hard. It hurt. She didn't flinch. What was he going to do now?

'I'm glad to see you're starting to get back into shape, sweetheart. Keep it up,' he said.

Tears ran down her face. She couldn't stop them. She hated

this. Hated it. She loved him, she really did, but this was too, too awful. It was bad enough when he'd only wanted oral sex, but this was a thousand times worse. What was wrong with her that she hated it so much? Was she really frigid, like Alan said?

'So what did you want to tell me, sweetheart?' Alan asked.

'Nothing. It's not important.'

She'd tell him when it was too late for him to make her have an abortion. She just had to hold out for another few weeks. Then he'd leave her alone, hopefully. She slept. Alan woke her later.

'I love you,' he said as he flipped her over.

She clenched her teeth.

CHAPTER 6
JOHANNESBURG, 1995

Brenda wilted in the chair in the waiting room at the clinic. Her eyes closed and she jerked them open. She was always so tired. Now that she had lost so much weight, she was almost as skinny as she had been before the twins, so Alan was starting to keep her awake a lot more at night too. Even if she'd taken an Ativan. Even if Zivah was crying. He just closed the door and let the baby cry. Zivah cried a lot. Having Thembi helped. Thembi had always been great with Zivah – and the twins. Right from the start, when she'd had to find a loo urgently and Thembi had offered to keep her place in the queue and watch the kids.

When she had got back, Thembi told her that mothers with babies didn't have to queue: they could go to the front and the officials would let them vote immediately. That was Thembi for you. She always knew everyone and everything, and she had never let her down. Brenda just wished Thembi would agree to sleep in. They had a perfectly good maid's room in the yard. It would save her a lot in taxi fares, and today, when the taxi strike stopped her from getting to work, she wouldn't have had to bring Zivah with her. She hoped the doctor wouldn't take too long. She had to fetch the twins at twelve-thirty. She needed the loo again.

'Mrs Silverman?' The nurse directed her to an examination room and handed her a little plastic container to wee into. Zivah waited in her pram in the corridor outside.

Dr Schwartz looked at the form she'd filled in.

'So, Brenda. May I call you Brenda? What seems to be the problem?'

'I think I have a bladder infection. I need to go to the loo all the time.'

'Any other symptoms? Could you be pregnant?'

'No, I had my tubes tied after Zivah was born. I'm just so tired, but I find it difficult to sleep. I suppose that's what you expect with a baby. She doesn't sleep through the night yet.'

'How old is she?'

'Sixteen months, nearly.'

'Do you have any other children?'

'Twins. They're six – next month actually.'

'No wonder you're tired. Okay, let's see if anything else is going on.'

Dr Schwartz pressed and prodded her, then looked at the results of her urine sample.

'Brenda, I'm going to send you for a couple of blood tests. You don't seem to have a urine infection, so I just want to check out a few more things. There seems to be some glucose in your urine.'

He handed her a form to take to the pathology lab and a prescription for "something mild to help you sleep". As she got up to leave, Zivah started crying.

'Would you like me to take a look at her?' Dr Schwartz asked. 'Maybe she has an ear infection that's keeping her from sleeping through. It shouldn't take long. Here. Let her sit on the exam table.'

She lifted Zivah out of the pram and held her on the table.

'Doesn't she sit yet?' Dr Schwartz asked, clearly surprised.

'No, not yet.'

He looked in Zivah's ears.

'When did she start crawling? Walking?'

'She hasn't.'

'Her ears are clear, but perhaps she should see a paediatrician, just for a routine check-up. I'll phone and make an appointment for you.'

Brenda sighed. Alan wouldn't be happy. He was still trying to get them onto a medical aid, but it was expensive and he was so busy trying to get the company sorted she really shouldn't bother him with this.

CHAPTER 7
JOHANNESBURG, 1999

Brenda peered blearily at the teacher. Avi's teacher. Or was she Yair's teacher?

'I'm sorry. You were saying…?'

'Are you okay, Mrs Silverman? You look a little…'

Brenda shook her head. God, she needed some coffee. How bloody stupid could she be – to run out of green Adaphens today, of all days. She hated coming to the school and having to make small talk with all the *kugel* moms. She needed her pills to get her through this. She needed some to clear out the cobwebs. Dr Schwartz was getting a little difficult about giving her another prescription, but, if she could just get to Randburg, Dr Viljoen would give her one for Yair's Ritalin, and that was almost as good. Or she could go to Dr Becker – he'd give her a script for the purple ones, but then she'd need more, because they weren't strong enough, and it was such a schlep to Alberton. She still had some yellow Ativans. So she at least would sleep tonight, unless Alan insisted… She shuddered.

'I'm fine. Just a bit of a migraine,' Brenda said.

'Poor you. Shame. Look, I'll be brief so you can get out of here. Aviva is doing really well. She's a delightful child, mature, very self-assured. Her reading is… Very pleased with… Hebrew… Excellent… A little leader… Very proud…' The woman's voice faded in and out.

Sweat trickled down Brenda's back.

'Yes, we are very proud of her,' Brenda muttered.

'I'm glad to hear that, Mrs Silverman. What I was saying is that we'll be very proud if Avi is chosen to represent Gauteng. It's a great honour for the school.'

'When was that? Why wasn't I told?' She felt awful. She'd skip going to Yair's teacher. Or had she already been to her? God, she hated parents' evening. Alan had said he'd come with her, but with the listing coming up – or had it already happened? Or was she confusing that with the Jewish businessman thingy? She'd been so disappointed for him. He worked so hard. He was such a good husband, such a wonderful provider. She was so lucky.

She smiled at the teacher, thanked her for all her hard work with Yair, and walked out. She needed to sleep. Stembiso was waiting to drive her home. First thing tomorrow, she'd go to Dr Fourie… No, wait, he was for Ativan and she still had some. She'd go to Dr Schwartz – no, Dr Viljoen. She mustn't get them muddled. She'd sort it all out in the morning.

***

Brenda couldn't sleep. She couldn't remember if she'd taken her slow-acting insulin. The Protophane. She'd better not take any more. They'd warned her about it when they showed her how to inject herself that first time. She'd test her blood in the morning. She took a white Ativan, just to chase the yellow one along a bit.

Alan came in.

'Hey, Brenda. You awake? We closed nearly ten rand up on the initial offer!'

'Tha...That's nice. Is that nice, Alan?' He'd been drinking. She could smell it on him. He'd been smoking again too. She really should tell him to stop.

'Of course it's fucking nice. It's a fucking twenty percent gain – on the first fucking day. If this keeps up, I'll sell off a few more of my shares – it won't affect my control of the company – and we'll buy that house... Brenda, are you listening?'

'Tha's nice, Alan.'

'Oh, what the hell am I trying to talk to you for?'

He flipped her over and tugged up her nightie. She no longer bothered with panties in bed. She buried her face in the pillow and prayed for the little yellow pill's precious gift of oblivion.

CHAPTER 8
JOHANNESBURG, 2005

Brenda stared in dismay at the blue plate in the meat kitchen sink. The blue plates were for milk. Zivah must have made a mistake again. But she couldn't blame Zivah. Trying to keep kosher was so confusing. There was so much to remember. She had found it so difficult, at first, after Alan came home from a *shiur* at the *shul* one night and announced that, from now on, they would be *frum* and she would have to keep kosher. Leah Rosenberg, Rabbi Rosenberg's wife, had been so patient with her, but she still kept getting things muddled. They all did.

Except Avi. Avi took to it all like a duck to water. She hadn't even objected when Alan said she could no longer wear jeans or strappy vests. Yair, on the other hand, had complained bitterly, but, after Alan increased his pocket money, he'd tried a little harder and now he mostly remembered to wear his *yarmulke*, and to more or less behave himself, although sometimes Brenda got the feeling that there was something not quite right with him. He was always burning incense in his room. She could smell it when she walked past. He wouldn't allow anyone to enter his room, except Thembi to make the bed, change the linen and tidy up a bit. Brenda also sometimes worried about Yair's friends. He never brought them home to visit anymore. He had a lot of friends, she knew. He was always going out with them. Stembiso was so kind to fetch him at all hours of the night, especially on weekends. The problem with Yair was that he went out far too much. She would really have to make good on her threat to ground him if his marks didn't improve.

Avi, however, seemed quite happy to stay home, even on Saturday nights after *Shabbos* came out. She also hadn't seemed to mind when Alan insisted that she give up gymnastics because it was wrong for her to perform "half naked" in front of men. Brenda had objected, though: Avi was really talented and she loved gymnastics. However, the very next day, Avi told her coach that she was giving up. Brenda only found out when Miss Levy phoned her and begged her to speak to Avi and persuade her to change her mind. Avi, however, said that, if that was what Daddy wanted, that was what she would do. Avi adored her father; it was actually very sweet to see, and Brenda was relieved that at last Alan was showing an interest in at least one of the children.

It had been Avi's idea that they build a second kitchen so that they would have one for meat and one for milk. Initially, Alan objected, but Avi pointed out how impressed everyone in the community would be. Brenda didn't care about that, but Avi had also been right when she said that it would make their lives so much easier. Avi had also suggested that they paint the door to the milk kitchen blue, to help Zivah remember. That hadn't been as successful.

When the renovations were finished, Alan asked Rabbi and *Rebbetzin* Rosenberg to help him to *kasher* the kitchens. Even the new stoves and dishwashers and microwave ovens had to be blessed. Then Avi went with Alan to *kasher* all the plates and glasses and everything at the *mikvah*. Yair stayed in his room and listened to some awful pounding music, the smell of incense permeating the entire house. It had made her feel so ill that she had gone to lie down.

Brenda had never heard of a *mikvah* for things. She thought only women went to the *mikvah*, although she'd never understood how being dunked in a communal bath could possibly be healthy. However, the first time she had gone – Alan had insisted – *Rebbetzin* Rosenberg had explained that the *mikvah* was not about bathing. 'You don't enter the *mikvah* to clean your physical body. It's about purity and holiness,' *Rebbetzin* Rosenberg had said.

Brenda found the whole ritual embarrassing: the *rebbetzin* examined her nails and checked that she was absolutely clean before allowing her to enter the ritual bath, which was really like a small swimming pool. She had to dunk her head right under the water. Brenda hated it, but *Rebbetzin* Rosenberg said she should go to the *mikvah* every month, after her period ended. She didn't want to, but Alan said it was expected of her. He went to the men's *mikvah* regularly too, although there was no real need, but he said it made him feel good and it gave him a chance to rub shoulders, as it were, with some of the really important people in the community.

Brenda took the offending blue plate out of the meat sink and sneaked it into the milk kitchen. There. No one would be any the wiser. She rinsed it under the tap and left it to dry. Thembi could put it away later. They wouldn't be using the milk kitchen again today, anyway. They always served a meat meal for *Shabbos* dinner.

She glanced at her watch and hurried to her bedroom. She had to get ready. She wondered if she would ever get used to the *Shabbos* dinner ritual. Alan always invited a huge crowd. Tonight, if she remembered correctly, there would be twenty of them, including Rabbi and *Rebbetzin* Rosenberg. Thank heavens only five of their children would be coming too. However, having the rabbi for dinner meant everything had to be perfect, and even more elaborate than the last time the Rosenbergs had come over. Brenda groaned quietly to herself.

She went into her bathroom and swallowed a green Adaphen. There. That would make the evening more bearable. She just had to remember to take her Ativan as soon as dessert was served. Otherwise, when their guests went home and Alan performed his husbandly duty, it would be unbearable. But if she took the Ativan too early, and the guests decided to stay and chat, she would fall asleep in front of them. It was a delicate balancing act, but she'd pretty much perfected it now. Anyway, if she did get it wrong, she could always blame it on her erratic sugar levels.

In the dining room, Thembi had already started setting the table under Avi's supervision. That meant everything would be perfect. For a fifteen-year-old, Avi was frighteningly meticulous. Sometimes, Brenda wondered if she shouldn't just go away and let Avi get on with running the household. Her daughter would probably do a far better job than she ever could.

'Why are you using the Royal Doulton dinner service tonight?' Brenda asked.

Avi ignored her and carried on putting the side plates next to each place setting.

'Avi, I'm speaking to you. Why are you using that set? You know I prefer the Country Roses,' Brenda said.

'We don't have enough Country Roses soup bowls. You broke three of them last week, remember?'

Brenda pursed her lips and walked out. She didn't remember.

She hurried to the kitchen where the caterers were setting up. The hot trays had been plugged in, the time switches set to turn off at midnight, and switch on again at eleven tomorrow morning so that lunch could be warmed up in time. They were expecting another big crowd after *shul* tomorrow. She hoped the caterers had brought enough food.

'It's all in hand, Mrs Silverman,' said Delores, of Delores' Delishus Delights (Kosher). 'Avi checked. It's not the same menu as the last time Rabbi Rosenberg came. And I've brought an extra tray of *tzimmis*. You just have to remember to cover it with additional tinfoil before you put it on the warmer tomorrow. Avi knows what to do...'

'And me. I also know how to put the food on,' said Zivah from her perch next to the kitchen table where she was pretending to feed her doll.

Brenda smiled at her younger daughter, but Zivah ran past her and launched herself at Yair as he came in through the back door. He caught her up in his arms and swung the little girl around as easily as he had done when she was a baby. Brenda couldn't believe Zivah was already eleven.

'Yair, you're filthy,' Brenda said. 'You'll make Zivah's dress all dirty and then she'll have to get changed. Where have you been? You're late. You'll be late for *Shabbos* and you know your father won't tolerate that.'

Yair ignored her and sauntered out of the kitchen, Zivah chattering excitedly at his heels.

Brenda sighed. Why couldn't she connect with *her* children when she got on so well with the kids in Alex? Those kids appreciated her. They loved her. They kept her sane.

***

Brenda hadn't wanted to go with the Union of Jewish Women into Alex Township to deliver food parcels, but Alan reminded her that, as Mrs Alan Silverman, she had a responsibility to do meaningful community work. So she had gone. It was so hot. Her *sheitel* made her head itch, but Alan said that, if *Rebbetzin* Rosenberg could wear one, so could she. She could feel the sweat dripping down her legs. It was ridiculous that Alan insisted that she wear thick stockings under her long skirt, and that her sleeves had to cover her wrists. Lots of *frum* women just covered their elbows, but Alan said she had to do it all properly. He said she had to set a good example to the children.

She'd seen something of the old Alan's boyish enthusiasm when he put on his new black broad-brimmed hat and black suit for the first time. He was so proud of his new "uniform". 'They like me, Brenda. They accept me – us. They don't care about my accent or where I grew up. When I'm dressed like this, I'm one of them,' he said. Then he'd presented her with her first *sheitel*.

There wasn't a tree in Alex and the sun burned down on the dusty playground. Brenda looked longingly at the little girls' dusty bare feet as they stamped and sang and kicked their legs high, so high. She'd never seen such flexibility, such talent in so many small children. The rhythm pumped through her veins. For the first time in years, she felt alive.

'Who is your dance teacher?' she asked a young girl as she handed her a Checkers packet with mealie meal, sugar, salt, soup powder, a bottle of sunflower oil and some washing powder.

'I am,' the child said. She introduced herself as Miriam Mazebuko. 'I love to dance.'

'What kind of dancing do you teach, besides traditional?' Brenda asked.

The girl shrugged.

'What about ballet?'

'What's that?' Miriam asked.

A week later, Brenda persuaded Stembiso to drive her to Alex again. With *The Turning Point* downloaded onto her laptop, she introduced Miriam to ballet. It was a match made in heaven.

Now Stembiso took her to Alex at least twice a week, more if possible. For a few hours, she was Brenda Jones again, but, at 4:30, Stembiso would come and transport her back to the suburban prison she shared with Alan.

PART 10
ALAN

CHAPTER 1
Johannesburg, 2012

Alan swallowed his decaf coffee. It was like drinking piss, but the good stuff would send his blood pressure soaring and give him heart palpitations. He looked at the papers waiting for him on the table. He'd swear Thembi had been smirking when she'd put them down – the *Daily Express* on top, with its screaming headline: "Alan Silverman – adulterer and wife abuser?"

That skinny, red-haired reporter was really gunning for him. And the photograph of him was revolting. It made him look like a guilty fugitive when all he'd been trying to do was follow Gideon through the throng of journalists and photographers lying in ambush for them on the Ntemi Piliso Street pavement. However, the picture of Yair was worse – he looked wasted. Good. The little fuck had really tried to screw him. Just wait till this was over. He'd chuck him out on his ear, for good this time.

He read the story. At least they hadn't named the women that fucking Ingrid Lamont had listed in her affidavit. The bitch. Who would have thought she would be so fucking vindictive? He should have known she'd be bad news the moment he'd laid eyes on her.

***

Johannesburg, 1996

She strode into Alan's office, hand outstretched, blood-red lips framing pearly teeth, blonde hair artistically cascading to just above her shoulders.

'Mr Silverman,' she said, her voice a sort of Marilyn Monroe growl. 'Ingrid Lamont. Thank you for the opportunity.' She seated herself prettily in the chair he indicated, crossed her ankles, smoothed her black skirt and looked at him appraisingly.

On closer examination, she wasn't as young as she had first appeared. There was just the slightest hint of sagging at the jaw line, but, with the top button of her white shirt giving a subtle hint of what he suspected had been carefully and expensively enhanced below, and the flawless perfection of her face, there was no doubt that she invested considerable time and money in presenting herself in the best possible light. He admired that. It indicated that she understood the importance of presentation. He hoped she would devote as much passion and energy to Silver Properties.

'Miss Lamont. Thank you for your time. You come highly recommended.'

Her lips pulled back a smidgen to reveal a few more pearly whites. 'Please, call me Ingrid.'

'I'm Alan.' It had taken a bit of getting used to, the way everyone in Jo'burg was on first name terms, from the tea girl to the CEO. Very different to London, but perhaps it had something to do with the new democracy – or because no one could pronounce the surnames of the new black elite.

She nodded, flipped open a black folder, poised her gold Cross pen over a blank page, and waited.

He gave her the spiel about how he had started the company with some seed capital – funny how hardly anyone ever asked about where the money had come from. When they did, he just told them he'd brought it back from his time in exile. He just had to say the word "exile" and he could see the admiration on their faces. Every single time.

'I want to take Silver Properties public in the next couple of years. Certainly before the end of the decade.'

She looked around his little office as if she had a smell under her nose. So, all right, the office was what charitably could be called "bare basics", but what more did he need? The old brown wooden desks and chairs he'd inherited with the building did the job, and he hadn't had time – or the money – to run about with fancy decorators. He had to get a business up and running. Every spare cent had been ploughed into finding and buying up the right property in the right areas at the right price. Potential investors would be far more impressed with a flourishing property portfolio than ergo-whatever chairs and a schmancy logo. He didn't care what this *alter kocker* bimbo thought. She'd be thinking something very different in a few years' time. If he employed her.

'Your job,' he said, 'would be to help ensure that the listing is successful. And that means Silver Properties must become a household name in the next two years. When we announce the IPO – I'm looking at mid-1999 – I want people to scramble for a slice of the action. I want it to be oversubscribed by a factor of ten. Get it right, and you could be a very wealthy young woman.'

She leaned back in the chair and her black jacket fell open, revealing what he could now see were undoubtedly enhanced assets below.

'Alan, I'm your girl.' She turned up her hard sell a notch. 'I've handled several listings in the last few years. A couple of them offshore. One of my clients is listing on the JSE main board next week.' Her client's wolfish face grimaced at him from the cover on the *Financial Mail* that lay in its plastic folder on his desk. He'd met that CEO at the charity auction at the Johannesburg Country Club and he'd warmly recommended Ingrid Lamont for her PR – and other – services.

Alan hoped he could inspire her loyalty and dedication without having to resort to the other. She really wasn't his type. Far too desperate. Too old… and a little too surgically enhanced. Anyway, Annette came up to Jo'burg from Cape Town on her constituency visits fairly regularly, although she was starting to be a little difficult again, probably because she was still hoping to have a child with poor Charles before her biological clock ran out. Meanwhile, Julia and Suzaan were filling in fairly satisfactorily. Susan too, when she was around. Things had improved with Brenda as well. She was trimmer and firmer than she had been in years, and she was also far more accommodating lately – if he got to her before she fell asleep. She still cried a lot, though. He'd told Dr Schwartz she needed stronger happy pills, but Schwartz said she also had to sort out her sugar levels, because that was what was affecting her moods.

'That's great, Ingrid,' he said. 'Send me a detailed proposal – and let's see if we can get this show off the ground sooner rather than later. We've only got a couple of years.'

***

Johannesburg, 1998

Ingrid reached over and stubbed out her cigarette. Alan wished she wouldn't smoke. It made his clothes smell. Brenda even complained at times that he should give up smoking. Ingrid's Sandton townhouse was always filled with ashtrays overflowing with red-ringed *stompies*, contrasting vividly with her decor. Everything in her townhouse was white – the tiles, the rugs, the furniture, the curtains – with some tasteful black or red bits and pieces artistically placed here and there. It was like being in a fucking cloud, or art gallery. She also

352

tasted like the bottom of a budgie cage.

The white sheet – one hundred percent percale cotton – fell away from what she liked to describe as her "perky" boobs as she swung her feet to the floor and stood up. He grinned as she quickly sucked in her stomach. No amount of circuit training could disguise the slight thickening of her waist.

'I've had a brilliant idea,' Ingrid said.

'You're always full of brilliant ideas. What's this one going to cost me?'

'Nothing you shouldn't be spending anyway. You're going to be nominated for the 1999 Jewish Businessman of the Year Award.'

She'd lost it. She had totally fucking lost it. Who the hell in the Jewish community would nominate him?

'You don't have to be Jewish to nominate anyone. I checked. You just have to be Jewish to be nominated. So I'm going to nominate you.'

'Waste of time. I'll never win.'

'Who said anything about winning? It's the nomination I'm after. And we've got just over a year to get you in shape. Look, it'll be a great hook to generate all kinds of positive stories about you and Silver Properties in the run-up to the listing. Let's get back to work, shall we?'

He watched, amused, as she reverse strip-teased back into her regulation black suit, white shirt and high heels, repainted her lips and fluffed out her platinum hair. He'd done his duty, so he also dressed and joined her downstairs in the

Ingrid Lamont and Associates offices. She was peering at the computer screen. She refused to wear glasses and she was still waiting for her new contacts to replace the ones she'd lost when Larry Goodman's wife had arrived at his office early to collect him for their theatre date. Larry had boasted to him about it at the gym. Poor sod actually thought Ingrid had the hots for him.

Alan liked Ingrid. Correction. He didn't like her at all. She was a fucking piranha. He admired her. Particularly, her single mindedness at using all her assets to promote herself, her business, her clients and, most importantly, to snare a husband – suitably able to keep her in the style to which she would love to become accustomed. She just might get her wish too. Larry was seriously contemplating divorcing his wife, and was in heavy discussions with Joe Rabinowitz to develop a plan of action that would limit the damage divorce would cause to his cash flow, and thus drive his intended – Ingrid – into the arms of another less financially encumbered bastard. Larry was nothing if not a realist.

Alan hoped that *shyster* lawyer wouldn't solve Larry's problem before the listing. She was good, was Ingrid. She couldn't write a parking ticket, let alone a press release – she employed freelance writers to handle that side of her operation – but she was well in with most of the influential financial journalists in Jo'burg. The male ones, anyway. Plus, her hare-brained promotional ideas usually worked. He had a file full of press clippings to prove it. So he'd continue to fuck

her for now, and consider her crazy Jewish Businessman of
the Year Award idea.

***

'Look at it this way, darling,' Ingrid said as Alan settled into
the black leather client chair on the opposite side of her shiny
white desk.

He suppressed the mild sense of panic that always
threatened to choke him as the chair wrapped itself around
him, sucking at him, pulling him into its softness. He forced
himself to think of it as a continuation of what they'd been
doing upstairs, only quieter, where he was on top. One night,
after a superb bottle of Hamilton Russell Pinot Noir, she'd
confessed that she had chosen that chair deliberately. 'It makes
whoever sits there more vulnerable,' she'd said. He thought
claustrophobic smothering would be a more apt description.
It reminded him of his mother, but he wasn't going to tell
Ingrid that. He'd never tell anyone about that, ever. He let
Ingrid think she was in charge – at least in her office. In her
bedroom, it was a different story. There, she was amazingly
compliant.

Alan lifted the translucent white mug of strong, hot coffee
she'd prepared for him and sipped. Just the way he liked it. He
smiled. Ingrid always paid attention to detail.

'You need the support of the Jewish business mafia to
ensure the success of your IPO,' she said.

'What about my ANC buddies?'

'They don't invest. They don't have the money. Not yet. They just want their share.'

'Which I am going to have to give them.'

It wasn't a question. Alan knew it was rapidly becoming the reality of the "new" South Africa. Even ANC guys he'd known in London now didn't give him the time of day unless there was something in it for them. At least four of the property tenders he'd gone after in the past six months had come with unofficial "incentive" or "commission" requirements attached. And the amounts where getting bigger all the time.

'They're getting fucking greedy,' Alan said. 'And when Mandela retires, it's going to be a thousand times worse – you just mark my words. Everyone will be scrambling to fill the old man's shoes and that will take money – from *schmucks* like me.'

'So who're you going to back?' Ingrid fancied herself as a political analyst, but all she really did was parrot whatever her latest fuck had told her. 'I think Mbeki would be the obvious one,' she said.

Ah hah. So now he had a pretty good idea of who she'd been *shtupping* last night. Not that he cared. However, Ingrid was pretty useful for spreading opinions and snippets of information to the right ears. Alan had learned that the hard way when he had heard one of his more outrageous rants being repeated to him, almost word for word, by Larry in the gym one day soon after Larry decided, again, that it was too expensive to divorce his wife.

'Mbeki's certainly the obvious choice,' Alan agreed. And then he decided to stir a bit. 'But I'm not sure he's the right choice. He's too cold. I met him a couple of times in London. He doesn't inspire loyalty like the old man does. Nah. I dare not put all my eggs in the Mbeki basket. It'll be tricky, but I'll have to keep my options open – spread it around. Bloody hell.'

Ingrid gave him one of her self-satisfied, smug, "aren't I just so clever" smiles.

'Of course you have to give to them. They hold all the strings, remember. But, in return, they'll ensure you get the tenders you want. So, yes, you have to go after the Jewish vote – and money – but you also can't neglect your ANC *chommies*. Don't look so pained, Alan. It won't cost you nearly as much – at least not financially – to become an admired member of the Jewish community.'

'I'll *schmooze* them if I have to, but I'm not going to wear a fucking black hat, if that's what you're suggesting.'

She looked utterly bewildered. Ah, he'd found something this know-it-all didn't know about.

'A black hat?'

'It's what those ultra-*frum* nutcases wear. They still dress like they're living in medieval Russia or something. I'm not going to be like that. Can you see Brenda in a *sheitel* – those wigs the strictly observant Jewish women wear?'

Ingrid threw back her head and her gurgling laugh tinkled

like ice cubes onto her desk.

'No one said you had to be like that. Just be more of a nice, committed, generous member of the community. You know – be a *mensch*.'

Alan wondered which of her clients had taught her that word. He'd bet anything the *oke* wasn't being much of a *mensch* at the time either. Whoever it was had probably let her climb on top of him. That's when she gave her best advice, Larry said. However, Alan would never let her, or anyone else, mount him. Never again. But he made sure he gave Ingrid just enough in the bedroom, and the bank, to carry through to her goodwill in the office.

'You have to support the Jewish charities,' Ingrid said. 'And let it be known at that you support them. Anonymously, of course. That kind of thing.'

Alan nodded. He could do that. He already did it. Maybe he'd just have to step it up a little; maybe refurbish the gym at the twins' school.

'One more thing,' Ingrid said.

'What?'

'You're going to have to avoid doing anything that could tarnish your reputation as a nice, devoted Jewish family man.'

That was a joke, coming from her. 'Meaning?'

'Once you become a public figure – and you are going to be a very public figure even if it kills me – your private life becomes fair game.'

'Meaning?' Alan knew exactly what she meant.

She'd given Larry the same spiel. 'She fucking told me that while I was in the middle of *shtupping* her, would you believe,' Larry had said. They'd laughed so much that all the guys in the gym cloakroom had stared at them.

'Do I have to spell it out?' Ingrid asked in a coy little girl voice.

He nodded, enjoying her feigned discomfort.

'Okay. No more screwing around,' she said.

'With you?'

'No, of course not. Just not with anyone who could land you on the back page of the *Sunday Times*. If Brenda's not enough for you – and it certainly doesn't seem like she is – then play safe and keep it in the family, as it were.'

'And you're family, I take it?'

She smiled. 'I'm family.'

Official business over, he let her lead him back upstairs.

***

Johannesburg, 2012

Alan had been so right about Mbeki and the ANC. He should have written a book back then. They'd be calling him a prophet now, instead of writing all this crap about him in the papers, but at least they hadn't named the women in Ingrid's affidavit. It would kill whatever credibility he still had with the ANC if they ever found out how many of their esteemed female leaders were more than willing to go above and beyond the call of duty to keep a comrade happy. However, none of them – not Annette, not Susan, not any of the others – deserved to be pilloried for it, and neither did he. It was all just good, albeit not so clean, fun, and it didn't hurt anyone.

CHAPTER 2
ENGLAND, 1988

Alan rolled off the girl and walked into the bathroom. What the fuck was her name again? Miriam? No, that was the one in Manchester. Or was it Liverpool? Patsy – no, Portia…. Damn. He'd have to ask her for a business card.

'Be right back, sweetheart,' he said as he closed the door.

He was losing track of them. She hadn't been too bad, this one. Better than most. Not as good as Brenda – as Brenda used to be before she got all gross and fat and revoltingly pregnant. In fact, she'd been pretty damn good. Perhaps he'd see her again. She said she lived in London. She was only visiting Leeds for a few days, on business. Like him. He'd seen her at the WOAH talk. It was hard to miss her. She was quite beautiful if you liked that sort of look. A sort of grown-up Pretty. The same silky chocolate complexion. Still very slender. Unusual for a black woman. Unusual woman, period. She didn't fawn all over him, like all the others. She'd just looked at him, smiled and left the hall.

He was pleasantly surprised when she came up to him in the pub at the hotel later.

'Good talk,' she said. Then she perched on the stool next

to him and looked at him appraisingly.

They chatted. It turned out she was South African too. She said her parents had gone into exile after Sharpeville or the Rivonia raid or trial or something. Her dad's name sounded vaguely familiar. She'd been born in England. She said she'd always wanted to fuck a *boer*. So they went up to her room.

***

She smiled at Alan as he rolled back to his side of the bed.

'You're quite something, you know that, Alan? You're more than just a pretty face too. But if I don't get something to eat soon, I'm going to die of hunger. Love can only sustain you for so long, you know.'

He grinned at her. 'Okay, sweetheart, I get the hint. I'll go now. I have to be getting back to London early in the morning anyway.'

'Wifey waiting, is she?'

He frowned. Of course she'd be waiting. Brenda was always bloody waiting with that huge stomach that was getting more and more obscene by the day, and no wonder. She wasn't only going to inflict one howling brat on him. No. She was having twins. She'd even tried to blame him for it, saying it showed how strong and virile he was. Bullshit.

'You know what?' He pulled her back down next to him. 'I'm not in any rush. And I'll feed you after this, if you're a good girl.'

She was a very good girl. Very willing. Not like Annette. In fact, when he and Annette had done it in the WOAH offices after he found out about Brenda being pregnant and she'd comforted him on the sofa, it had been a bit of a disaster. Annette clearly hadn't grown up. She still regarded sex as a battle for domination. No wonder she had married Charles. She could dominate him, the poor sod. However, this little black beauty had the right idea. Even if she wasn't Brenda. None of them were.

As they finished their very late breakfast in the hotel restaurant, he said, 'You know. This is fun. Why don't I call my office and tell them my car has broken down? What do you say, sweetheart?'

She got up and walked to the payphone.

'I'll tell my husband I'll be home tomorrow, or maybe on Friday. That it's taking longer than I expected to close the deal.' She winked. 'And my name is Susan.'

***

Alan pushed open the flat door. He picked up a scrap of paper lying on the floor and put it on the entrance table. Brenda was getting sloppy. He walked into the bedroom. *Fuck.* What the hell was going on here? It was after lunch and the bed was still a mess. There was a damp towel on the floor. Brenda was normally so tidy. He walked into the bathroom. There were towels all over the place. In the kitchen was a trail of instant coffee from one side to the other. Where was Brenda? She knew he didn't like coming home to a dirty flat.

He phoned the Shapiros. No reply. Brenda must have gone out to do more last minute baby shopping with Ruth. He phoned the office.

'Mr Silverman!' the switchboard operator squeaked. 'Where on earth have you been? Mr Shapiro just asked me to call the police.'

'Why, what's wrong? I told you that I had car trouble. I've only just got home.'

'Didn't you see the note Mr Shapiro put under your door? You'd better get to the hospital.'

'What's happened?'

'Just go. Mr Shapiro is waiting for you there.' She put down the phone. Fat bitch. Something must have happened to Brenda. Now he'd have to explain why he was so late. Shit. Oh well, at least he'd had fun. Susan was a really good sport. They had arrangements to meet at that new little restaurant in Soho tomorrow night. Her husband was on his way to Moscow. He'd be gone for three weeks, she'd said.

He read Ben's scribbled note. *Oh fuck.* Why did this have to happen while he was out of town? He hoped she was okay. He loved her. He didn't want anything to happen to her. Women didn't still die in childbirth, did they? He hoped she'd have had the brats by now, because Ruth would expect him to hold Brenda's hand through the whole messy business and he couldn't imagine anything worse. It had been so civilised in the olden days when the fathers were expected to pace the corridors and smoke cigars. Now they had to be supportive and help their wives. Yeah right. What a load of crap.

He remembered to buy a bunch of flowers from the flower sellers outside the hospital. Then he hurried into her ward. Ben and Ruth were there. Ben looked like thunder. Ruth looked exhausted. Brenda looked terrible. Her face was puffy and all splotchy. She'd obviously been crying. There was a drip in her arm. From the heap under the blankets, she didn't look so pregnant anymore, so the babies were gone. Thank God.

'Where the hell have you been?' Ben asked.

'Shh, Ben,' Ruth said. 'He's here now. That's all that matters. Let's leave the children alone.'

Alan put the flowers down and looked at Brenda who was propped up on pillows. She was crying again. He didn't know what to say to her.

'So you had them.'

'Yes.'

'And you're okay?'

'Yes.'

'Good.'

'They're in the nursery. You can go and see them if you want.'

'That's okay. Maybe later.'

'Don't you want to know what they are?'

'Huh?'

'I mean, don't you want to know if they are girls or boys?'

'Oh, right.'

'We've one of each. A girl and a boy.'

'Oh.'

'They were born this morning. At about two o'clock.'

'What time did you come to the hospital?'

'Dunno. About nine o'clock, I think.'

'So it didn't take very long.'

'Nine o'clock yesterday morning, Alan. I was in labour all day. And all night. And then they had to do an emergency Caesar. It was terrible. Where were you? I needed you. I was so frightened.'

He groaned inwardly. 'Oh, for Christ's sake, Brenda,' he snapped, his guilt making him more brusque than he intended. 'You're not the first woman to have a baby. Babies. Don't make such a fucking big deal about it. I'm here now, aren't I?'

She looked at him. She just looked at him. He didn't know what else to say.

'Look, I'm tired. I didn't sleep much last night.' Susan hadn't let him. 'I'm going home to shower and catch a bit of kip. I'll see you tomorrow.'

She obviously needed a chance to get over it. The good thing was, now that she'd had the kids, she would soon be his beautiful little Brenda again and maybe it wouldn't be so bad being married. He glanced back as he reached the door. Her white, tear-stained face peered at him over the sheet she had pulled up under her chin; her dark curls were haloed around her head on the white pillow. His breath caught in his throat.

She had never looked more defenceless. He felt himself stirring and hurried down the corridor.

***

Brenda's vulnerable little face stayed with Alan all the way back to the flat. By the time he'd showered and tidied up, it was late. He walked down to the local pizzeria and ordered supper. He'd let Brenda have a quiet, peaceful night. She clearly needed it. He'd visit her in the morning. It was Saturday, so he didn't have to go to the office. He went to bed, crushed her pillow in his arms and breathed in her scent. He dreamed of her. His old dream. The way she had been on the kibbutz. The way she had been when they first got to London. The way she was going to be again. His beautiful, vulnerable, sweet little Brenda. She was back.

He stopped at Boots on his way to the hospital and bought a bottle of Charlie perfume. A large one. She loved Charlie. She'd had a rough time, poor little thing, so this would cheer her up.

He rushed down the corridor to her ward, pushed open the door and walked in, smiling. Brenda was propped up on the bed. Two enormous mounds of pasty lard etched with thick blue lines spilled out of her nightie. A nurse was standing next to her, holding a bundle of baby blankets. A second bundle appeared to be attached to one of the mounds.

'Alan,' Brenda said. 'You're just in time to see me feed

them. Look, I'm starting to get the hang of this.'

The perfume crashed to the floor and he stumbled back. In the corridor, he propped himself up against the wall, gasping for air.

'Are you feeling all right? Let me get you a chair,' a nurse said.

He put his head between his knees, his heart hammering. That was horrible. That was the most disgusting thing he'd ever seen since, since... since... He was crying. He wrapped his arms around himself and rocked, backwards and forwards, trying to blot out his worst, recurring nightmare. Those... Those grotesque white and blue appendages that had burst, alien-like, from Brenda's beautiful chest... it was horrible. Revolting. Disgusting. Bile surged up his gullet. He clamped his hand over his mouth and ran down the corridor to the gents' he'd passed on his way in.

He slid down the cold tiled walls and lay on the floor, his arms wrapped around his knees, shaking, sweat pouring from his forehead, down his back. He couldn't go back into that ward. Not while it... they... were still there. Pulling at her. Sucking. Sucking, suck, suck, suck. Suck hard, suck harder, harder, harder and she was panting and groaning and throwing back her head and moaning and squirming and rubbing herself against him, faster and harder until he couldn't help it. He tried to control himself, he really tried, but he couldn't and he came and she smacked him and then she heaved herself up on top of him again and squirmed, and rubbed and moaned, then she dug her nails into his head and he had to lick and suck and suck and then she shuddered and climbed off him and then... and then she was bending over him again, forcing him to suck, suck, suck the soft, pasty white blubber, smothering him, drowning him in fat and flab, but she wouldn't let him go; he couldn't break free; he was suffocating, choking, sucking, sucking... He couldn't do it, not anymore... He had to hide. Somewhere she couldn't find him. He had to run, to find somewhere to hide.

'You okay, guv? Did someone die?' An elderly man was regarding him curiously.

Alan took a shuddering breath. He had to get control of himself. He had to calm down. He had to deal with this. He sat up, his back against the wall, and pushed himself to his feet. Swaying, he tottered to the basins and splashed cold water on his face. He waited. How long would it take?

He peered around the door of the gents'. Eventually, Brenda's door opened and he saw the nurse wheeling a basket down to the nursery. Good. They were gone.

He took a deep breath and peeped into her ward. Thank God. Those monstrous white breasts with their swollen blue veins were covered by the sheet... but they were there, they were still there, just waiting for him. He could feel sweat starting to drip down his back again.

Brenda looked at him sadly. 'What's the matter? Why did you leave? I was doing my best to feed them, but it's not easy. It hurts.'

'Then don't do it,' Alan said. 'You really don't have to. They can't expect you to feed twins. Just give them a bottle or something.'

'You won't think I'm a failure if I don't breastfeed?'

Hell no!

'You're all that matters,' Alan said. 'If you can't do it, you can't. That's all there is to it.'

'You're sure? I don't want to disappoint you.'

'Sweetheart, I want my girl back. That's all. My girl doesn't breastfeed. Okay?' The trusting, grateful smile she gave him made his heart turn over. It was going to be okay. As soon as she was back to normal. As soon as she got her little ballerina tits back.

***

There was a gentle knock at the door and the Shapiros walked in.

'So, Daddy Silverman, what do you think of your angels?' Ruth asked. She looked at him curiously. 'Are you feeling all right, Alan? You look a little pale.'

Ben didn't say anything.

'I'm fine, 'Alan said. 'And the babies are just perfect. Like their mother.' He wasn't going to tell the children's self-appointed grandparents that he hadn't seen them yet. Not properly.

Ben smiled at him. Good. He'd got over his anger – he

always did. They chatted. It was getting late. Alan watched impatiently while Brenda held the little bottle and fed one bundle while Ruth fed the other one. The nurse showed her how to burp it. Milk dribbled out the corner of its mouth. Alan turned away in disgust. The Shapiros left. He watched them disappear into the lift. Then he really couldn't wait any longer. He counted to ten. He hurried to the tube station. He just had enough time to get home, change and get to Soho... and to dark, adventurous Susan with her silky, dark, taut little breasts and generous spirit.

CHAPTER 3
LONDON, 1990

This was a nightmare. Alan felt as if he was caught up in some cruel surreal acid trip. His beautiful Brenda was still trapped inside a gross slut. Ruth said it could take a while for Brenda to regain her figure. She didn't say how long a while was, but he was an optimist. Things would get back to normal. Eventually. They had to. Meanwhile, he couldn't bear to touch her. He could hardly bear to look at her. She was fat and flabby… and clingy. She smelled musty and stale too. She had turned into a weeping, spineless version of *Ma*.

However, he knew that somewhere in that sodden lump of flab was the only woman he'd ever truly loved, the only woman he'd ever really wanted… and she loved him. So he forced himself to let her blow him. That's all he could stomach. She wanted to. Needed to. She loved him so much, and he loved her. He really did… but she was always bloody crying. All the time. Like her bloody brats. Especially the girl. That kid didn't stop, and, when she did, the boy started. And Brenda was hopeless at keeping them quiet. She was just hopeless, period. She moped around all day in a dirty dressing gown. There was always a huge pile of dirty nappies in the bathroom. She was constantly nagging for disposables, but they were too damn expensive. The bonus Ben had given him – richly deserved, Ben said, and who was he to disagree? – was great. He'd put it into the rainy day account for when it was really needed. He was certain it would be needed at some stage. If there was one good thing his mother had taught him, it was that there would always be rainy days, often when you least expected it. So there was no way he was going to spend his hard-earned salary and commissions on disposables when she could bloody well wash real ones. She had nothing else to do all day. She didn't clean the flat. She hardly ever even made his supper anymore. They were living on Chinese takeaway and it was beginning to show.

He'd had to start jogging again. It would help him keep in shape... and get him out of the flat. Thank heavens Shapiro & Son was still so busy, which meant he had to work longer hours as well. It gave him an excuse to go out without arousing Ben and Ruth's suspicions. Brenda was so out of it she barely noticed whether he was there or not. When he made a detour to Susan – her husband travelled a lot – or Jenny or Vivian, he could also catch some kip and no one was any the wiser.

It was getting so bad lately that even being alone with Annette was becoming increasingly difficult, but he couldn't go there again. A bit too close to home. Maybe. Or possibly more convenient? Perhaps. Susan's husband was going to be home for the next few months.

'Bye, Brenda. I'm going now,' he called. He didn't think she heard.

Both kids were screaming. She was probably late with their bottles again. They'd screamed all night. He'd battled to wake her to deal with them. No wonder he was irritable. Now he was exhausted. It couldn't go on like this.

He slammed the door behind him. Annette was meeting him down at the Anti Apartheid Movement offices. She had sounded really excited when she had phoned him. Apparently FW was going to be making some big announcement. Not that he cared.

***

Annette tucked her arm through Alan's as they made their way up to WOAH's offices.

They settled down companionably on the sofa. He relaxed. Annette was comfortable to be with. She never made demands on him. She felt nice and warm against him. FW droned on and on.

He dozed off. He felt her hard, neat little body snuggling against him and smiled. Brenda always liked to snuggle. He slipped his hand up under her shirt and massaged her little breasts. They felt nice, so nice...

She jumped up. He blinked.

'I don't believe it. I don't believe it!' she said.

'What?' Oh shit. She wasn't Brenda.

Annette threw herself at him. He put his arms around her. What the hell, why not?

Afterwards, he smiled at her. So she wasn't Brenda, but she wasn't too bad this time. Charles must have taught her a thing or two. Who would have thought?

***

Alan got back to the flat in the early hours. Brenda was fast asleep and so were both twins, for once. She looked so vulnerable with her curls spread across the pillow and the sheet tucked up under the chin. Oh God, he still wanted her, so much. He needed her. He'd missed her so badly. He reached out for her.

'Brenda,' he whispered. 'Sweetheart, wake up.'

'Alan,' she murmured and turned towards him.

He felt her flabby stomach and boobs rubbing against him. The familiar nausea welled up in his throat. He turned his back on her so she wouldn't see the tears of frustration that rose, unbidden, in his eyes. He couldn't bear this. She was still crying when he fell asleep.

CHAPTER 4
LONDON, 1994

Alan was content. Almost. Things were going well at Shapiro and Son. Since Jeremy's death, Ben was taking less and less interest in the business. Which more or less left him free to run it as he liked. Ben trusted him. Ruth adored him – and Brenda. They regarded the twins and Zivah as their grandchildren. Spoilt them like that too. So he insisted Brenda take them to the beautiful Golders Green house as often as possible. But they hadn't been there for *Shabbos* supper for ages. Not since Zivah was born.

The fifty thousand pounds the Shapiros had given the twins at their birth and another twenty-five thousand for Zivah – "for their education", Ben had said – had been generously supplemented on each of the twins' birthdays. He'd opened a special investment account for each of the kids at Ben's bank on the advice of Ben's bank manager, who he had met at Yair's *bris*. He'd deposited some of Ben's gift into the accounts. The banker assured him that it was a solid long-term investment that would grow steadily until the children needed it in eighteen or so years.

The bulk of the children's "education fund" was safe in his "rainy day" account, which was growing nicely, supplemented by the bonuses and dividends he declared for himself as well as the commission he was entitled to for all the overtime he put in on the really big deals.

Yes. Things were going really well at work… and then he went home. To Brenda.

***

Brenda. Her body was slowly getting back into shape, thanks to the hours she was putting in down at the community centre, but it wasn't the same, and no amount of exercise would remove that hideous Caesar scar or take away the tuck of tummy that folded over it. He suggested a boob job, but she refused. She said she was scared of more surgery, but he couldn't really complain. He still couldn't do it missionary style with her, but now she enjoyed it when they did it the new way. She said she hadn't liked it very much at first and sometimes still pretended she didn't want to. It had become something of a game that just made it all the more exciting for them. God he still loved her so much. And she loved him.

Sometimes, he saw glimpses of the old Brenda and that gave him hope, which helped him deal with the other times, like when she'd fall asleep almost before he got going. It frustrated the hell out of him. He liked her to be still and quiet after their game playing, but sometimes he suspected she actually fell asleep on the job as it were. She often didn't even hear – or pretended not to – when one of the kids started screaming in the middle of the night, which meant he had to get up and go shut the brat up before it woke everyone in the building. That wasn't fair, because he still had to go to work in the morning.

He also missed Annette. She had been a lifesaver. Especially after Susan and her husband had gone back to South Africa.

'Our exile is over,' Susan had said.

'But you've never been to South Africa. You have no idea what it's like. Not all the whites there are like me. If you think they are just going to hand everything to you on a silver platter, you're in for a shock.'

'It's our country, Alan. We are going to be needed to reclaim it and then rebuild it.'

He'd wished her luck.

Then Annette had gone back to South Africa too. He'd thought he and Brenda would be fine again, but then Brenda went and fell pregnant and she didn't realise until it was too late to do anything about it. But there would be no more accidents, no matter how passionate they got. He'd made jolly sure of that.

***

'Alan, I had a call from the auditors this morning. They want to go over the figures with us,' Ben said.

Fuck, fuck, fuck. 'Is there a problem?'

Alan knew damn well there was a problem. He'd meant to deal with it, like he had last year before the annual audit, but he'd been so busy making Ben even more money and coping with the twins and Zivah and everything. Stupid, stupid. He'd hoped they'd overlook it, but he might have guessed that that arsehole Max Lieberthal wouldn't miss a fucking thing. Now it was too late. He had to delay the meeting for as long as possible. They set the meeting for next Thursday. Alan walked back to his office and buzzed Josephine Smith. She was standing at his desk, shorthand notebook and pencil in hand virtually before he'd taken his hand off the button.

'Yes, Mr Silverman.' She was secretly in love with him, silly old cow. So he sent her flowers on her birthday and "accidentally" touched her hand whenever the opportunity arose.

'Miss Smith, please get Mr Jenkins on the line for me. And after I've spoken to him, I have to go out.'

Mr Jenkins was in conference, but his secretary at the Cayman National Bank and Trust Company (Isle of Man) said he would return the call. She and Miss Smith had set up a tentative time of around 4pm.

Alan beamed at her, touched her gratefully on her shoulder and walked out of the office. Miss Smith, the perennial blush seeping up her crepey, wobbly neck into her puffy, over-rouged cheeks, was too overcome to ask where he was going or when he'd be back.

He caught a taxi to the travel agent he had spotted in Patten Street, not far from the ANC's offices. The first available flight was on Sunday. He paid for the tickets with his Shapiro and Son credit card.

Later, after a meeting with the Liverpool developer, and the managing agent of the new office block they'd acquired in Bath, he gave Mr Jenkins precise instructions about his rainy day account.

Then he went home.

***

'We're going home,' Alan told Brenda when she had finally managed to put the twins and the baby to bed.

She looked terrible. She was still in the throes of her annual winter cold. She was constantly whining about how hard it was to deal with three kids under the age of five, one an eleven-month-old baby, and how tired she was.

'Brenda, did you hear me? We're going home.'

'What are you talking about?'

'We're going to South Africa. Home.'

He chuckled at her stunned expression.

He hadn't told her that he'd started making enquiries back in December, when the South African Government had announced the end of national conscription. The clerk at the embassy had told him, quite rudely, he thought, that it was unlikely he would be prosecuted if he returned.

Brenda put down her bottle of pills. 'When?'

'Sunday.'

Her mouth opened, then closed. Then opened again. 'Sunday? This Sunday?'

'What's your problem? All you have to do is pack the clothes. Everything else can stay. We'll buy what we need when we get to Jo'burg. It will be a fresh start, sweetheart. You'll get the nanny you've always wanted. And, with help, you'll feel better and be back to your old self in no time.'

He thought that would make her happy, but she kept asking questions. He hoped she wouldn't ask him about Ben and Ruth.

She asked, 'What did Ben say when you told him? You didn't tell me you'd given in your notice. When did you do that? Are they getting a replacement for you?'

'I haven't told him – anyone – and neither will you. I cannot abide soppy, weepy goodbyes.'

She objected. She argued. She cried. He really didn't want to deal with this. Anyway, why should he explain anything to her? She was just damn lucky he was taking her and her brats with him. He could leave them behind. Perhaps he should just leave them… but she loved him, and he loved her. They belonged together. And there'd be no more children, ever. He should have insisted that she get her tubes tied after the twins were born. Then it wouldn't have mattered that he'd been so damn upset about Annette leaving him that he forgot to take care when he got home and saw her looking so fucking seductive under the blankets. He had yanked the blanket off her and ripped off her nightie. God, he wanted her so badly, right there, as she lay looking at him with her big, beautiful eyes, but her boobs... her flabby stomach... he just couldn't. Frantic now, he flipped her over, as usual, and drove into her, again and again and it felt so soft and wet and amazing. He realised he was in her vagina but it felt so good after so long... and then he took her again, the other way and it was pretty damn good as well. It always was… and she had loved it. She had pretended not to, of course, because she knew how much that excited him. But then she'd gone and got all bloated and revoltingly pregnant again and they'd had to be satisfied with oral sex only for fucking ages.

However, she was almost over the pregnancy now. She'd lost weight and firmed up a lot and was his little Brenda again. Almost. Plus, she was his wife. The others really didn't mean anything.

He reached out for her. She groaned in anticipation.

'No, Alan,' she teased. 'The kids. Zivah will wake any minute – you know she doesn't sleep through the night yet.'

He smiled at her. She was still so shy sometimes, so worried one of the kids would walk in on them. He got up and locked the door – to make her feel more secure so that they could both really enjoy themselves. Then he lifted her off the bed and gently positioned her over the dressing table stool just the way she liked, her cute, white little bottom all ready for him.

***

On Friday, Alan surprised Miss Smith with a little posy of flowers on her desk.

She brushed back her greying hair and glowed. 'Oh, Mr Silverman, you are so good to me. Thank you. It's not my birthday, so why?'

'Because you are my rock, Miss Smith. I could never manage without you. Finding you in the typing pool was the best thing that ever happened to me – apart from Mrs Silverman, of course.' They both laughed. 'I just want to remind you how much I appreciate you and everything you do for me. I know you'll hold the fort for me next week. I have to go check on the Birmingham project again.'

Her pale eyes glowed. 'Mr Silverman, if you would pardon my presumption. I do believe you are the best thing that ever happened to Shapiro and Son. Honestly, I do. Joan over in personnel agrees.'

He was tempted to give her a peck on the cheek when he left the office that evening, but didn't. The old girl would have had an orgasm on the spot. Probably the first in her pathetic little life. And he was through making fat old women come.

On Saturday, he left Brenda in peace with the kids to finish packing up the flat while he went to say goodbye to Elizabeth. It had taken him a while to find her. In fact, he had been through quite a few after Annette had left and Brenda had told him she was pregnant again. He'd been so upset that he'd walked out and couldn't bring himself to go back for three days. Brenda had given him a blow job to die for when he returned.

Elizabeth was a good sport too, undemanding and accommodating. He'd miss her.

'Same time next week, my love?' Lady Elizabeth confirmed as she let him out the Mayfair flat her husband had bought for her, for when she had to come down from the country for one or other of her charity functions.

He nodded and kissed her lightly on the lips. 'Same time.'

The next morning, the taxi arrived promptly at 9am to take them to Heathrow. It was a squash with their luggage and all the baby's paraphernalia. Brenda was pale and weepy. He'd had to be quite forceful when persuading her that she didn't have to phone Ruth or Sally or that stupid cow down at the community centre to say goodbye. The twins were quiet, for once. The baby slept. Fortunately, she hadn't started crawling yet – a late starter, Ruth always said – so they could just strap her in the pram where she slept or gazed around with her large brown eyes. The plane took off and he looked down as the city receded. He wondered if he'd ever see London again.

CHAPTER 5
JOHANNESBURG, 2012

Alan had never gone back to London. After Ben's fucking revelations, he supposed he never could – even though he hadn't done anything wrong. He'd just taken what was due to him, seeing Ben was such a bloody miser. What on earth had made Ben come after him like that? After so many years. It didn't make sense. Ingrid was a different kettle of fish. Apparently, her business had fallen apart after he had fired her. But it was so worth it – almost.

***

Johannesburg, 2000

'But we knew you'd never win,' Ingrid protested.

'Big mistake, that, Ingrid. Big mistake. I don't like losing. It makes people think I'm not a winner.'

She frowned. 'If you remember, Alan, the whole idea of entering was just to get you good publicity for the listing.' He did remember, but he wasn't going to tell her that, and it had been a good listing. It had been hailed as one of the most spectacular listings of the year.

'Really, you're just being difficult.' She leaned back and glared at him.

He slammed his hand on her white desk and struggled out of the smother chair. He'd perched himself right on the edge, in preparation for this scene, but the chair still got the better of him. It helped to fuel the anger he'd been working himself up to for the last few days.

'Watch it, Ingrid. I'm your client. If you can't do your fucking job properly, don't blame me. I wanted to win Businessman of the Year. You were supposed to make it happen – that's what I pay you for.'

That hurt her, he could see. Good. She was way past her sell-by date. He was seriously considering changing agencies. It was getting more and more difficult to keep fucking her. She made him sick. She made his skin crawl. She was old and soft and flabby, getting more and more like *Ma* by the day, only not as fat, yet. She was also becoming increasingly needy and whiny. Some of the humiliating things she was willing to do for him, to let him do to her, startled even him. It was depraved at times – there was no other word for it. He certainly didn't enjoy it – he was just curious to see how far she would go.

She was also delusional. She was starting to drop some not so subtle hints about Brenda, especially since Larry's divorce had fallen through – again – and Jack had gone and married that little floozy who was probably young enough to be her daughter. She was also starting to do crazy things, like scratching him or leaving lipstick on his shirt – anything, she obviously hoped, that would upset Brenda. Fortunately, Brenda never noticed the subtle, and not so subtle, telltale signs. Anyway, Brenda trusted him; Brenda loved him.

However, the biggest problem with Ingrid was that she was losing her influence with the business journalists, who were getting younger – and darker. From a purely business perspective, five years with one agency was already too long. All the marketing books said so.

Now, she grovelled. 'I'm so sorry, Alan,' she said, her smoke-tinged voice more raspy than usual. 'I didn't mean to… Look, I'll think up a strategy and we'll get you an even bigger award. Let's go upstairs and work on it.' She held out her hand, her red-tipped talons contrasting vividly with her deeply moisturised white hands, the wrinkled white breasts spilling over the top of her too-tight silvery top heaving with undisguised desire. He felt the familiar nausea rise in his throat.

'Sorry, Ingrid. I have to get home. Brenda and I are going to Tokyo and Judy for dinner. You need to start working on that new strategy for Silver Properties – something original for once. Have it ready for me tomorrow. Bring it to my office. I want Arno to look it over as well. He's going to be getting a lot more involved in marketing.'

He glanced back as he walked to the door, and noticed

what looked like a tear sliding down her face. What a rush! He could barely wait to get home to Brenda.

***

'Sweetheart, who's Dr Viljoen?' Alan asked as he stepped back into Brenda's bedroom, his hair still damp from the shower he'd needed after their amazing love making.

Brenda was still pretty damn good if he got to her before she fell asleep, even if she was also starting to show her age. He'd seen her swallow one of her yellow tablets as he walked in to her bedroom, but she seemed to be okay. It would have been a fucking disaster if she wasn't able to stay awake – and not just because he needed her after his run-in with Ingrid. They had a big night ahead.

'Dr Viljoen? Why?'

'His office called this morning. Apparently you forgot to sign your cheque when you were last there. Why are you paying a doctor with a cheque? Who is he?'

'Oh, just a new doctor I'm seeing about my headaches. I heard he was really good, and he is very nice.'

'But why the cheque?'

'Oh that. Well, he prefers it and we're already claiming so much from medical aid what with Zivah's therapists – she has to go to extra occupational therapy now as well – that I just thought it would be easier to just pay him myself.'

He frowned. Zivah's medical bills were getting beyond

a joke. The teachers at the nursery school probably got fat kickbacks from all the medical professionals they constantly referred her to. There was absolutely nothing wrong with the child. She was just a little slow. She'd catch up once she went to primary school. Anyway, all the physio, speech therapy, play therapy, this therapy, that therapy – wasn't helping. Not that he could see.

He watched Brenda carefully repairing her make-up, most of which was now smeared on the white pillow case, and grinned. She'd protested quite strongly that he'd mess her make-up and complained that she wouldn't have time to fix it before they'd have to leave for the Sexwales. Well, they could be a few minutes late. This was Africa. She put on fresh underwear – they looked really sexy, but they were so damn flimsy – and stepped into a demure little black dress. If he didn't look too hard, she was almost the woman he'd fallen in love with, but she wasn't a spring chicken anymore. She was pushing thirty-three – or was it thirty-four? God, what he wouldn't give to have the old Brenda back with her fresh, taut body and tight little breasts. He ached for her. He really needed to find someone. Annette wouldn't do anymore. She was also getting on. Perhaps Avi's gym teacher; she was making all the right signals, although he'd have sworn she was gay. She was a little too muscular for his tastes. Maybe she was gay, but wanted to spread her wings a bit. It could be fun to find out, especially if she'd never been properly fucked. Christ, it had been so long since he'd had a virgin. He'd thought that Larry's daughter would be one, but boy had he been wrong. That little girl had a lot more tricks up her sleeve than Joan, who Larry had still not managed to divorce. What Alan wanted, needed, so badly, was a pretty little innocent with baby tits and a tight little cunt who'd look at him with adoring eyes and let him break her in, his way. Like Brenda.

'..And the coach said Avi – and probably Yair as well – could be selected for the provincial team again....' Brenda was prattling away. She was in good form for a change. It was going to be a good evening; he was confident of that. He might even be able to close that deal if the guys from Chancellor House were also there. On balance, life was pretty damn good. Whoever said you couldn't have it all was a fucking loser. He just had to put his mind to finding his sweet little virgin and then he really would have it all.

***

'Alan, who's that nice-looking young man? He looks familiar,' Brenda said as they walked past Arno's glass-fronted office to the foyer.

Alan examined their reflection in the huge gilt-framed mirror behind the reception desk. They still made what *You* magazine described as "a striking couple". The sandblasting of the logo on the mirror had cost a fucking fortune, but, he had to admit, it looked good. Brenda had been really impressed. She hardly ever came into Silver Properties – this was her first time since the renovations – but they were going to the twins' prize giving and concert. Stembiso was waiting for them downstairs in Brenda's car. His was in for service. The twins had already been dropped at school, Brenda said. Zivah was at home with Thembi.

'That's Arno. My assistant. He's been with me almost a year now.'

He hadn't been looking for an assistant when Arno's CV had landed on his desk. He had Mabel and she was just fine. Arno had applied for a job in sales and Alan had been about to scrawl "no" on the CV when he'd noticed that the candidate had matriculated at Driespruitfontein Hoërskool. HR had been surprised when he'd insisted on interviewing the candidate himself.

Alan had liked the look of young Arno the moment he walked into his office. Tall, well built, blond hair neatly combed, clean shaven – and desperate. Despite his B.Com (Marketing) from Tukkies, he couldn't find a job. Any job. Too white. Too Afrikaans. But if he didn't find something soon he'd have to go back to Driespruitfontein – and he hated farming.

Arno told him that they'd only moved to the farm from Bloemfontein when his ma's father had died when he was in standard four. 'My younger brothers can run the farm with Ma,' he said. 'I think I got my Pa's genes more. He's didn't grow up on a farm either. He prefers to run the farm school and coach rugby.'

Who were his parents, Alan asked, although he had a

pretty good idea.

'Annamari and Thys van Zyl,' Arno responded.

After checking Arno's date of birth, Alan knew for sure that the boy had as much interest in farms and farming as his father. He'd studied Arno's guileless, open face: yes, there was something of Annamari there. Alan smiled when he remembered how he'd sometimes wonder if Annamari remembered him. Now that he'd seen Arno, he was pretty sure she did.

Arno looked at Alan curiously.

'Silverman,' he said. 'The general dealer in Driespruitfontein is Silverman's.'

'Yes,' Alan said, curious to see what, if anything, Annamari and Thys had told him.

'I never met them,' Arno said.' I heard they had to move away after their boy chickened out... oh.' Arno's fair hair contrasted vividly with his bright red cheeks and made his blue eyes appear even brighter. Alan burst out laughing. Arno's flush deepened.

'Uh-huh. Me, I'm afraid. But if you've no objection to working with an old draft dodger, I'd like to offer you a position at Silver Properties.'

It was a joke, really. Curiosity. He had had no intention of keeping the boy on permanently, but Arno had surprised him. He'd managed to get rid of Ingrid like an old pro. If he ever bumped into the boy's mother – unlikely – he'd congratulate Annamari on a job well done.

***

Rabbi Rosenberg pushed through the crush of parents towards Alan. The principal had invited them all to "enjoy refreshments" after the prize-giving and Alan hastily put down his cup of coffee to shake the rabbi's hand. It was hard to break the schmoozing habit. He'd been schmoozing left and right since the start of the long, boring evening. Avi had walked off with all the academic prizes, as usual. She really was turning into a little beauty, growing more and more like her mother every day, but it was Yair's achievements that had stunned him. Who would have thought the little *pisher* had it in him? It was probably the generous anonymous donation he'd made for refurbishing the gym that had earned Yair the position of vice head boy.

'You must be extremely proud, Alan,' the rabbi said.

'Absolutely. Especially about Yair. Avi's always been an achiever, so I'm not surprised. But Yair – that was a shock.'

The rabbi bared his teeth, just visible through his beard. 'You underestimate him, Alan. He's a clever youngster. Preparing him for his Barmitzvah will be a challenge, because he asks lots of questions, although I suspect that is only to waste time rather than do actual work. I think he'll surprise us all one day.'

'Barmitzvah already?' Shit, he sometimes forgot Yair and Avi were twins. She was so much more mature. Brenda should have told him that Rabbi Rosenberg was Yair's *cheder* teacher. He wondered if Yair would celebrate his Barmitzvah like he had. It was still a way off, but he doubted it. Thembi was no Johanna and Yair was such a *pisher*.

'They grow up so fast,' Rabbi Rosenberg said. 'But one is never too young to learn – or too old, Alan. Never too old.'

'I never had much opportunity to study Torah when I was young, you know, Rabbi, growing up in a Free State *dorp* and everything. I'm sad to say I hardly remember my Barmitzvah.' Like hell he didn't. Okay, not the Torah bit and all that, but afterwards. That, he'd never forget.

'Perhaps you'd like to come along to our *shiur* meeting next Tuesday. Nothing too hectic, just some learnings from the Talmud, good debate and good company.'

Shit. It sounded terrible.

'I'm not *frum*, Rabbi. I wouldn't know what to do.'

'Come along. If you don't enjoy it, you needn't come back. I won't be offended. And perhaps your dear wife would like to go to the women's *shiur* with my wife. I'm sure she'll enjoy it.'

Alan smiled at the older man. He liked Rabbi Rosenberg. He was so non-judgemental and accommodating... and he really should market himself more to the ultra-Orthodox community. He'd been right. With Mbeki running the show – even if the old man, Mandela, hadn't retired yet – his struggle credentials were not as much of an entree to the emerging black elite as they used to be. He really did need to hedge his bets. This was Africa, after all, and, regardless of Archbishop Tutu's rainbow nation notion, and the ANC's proclaimed vision of a "non-racial, non-sexist, democratic" blah blah blah society, the bottom line was that he was white and they were black.

Brenda came over. Her eyes were starting to look a little glazed and there was a faint gleam of sweat on her top lip. Time to take her home. Quickly. He'd obviously be getting nothing from her tonight either – well, nothing worthwhile. Damn.

'Sweetheart, Rabbi Rosenberg says you should go to the *rebbetzin's shiur* next week – when I go to the men's.'

'You must, Mrs Silverman,' the rabbi said. 'Aviva is already attending Batmitzvah classes with my wife. We can't have the daughter teaching the mother, can we?'

Brenda looked at him in shock. She'd obviously not given a thought to what Avi's Batmitzvah was all about, apart from the party, of course. It was going to be quite a party, if the bills for the deposits for the band, and the venue, and the food, and the decor and the invitations and the this and the that were anything to go by. It was going to be bigger than a fucking wedding. He hoped the returns would be worth it, but it never hurt to have a back-up plan. 'What time, next week, Rabbi? We'll both be there,' he said.

***

One of the first lessons Alan learned at the *shiur* was that a black hat in Jo'burg meant more than just being ultra *frum*. It was a kind of visible secret handshake into a select society, a group of people who looked out for each other, did business with each other and supported each other. He also learned after deciding to join that select group, that it wasn't easy. Getting up early for morning prayers and giving up on prawns and lobster and having to drink black coffee after a good steak meal had been a pain… but it had been worth the effort, and it could have been worse. At least macon tasted a lot like bacon.

Plus, just look how the *frum* community had all turned out to support him in the difficult months since Brenda's death. Their fridges and freezers had almost burst with the stews and lasagnes and cheese cakes and grilled chickens the women delivered to the house daily. Just look how they were still supporting him – writing letters to the editor and editorials in the *Jewish Voice*, and packing the public gallery at the court. Making life difficult for that little bitch reporter. He'd see her run out of town by the time he was finished with her. Just wait till the inquest was over. He'd instructed Gideon Feinberg to make chopped liver out of Yair on the stand today.

PART 11
YAIR

CHAPTER 1
JOHANNESBURG, 2012

Yair tried to pull himself together. He knew he was making such a fool of himself, in front of everyone, in front of Dad, which was so lame. And Red. She'd smiled at him when he arrived in court. He didn't deserve that. He had never been particularly nice to her. Did she still remember that night at his Barmitzvah?

***

Johannesburg, 2002

Red was such a tall, scrawny thing it was easy to make fun of her. Everyone did. Even though Daniel was such an arsehole, Yair had laughed as loudly as the others, although he didn't think Daniel was very funny. He actually thought Daniel was a bastard, calling her a totem pole. Daniel was stupid – it was a beanpole. Poor Red. She was actually very sweet. He liked her, not that he would ever admit it to anyone. Daniel and the others said she was a swotty nerd. Avi and her crowd said she was a drip, but she sat next to him in history and she was nice… and funny. Plus, she was really clever, although she never made a big deal about that. She wasn't as clever as Avi, though, but no one was. Certainly not him, as the teachers always reminded him.

'Yair, why can't you be more like your sister? Yair, why don't you ask your sister to help you with equations? Yair, it's hard to believe you and Aviva are twins – she is so conscientious. Yair, Yair, Yair...' Even Dad was taking notice of Avi lately. They'd grown up used to being totally ignored by him, Mr Alan fucking big shot Silverman. It was like they didn't exist. He and Avi had never really got on – she was such a bossy goody-goody – but at least they'd had each other when things were really bad with Mom. The only thing he and Avi ever seemed to agree on was Zivah – she was their special joint project. They took turns watching out for her.

But now Avi was Dad's little pet all of a sudden. Ever since her Batmitzvah. Dad had even danced with her at her Batmitzvah party in the big hall at the HOD centre. Dad had made the most brilliant speech about her and Avi had blushed and beamed. Now Dad and Avi were always together, chatting and laughing and leaving him out. He'd honestly thought that if he did really well at his Barmitzvah, Dad would also be proud of him, but, today, although everyone said how well he had sung his portion in *shul*, and although Rabbi Rosenberg told Dad how well he had done in his Barmitzvah exams, Dad had virtually ignored him, except when he'd had no choice like on the *Bimah* during the service. Dad had made a big fuss of Avi though, telling her how grown-up she looked in her stupid dress that probably cost a hell of a lot more than his new pants and shirt. It wasn't fair. He felt tears prick his eyes. He supposed he should be thankful that Dad had at least let him have this party. Mom sort of explained that it wasn't nearly as big and fancy as Avi's Batmitzvah party had been last year because they hadn't been *frum* then. He hated having to be *frum*.

Daniel passed him the zol and he inhaled deeply. He felt himself float away. Someone switched off the light. This was so cool. He must remember to ask Daniel where he got the stuff. It was *so* cool. Christ, he'd had to fight Dad to allow girls to come to the party. Dad really was taking this whole *frum* thing far too seriously. It was so damn irritating... What the? One of the girls was kissing him. Shit, she was putting her tongue in his mouth. Tiffany. Would she let him grope her? Of course she would. She let everyone grope her. Anyway, it was his party. He wondered how far she'd let him go. He could hear the others, giggling and gefuffeling and whispering. Fuck, he hoped Mom wouldn't take it into her head to walk in. Nah, she was probably already passed out in her room. Zivah was also probably fast asleep in her bedroom, and Avi was no doubt still sucking up to Dad… and Dad never came to his room.

Yair shoved his hand down Tiffany's jeans.

'No,' she said. She wiggled away.

Oh bloody fuck, she wasn't going to let him. He'd tell Daniel he was wrong – she didn't grope everyone. Shit, no, he couldn't tell Daniel that. Daniel would tell everyone that he was a loser who couldn't even feel up the school mattress. She was lying next to him again. She took his hand... Christ, she'd unzipped her jeans. He stuck his fingers right inside her panties and his mouth went dry.

'There are too many people in here,' she whispered in his ear. 'Can't we go somewhere?'

He got off the bed, trying to hide the huge bulge in his pants. They sneaked down the passage to Avi's room. It was locked. She always locked it, but he knew where she hid the key. He couldn't believe this was happening to him. Screw Dad. Stuff Aviva. This was his party and, for once, he was going to be the winner. He locked the door – he didn't want Avi walking in on them. She didn't like Tiffany. He didn't like Tiffany very much either, but, right now, he loved her... and she seemed to know what she was doing. She helped him pull off his pants. He wondered how old Dad had been when he'd had his first fuck.

***

Yair couldn't wait to get to school on Monday and tell Daniel and the others what he'd done. They probably already knew, because, when he had gone downstairs to say goodbye to everyone at eleven when their parents came to fetch them,

Daniel had high-fived him. Tiffany's mom had only arrived after twelve and he'd had to sit and talk to her while they waited, all stiff and formal and absolutely nothing to say to each other. She really was thick. No wonder she had failed last year.

Avi had already gone to bed. Dad told him to lock up and went off to his room. Yair picked up the bottles lying on the carpet and took them down to the kitchen. The last thing he wanted was Thembi moaning at him that she had already had enough cleaning up to do when she came in, in the morning. He hoped she wouldn't tell Mom about the hole some idiot had burned in his duvet cover. Oh, who cared? Mom certainly wouldn't. They could buy him another one.

He heard Dad's door open. It squeaked. Where was he going? Probably down to the kitchen for something to eat. He was really hungry too, but he didn't feel like getting up, or facing Dad again. He replayed fucking Tiffany over and over in his mind. It had been pretty awkward at first, but then he'd got the hang of it. He wished it hadn't been with her. He didn't really want to do it with her again – unless there was no one else. He couldn't think of which other girl would let him. He wondered about Red. Nah, after what they'd done to her, she'd probably never speak to him again, and anyway, she wasn't that kind of girl. He wondered if Daniel knew which other girls were easy. He wondered if Daniel knew how to get hold of condoms… and more weed. He slept.

CHAPTER 2
JOHANNESBURG, 2004

Yair tried to focus on the lock in the back door, but he couldn't figure out which hole to put the key into. Eventually, he got it right. He quietly turned the key and pushed the door open and jumped. Pheeeeeee. Shit. He'd forgotten about the alarm. The warning beep was so loud. It would wake everyone in the house. He had to get to the alarm panel in the passage before the real alarm went off. He bumped into the kitchen table; something fell onto the tiled floor and smashed. He stumbled into the passage. The alarm panel was miles away, down near the entrance hall. His father materialised in front of him. He seemed to have a gun in his hand.

'Jesus, Yair, I could have killed you. What are you doing? It's five o'clock in the morning. Don't tell me you've just got in. Where the hell have you been?'

Yair blinked, but his father remained all blurry. He felt awful. Sick. Really, really sick. If he didn't get to the bathroom, he'd throw up right here, in the passage.

'Not so fast,' Alan said as he punched the secret code into the alarm panel. 'I want some answers'

Yair shook his head. 'I don't know.'

'What do you mean you don't know? Where have you been? What have you been doing? How did you get home?'

'I don't know,' Yair said. 'Really, Dad. I don't know. Please, I feel sick. Let me go.' He pulled his arm out of his father's grasp and staggered into the guest toilet, stuck his head in the bowl and heaved.

When he looked up, Alan was standing in the doorway, glaring down at him.

'Please, Dad. I don't know. I... I was at a party. And then... I don't know. I was home. I don't know how I got here.'

'Don't lie to me, Yair. It's bad enough that you go out drinking and drugging with your unsavoury friends. But do me the courtesy of not lying about it.'

'I'm not lying. I don't remember anything. I really don't.'

'Get to bed, Yair. Go sleep it off. We'll talk about it when you've sobered up. Go back to your room, Avi,' Alan said as Avi appeared at the top of the stairs, still belting her dressing gown around her. Avi retreated.

Yair watched his father disappear up the stairs. He waited until he heard his father's bedroom door close before tackling the staircase himself. When had it got so steep? He felt as if he had just crawled out of the bottom of a scrum.

He fell on his bed and tried to remember.

He remembered Stembiso dropping him off at Daniel's house. He remembered Daniel sneaking some beers out of the fridge. He remembered drinking a beer, and smoking a bit of weed. He remembered climbing onto the back of Daniel's bike. He remembered arriving at the party. It was in a house somewhere in Sandton, he thought, but he wasn't sure where. He remembered taking off his *yarmulke* and putting it in his pocket. He felt in his pocket. His *yarmie* was still there. So was his cell phone and wallet.

He remembered walking into the party. There had been so many people. He had recognised a couple of the kids from school, but most of the people there were adults, university students, possibly older. He remembered this really pretty girl; no, she wasn't a girl; she was at least twenty. He hadn't been able to believe it when she came over to him.

'Come dance with me,' she'd said.

They danced. She was gorgeous. She said her name was Diana... something like that.

'I need a drink,' she said. 'Let's go find the bar.'

They went towards the bar.

'Here, have a vodka cocktail.' A dark-haired guy with a moustache handed him a tall glass with a greenish drink inside. It tasted nice, but boy, it had one hell of a kick. He staggered. He felt so drunk. Diana was laughing at him. He nearly fell. Someone really strong seemed to be supporting him, helping him get outside.

And then... and then... he couldn't remember. He couldn't remember anything until ... think, Yair, think.

He got up and went to the bathroom. He stripped off his clothes. There was blood on his pants, on his underpants. Shit, he'd better throw them out before Thembi told his mother he'd been fighting again. He was aching all over. He climbed into the bath. The water was so soothing.

Dripping, he crawled under his duvet and went to sleep.

***

Yair woke to the sound of his cell phone ringing.

'So how was it, dude?' Daniel asked.

'What?' Yair asked.

'Aw cummon, Yair. I want all the details. That hot bitch. She was all over you, you lucky bastard. And then when I looked for you later, you were gone. So I schemed you'd gone home with her. How was it?'

'Oh. Yeah, it was great. Amazing,' Yair said.

'So when you seeing her again?'

'I don't know.'

'Well, when are you going to phone her?'

'I don't think I have her number.'

'Are you fucking stupid? So how you going to get hold of her?'

'I don't know.'

'Are you fucked in the head?' Daniel yelled.

'Sorry, dude. Gotta go.' Yair cut the call, just as his father walked into his room.

'Okay, Yair. Time to explain yourself. You are only fifteen years old. You cannot stay out till all hours partying with your friends. You can't expect Stembiso to have to wait around until you are good and ready to come home. It's not fair on him and it's disrespectful to me and the entire family. Now, where were you?'

Yair sat up and looked appealingly at his father. 'I don't know, Dad. That's the truth. I don't remember anything. Please. I think something happened to me. I can't remember...'

'You are quite right, Yair,' Alan said. 'Something did happen to you. It's called a blackout. You went out, had too much to drink, and probably doped yourself up on some drugs. And then you passed out and now you can't remember. That's what happens when you drink too much, when you take drugs.'

'I didn't. I didn't. Really, Dad, you have to believe me. I didn't drink too much.'

'Oh, please, Yair. Don't lie. Please don't lie. The guard saw you staggering down the road, pissed out of your mind and as high as a kite at about three o'clock. He said you were reeking of booze – I smelled it on you too. You were so far gone you collapsed in the guardhouse and he let you sleep it off because he didn't want you to get into trouble by calling me.'

'I slept in the guardhouse? Who dropped me off?'

'What's the matter with you, Yair? Why can't you be more like Avi? Your mother and I give you everything, and this is how you repay us? I'm warning you, my boy. If you do this again, if I ever catch you drinking and drugging again, I'll pack you off to rehab so fast you won't know what hit you. Do you hear me?'

Yair didn't answer as his father turned and walked out of his room. He felt terrible. His head was throbbing. This was a hangover from hell. Except, he couldn't remember drinking all that much. It wasn't as if he had never been drunk. Of course he had. But he'd never had a blackout before. At least, he didn't think so. So what had happened? He wished he could remember.

CHAPTER 3
JOHANNESBURG, 2008

Yair lay on his bed watching the smoke curl up towards the ceiling. He inhaled again, held the smoke in his mouth, and exhaled slowly. The smoke curled again. Like it always did. Avi put her head around the door.

'Shit, can't you fucking knock first?' He retrieved the zol from where he'd dropped it and relit it. 'What do you want? Don't give me a fucking lecture, okay. I'm not in the mood.'

She didn't listen. She gave him the lecture. Again. He virtually knew it by heart. About how he was wasting his life being stoned all the time. About what dagga would do to his brain – bullshit. There was nothing wrong with his brain. He was doing okay, but varsity was so fucking boring. He was seriously thinking of dropping out while he decided what to do with his life. He supposed he could go into the business – most of the guys in his class were going to go into their family businesses – the white ones anyway. But he really didn't want to spend any more time with Dad than he had to, and anyway, that prick Arno van Zyl was so far up Dad's arse, he'd probably take over one day and where would that leave him? Avi thought Arno was fucking wonderful, though. She was coming to the part in her lecture when she would start comparing them.

'... Look how Arno managed to get his degree and a good job. You'll never get anywhere, Yair. And you've got so much going for you...'

He wondered if Avi had ever kissed Arno. Nah, he was too old... and anyway, Arno wouldn't be so stupid to lay a hand on her. Dad would go ballistic if he did – Arno wasn't *frum*. Shit, he wasn't even Jewish and Avi would have to marry the nice, *frum nebbish* that Daddy dearest would pick out for her. Probably as soon as she graduated. Or maybe even before. A lot of the *frum* girls were married off almost as soon as they finished high school. He had been so surprised when Avi had told him when they were in Matric that she was ready to marry whoever Dad chose for her, but then she'd confided that she really hoped it wouldn't be too soon. So, when she had won the scholarship to Wits, she had been thrilled when Dad said she could go and that she wouldn't have to get married for a few years.

Yair, of course, hadn't won anything. He had no idea how he had managed to get through Matric. He literally hadn't opened a book. He was having far too much fun hanging out with Daniel and the other guys – and some of the girls. Even Tiffany joined them sometimes, although she had had to leave school when she failed Grade 11. She said she was trying to do Matric through some correspondence college, and in the meantime she had a job at the Chevrah Kadisha, filing or something. He still didn't like Tiffany, but she was always available and somehow she always had a ready supply of weed.

However, if Dad thought he was going to marry any girl he chose for him, he had two chances – zilch and nada. He'd go through the motions Dad expected him to – the dumb clothes, the stupid hats, the keeping kosher – even when he went out, in case someone saw him eating pork or other *treif* and told Dad – but he wasn't going to get married any time soon, and not to some *frummer* daughter of one of Dad's business associates.

***

Avi sat down on the bed. She put out her hand as if to take Yair's, but then she withdrew it, embarrassed. Jewish girls didn't touch Jewish boys or men, not even their brothers or fathers. How stupid was that? He wasn't even supposed to hold Zivah's hand. He had been supposed to stop as soon as she had had her Batmitzvah, when she was twelve. It was hard to believe she was fifteen already, but she was still a child. So he wasn't going to stop. Anyway, she was the only person in this house who loved him. He would continue to read to her and tell her stories and hold her hand when it stormed. Lightning and thunder terrified her. If Dad didn't like it, too fucking bad.

'Yair, I need to talk to you,' Avi said.

'So what have you been doing for the past half an hour?'

'Don't. Listen, this is serious. I don't know who else to talk to. It's about... Yair, have you ever made love to a girl?'

He couldn't believe it. What the hell had got into her – and it was none of her business, anyway.

'You mean had sex? Of course,' he said.

'With Jewish girls?'

He stared at her. 'Of course with Jewish girls.' All the girls at school had been Jewish and he'd had quite a few, apart from Tiffany. Even after Matric. Especially after Matric.

'With *frum* ones too?'

What was this? She couldn't be messing around. He wouldn't have thought she'd even consider it. Not Avi, who hadn't even gone to the Matric dance, although she'd had lots of invitations. All the guys thought she was really hot, and, he had to admit, she was quite pretty, even if she was his twin. He'd thought about inviting Red to the Matric dance, but then he'd thought better of it. She was fun to talk to in class, but the Matric dance was when girls were supposed to put out, and Red really wasn't the type. So he invited Deborah and they'd had a really good time. He hadn't seen Red at the dance. Maybe she had also decided not to go, like Avi.

He'd have bet the house that Avi would be a virgin when she got married. It was what was expected of nice Jewish girls, and Avi always did what was expected of her.

'What's up, Avi? Tired of being a virgin?' he asked, then

stared in shock as his twin sister blushed and looked away.

'Who's the lucky man? Did you meet him at varsity? Have you asked Dad for permission? Do you want me to ask him? Christ – you're not pregnant, are you?'

'I haven't... I won't... I just thought I could speak to you, but obviously I was wrong,' Avi snapped.

She walked out and slammed the door. Yair laughed. He loved it when he managed to upset her. It helped to make up for all the times, growing up, that she had made him feel like he was an insignificant nothing.

A week later, she disappeared.

CHAPTER 4
JOHANNESBURG, 2009

Hava neranenah.
Hava neranenah.
Hava neranenah ve-nismeha.

Yair watched Zivah happily twirling around and around the *hora* circle, her blonde hair flying around her animated little face. He stood outside the ring, clapping in time to the throbbing music. His father was watching from the other side of the room, a sleek, self-satisfied smile on his face. Zivah was so happy. She loved the attention she was getting from everyone. She'd come into his room at the crack of dawn this morning – before dawn, actually, because it wasn't quite light yet – and bounced on his bed, waking him.

'I'm sweet sixteen today, sweet sixteen today. Where's my present, Yair?' She'd flung herself at him and tickled him until he had to squirm away, laughing.

'Shh, Dad will hear you in here and then I'll get into trouble,' he whispered, and handed her the present he'd hidden in his cupboard.

He was sure she'd known it was there. She'd probably already figured out what it was – there were some grubby fingerprints on the shiny wrapping paper. She ripped off the paper and turned her glowing face up to him, delight oozing out of every pore as she hugged the giant pink teddy bear. Then she dropped the bear and flung her arms around him. 'Oh, Yair, I love it. I love you. Thank you.' He felt her little breasts pressing against him through her thin shorty pyjamas.

He shooed her out his room and tried to go back to sleep. It was no good. He was wide awake and anyway, he wanted to spend as much of the day as possible with his precious little sister. He loved her so much, his heart ached as he watched her dancing and clapping and smiling.

Brenda tottered into the room carrying a platter of food. Why was she doing that? There was more than enough food on the table already. Christ, she was wasted, as usual. He hoped she'd be able to hold it together until everyone went home or Dad would be furious... and embarrassed. Though why on earth he'd invited all those stuffed shirts to Zivah's birthday party, he had no idea. Probably to show everyone what a happy family they were – even though they still hadn't heard a word from Avi. Not once. Not in five months. Not even today for Zivah's birthday. She'd just packed her clothes and disappeared off the face of the earth. Dad told everyone she'd gone to a *yeshiva* in Israel. Everyone seemed to believe it too.

Yair felt terrible about it. He wondered if he could

have stopped her… but then, he didn't know why she had gone – she'd obviously been trying to tell him, before she disappeared, but he had just been a real bastard to her. He should have listened to her. He'd never seen Dad in such a state about anything. Mom had just gone to her room and shut the door. She hardly ever mentioned Avi's name anymore. Neither did Dad. It was as if she'd died, except they hadn't sat *Shivah* for her.

He watched his mother make it to the table and somehow set the platter down, right side up, without too many little salmon lox on rye slices sliding off. He breathed a sigh of relief. He wondered if he should go over to her, help her upstairs. She was wobbling on her high heels. Better not. She had been in a foul mood all day. He'd heard her moaning at Zivah about putting on weight. That was so unfair. Zivah was filling out a little, but so what? She wasn't a little girl any more. She was gorgeous. She was dancing with one of the girls in her class now; they were holding hands and whirling around and around, and oh shit. Zivah's dress had torn, right down the back. She looked so embarrassed. He took his jacket off and put it around her shoulders.

'Quickly, go get changed,' he told her.

She scampered up the stairs. The dancing continued. He helped himself to some rye bread with lox, a few falafel balls and a good dollop of hummus. Then he topped up his Bells with more soda, and went outside onto the patio to enjoy some peace and quiet. It was a beautiful night. The fairy lights strung through the trees winked and twinkled. He wished he was back in Cape Town, on Lion's Head, enjoying the lights of the city. He wanted a joint so badly, but he'd promised himself he wouldn't. It had been eleven days since his last one. He went back inside.

'Yair, have you seen Zivah?' Mom looked worried.

'There she is.' He pointed at his sister. She had changed into a white skirt and a white top. She was dancing again. There was a red stain on the back of her skirt, and it appeared to be spreading. Oh God no, she was having a really bad period, poor kid. He remembered her first one. How frightened she'd been. He'd tried to explain it to her and then Avi had taken over.

Dad took her upstairs again. Everyone went home. Dr Schwartz arrived. They took Zivah to the clinic.

***

Yair was lying on his bed, worrying about Zivah, when his parents walked in. Together. Brenda was crying. Alan looked furious.

Brenda asked, 'How could you, Yair? She's your sister.'

He was stunned. What was she talking about? He looked at his father.

'Zivah was having a miscarriage. They had to do a D&C to clean up the mess,' Alan said.

No. Impossible. Why were they looking at him like that?

Surely they didn't think he'd...

They did. Both of them. Alan said he must have raped Zivah when he was high or drunk or both. His father said he probably hadn't known what he was doing. His father said Zivah wouldn't tell them who did it to her, but it was obvious. He was always in Zivah's room and she was always in his room and he was always touching her inappropriately. Yair remembered how she'd pressed herself against him this morning... yesterday morning... and went cold. No. His mother couldn't bear to look at him. She walked out of his room, sobbing.

They were going to send him away, his father said. Dr Schwartz had arranged for him to be admitted to a rehabilitation centre in the Cape. It was that or they'd have to have him arrested – for rape. Tough love. If he made a full recovery, if he stopped using, they'd let him come back, but he had to promise never to be alone with Zivah, ever again.

'It wasn't me,' he cried. 'I wouldn't do that.'

'You just don't remember,' Alan said.

'Ask Zivah – she'll tell you it wasn't me.' It couldn't be. He wouldn't... He couldn't.

Alan said they weren't going to force her to answer any questions. She was frightened enough as it was. Of course it was him.

Yair felt sick. Surely, if he'd done that to his sister, he'd remember? He tried to remember. He really tried. He couldn't remember. He couldn't. He put his head in his hands and wept.

CHAPTER 5
JOHANNESBURG, 2012

Yair forced himself to walk back into the court. He felt about a thousand years old. He hadn't slept. He dreaded facing Gideon Feinberg.

He gripped the rail on the witness box and tried to stare down the *shyster* lawyer as he adjusted his *yarmulke* and squared up to him. He hoped Feinberg would remember that he was supposed to represent the entire family.

Feinberg picked up where Ms du Toit had left off. 'You've testified that you saw your father forcing your mother to engage in oral sex. Is that correct?'

'Yes.'

'When was that?'

'I'm not sure. A few years ago.'

'Are you aware that oral sex between two consenting adults is not illegal?'

'Of course I know that. But it wasn't consenting. She wasn't consenting. She was crying and trying to pull away.'

Feinberg shook his head and looked around the court, smiling.

'Okay, let's move on,' the lawyer said. 'Since then? Did you ever see any other indications that your mother was being abused?'

'Yes.'

He gripped the witness box rail. He wanted to run. He couldn't stand here, in front of all these people and tell them what he'd seen. In front of all those *frum* people. He knew them, for God's sake. They'd looked shocked, stunned, horrified – and embarrassed – when he'd told them about what he'd seen that first time. He'd bet anything none of the women had even heard of oral sex, let alone practised it themselves. He could feel himself shaking. Gideon Feinberg was insisting he tell about the other times. He couldn't. He just couldn't. He had to.

'Another time – last year, sometime – I heard her again,' he said. 'She was crying and saying something like "no, Alan, no". I opened the door to her room. She was by her dressing table – and he was, he was…' He stopped.

'Mr Silverman,' the magistrate said. 'Please tell the court what you saw.'

How was he going to say this? He said it. He just fucking said it.

'He was sodomising her. Okay? Are you satisfied? He was fucking sodomising her, like she was a bloody dog or something. And she was crying and begging him to stop, but he didn't. He's a fucking pig, a bastard, a sick, sick bastard…'

The courtroom erupted. One of the religious women had

her head down between her knees. Another was fanning herself with her hand. Two of the black hats were on their feet shouting and shaking their fists. Who were they shouting at? The magistrate pounded her gravel. His father was yelling at him. He screamed back. He could see the reporters' thumbs flying over their smart phones. Red was staring at him – her mouth open.

***

After the short recess, Gideon Feinberg unleashed himself. 'You see a lot of things, Yair, don't you?'

Ms du Toit objected.

Feinberg nodded, smiled and continued. 'Did you see your father inject your mother with insulin?'

Ms du Toit had told him to keep his answers short and to the point. That's exactly what he would do.

'No.'

'Did you see your father force pills and other medicines down her throat?'

'No.'

'So you didn't see your father kill your mother, as you claim.'

'I didn't see that, but, the way he treated her, he could have… He made her life unbearable.' Damn, that sounded so pathetic, but it was true; they had to see that.

'But you didn't ever actually see him do the actions that

led directly to her death, did you?'

'No.'

'So what you really mean is that you believe your mother committed suicide – possibly because of what you say was your father's abusive behaviour?'

No, he screamed silently. *Don't twist my words.*

'I don't know. I didn't say that,' he said.

He watched Feinberg look at something in the big fat file on the desk in front of him. He tried to stop his legs from shaking as his father's *shyster* lawyer – because that's what he was – smirked like a smug tiger. What now?

'When did you first start abusing drugs, Yair?'

Oh shit. Of course. Dad would have told him everything, and now everyone would know. Ms du Toit objected. The magistrate ordered him to answer the question.

'I'm clean now. I have been for months.' That sounded like he was whining. He wasn't. It was true.

'That's not what I asked. I asked how old you were when you first started abusing alcohol and drugs. You surely don't deny that you are – or were – a substance abuser?'

'I'm not sure. It depends what you mean by abusing.' Oh damn, the words tumbled out before he could stop them. Stupid, stupid. Now Feinberg would really let him have it.

Feinberg glared. 'Okay, let's talk about using. When did you first start using illegal substances?'

Yair gripped the witness box rail. His knees felt like rubber. 'I was about thirteen or fourteen when I started smoking.'

'Not cigarettes, Yair, correct? You're referring to dagga?'

'Yes.'

'And other substances? Cocaine?'

'I've tried cocaine.'

'And crack. Crystal meths?'

'No, I've never tried that.'

'Really? That's not what your father told me.'

'Well, my father's wrong.'

'Really?'

The smile Gideon Feinberg gave him made his blood run cold.

'But you have had blackouts Yair, haven't you?'

'Once – a long time ago. And it wasn't...' Dread settled in his stomach. No, his father couldn't have told him that.

'Are you sure it was just once? Perhaps you just don't remember.'

Ms du Toit interrupted, 'Your Honour, what has Mr Silverman's alleged substance abuse got to do with anything?'

'I'd like to put it to Mr Silverman that what he claims to have seen in his mother's bedroom was probably nothing more than a figment of his drug-induced imagination Well, Mr Silverman, was it?' Feinberg snapped.

How was he supposed to answer that? Of course it wasn't. He never hallucinated – at least, he didn't think he did.

'I know what I saw. I know what I heard. That time, when he was... you know... sodomising her. I'd just come out of rehab. I was clean. I was stone cold sober. I know what I saw,'

Yair said.

'And how many times have you been in rehab?'

'Three times.' The first time – that was after Zivah's party. The dread in his stomach danced up into his throat. Oh shit, he knew what was coming.

'Who paid for you to go to rehab?'

'My father, I suppose.'

'And when was the last time you were in rehab?'

'I just got out. But my father made me go. He wouldn't even let me sit *Shivah* for my mother. He just wanted to get rid of me because he saw me talking to a journalist. I was clean, but he phoned Dr Schwartz and they made me go back to that place. But I was clean. I was clean. I was clean. You gotta believe me. I was clean.' He couldn't help himself; he was crying like a fucking two-year-old.

Feinberg wasn't finished. 'Do you know what perjury means, Yair?'

'Of course. I'm not stupid.'

'No, you're not. So why did you drop out of university? Why have you never held a job for longer than a couple of weeks? Drugs, right?'

Ms du Toit objected again. Yair didn't answer. What was the point?

'Yair,' Feinberg continued. 'Your father has tried desperately to help you, yet you stand here in this court and lie about him and your dear mother.'

'I'm not lying. It's the truth. And he never wanted to help

me. He just wanted me gone. He never gave a damn about me. He loves my sisters. Not me. Never me. Only my mother loved me.'

'Don't you realise that by saying what you have said – out of spite and hatred for your father – that you are desecrating her memory?'

Ms du Toit objected once again. Yair heard the magistrate warn Feinberg that she would not tolerate such tactics in her court, but he didn't care. He just didn't care anymore.

PART 12
TRACY

CHAPTER 1
JOHANNESBURG, 2012

Tracy watched, horrified, as Yair crumpled to the floor inside the witness box. His wracking sobs ripped through the deathly pall that shrouded Court 15.

She started to tweet, then stopped. She didn't know what to say. She hadn't known he'd been in rehab. She'd never have thought he'd become an addict. She watched Ms du Toit help Yair to his feet and lead him out of the court room. She walked out of the court in a daze. Poor Yair. She wished she could say something to comfort him. She wouldn't know what to say.

***

Yair gave Tracy a wan smile as he walked back into court after the extended lunch break. He didn't join his father at Gideon Feinberg's table. Alan Lookalike – Arno van Zyl – was there too. Feinberg wasn't there yet. Nor was Marie du Toit at her table. Yair squashed himself onto the media bench opposite and looked down at his clasped hands. She tried to catch his eye, but he never looked up. The public gallery was pulsing, every square centimetre radiating expectancy. There were considerably more black hats than before, but there seemed to be fewer religious Jewish women. Friday. They were all probably busy preparing for *Shabbos*.

Feinberg and Ms du Toit hurried into the court, followed closely by the magistrate.

'I have had a request,' the magistrate said, 'from Mr Feinberg that the next witness be heard in camera. I have considered the matter, but I can find no reason in law to grant his request. Legally, the witness is a competent adult. However, I understand Mr Feinberg's concern and I am, therefore, clearing the court of all spectators with the exception of immediate family and the media. For the family's sake, I would like this inquest to be completed with the least possible controversy, so I do not want to have a delay resulting from a challenge from the media – which I have no doubt would result should I exclude them from any part of this hearing. However, I am putting the media on notice now. Any evidence provided by the following witness, Miss Zivah Silverman, is protected and may not be reported on in any manner whatsoever. If, after Miss Silverman has completed her testimony, I feel it is in the public interest to release it, I will so rule. Until then, I instruct the media to respect the "in camera" status of this witness. That means no tweeting or sending other messages about today's proceedings until I say so.'

The public gallery emptied noisily. Arno van Zyl stood,

briefly touched his boss on the shoulder, and walked slowly out the side door. Yair continued to contemplate his shoes.

Zivah Silverman drifted into the court and stopped. She looked like a startled rabbit caught in the headlights of an oncoming car. Gideon Feinberg got up and gently led her to the witness stand. Once again, she was dressed all in white – long skirt, long-sleeved blouse buttoned to the neck – her long blonde hair tied back in a ponytail.

'How old is she? She looks about twelve,' the *Beeld* reporter muttered.

'Dunno. She must be at least eighteen or we'd all have been chucked out already,' *The Star* reporter said.

Yair stared at his little sister as she gripped the witness stand rail, and then put his face in his hands. Alan Silverman smiled encouragingly at her.

Her monosyllabic replies to Gideon Feinberg's gentle questions were barely audible. Feinberg was obviously using her to counter the worst of Yair's damning testimony against their father.

No, she had never heard her mother cry. No, her mother had never complained about her father.

'Daddy is the best in the world,' she said. 'He loved Mommy. He told me. He would never hurt her just like he would never hurt me. He loves me.'

Ms du Toit took over, gently coaxing answers from the young girl, who seemed to be starting to relax.

'Zivah,' Ms du Toit said. 'I want you to pretend there's no

one else in this room. Just you and me, okay? Do you think you can do that?'

Zivah giggled. 'I think so.'

'Good. Now tell me, Zivah. Did you ever hear your mother and father fighting?'

She shook her head. 'Daddy would never fight with Mommy. He never hurt Mommy.'

'Did you ever hear them shout at each other?'

Zivah hesitated, and looked at her father. He smiled at her.

'I did hear them shout once.'

'When was that, Zivah?'

'Oh, I don't know. Before she died.'

'How long before she died?'

'Not so long.'

'Did you hear what they were shouting about?'

Zivah looked frightened. 'No.'

'Zivah, you promised to tell the truth. Did you hear what they were shouting about?'

Zivah looked at her father. Her big blue eyes brimmed.

'Never mind. You don't have to answer that,' Ms du Toit said. 'Now, Zivah, I need you to think very carefully before you answer this question. You say your father loves you.'

'Oh yes.'

'And does he also love your brother and sister?'

'Not Avi. She's gone.'

'And Yair – does he love Yair?'

'He sends Yair away. I don't like it when Yair goes away. I

miss him. I love Yair.'

Yair smiled at her.

'Do you know why Yair is cross with your father? Look, they aren't even sitting next to each other.'

Gideon Feinberg jumped up. 'Objection, Your Honour. We cannot expect this child to read her brother's mind.'

'Oh, I know why Daddy and Yair are cross with each other,' Zivah said. 'It's because of the baby.'

Yair half stood, then sat heavily and buried his face in his hands. 'Zivah, no,' Alan Silverman shouted.

Gideon Feinberg grabbed his arm and pulled him down.

"BABY", Tracy wrote in her notebook. Baby?

'What baby?' Ms du Toit asked.

'My baby.' Zivah beamed at the prosecutor.

'You have a baby?'

'No. I lost it.' Her blue eyes overflowed.

Tracy looked around. Most of the reporters had stopped writing and were staring at Zivah. Tracy glanced at Yair. He was as white as a sheet. Even from across the courtroom, she could see he was sweating. He'd clasped his hands. She looked at Alan Silverman. He was pale. He was whispering in Gideon Feinberg's ear, frantically.

'Where did you lose it?' Ms du Toit looked perplexed.

'I don't know. Mommy was cross. Daddy was soooo cross.'

'Zivah,' the magistrate said softly. 'Are you telling us you had a baby?'

'No. Dr Schwartz said I was too little.'

Tracy was confused. The prosecutor looked as confused as she felt.

Ms du Toit tried again. 'What did your mother do when you lost your baby?'

'Oooh, she shouted at me.'

'And your father? What did he do?'

'He sent Yair away.'

Yair stumbled out of the court. Tracy stared after him. Horror settled in the pit of her stomach, then uncurled and wound its way around her heart. Her hand moved to cover her open mouth. She swallowed her retch.

'Daddy was also cross, but then he said he was sorry. He said he only shouted at me because he was upset, but he said Dr Schwartz would make everything all right. So everything was all right after that and now Dr Schwartz gives me injections so I won't have a baby until I'm bigger.'

Gideon Feinberg rose to his feet. Tracy groaned. Feinberg was going to ask the magistrate to throw the media out. She just knew it. He couldn't do that. This was a big story. She hoped he would throw them out. She didn't want to hear this, to have to report it.

'Your Honour, please. What has this line of questioning got to do with the inquest?' Feinberg asked instead.

'I don't know, Mr Feinberg, but we are in search of the truth and who can tell what is truth until we hear it? Proceed, Ms du Toit.'

'Zivah, do you understand the word "sex"?' Ms du Toit asked.

Please, please, please let her answer be "no", Tracy prayed. Let us find out that she's muddled and she's got it all wrong and she was never pregnant and there was no baby...

'Of course. Daddy says I'm not retarded or dumb. I'm just a bit slow sometimes, but I go – I went – to ordinary school. I don't need to go to a special school for retarded children. It's just that sometimes I don't understand things as quickly as other children. Then Daddy says I must just ask you to explain it to me nicely and I will understand. But you don't need to explain about sex to me. I know about sex.'

'Who did you have sex with?'

'Ooooh I didn't. I don't have sex with anyone. That's dirty.'

Tracy let out her breath. Thank God. Thank God. Zivah obviously had it all wrong. She hadn't been pregnant at all. The horror let go of her throat and settled again in her stomach.

'Then how did you get pregnant?'

'Don't you know? And you're a grown up and everything.'

The reporter next to her sniggered. It wasn't bloody funny.

Ms du Toit smiled. 'I apologise, Zivah, for not being more specific. Can you explain to Magistrate Ngubane how babies are made?'

'Yes, oh yes, I know that.' Zivah smiled proudly. 'Babies are made when a man loves a girl and when a girl really, really, really loves him, but she forgets to take her pill and Dr Schwartz hasn't given her an injection and he does things and...'

'Who? Dr Schwartz?'

Zivah giggled. 'No, silly, not Dr Schwartz; he's a doctor.'

'Did someone love you and make a baby with you, Zivah? Who was it?'

Shit. Why did the prosecutor have to ask her that? Tracy wanted to cover her ears. She didn't want to hear this. She really, really, really didn't. She knew anyway. She just didn't want to hear it. It was sick. Really, really sick. No one was going to believe this.

Zivah paled. She shook her head. 'I can't tell you. It's our special, special secret,' she whispered.

The magistrate pounded her gravel. 'That's enough. Before you continue, Ms du Toit, I need to ask Zivah a very important question. Now, Zivah. How long ago was all this – when you lost your baby?'

'I don't know. Oh yes, I do. I remember now. It was when I had my sweet sixteen party. I remember because the pretty dress Mommy bought for me was too tight and the zip popped when I was dancing and Yair had to give me his jacket and...'

'All right, Zivah. That's enough.' The magistrate paused.

The media bench held its breath. Gideon Feinberg and Marie du Toit sat down. Alan Silverman stared at his daughter. She looked bewildered and frightened.

Magistrate Ngubane spoke. 'Everyone will clear this courtroom immediately. My ruling about the protection of this witness' testimony stands. If any of you, in any way, publishes or broadcasts any aspect of this testimony, or causes any aspect of this testimony to be published or broadcast – either directly or indirectly – you will be charged with contempt of court and anything else I can think of in terms of the Child Protection Act and any other Act I can lay my hands on. If you don't like my ruling, take it to the High Court, but I don't think any judge will overturn it. Mr Silverman, that goes for you too. Only officers of the court may be present during the remainder of this witness' testimony. This hearing is now in camera.'

Tracy was numb. She followed the other reporters as they trooped out the side door of the courtroom. Alan Silverman looked grim and refused to answer any questions. He walked off with Arno van Zyl, who had been waiting outside. There was no sign of Yair.

Swallowing her nausea, Tracy tweeted:

Today's testimony at Silverman inquest held in camera
#silvermaninquest

CHAPTER 2

There it was. Tracy's journalistic dream. The front-page lead of the *Weekend Express*. Headline in 64-point type.

They didn't teach you to write stories like this at university. She'd started and restarted it; written it; deleted words, paragraphs; started again. Tried a different angle. Mafuta yelled at her. Screamed at her that she was just writing a fucking court report, not a Pulitzer fucking novel. There was a deadline to meet. She couldn't do it. She couldn't demolish Yair. She had to. No matter which way she tried it, she would destroy him... and he was her friend. Okay, not really her friend, but he'd always been pretty decent to her. When the other kids at school had called her Carrots, he'd softened it to the nice, warm 'Red'. He'd greeted her when the other kids, including his snooty twin, ignored her... but how well had she really known him? Not very well, it seemed. However, she was a professional... and objective. So, finally, she just wrote it.

'SILVERMAN THE SODOMISER' – SAYS SON

By Tracy Jacobs

Shocking testimony of rape, sodomy and yet more drug abuse in the Silverman household, one of Johannesburg's most respected Jewish families, rocked Court 15 at the Johannesburg Magistrate's Court where the inquest into the untimely death of Mrs Brenda Silverman (44) is unfolding.

Mr Yair Silverman (23), only son of millionaire property mogul, Alan Silverman (50), and the deceased, accused his father of killing his mother.

Testimony by a second witness yesterday was heard in camera and the *Weekend Express* cannot report anything about these proceedings.

Members of the ultra-Orthodox Jewish community, in court to support the family, appeared visibly shocked when Yair gave the court graphic details of how he said his father had sexually abused his mother.

This abuse, he added, included sodomy and oral sex,

to which Mrs Silverman had clearly objected.

Aggressively cross-examined by Mr Gideon Feinberg, who is representing the Silverman family, Yair Silverman admitted that he had abused drugs and alcohol from his early teens, and had been in rehabilitation several times.

However, he denied Mr Feinberg's assertion that the sexual assaults he claimed to have seen were the result of drug-induced fantasies.

Magistrate Patricia Ngubane had her hands full trying to control the emotion-charged proceedings, which, at times, were drowned by outcries of shock and horror from the public gallery. At one point, the hearing degenerated into a shouting match between the Silverman father and son.

However, the courtroom was eerily quiet when Yair Silverman broke down and admitted that he hated his father, who – he said – had

438

never had any time for him.

He also admitted that he had never seen his father inject his mother with insulin – Mrs Silverman died of an insulin overdose after ingesting tranquilisers.

In addition, Yair Silverman confirmed that he had not seen his father give his mother any of the medication to which she was alleged to have been addicted.

Large quantities of prescription tranquilisers and stimulants were found in Mrs Silverman's bathroom cabinet after her death.

The inquest continues on Monday.

***

Tracy forced herself to read it. Horrible story, but what else could she have done? Thank heavens she wasn't allowed to write about Zivah's testimony. She had no idea how she would have handled that… and Maxine was already complaining about the stuff she *had* written. If her mother only knew.

Maxine barged into the kitchen, clearly looking for a fight. Tracy sighed. She didn't need this. She really didn't.

'Morning, Mom.'

'Tracy. Are you *meshugga*? Are you out of your mind? You have to stop this. Right now.'

'Stop what?'

'Writing those terrible things about the Silvermans. How can you? I thought Yair was your friend?'

'It's my job. I'm just reporting what was said in court.'

'Even if it's all lies? How can you just write lies like it's the truth? You are destroying that beautiful family.'

Oh not again. Leave it. Just leave it. But Maxine wouldn't leave it. She went on and on.

'Mom, please,' Tracy said in desperation. 'I'm not destroying them. They did it to themselves. Look, maybe not everything is the truth, but some of it certainly is. It must be. It's not for me to decide what's true and what's not. I'm just a reporter.'

'You're not just a reporter. You're a human being. If you had a shred of decency in you, if you've learned anything about... about anything, you wouldn't be doing this. It can't be true. Things like that just don't happen in Jewish families. You know that. Not people we know.'

Tracy snapped. 'Well, Mom, it seems like they do. And you don't know the half of it.'

'Tracy, listen to me. Stop this. Please. I've already had Doris, and Joan, and Sheila – oh and even Gloria, who I haven't spoken to in years – all on the phone to me this morning talking about what you are doing. They all say it isn't true. I know that. You know that. So stop. Or I'll never be able to show my face in this town again.'

Her mother turned on her heel and sailed out of the door, indignation crackling in her wake.

Tracy wanted to weep in frustration. She climbed into the bath and shaved her legs. Perhaps she should slit her throat too. Would that satisfy everyone?

***

Tracy curled up her legs on the armchair and fished another shortbread out of the Eet-Sum-More packet.

'That's your third biscuit, Tracy. Do you intend to finish all of them?'

'Yes,' she said, glared at her mother and bit into the shortbread square. So much for a peaceful Saturday afternoon. Maxine was obviously not going to let it rest.

'I warned you, Tracy. I told you no good would come of it.'

Tracy picked up the remote control and changed the TV channel. Athletics. Boxing. More old rugby matches. Soccer – did they think sport was all anyone watched on Saturday afternoon?

'You know Rabbi Rosenberg had another go at you in *shul* this morning,' Maxine said. 'Doris Friedman called me and told me as soon as the *brocha* was finished. As if last night wasn't bad enough.'

Her mother continued her blow by blow account of what Rabbi Rosenberg had said about her to his congregation last night – as recounted in lurid detail at the hair salon this morning… and it seemed Rabbi Rosenberg wasn't the only one defending the honour of the Silvermans, and, by extension, the whole community. She had been pilloried – or at least the media in general had come in for scathing criticism – in at least three different *shuls* last night. That she knew of. There were probably more.

'It was Doris' sister-in-law's grandchild's Barmitzvah and everyone was talking about you,' Maxine said accusingly, as if her delinquent daughter had single-handedly ruined some brat's big day. 'Doris said Rabbi Rosenberg had another full go at you again this morning. He said your article in today's paper was a disgrace. He said your newspaper should be banned. He said this kind of trash was to be expected from the media, but not from a Jewish journalist like you. Doris said he said it was hard to believe you were Jewish.'

'Doris Friedman was supposed to be praying, not gossiping. And since when does Rabbi Rosenberg read the *Weekend Express* on *Shabbos*?'

'Don't be facetious, Tracy. It's not a joke. Doris said the rabbi said it was a sad day when one of our own turns against the community and slanders one of our most prominent families. Doris said he said it makes it easier for the anti-Semites to run us down.'

Tracy wanted to cry. Why wouldn't her mother defend her? Why couldn't she see that all she was doing was her job? And that she wasn't the bad one. The Silvermans were. Her father was no better. His first phone call to her in how many months? And all he'd done was yell. Told her she'd ruin his firm – like she gave a damn. She could just picture his face when she'd told him to sue the *Express*. He'd slammed the phone down. The fat hypocrite. He and Alan Silverman were two of a kind... and he also got away with it because he was such a big, fat, rich, pillar of the community. The fact that her mother had had to fight him for every penny, the fact that he had stopped paying maintenance for her the day she had graduated – nice graduation present, thanks, Dad – the fact that his new family went on holiday to London and Paris and Seychelles and Israel, and she and Maxine hadn't been able to afford to go to anywhere for years, not even to Durban – none of that mattered to the fucking community she was supposed to be a part of. No, they all just pretended they didn't know what an arsehole her father was.

'…And I told her that I'd told you to stop and…' Maxine was still at it.

Tracy had had enough. Maybe there was something she was missing. It didn't make sense why her mother, the rabbis, everyone in the entire fucking community was so convinced the stories about Alan Silverman weren't true.

She got up, walked to the window and gazed out. The garden was dusty brown and sad. The street trees were bare and gnarled. She wished the jacarandas were out. That was the best time of the year, when Jo'burg was draped in a beautiful purple cloth. It looked so calm. So peaceful. Jo'burg had more jacarandas than Pretoria, yet Pretoria claimed the title "Jacaranda City". Perception. Propaganda. Say something often enough and people believe it. People believe what they want to believe. What makes them comfortable and happy. Ostriches are happy. However, people aren't fucking oversized birds with tiny, stupid heads.

She swung around. 'Mom, explain it to me. Tell me why you insist Alan Silverman didn't do it – any of it – apart from the fact that he's Jewish. And rich.'

Maxine spluttered. 'Because... well, because Jews just don't do that kind of thing. You know that. I mean, I know Alan Silverman isn't really one of us – I mean, Doris said he grew up Afrikaans. In the Free State, somewhere. But still. Jews don't do that. Especially not *frum* ones.'

Tracy wanted to laugh, but she remembered that she'd thought exactly the same, until she'd done some research. She'd thought the Silvermans were freaks, but, when she'd googled "Jewish domestic violence", she'd been shocked to discover that there were homes and shelters for abused women in Israel. To be perfectly honest, her first thought was that those shelters must be for the Arabs, or for the other Jews – the ones from Yemen and Ethiopia and Nigeria.

But then she'd read that they were for everyone. And, there were even shelters for ultra-religious Jewish women with all their dozens of kids too.

'Mom, if these things don't happen in our precious community, tell me why there's a shelter for abused Jewish women right here in Johannesburg?' Tracy asked, sharing the titbit of information that had stunned her when she'd found it, quite accidentally, in her rapid research frenzy.

'Nonsense. I've never heard of such a thing. You must be mistaken,' Maxine said. 'I can't imagine why there's a need for such a thing.'

'It does exist. It's called Shalom Bayit. I don't know where it is, but it's run by Jewish Community Services. After the Silverman inquest is over, I'll pay them a visit and see if I can do a story about how widespread abuse is in our precious community. They're near here at Sandringham Gardens.' She paused. Something rang a bell... Something had been said in court about Sandringham Gardens and Brenda Silverman. What was it?

'Why? Why stir up more trouble? What's the point? If we have a shelter for Jewish women – and I really don't believe we do – then that's something that should stay in the Jewish community. It doesn't need to be broadcast to the world.' Maxine was off again.

'Mom, Jews are no different to anyone else. I admit, I was surprised to find out that there are abused Jewish women everywhere – America, England, Israel – and South Africa. But they will carry on being abused, because we have such a stupid culture of denial about it. We say it doesn't happen to us. Bullshit. Sorry. But it does. Jewish men are not angels, as you very well know. They're just men. I bet Brenda Silverman thought no one would believe her if she complained. I bet she thought she had no choice but to stay with that creep and be abused.'

'She wasn't abused, Tracy. She couldn't have been. That was just that druggie son of hers saying that. And you'll just make everything worse by putting more nonsense about our community in that paper of yours.'

'Oh, Mom, let's just drop it. Please. Just drop it. Here, what's this on TV? A rerun of *The Amazing Race*. Let's watch.'

She shook the packet of biscuits. Empty.

CHAPTER 3

Tracy's iPhone beeped. What was Kingmaker doing – WhatsApping her so early on a Sunday? On her weekend off, too. She found her glasses and read: "*T.T. – big stuff breaking re our man. NPA chief holding press conf. Mon. am. No details, but prob. gonna charge him. Heard corruption, etc, etc, etc. Trying to confirm. Check tomorrow's paper :)*".

Tracy turned up the volume on the radio and plunged into the shower. She loved the music they played on Sundays. All the old stuff her mother used to play on her cassette tapes in the car when she was little. She sang along loudly. She heard banging at the front door. Maxine must have left her keys behind again, along with whatever it was she'd come back to fetch. Tracy wrapped herself in her threadbare pink dressing gown, turbaned a towel around her head and dripped to the door.

'I'm coming; I'm coming.'

She pulled the door open and blinked. Yair Silverman, his fist raised, was about to pound on the door again.

'Hello, Red. Can I come in?'

She backed away. He followed her down the passage to the kitchen.

'I need to speak to you. Please,' he said as she shook her head.

She shook her head again. This was surreal. She was barely decent, puddling on to the floor with a towel around her head and the guy she thought she'd been madly in love with, but couldn't possibly have been, because she couldn't possibly love a rapist who screwed his own, poor retarded little sister, was standing in her mother's kitchen wanting to speak to her.

'I didn't do it, Red. It wasn't me,' he said.

She tried to read his expression, but his face was blurry.

'Wait. I can't talk to you like this. I'm going to put some clothes on.'

She fled down the passage to her room, used the damp towel from her hair to dry herself and pulled on underwear, jeans and a hoody. She dragged her fingers through her hair – shit, it would frizz like anything – put on her glasses and padded back to the kitchen, her sheepskin slippers slip-slopping on the tiles. Yair was reading the takeaway menus on the fridge door. She cringed – none of them were for kosher restaurants. He looked exhausted. His white shirt was rumpled, his black jacket stained. He'd removed his black hat and it sat accusingly on the kitchen table. A small blue *yarmulke* was clipped to his hair. He'd started growing a beard – or he hadn't shaved.

'What do you want?' Tracy asked.

'Red, please. You have to believe me. It wasn't me.'

She wanted to believe him. She really did. She glared at him and waited.

He stumbled on, 'My parents told me I did it. My father said I had a blackout and didn't remember, but that's not true. I've thought and thought about it. I even asked the therapists at the rehab centre to hypnotise me. I never laid a hand on Zivah. I swear. She's my sister, for heaven's sake. I might have used dope, but I'm not sick.'

'But you admitted that you'd had blackouts.'

'Once – only once.'

'How can you be so sure?' Tracy desperately wanted to believe him, but how could she?

'Please, Red, just listen to me. This time, when I was in rehab, I told the therapist about that blackout. It was quite a long time ago – I was still in school. It was after a party. I'd gone with Daniel and...'

'Daniel? He was always bad news.'

'He wasn't so bad. Anyway, I told the therapist that I'd had this blackout and she asked me to describe exactly what I did remember and all the symptoms afterwards, and she said it sounded like I'd probably been drugged with Rohypnol.'

'The date rape drug?' Tracy was sceptical. 'I've heard of girls having their drinks spiked with Rohypnol – we had a story in the *Express* about it a few weeks ago – but I've never heard of guys. Are you sure? Why didn't you say something? Why didn't you tell your parents? Why didn't you explain that in court?'

The look Yair gave her was so desperately sad, Tracy's heart turned over.

'My father was absolutely convinced I'd had too much to drink. He was furious with me,' Yair said. 'I didn't understand it myself. And anyway, who would have believed me? I can't prove that's what happened to me. I can't prove that I never had another blackout after that. All I know is that I didn't hurt Zivah.'

'Well, someone did,' Tracy said.

'I don't know who.'

'You knew that she was pregnant?'

'Only after – after the – you know. And Zivah was crying when she came home from the clinic. She'd wanted the baby. She thought it would be nice to have a real live dolly to play with.' He smiled sadly. 'I had no idea she had a boyfriend or anything. Then Dad sent me to rehab and, when I got out, well, I didn't want to upset her all over again, so I left it. She seemed perfectly happy. Please Red, say you believe me. Please. No one else does, except that therapist. *Shabbos* was a nightmare. I don't know what to do, where to go…'

She watched, horrified, as he cried. Huge gulping sobs wracked his thin frame.

'Are you hungry? Have you had breakfast?' God, she sounded like her mother.

He shook his head. She pulled out a kitchen chair. He collapsed onto it. She rummaged in the cupboard for a paper cup and plate, poured him some Coke and handed him an unopened packet of Eet-Sum-More.

'Sorry, that's all we have that's kosher. Oh, and here's some Kiri cheese too and I think these rice cakes are okay as well,' she said, noting the kosher stamp on the wrapper.

'It's fine. Thanks.'

She made herself a mug of coffee and nibbled on an Eet-Sum-More as he wolfed down the cheese and rice cakes.

She shifted uncomfortably on her chair and waited for him to speak. Her heart was thumping. After what seemed like forever, he raised his head and looked at her. His blue eyes pierced her heart.

'You do believe me, don't you?' he asked.

'Why should I? You walked out of court while Zivah was testifying – you looked as guilty as hell.'

'I couldn't bear it. I've always tried to protect her; she's so special and so fragile. When I heard she'd been pregnant – she miscarried, you know; it wasn't an abortion – I felt so, so useless. And in court, I felt like that all over again. So I left. Some brother I am, huh?'

'So who made her pregnant? Because, from the sound if it, he's still doing it to her. Although I suppose it's legal now she's over sixteen. That is, if it isn't you.'

'It's not me. It's not.'

'Well, whoever it was – is – deserves to go to jail. He raped her. She was just a kid. Is still just a child, really.'

'I know. I don't know what to do. I can't go near her. Dad

has chucked me out. Can we talk about something else?'

'Yair, you started it. You came here – how did you get past security, by the way?'

'A black hat is an open sesame in this area; didn't you know that?'

'Figures,' she said. Jeez, even the security guards were no different to anyone else around here – if you were Jewish, you were okay; if you were *frum*, you were beyond reproach. Tracy looked at him. He looked back. She felt herself blushing.

'You must believe me, Red. I need you to believe me. No one else does. You know me. You know I wouldn't do it; I couldn't do it.'

She wanted to believe him. So much.

'Yair, I don't know you. I know nothing about you, other than that you happened to go to my high school years ago and that you're a drug addict, who's been in and out of rehab.'

'I'm perfectly clean and sober now. I haven't even touched a beer for months and I can't remember when last I had a zol. I promise. And I'm not a rapist. For God's sake. I don't sleep with little girls. What do you take me for? Okay, don't answer that.'

The silence quivered between them.

'Red. I'm a good person. I'll prove it to you, if you'll let me.' He reached over the table, as if to take her hand. She grabbed her coffee mug and took it to the sink.

She wanted to believe him. She really did. But who else could it have been? Alan? Yair said he had seen his father abusing his mother. Surely Yair would also have had some indication that Alan was abusing his sister? Then again, who said Brenda Silverman really had been abused? Who was to say that what Yair saw – or thought he saw – was not just two consenting adults playing games? Some people liked it rough, she'd heard. Maybe he hadn't seen anything at all. Maybe he'd just imagined it. What kind of sick person thought *that* about their parents? It was too awful to think about. She was tired, so tired of the whole sick, awful, awful mess. She just wanted it all to go away. She wanted it all to be the way it used to be. Except...

She'd play pretend for now – she'd pretend they were back in high school and Yair was just a friend – maybe more. There was no inquest, no Alan Silverman, no Zivah. Just the two of them. Her high school fantasy. Just for today.

CHAPTER 4

CORRUPTION CHARGES FOR ALAN SILVERMAN?

By Tshepo Buthelezi, Political Editor

Millionaire businessman Alan Silverman is expected to be charged with corruption and a host of other crimes this week, sources close to the National Prosecuting Authority (NPA) confirmed to the *Daily Express* at the weekend.

The NPA is scheduled to hold a media conference this morning, but the subject of the conference has not yet been made public.

However, the *Daily Express* understands that investigations into Mr Silverman (50), founder and CEO of JSE-listed Silver Properties, have been going on for some time.

Silverman was once regarded as an intimate of many in the highest echelons of the ANC, many of whom he met while living in exile in London during the apartheid era. He is believed to be a major financial supporter of the ANC, as well as key individuals within the party.

He started falling out of favour with the party after backing former President Thabo Mbeki in the run-up to the 2007 ANC elective conference in Polokwane.

Mbeki lost the leadership of the ANC to Jacob Zuma at that conference. That led to Mbeki's recall as president and opened the way for corruption charges to be dropped against Zuma, and his (Zuma's) appointment as South African President.

According to Silver Properties' latest annual report, Khaya Silver Development – a Silver Properties-Khaya Trust joint venture – is involved in several RDP housing developments in Limpopo and Mpumalanga. Khaya Trust members include prominent members of the anti-Zuma faction of the ANC.

'They're going after Alan Silverman as a warning to others to toe the line at the ANC elective conference in Mangaung in December,' an ANC insider told the *Daily Express*.

Meanwhile, the inquest into the death of Silverman's wife, Brenda Silverman (44), continues in the Johannesburg Magistrate's Court this morning.

The rest of the report was a rehash of Tracy's *Weekend Express* story. She shoved the paper into her bag and hurried into court. The media benches were already filling up, as was the public gallery. The first three rows were packed with black hats on the left and *frum* women on the right. Alan Silverman was not in court. Arno van Zyl was back in his seat next to Gideon Feinberg. Marie du Toit wasn't there yet. Yair was. She almost didn't recognise him. He looked so different, clean shaven and without his black suit and hat. The *frum* women were staring at him, pointing and whispering.

'I'm surprised he hasn't been arrested yet,' the *Beeld* reporter whispered in her ear.

'They haven't had the press conference yet,' Tracy said.

'No man, not Alan Silverman. Him – the son. Over there. I wouldn't have thought he'd have the balls to show his face in court today.'

'Why not?'

''Cos of what he's been up to with his little sister – it's sick.'

Tracy bristled. 'Who says it was him? There's no evidence it was him.'

'Aw come on. What more evidence do you need? It had to be him.'

She swallowed her retort and pretended to study her notes. She couldn't defend him. She was a professional. She couldn't let the great pretend day they'd had yesterday compromise her objectivity. She'd think about it again tonight – about how they had sneaked off to Mr Price to get him civvies… and then to Schafflers Under the Trees Garden Cafe for lunch, where they'd sat at a secluded table in the beautiful garden. He'd had a salad, freshly picked from the garden, and a Coke. She'd had a brilliant homemade chicken pie and… She looked up as a sudden hush descended. Alan Silverman sat down next to Arno.

The court hummed again. Speculatively. Accusingly? Marie du Toit took up her position. The magistrate arrived. Showtime.

***

Dr Irwin Schwartz was sworn in. A short, beaky little man with bottle-black hair and an air of arrogant confidence. Mr

Feinberg led him gently through his testimony. Yes, Brenda Silverman had been his patient. For nearly fifteen years. No, she wasn't abusing the medications – they were not drugs – he prescribed for her. She was depressed. She couldn't sleep. She was in pain from a former knee injury. No, she had never given any indication that she was being abused. Yes, she was happily married. She told him so. Marie du Toit objected. Hearsay.

Then it was Marie du Toit's turn to question him. Schwartz crossed his arms over his pigeon chest. Painfully, slowly, testimony was dragged from his thin lips. No, he hadn't asked Mrs Silverman why she was depressed – she was rich, she was happily married, she had beautiful children and an active social life. People get depressed. Medication helps. No, she couldn't possibly have been abused. How did he know that? Because he knew – he was their family doctor, after all, and he'd never seen even the smallest bruise on her. They were a perfectly normal, happy, healthy family. No, she never received renewals of her prescriptions more frequently than she should have. He'd checked. She must have got more from other doctors. No, he didn't check on that – how could he? No, he never checked her blood levels for Methylphenidates or diazepam or opiates before refilling her prescriptions – why should he? He sent her for blood tests once a year to check on her diabetes. That's all. Based on his knowledge of her – and this was what he would call "informed speculation" – it was quite possible, no, probable, that Mrs Silverman had ended her own life either deliberately or – more likely – accidentally.

Ms du Toit stood and stared hard at Dr Schwartz. She remained quiet. Tracy mentally crossed her fingers that Ms du Toit wouldn't decide not to cross examine him further. He looked like such a smug weasel. She'd rather die before she'd go to him for anything, not even a broken fingernail.

Ms du Toit's cross-examination of Dr Schwartz continued. Yes, he knew Alan Silverman well. He knew the whole family. He was their family doctor. He treated them all – for coughs, colds, flu, that kind of thing. That's all. No, he'd never performed surgery on any of them. He wasn't a surgeon.

Yes, he had tried to help with Yair's addiction. He had recommended the rehabilitation facility. Yes, he had a very small shareholding in the facility. Yes, he'd signed the order to have Yair readmitted to the facility after Mrs Silverman died, and before that too. Twice. No, he hadn't checked Yair's blood or urine the last time. He could see Yair was using again. He knew him well… and he was a doctor. With thirty years' experience. It was obvious the boy had had a relapse. Addicts always relapsed.

Yes, he could see Yair sitting in the court. No, he wouldn't presume to speculate whether or not Yair was using drugs again at present. He hadn't spoken to or examined him. No, he didn't take instructions from Alan Silverman regarding the health and treatment of the Silverman family. Gideon Feinberg objected. Ms du Toit withdrew her question.

The prosecutor had nothing further for Dr Schwartz.

However, she would be sending a report to the Medical Council and the National Prosecuting Authority requesting an investigation into Dr Schwartz's treatment of Brenda Silverman, Yair Silverman and Zivah Silverman.

Yair smiled at her. Tracy gave him – and Ms du Toit – a mental thumbs up.

Tracy tweeted:

> Brenda not addicted. Committed suicide or overdosed – doctor #silvermaninquest

***

After the tea break, Tracy was surprised to see that a TV had been set up in the court.

'Wonder what that's for?' the *Beeld* reporter asked.

'Maybe they're going to show us the NPA press conference,' said *The Times* reporter.

'Hasn't started yet. Just got a WhatsApp from my political editor. They're running late,' Tracy said.

The court orderly called the next witness.

A slim young woman, a sleek dark cap of hair framing her white face, glided to the witness stand. She gripped the handrail; she stared at Alan Silverman.

He jumped to his feet. 'Avi!' he gasped.

CHAPTER 5

Aviva Silverman hadn't changed much since school. She'd cut her hair and looked like something from a Foschini Young Professionals catalogue in her knee-length black pencil skirt, shiny silver-grey blouse and short black jacket. She looked taller, probably because of those spiffy heels that had click-clacked across the court floor. However, that old, cold snootiness, that "I'm better than you" self-assured arrogance that had always made Tracy feel so small even though she'd towered over Miss Bloody Perfect Silverman – that was still there. In spades. Tracy poised her pen over her notebook, trying really hard to regain her objectivity.

Gideon Feinberg was on his feet, objecting. 'Aviva Silverman has been estranged from her family for almost three years. She has had no contact with any of them since she disappeared. She could not possibly have any evidence that would shed light on Mrs Silverman's untimely passing.'

'Let's find out, shall we?' said Magistrate Ngubane.

Aviva Silverman was sworn in. She confirmed that everything she had to say could be said in open court and reported in the media. She had thought about this for months – since her mother's death – but she had never seriously considered coming to South Africa to testify, until Friday when she realised that Zivah had testified in camera.

'I knew then that the full story about why my mother died would never come out. Not unless I came forward. So I managed to get on a plane yesterday, and I landed this morning. I came straight from the airport to the court and spoke to Ms du Toit. And here I am.'

'Aviva,' Ms du Toit said. 'When did you last speak to your father?'

'On the 25th of October 2008.'

'Why do you remember that date so clearly?'

'That was the night my father sodomised me – for the first – and the last time.'

Pandemonium. Gideon Feinberg was on his feet objecting. Alan Silverman was slumped over, his head in his hand. Yair looked shell shocked. The magistrate pounded her gravel, shouting to be heard. Aviva stood calmly in the witness stand, immune to the cacophony of disbelief and shock.

Tracy tweeted with shaking fingers:

Surprise witness Aviva Silverman claims dad Alan sodomised her #silvermaninquest

***

The magistrate issued a stern warning that no more such interruptions would be tolerated. Then she instructed Marie du Toit to continue.

'Was that the first time your father had sexually abused you?'

Gideon Feinberg objected again.

Before Ms du Toit could say anything, Aviva answered. 'He didn't abuse me. Let's call a spade a spade, shall we? And say what really happened. He raped me. Regularly. From the time I was thirteen years old.'

The court was stunned into silence. Tracy scrabbled on the floor to retrieve her pen again. Yair's mouth was hanging open. Gideon Feinberg was trying to pull Alan Silverman down.

Alan Silverman was shouting, 'I didn't; I didn't; I loved her. I never raped her.'

The magistrate banged her gravel and warned him to sit down and shut up. Aviva looked directly at him – and smiled.

Gideon Feinberg coiled in his seat, a snake ready to strike. Alan Silverman didn't move. Nor did Arno van Zyl. Then, coldly, clinically, in a flat voice totally devoid of emotion, Aviva Silverman took control of Court 15.

'The first time was the night of Yair's Barmitzvah party,' Aviva said.

Tracy gasped. She had been there that night. She'd seen Alan Silverman with Avi on the front patio. She'd felt so envious of the way Mr Silverman had his arm around Avi's shoulder, the way Avi had been pressed into his side. She'd wished her father loved her like that. She felt sick. She stared at the poised woman in the witness stand.

'It was the week after our thirteenth birthday,' Aviva Silverman continued. 'Daddy told me it was time for me to become a woman. Looking back, I realised that he had been preparing me for this since my Batmitzvah. Girls have a Batmitzvah when they are twelve; boys have their Barmitzvah when they are thirteen,' she said. So matter of fact. So cool, calm and collected. Tracy couldn't bear to listen. She clenched her pen and wrote down the horror that flowed from Aviva's pearly pink lips.

'I was so happy when he finally started taking notice of me. He would come to my room and sit on my bed and talk to me. And then he would stroke my hair, and hold my hand, and put me on his lap and tell me how much he loved me and how proud he was of me. I loved the way he really cared about me. He cared so much he even got Dr Schwartz to put me on the pill so my periods wouldn't be painful or interfere with my gymnastics.' Her face twisted in a grim smile, and then went blank again.

'And then, that night, when everyone had gone home after Yair's party, he came to my room again, but this time he taught me how to be a woman. I don't remember much about it – that first time. It's all a bit of a blur. But afterwards, when he came to my room again, I began to enjoy it.'

The court convulsed in a collective heave of shock,

disapproval and disbelief. The horror Tracy felt was mirrored over and over again in the public gallery. Even Ms du Toit and the magistrate seemed shocked.

Aviva swallowed, and then continued, 'It's taken me a long time to stop hating myself for that. Apparently, I'm not unique, not according to my therapist.' She paused. Took a sip of water. How could she remain so calm? 'Anyway, I would look forward to it.'

This was sick. Perverted. Tracy glanced at the public gallery. The *frummers* looked as anguished as she felt.

'Why wouldn't I enjoy it?' Aviva's voice never changed. There was no anger, no emotion whatsoever in her tone. Her very matter-of-factness tore through Tracy, shredding her soul. 'He never hurt me. I believed him when he told me how lucky I was that he was prepared to do this for me. He told me that this was what religious, observant fathers were supposed to do. He said the rabbi had told him we must do this together. He said a lot of fathers – *sheigetz* – what you'd call sinners, I suppose – he said they didn't obey the Talmud and the Rabbinical Laws and so their poor daughters were totally unprepared to be good wives and mothers.'

A wail issued from the public gallery. 'That's nonsense. That's an abomination.'

Tracy looked up to see who had shouted.

Aviva continued as if she hadn't heard it. Perhaps she hadn't. She almost appeared to be in a trance, unaware as her words plunged the court into a vortex of horror.

'I believed him. He was so clever and he went to lessons with the rabbi all the time. I believed him when he said it would just make my friends jealous if I told them about our special lessons. He said religious girls did not discuss sex with anyone anyway, except their own parents. And Mom wasn't well enough to discuss it with me. He said there was no need for me to attend the sex education classes at school. That was for the daughters of sinners and the unobservant, not for a Silverman. Yair could go, because he needed extra lessons, as usual.'

Yair went red, and gazed at his shoes. Aviva's cool facade cracked, slightly, just for a second.

Then she composed herself and continued. 'My God, sometimes I still can't believe how naive and stupid I was. I believed, I truly believed him. I believed that he loved me so much he was preparing me for my future husband, like all good religious Jewish girls should be prepared – are prepared.' She shook her head and her hair fell forward. She swept it back.

'I didn't care when he said I couldn't go to my Matric dance, not even with one of Yair's friends. Do you remember, Yair? You set it all up and Daddy said no and shouted at you for interfering. I was pretty cross with you too.'

Ms du Toit instructed her, gently, not to address her remarks to anyone in the courtroom, only to herself and the magistrate.

Aviva apologised and continued. 'I didn't care that I didn't have any real friends. I didn't need friends. I didn't need my brother. And I didn't care about my mother. I had Daddy. I loved him so much. He made me feel so... so... special and happy.'

Yair looked up at his twin, and shook his head. Disbelief? Sympathy? Guilt? Tracy couldn't tell.

'The girls at school all said how lucky I was that Alan Silverman was my father,' Aviva said. 'They all wished their fathers were as handsome as mine, and also came to their concerts, and prize givings, and events and everything.'

A memory stirred for Tracy. She remembered how Alan and Brenda Silverman hadn't attended when Yair had the lead in the school musical, and how upset he had been. Aviva, if she remembered correctly, hadn't auditioned for a part. Not that she would have got one. She couldn't sing to save her life.

'I'd look at the other girls' fathers,' Aviva went on, 'and I couldn't imagine anything worse than having to make love with those fat old men, even if the Talmud said you had to. I felt so sorry for them. So I didn't want to ask them about their lessons with their fathers; it would just have made them jealous about mine.'

She paused again, as if gathering herself together.

Tracy looked down at her notebook. She couldn't bear to watch Aviva, or Yair. Alan Silverman was a statue – a hard, marble, unflinching, unfeeling, emotionless statue. It was as if he couldn't hear what his daughter was saying.

'But sometimes,' Aviva said, 'if I wasn't pleasing him...'

She made quote marks in the air with her fingers. '… He would snap at me and call me Brenda.'

A collective gasp shivered through the court, quickly hushed.

'It was only when I got quite a lot older that I began to wonder if he really loved me, or if I was just a substitute for my mother, because we looked so much alike and she was so useless. But mostly he called me sweetheart.'

Yair's strangled gasp echoed around the court. 'He called my mom sweetheart, all the time. That's so sick,' he hissed.

Alan Silverman didn't move.

The magistrate banged her gravel and ordered Yair to be quiet or to leave the court.

'Anyway,' Aviva said, 'when I got to university, I finally began to realise that something was wrong – no, that's not it. I still loved what we were doing. But I realised that making love with your father wasn't… wasn't quite kosher. Sorry.' She looked at the public gallery. 'I can't think of another way to say it. I went to one of those lectures during initiation when they spoke about sex and Aids and that kind of thing. And the topic of incest came up. I couldn't believe it when they said that what Daddy and I were doing was incest. And that it was illegal. And a sin. I just couldn't believe it. How could something so… so… nice be wrong? And what about the Talmud and everything? So I used the university computers in the library to do some research on the internet.'

Aviva stopped. For a fleeting moment, her stony face

reflected the confusion she must have felt. For the first time in her life, Tracy felt sorry for Aviva Silverman.

'I realised my life was a lie. But I didn't know what to do. I couldn't tell anyone. I suppose I didn't really want to tell anyone. I mean, what was there to tell? I loved my father and, if I told, they'd stop us. And what if they took Daddy away from me? And I was scared that they'd send him – and me – to jail. I thought about asking Mom, but she was so out of it. She didn't care about anything except her pills. I even approached Yair once.'

She stopped. The court waited… and waited. Tracy glanced over at Yair. He was staring at his twin, anguish written all over his white face.

Finally, Ms du Toit asked, 'So what made you leave?'

Aviva swallowed. She closed her eyes. Then she looked up and stared directly at her father. 'As I said, he sodomised me.'

Alan Silverman stared back at her. Tracy couldn't believe how he could just sit there, so unmoved, unflinching. What was wrong with him?

'It was horrific,' Aviva said. 'I have never felt so much pain. I screamed and he just put his hand over my mouth and told me to be quiet. He said I didn't please him anymore. He said I was fat and flabby because I'd stopped gymnastics. But he'd made me stop. He said it was wrong for me to "flaunt my body" like that. But then he said he couldn't love me if he had to see and feel my fat boobs, so we had to do it this new way. That way, he could still love me. But I knew, I just knew. For the first time, I knew. I knew he didn't love me. That I was a fool. That he was sick. We were sick. I knew that, if I didn't get away, he'd destroy me. That I'd end up like my mother.'

She stopped.

Tracy felt drained. She glanced at her notebook. The page was blank. When had she stopped taking notes?

'So after he'd gone back to his room,' Aviva continued, in the same measured voice, 'I cleaned myself up as much as I could – I was bleeding. I packed a few clothes and I contacted POWA – People Opposing Women Abuse. They had posters on campus. They took me to a shelter. I stayed for a few days, but I knew he would find me. He's a powerful man, my father. So I left the country.'

Gideon Feinberg hauled himself to his feet. He looked ill. 'Your Honour. This is all very touching. But how do we know any of it is true? And what has any of this to do with Brenda Silverman's death?'

Marie du Toit jumped in. 'We're getting to that.'

The magistrate looked at her watch. 'I think now will be the perfect time to adjourn for lunch. Ms du Toit, I've given you a great deal of leeway, but I agree with Mr Feinberg. If you cannot show a link between what this witness had to say – much as I sympathise deeply with her – and Mrs Silverman's death, I will have to disregard her testimony. Meanwhile, I would like to warn the media that Miss Silverman's testimony is just that – untested testimony.'

Everyone filed out of the court in silence. Tracy looked

back. Alan Silverman was still in his seat. He fiddled with his iPhone.

Tracy checked her iPhone. Still nothing from Kingmaker about the press conference.

She tweeted:

Alan Silverman raped her repeatedly from age 13 says daughter Aviva #silvermaninquest

CHAPTER 6

The court was bulging. Aviva Silverman was back in the witness box, one perfectly manicured hand resting lightly on the rail in front of her. She had walked back into the court with Arno van Zyl. He touched Aviva's shoulder and started towards his seat next to Alan Silverman. Then he hesitated, turned and squashed himself on the media bench next to Tracy.

'Seems I may owe you an apology, Ms Jacobs, but not quite yet. Let's see what else the lovely Avi has up her sleeve.'

'You know her?'

'Of course. I've been with Silver Properties for ten years. I always was very fond of her. I wondered why she ran away – she and her dad seemed so close.' He grimaced. 'That doesn't sound so good now, does it? Or perhaps she's just delusional and vindictive – like her brother.'

***

'Aviva,' Ms du Toit said. 'When did you last see your mother?'

'The day before she died.'

Gideon Feinberg was on his feet. 'Impossible, Your Honour. Aviva Silverman was not even in South Africa, then – was she?' For the first time, Feinberg faltered.

Tracy smiled to herself.

'No, Mr Feinberg is quite correct,' Aviva said. 'I wasn't in South Africa. I was in Israel, where I've been since leaving South Africa. I knew my father could never come after me there. He'd probably have been arrested. Mom and I skyped.'

'But weren't you and your mother estranged?' Ms du Toit asked.

'Yes. I hated her. But that changed. I understood, and forgave her.'

'Perhaps you'd better start at the beginning, Aviva. When did you and your mother "make up"?'

'It was about three months before she died. A counsellor at the abused women's shelter where I volunteer – it's near Tel Aviv – she told me that a social worker from South Africa – Carol Aronowitz – had been in touch with her and was looking for me. She explained that Carol was with Jewish Community Services and that my mother was her client.'

Ping. The penny dropped. Tracy realised that Carol – the "friend" Stembiso Tshabalala said Brenda visited at the Sandringham Gardens Jewish Old Age Home, didn't exist; Carol, a social worker from Jewish Community Services at Sandringham Gardens, did. Brenda Silverman had been visiting a social worker on the quiet.

'Anyway,' Aviva said, 'I agreed to speak to her. If she'd

made such an effort to find me, it was probably the least I could do. I had every intention of telling her what I thought of her and what her precious husband had done to me.' Aviva stopped.

'Would you like some water?' Ms du Toit asked.

Aviva nodded. A court orderly handed her a glass and she sipped a little, and then placed the glass carefully on the witness stand while the court watched in hushed fascination.

'I was really shocked the first time I spoke to her,' Aviva said. 'She was so different. Together. Sober, you know? She told me – and Carol confirmed it – that she'd been clean and sober for weeks. Months.'

Alan Silverman looked up and stared, open-mouthed, at his daughter. A murmur drifted across the courtroom. Tracy gripped her pen.

Aviva didn't seem to notice the effect her words had had. She continued, 'Carol sent her for regular checks and she was absolutely clean. The day before she died, when I spoke to her, she was clean. I swear it. She would never have accidentally overdosed. She hadn't taken one of Dr Schwartz's happy pills for six months.'

Gideon Feinberg objected.

Ms du Toit interrupted, 'I have an affidavit here from Carol Aronowitz, a senior social worker with many years' experience in substance abuse, confirming that Brenda Silverman had not taken any narcotics for a period of six months prior to her death. I also have laboratory records confirming the results of a series of drug tests on Mrs Silverman. The last test was done three days prior to her death. It was negative.'

The court was buzzing. Everyone was speculating, chatting... The magistrate called for order.

Aviva looked smug. Tracy knew that look. She was about to drop another bombshell.

'And she would never have killed herself,' Aviva said, 'because she was going to be starting a new life and she was so excited and happy about it. She was leaving my father and was coming to Israel, with Zivah.'

'No,' Alan Silverman said. 'No. She would never have left me. No. Avi, you're wrong. Why are you doing this? Why are you saying these terrible things about us? About me?'

Tracy looked across the court at Yair. He looked stunned. Gideon Feinberg was on his feet. 'Objection; hearsay. This is just a figment of Miss Silverman's highly overactive imagination – as has been the rest of her sad story.'

Miss du Toit smiled. She looked like the proverbial cat.

'Your Honour, may we play a video recording for the court?'

Feinberg objected.

'You can make whatever objection you like later. After we have seen it,' the magistrate said. 'I will consider your submission with due care at that time. For now, I just want all the evidence.'

The court orderly pressed a button on a remote control device. The TV set lit up. He pressed another button on a laptop. Brenda Silverman appeared. She was smiling. Yair Silverman stared at the screen, his mouth open.

'Brenda, Brenda.' Alan Silverman whispered. 'Oh my God. Brenda.' Tears flowed down his cheeks and dripped into his grey beard.

***

'Hi Avi, how are you?' Brenda says.

Aviva's voice answers. 'Fine, Mom. It's so soon now. You excited?'

'Not yet. I'm worried about Zivah. I told her this morning. She cried. She doesn't want to leave her father. Or Yair. I don't know how to make her understand. She thinks he loves her. She thinks I'm jealous.'

'Mom, I would have thought the same. Really. You have to make her come. Kidnap her if you have to.'

Both women laugh.

Tracy glanced away from the screen to Alan Silverman. His pain and anguish were palpable. Tracy jerked her eyes away, back to the TV screen.

'Have you told Dad?' Aviva asks.

'Yes. Last night. It was horrible. He couldn't believe it. We had a bit of a screaming match. I was worried Zivah would hear. He said he'd never let us go. He said he loved me. He actually doesn't think he has done anything wrong. Nothing. He thinks he's a great father. He's…'

'You are kidding. Really?'

'He's sick, Avi. He must be to have done what he has. He wasn't always like that, you know. He was the kindest, most gentle man. I loved him. And he loved me. We were like Romeo and Juliet.'

'They died, Mom, in case you forgot.'

Brenda laughs. 'Well, you know what I mean. Everyone would always comment on how much we loved each other. And he was incredibly handsome, and clever. I could never understand what he saw in me.'

'I've seen photos of you, Mom. You were beautiful. Still are.'

'But I grew up – matured, if you like. He didn't like that. When I first met him, on the kibbutz, all the girls were crazy about him. And, when we got to England, there was... you might remember her? Aunty Annette? She always had a thing for your father. But he chose me. Now she can have him, like Camilla finally got Charles. Except she married Charles first.'

They both laugh.

Tracy giggled, recalling that Annette Davies Smedley's husband was Charles Smedley.

'I never really understood why he married me, but it was the happiest day of my life – until afterwards,' Brenda says.

'Why – what happened?'

'I don't think I should tell you this. I mean – he's your father.'

'Mom, he's the man who raped and abused me. He

sodomised me, for heaven's sake. You can tell me anything you like about him.'

Brenda closes her eyes. Then she opens them and stares directly at the courtroom.

'When we got back to our flat after the reception – it was wonderful, in the garden at Ruth and Ben Shapiro's beautiful home – he carried me over the threshold. It was so romantic. But then... then...' She stops. Tears stream down her face, clearly visible on the big screen. She blows her nose. 'Sorry, Avi. It's still so hard to talk about it.'

'Mom, what happened?'

'That was the first time he... ' She stops.

'He what, Mom? Did he abuse you? Is that what he did?'

Brenda nods.

'Did he hurt you?'

'Not so much – not that time. It was just oral sex.'

Tracy glanced at Yair. He had shut his eyes. Alan Silverman was staring at his clasped hands.

'Aw come on,' the reporter next to her whispered in her ear. 'Oral sex! Big bloody deal!'

'Shut up,' Tracy hissed back.

'I was so shocked,' Brenda says. 'I'd never even heard of that kind of thing before. I didn't know it then, but it isn't the worst thing in the world. It got worse later, but not always. It depended what he wanted.'

Brenda pauses, chews her bottom lip and continues. 'Anyway, after he finished, he walked out. I was so scared. I thought he wasn't coming back.'

'Why? Why did you want him back, after what he did to you?'

Tracy stared at the big screen. The whole court stared at the screen, except Alan. He kept staring at his hands. Tracy wondered why on earth Brenda had wanted a man who had just abused her to come back. It didn't make sense.

'I was all alone,' Brenda says. 'I was pregnant and alone. I had no money, no family and no friends. Who would have believed me? Anyway, what did I know? Maybe what Alan did, maybe that's what all married couples did? I didn't know. Anyway, I loved him. I adored him. Maybe it was me who was wrong. Maybe I just had to get used to it.'

Alan was sobbing now. Tracy couldn't look at him.

'I was so lucky that he loved me,' Brenda says. 'I mean, he'd married me even after I'd been so stupid to fall pregnant and everything.'

'You didn't get pregnant alone. He had something to do with it,' Aviva says.

'No, I was stupid, Avi. I was careless. Not that I'm sorry now, of course. You kids are the best thing I've ever done in my entire life. But back then... oh God, I was so scared. But it was my fault, all my fault that he was angry with me.'

'Falling pregnant is no excuse to abuse anyone,' Aviva says.

Tracy agreed.

'But was it really abuse? I mean. He never hit me. Not

then. Even though he felt I'd betrayed him.'

'Oral sex. No smacking her around. Not abuse,' declared the reporter next to her.

Tracy kicked him.

'You never betrayed him,' Aviva says. 'How did you betray him? By falling pregnant and having his children?'

'I was no longer the girl he fell in love with,' Brenda says. 'When he... did those awful things, and later when he started to really hurt me, it was like he was punishing me for not being the way I used to be. When I was pregnant and then you and Yair were born, and later Zivah – poor Zivah, she was a godsend to me, but look what I did to her. I was such a coward and I damaged my baby.'

'Mom! You can't blame yourself for Zivah.'

'No, Avi. I should have been able to deal with it like an adult. But what did I do? I popped pills – and I kept popping pills, even when I was pregnant. So it is my fault, but I'll take care of her now. I promise. And I'll make it up to you, to all of you. I swear.'

There was a long silence. The only sound in the court was the quiet sobs of Alan Silverman and his son. Tracy thought the recording had ended, and then Brenda started speaking again.

'I tried everything, you know, so we could go back to the way we had been. But it didn't happen and then, after Zivah, I knew there was no way it was going to happen. He'd started... He was sodomising me regularly by then.'

Tracy felt sick. This was absolutely horrific. In one way, she was relieved that Yair was being vindicated, but how terrible was this for him? Aviva was sitting, seemingly unmoved, near the TV screen, watching her mother intently.

Alan Silverman, a pasty grey, fiddled with his phone. Even from where she was sitting, Tracy could see his hands shaking. He licked his lips, stared at the phone, then looked back at the TV set.

'He said that doing it like that... He said he didn't want to risk having another baby, even though he'd made me have my tubes tied... But I think the real reason was that I wasn't young and firm anymore. And I'd never be young again,' Brenda says.

'You know something?' Aviva says. 'I've just realised something. I know what it is about Dad – why he did... does... what he does, not that it's any excuse. I swear he's a hebephile.'

A what? Tracy looked around the courtroom. Everyone looked as blank as she felt. She didn't even know how to spell the word. Alan Silverman was staring at the TV, clearly shocked, his phone clutched in his hand.

'A what?' says Brenda.

'A hebephile. I heard about it at the shelter. It's like a paedophile, except you're not into little children. You like girls – and boys, in some cases – who have gone through puberty, but aren't, you know, adults yet. I mean, there was you – and then your body matured he started doing perverted things to you. And then he went after me – I was you as you used to be. And when I got too grown up for him, he sodomised me too. And then Zivah, poor kid... '

Alan Silverman was on his feet. 'That's a lie. That's a goddamn lie. I'm not a pervert. Your Honour, please. This is *meshugga* – crazy. How can you make us listen to this nonsense? I'm not a pervert. I'm not a pervert. Avi, please. I'm not. I'm not!'

Aviva jumped up and, for the first time since taking the stand, emotion wracked her.

'Accept it, Dad – you're sick. You are a pervert. And a damn criminal. I was a child, for God's sake. Hebephilia is not accepted as a legal defence anywhere. You're a pervert, a bloody perverted... I hate you. I hate you. You're a pervert, a pervert... '

'Avi, no. No. You can't. I love you. Avi, I love you. Please.'

The magistrate told them both to be quiet.

Aviva collapsed into her seat, crying.

'Avi, please,' Alan said, and then he half stumbled, half ran out of the court.

Tracy started to get up to follow him, then sat down again. She'd catch up with the pervert later. Tracy felt her phone vibrate. She looked down. A WhatsApp from Kingmaker. At last.

'... I was sick too.' Brenda was still talking on the TV. 'I don't know how you can forgive me. I'm so sorry. I'm your mother. I should have protected you. I'm so, so sorry. And

Yair, my poor, sweet, gentle boy. I believed Alan, you know. I made myself believe him. I had to. It was so much – easier, I suppose – to blame him for Zivah. So we sent him away. Your father said it was for his own good. And Zivah's. I don't know how I'm going to admit to him how wrong I was and how sorry I am. I should have defended him, because I knew…. I knew he didn't make Zivah pregnant. He couldn't have. He was away – in Cape Town. He'd dropped out and Alan was so angry with him and you'd just disappeared. Yair only got back to Johannesburg a week or so before Zivah had the miscarriage. So it couldn't have been him. But I didn't want to believe it. I couldn't. Because if it wasn't Yair, then… '

Yair's sobs echoed around the court. Tracy could feel herself beaming at him and tried to compose her face. She felt as if a ton of bricks had been lifted off her heart.

Aviva's voice breaks in. 'Mom, it wasn't your fault. You didn't know…'

'I did, Avi. I've never admitted it before. To anyone. I did know. Deep down, I knew. I didn't want to. But I knew. About you. And before. All the other women. But when he was with them – and you – he'd mostly leave me alone – so I just took another pill and pretended everything was okay. What kind of a mother lets her husband do that to her daughter? What kind of a mother doesn't protect her children? I'm sorry, Avi, really, really sorry.'

'Mom, I could deal with it. But Zivah? She's a child, a baby. Maybe, if I hadn't left, he wouldn't have… It's my fault too.'

'Don't even go there, Avi. You couldn't have known. And it wasn't your responsibility. It was mine, and I... I still don't know when he started abusing her. I mean, after you left, he was furious. He really took it out on me – no, don't apologise; you did the right thing, leaving. But he... he got worse. He wouldn't leave me alone. All the time. I could be sleeping – or passed out – it made no difference, and he'd... I honestly never thought that he'd start on Zivah too. I should have... He didn't try very hard to hide it –he came to me directly from her room once. I could smell her on him. That was when I realised... when I knew I had to do something because I knew he'd use her and destroy her. I had to protect her, it was the least I could do after what I'd done to her. I should have protected you too. You were also just a child. I'm so, so sorry.' Tears stream down her face.

'It's okay, Mom. Really,' says Aviva. 'I've worked with enough abused women here to know that it's really hard, you know, to get away. I admire you, Mom. I do. You've managed to stop drugging – that's huge. I mean, I've never known you to be sober. After so long, it's frigging amazing. And now you're actually going to leave the bastard. That's so incredibly brave.'

Brenda wipes her eyes and smiles. 'You set the example, Avi. We're booked on the 8:30 flight. Direct to Tel Aviv. I'm scared. But a happy frightened, you know? I think I'm going to be free for the first time in my life. Thanks to you. I just hope Zivah won't kick up too much of a fuss. She keeps telling me he loves her more than he loves me.'

'I was exactly the same. But Zivah? How can he? He's unbelievable.'

'You said it yourself. He's sick. I should have got her away from him months ago. But Carol said I should take care of myself first so I could be strong enough to take care of her. It's been so hard, now that I'm sober... I locked my door once, but, when I came out in the morning, he was... It was the worst, that time. He hit me – he'd never done that before. So now I pretend to be passed out and sometimes... sometimes, he just stands and stares at me and then he leaves and it's such a relief, but then... then... he goes to her room, I'm sure of it but I'm too scared to check. God, you have no idea how much I hate him.'

In the distance, somewhere in the building, there's screaming. A woman is screaming. Then what sounds like people running. Then more screams.

***

'Oh, Avi. I love you too.' Brenda is still talking. 'I'll do my best to be a good mother to you and Zivah. And Yair too. Poor Yair, I allowed Alan to damage him too. I see that now. I'll make it up to you all, I will. I hope Yair decides to come to Israel too. It's a big decision for him. But he has to make it. Not me. It's time I start acting like a mother. I'll speak to him tomorrow, after I've had another go at Zivah. Then, if she doesn't listen, perhaps he can speak to her too.'

'Mom, I'll just be happy if we can be friends. I've never had a friend.'

'I love you, Avi. I'll see you soon.' Brenda blows a kiss.

'Love you too.'

The screen went black. Tracy forced herself back to the present.

Aviva stood and walked back into the witness box. She was cool and composed once again.

Marie du Toit turned to her. 'Why did you record this conversation?'

'I was testing new Skype recording software, so all my Skype calls were recorded and…'

A police officer burst through the side door of the court.

'Your Honour, Your Honour. Sorry, Your Honour. Alan Silverman has just – *fock* – sorry, Your Honour. He *focking* took a dive off the roof. Head *focking* first into the pavement! Just missed a *focking* hawker. He's dead.'

Tracy finished reading Thepo's WhatsApp message: "… totally exonerated. No evidence against him. They're letting him get away with it to protect their own f*** hides. Wonder what this travesty cost him. Now we're going to have to apologise to the bastard".

No, Tracy thought. No, we're not.

EPILOGUE
AVIVA

Johannesburg, 2012

The wind howled across West Park Jewish Cemetery. Aviva huddled into her anorak. She'd forgotten how cold Jo'burg could get in winter. Thank heavens Yair had a spare pair of long johns for her to wear under her long skirt, and she'd found a pair of her mother's boots, and two pairs of socks. Yesterday's surprise snow had melted – she'd never seen snow before – and now only the cold remained. She still couldn't believe it. It was over. He was dead. That was him in the pine box pallbearers from the Chevrah – and Arno – were pushing up the steep path to his grave. Dear, dear Arno. He could have stayed away. Everyone else had. She hoped the powers that decide these things would have had the sensitivity not to assign him a grave near Mom. They turned left.

'Mom's buried down there,' said Yair, indicating to the right.

Relief. She'd visit Mom's grave when this was over. She'd place a little stone on it. She hoped she could find a nice, round smooth one. Yair said they still hadn't put up a tombstone for Mom. Perhaps they could do it before she went back to Israel. They could pour concrete over his grave, for all she cared.

Zivah was whimpering again. She sounded like a sick puppy, poor little girl. She'd hardly said a word since they had told her and the Hatzollah medics had come and given her a sedative. They couldn't call Dr Schwartz. Zivah had eventually quietened down and fallen asleep, but Aviva would never forget the poor little girl's shrieking, that broken, agonised wail. It would haunt her forever. She put her arm around her little sister's shoulders. Zivah shrugged out of it and moved closer to Yair.

They climbed higher. The Brixton Police barracks perched on the *koppie* at the edge of the cemetery glowered down. Avi smiled. The cops would be watching over Daddy dear forever. She fingered the business card in her pocket. They'd found it clutched in Alan's hand after they had scraped him off the pavement. On the back of the card, scrawled in black ink, he'd written "Avi. I'm sorry. I'll always love you. Daddy". Aviva crushed the card.

They reached the grave. The Chev men lowered the coffin and stepped away, but not too far. They needed a *minyan* for this. Yair and the Chev's appointed rabbi made up two of the ten men required; Arno didn't count, because he wasn't Jewish. So eight of the Chev men had to stay. They shivered around the edge of the grave. That journalist – Red, Yair called her – stood a little way off. What was her name again?

She had been such a nerd at school. Yair seemed to like her, so maybe she wasn't so bad. Aviva wanted to cry. How stupid was that? However, funerals always made her cry – and she'd missed her mother's. She felt tears run down her face. She supposed that she really was an orphan now. Odd, really.

Yair recited the mourner's *kaddish*. He might have shed his black hat uniform, but he still knew the drill. He threw his obligatory three shovels on the grave. Aviva reached into her pocket, pulled out the crumpled business card and threw it into the grave.

The rabbi wished them a long life. They walked away, back down the hill. Arno put his arm around her. She leaned against him. He felt so safe. The journalist – Red – hugged Yair. The sun shone in the washed-out blue sky. The wind howled. It was over.

***

'Zivah, sweetie, listen. You have to come with me to Israel. There's no one else who can take care of you,' Aviva said.

Zivah glared at her. 'Yair can. I love Yair and Yair loves me.'

'Yair can't. He said so. Anyway, he might be moving to Israel as well, eventually. He can't sort out everything here with Arno and worry about you. So you come with me and Yair will come next year.'

Zivah shook her head. She was deathly pale. She insisted on wearing white.

'Daddy said I should always wear white.'

'Daddy's dead, Zivah. He can't hurt you anymore.'

Zivah's big blue eyes brimmed. 'Daddy didn't hurt me. Why do you keep saying that? Mommy said so too. He didn't; he didn't. He loved me. You're just jealous. Like Mommy. Daddy sent you away so he could love me. He loved me more than he ever loved you. He told me.'

Aviva caught her breath. How was she going to make Zivah understand?

'Zivah, Daddy shouldn't have loved you like that. It's wrong.'

'It's not. It's not! He loved me.'

She tried again. 'Zivah, only men and women who are married are supposed to love each other like that.'

'I know that. So Daddy and me, we were going to get married.'

Aviva stared at her sister, shocked.

'When I got bigger and could have a baby, Daddy was going to marry me,' Zivah announced.

'Is that what Daddy told you?'

Zivah thought for a while and then shook her head, her ponytail wavering. 'No, but he loved me. And men always marry the girls they love. I saw on TV.'

'But Zivah, Daddy was already married. To Mommy.'

'But he loved me. Not Mommy. Not you. He said so. And now I've finished school, so I'm all grown up. And anyway, Mommy's dead.'

A chill slithered down Aviva's neck.

'Zivah? Did you help Mommy with her insulin?'

'I always had to help her. She couldn't see the dial. I made her decaf coffee too, with lots of milk and Canderel, not sugar. I know how to make decaf. I'm not stupid.'

'Oh my God. Zivah. What did you do?'

'Nothing. She was going to take me away from Daddy. She wouldn't listen to me. She was just going to get sick. She said that if she had too much insulin it would make her sick. That's why I had to help her. I put some of her happy pills in her decaf too, because she was so upset. But she was wrong. She was so stupid. She died. I got such a fright.'

Aviva went cold. Who was this girl?

'But it all turned out okay, really, because now Daddy and me were going to get married. But you came back and then he died. It's all your fault. I hate you. And now… and now… I won't let you. I won't!'

'What are you talking about?'

'I won't let you take me to stupid Israel. We're getting married. Daddy's dead, so now Yair and me, we can get married. He loves me – not that stupid, ugly girl with the red frizzy hair. She shouldn't have come to Daddy's funeral. She hugged Yair. She shouldn't have done that. He loves me. He told me. He's going to marry me.'

Aviva felt hairs rise on the back of her neck. Had Mom been wrong? Did Yair...? Had Yair…?

'Zivah – did, does Yair love you like Daddy loved you?

Did he...? Does he...? Did he touch you?'

'You really are stupid, aren't you, Avi? Of course not.'

'When...? Why...? When did he tell you he would marry you?'

Zivah flicked back her blonde hair and glared at her sister.

'Shut up, Avi. You're trying to mess everything up again. Yair loves me; he said so.'

'When? When did he say so?'

'He always says so. You've heard him. But Daddy loved me more than anyone and two men can't love you like that, not at the same time. Everyone knows that. It's so wrong. So Yair never loved me like Daddy did.'

Aviva was stunned, but hugely relieved.

Tears suddenly ran down Zivah's pale cheeks, and she sobbed as if her heart was breaking.

'Now Daddy's dead and it's your fault; it's all your fault. If you hadn't come back... Daddy said I mustn't tell anyone, and I didn't. I didn't. I didn't. I didn't. They tried to make me; they tried – in court. They said it was Yair's baby, but I told them; I told them it wasn't. I told them it was my baby, mine. I never told our secret, Daddy and my secret. But Daddy's dead, so Yair doesn't have to be jealous anymore.'

'Yair's jealous? Why's Yair jealous?'

'Of Daddy and me. Daddy said so. After the baby, Daddy said Yair was jealous, so he had to send him away, like he sent you away so you wouldn't be jealous. Because Daddy loved me the best.'

The silence stretched between them, vibrating with tension and confusion. Aviva didn't know what to say. She looked away, replaying her little sister's tirade, trying to make sense of it all. Her head jerked back as Zivah, her voice soaring triumphantly, declared, 'Yair can love me like Daddy now and we'll get married and we will have our own baby.' She paused, and then spat, 'And you can't stop us, Avi. You can't take me away. I won't let you. I'll stop you. I stopped her, so don't you dare, don't you dare even try. Yair is mine; he's mine; he's mine, all mine, not yours, never. You go away. He doesn't love you. He loves me.'

Aviva backed away, horrified at the fury that had contorted her little sister's pretty, gentle face.

'It's okay, Zivah. I won't take you away.' Her mind raced. 'I'll just get someone else to take care of you. Okay?'

'Okay.' The girl smiled, and then frowned. 'But only until me and Yair are married. See? Because when you're married you have to be together all the time. Maybe you can come visit us. But you can't stay for long, because Yair and me don't love you.' Zivah giggled.

'Of course.'

***

Aviva and Yair walked into Carol Aronowitz's office in Sandringham Gardens. Zivah followed, pulling along a big red suitcase, a slightly grubby giant pink teddy bear under her arm.

'Carol, this is Zivah. Our little sister. Take care of her,' Aviva said.

Outside, Yair and Aviva held onto each other as they cried quietly together.

'Please take care of yourself, Avi,' he said. Then he kissed his twin gently on the cheek, turned and walked quickly to his car.

Tears streamed down Aviva's face as she drove the hired car back to OR Tambo International Airport.

AUTHOR'S NOTES AND ACKNOWLEDGEMENTS

The idea for *A Beautiful Family* had its roots in a remark my late father made many years ago. We were visiting Israel and one evening, while strolling through Tel Aviv, we saw some prostitutes plying their trade on the opposite side of the road. "Jewish women don't do that," he said. I was a little surprised too.

Many years later, my husband – who was a member of our local Community Police Forum – told me that the police Station Commander had said that a particular problem in our precinct was domestic violence in the Orthodox Jewish community. Like my husband, I was stunned. Things like that just didn't happen in the Jewish community. So it was not surprising when, in 2010, the community was rocked by reports of a Jewish paedophile who had been arrested (and subsequently jailed) for "grooming" his own daughter as well as a 13-year-old girl from a religious family. But almost immediately, the community sought to distance itself from the man: he was mentally unstable; he was a crook who didn't pay his bills; he was an aberration - he really wasn't one of us.

I am well aware of the scourge of domestic abuse and violence in South Africa. But I'd never associated this with my community. Whenever the subject was raised – a dinner table discussion resulting from a news report on a brutal rape, a radio programme during the annual Sixteen Days of Activism against women and child abuse, and so on, the unspoken assumption was always that sexual abuse was confined to poor communities or perpetrated by uneducated men; that this type of violence was a social ill fuelled by poverty, ignorance, over-crowding and substance abuse. It didn't happen in the leafy suburbs, and certainly not in "good" Jewish families.

Or did it? My daughter, who had worked at the Teddy Bear Clinic in Johannesburg – a wonderful NGO that deals with sexually abused children – confirmed that many of the children referred to Teddy Bear came from what could loosely be termed as "middleclass" families and communities.

Could the Jewish community really be immune to such a pervasive social ill?

I googled "Domestic Abuse in South African Jewish families". Not surprisingly there wasn't much to be found, at least not with regard to South Africa. However, what I did find was illuminating and set me on the path to formulating my themes for *A Beautiful Family*. In particular, I drew heavily on (and I am deeply indebted to):

- *Perspectives of Orthodox, Jewish women regarding the*

perceived effects of Jewish religious and cultural values on women's choices in abusive relationships by Kim Lindy Serebro. This enlightening research report was submitted to the Faculty of Humanities, University of the Witwatersrand, Johannesburg, in partial fulfilment of the requirements for the degree of Master of Arts (Community-Based Counselling) degree in 2011.

- *Domestic Abuse and the Jewish Community: Perspectives from the First International Conference.* Edited by Rabbi Cindy Enger and Diane Gardsbane. Published by The Harworth Pastoral Press and co-published simultaneously as the *Journal of Religion and Abuse, Volume 6, Numbers 3 and 4 2004.* This book contained information about domestic abuse in Jewish communities from around the world.

- Of particularly interest was the chapter: *"Domestic Violence in the South African Jewish Community: A Model for Service Delivery"* by Brenda Solarsh MA, MS (then the Director of Social Services for the Johannesburg Chevrah Kadisha and co-founder of the Johannesburg Shalom Bayit project) and Jane Frankel (a Social Worker at Jewish Community Services, a division of the Chevrah Kadisha in Johannesburg).

Any misinterpretation of these sources is entirely due to my own inadequacies.

I also trawled the internet in search of information about paedophilia, incest and the sexual abuse of sons by their mothers. This took me to some interesting and, at times (for me), harrowing websites. (I am eternally grateful that no one took it in to their heads to monitor my web surfing at this time).

My research led me to a term I had never heard before: "hebephile". I realised that this was exactly the condition I had imagined for Alan. He was not a paedophile in the widely accepted sense of the word, because he did not prey on small children.

At one point, while trying to find out more about this aberration, I found myself in an online hebephile chatroom. I stuck around long enough to realise that most of the participants considered their sexual predilection perfectly normal – even beneficial to their victims.

Researching incest was even more horrifying, particularly what I learned about mother/son sexual abuse. I drew on the descriptions and discussions of incest I found on several medical and psychological websites as well as in research papers, when developing Alan's character. It's believed that mother/son incest is far more unusual than other types of incest (brother/sister or father/daughter). However, some researchers believe that could also be because, like male rape by a female, it is less likely to be reported.

And so on to the writing of *A Beautiful Family*.

I am deeply grateful to:

Author **Jo-Anne Richards** and **Richard Beynon** of **Allaboutwriting** for helping me to find my fiction voice and giving me the encouragement I needed to tackle a full-length novel. I drew on many of the hints and tips imparted during their lively Creative Writing course and I believe *A Beautiful Family* is a much better novel as a result. Richard's insightful critique of my initial draft resulted in *A Beautiful Family* being entirely rewritten – for the better, I believe. Any shortcomings in the novel, however, are entirely due to my own inadequacies.

Francois Engelbrecht, my colleague and friend, a hugely talented, creative and literate designer, who volunteered his time to come up with a cover for *A Beautiful Family* that is absolutely perfect. Words cannot express my gratitude deeply enough.

My friend and walking partner, **Janet Perch**, for her endless encouragement and for listening politely as I bent her ear and bounced my thoughts off her while we tramped tens of kilometres through Johannesburg's streets. Another friend whose literary opinion I respect enormously, **Frances Richardson**, also gave me much appreciated encouragement and support.

A colleague, **Dylan Mclaren**, assisted me with some of the legal issues in the book; and **Dr Hilda McLoughlin** checked the pathologist's testimony and corrected my mistakes. Any factual medical and legal errors that may still be present in the book are entirely my own fault.

My thanks and love to my family: My sensitive, caring Social Worker daughter, **Jessica**, who gave me support, love, insights, information, suggestions and extremely useful feedback; my older daughter, **Laura** – warm, caring and observant – who enabled me to see and experience at first hand the incredible warmth and support that is such a remarkable feature of sections of Johannesburg's religious Jewish community; and my long-suffering husband **Poen**, who put up with my mid-life crisis decision to write a novel and go back to class to figure out how; encouraged me to keep writing and to get my book published; and meticulously proof read the entire manuscript – twice.

Finally, I would like to pay tribute to the many, many strictly observant Jewish men and women in Johannesburg who embody a true spirit of *tzedakah* (best translated as justice or righteousness, but also often meaning charity); as well as organisations like the Chevrah Kadisha and Jewish Community Services for their amazing work within the Jewish community – and often beyond.

I so enjoyed writing my first novel that I have started on a second. It features several of the characters from *A Beautiful Family*. I hope to publish *When Time Fails* in 2015.

Marilyn Cohen de Villiers

GLOSSARY

Alter kocker	(Yiddish) old fart
ANC	African National Congress
Baas	(Afrikaans) Boss/Sir
Babbeleh	(Yiddish) Baby
Bagel	(Yiddish) A ring-shaped bread roll, but also a pejorative term for a spoilt Jewish youngster (the male equivalent of a *kugel*)
Barmitzvah	(Hebrew) Religious ceremony marking the coming of age of a thirteen-year-old Jewish boy
Baruch Ha'Shem	(Hebrew) Blessed be name of the Lord – used like "God willing"
Bashert	(Yiddish) Destiny/Fate
Batmitzvah	(Hebrew) Religious ceremony marking the coming of age of a twelve-year-old Jewish girl
BEE	Black Economic Empowerment
Beth Din	(Hebrew) The rabbinical court of Judaism
Bimah	(Hebrew) The platform/podium in the synagogue from which the Torah is read
Bobba	(Yiddish) Grandmother/Granny
Bobbemyseh	(Yiddish) Old wives' tales/Nonsense
Boer War	South African War fought between the Boer Republics and Great Britain; 1899-1902

Boer/boertjie	(Afrikaans) Literally: farmer. Often used to refer to a person of Afrikaans heritage
Boereseun	A farm boy or an Afrikaner
Bris	(Hebrew) Circumcision ceremony, performed on a boy on the eighth day after birth
Brocha	(Hebrew) Prayer/Blessing
Bru	Brother (affectionate term)
Bubbeleh	(Yiddish) Term of endearment (like dear; pet; honey)
Cheder	(Hebrew) Jewish studies (often in preparation for Barmitzvah or Batmitzvah)
Challah	(Hebrew) Literally: bread. Here used to refer to the plaited bread eaten on the Sabbath, which is also sometimes referred to as a *kitka*
Chommies	(Afrikaans) Friends
Chupah	(Hebrew) The canopy used during a Jewish wedding ceremony; the wedding ceremony itself
Dankie	(Afrikaans) Thank you
Dingus	(Afrikaans slang) Thing
Doek	(Afrikaans) A square cloth, usually worn by black women to cover their hair
Dominee	(Afrikaans) Pastor/Reverend
Dorp/dorpie	(Afrikaans) Village/hamlet
Dreck	(Yiddish) Something that's cheap; shoddy; useless
Feiglings	(Yiddish) Cowards
Frum/frummer	(Yiddish) Religious/Religious person

Gonif	(Yiddish) A thief; crook; swindler
Hoërskool	(Afrikaans) High school
Ha'Shem	(Hebrew) God; literally: "The Name". Jews consider that saying, or even writing, the name of God is blasphemy
Hora	Israeli folk dance performed in a circle
Jislaaik	(Afrikaans) An exclamation of surprise
Kaddish	(Hebrew) A blessing
Kaffir	(Afrikaans) A black person (extremely pejorative)
Kasher	(Hebrew) To make kosher
Kaynahora	(Yiddish) Expression used to ward off the evil eye
Khaya	(Zulu) House. Often used to refer to domestic workers' quarters
Kibbutzniks	(Hebrew) Permanent members of the kibbutz community
Kinderlach	(Yiddish) Children
Kitah	(Hebrew) Class/Grade
Kitah Aleph	(Hebrew) First Grade (Grade A)
Kitah Bet	(Hebrew) Second Grade (Grade B)
Kitah Gimmel	(Hebrew) Third Grade (*gimmel* is the third letter of the Hebrew alphabet)
Klap	(Afrikaans) Smack
Kleinbaas	(Afrikaans) Literally: little boss or little master. Usually used by a black employee when referring to the male employer's (the *baas'*) son
Kleinboetie	(Afrikaans) Literally: little brother. Usually used to refer to the younger brother in a family
Koppie	(Afrikaans) A small mountain/hill

Kosher	(Hebrew) Food that complies with the Jewish dietary religious laws. By extension, anything that is pure, good, legitimate and genuine
Kugels	(Yiddish) Spoilt teenage Jewish girls
Laaities	(Afrikaans) Little boys
Laerskool	(Afrikaans) Primary/Junior school
Le chaim	(Hebrew) To Life. A toast when drinking, like "cheers"
Lokshin	A literal pronunciation of the term "location", usually referring to dormitory townships for black workers on the outskirts of white towns
Lox	(Yiddish) Smoked salmon
Macher	(Yiddish) An important or influential person
Mazeltov	(Hebrew) Congratulations; well done
MEC	Member of the Executive Committee – the "Cabinet" of the Provincial Government
Melktert	(Afrikaans) Milk tart – a popular dessert
Meneer	(Afrikaans) Mister/Sir
Menorah	(Hebrew) The seven-branch candelabra used to celebrate the festival of Hannukah
Mensch	(Yiddish) Man of fine qualities; a real man
Meshugga	(Yiddish) Crazy/Mad
Mevrou	(Afrikaans) Mrs
Mikvah	(Hebrew) Bath used for the purpose of ritual immersion
Minyan	(Hebrew) The quorum of ten men required for holding public prayers

Mishpocheh	(Hebrew) The entire family network of relatives by blood or marriage
Mlungu	(Zulu) A white person (can sometimes be used pejoratively)
Momzer	(Yiddish/Hebrew) A bastard/illegitimate child
Morah	(Hebrew) Teacher
Moshav/ moshavim	(Hebrew) A collective farm/s similar to a kibbutz
Mohel	(Hebrew) The religious man who performs ritual circumcisions
Naches	(Yiddish) Pride; pleasure; good fortune
Nats	Members of the National Party
Nebbish	(Yiddish) A loser
Neft	(Hebrew) Paraffin
Neshomeleh	(Yiddish) Sweetheart/Darling
Nu	(Yiddish) Well? So?
Oke	(Afrikaans) Man/Guy/Bloke
Olim	(Hebrew) Immigrants to Israel
Ou	(Afrikaans) A boy or man
Ouma	(Afrikaans) Grandmother
Peter Hain	Anti-apartheid activist and chairman of the "Stop All Racist Tours" campaign to isolate South African sport
Pisher	(Yiddish) An inexperienced or insignificant person
Ratel	(Afrikaans) A type of armoured military vehicle
Rebbetzin	(Yiddish) Rabbi's wife
Rock/ Rockspider	Pejorative names for Afrikaners

Rooi Rus	Brig. Theuns Swanepoel – one of the most feared interrogators of the SA Security Police in apartheid South Africa
Sabra	(Hebrew) Native Jewish Israeli
Schmuck	(Yiddish) A fool; a jerk
Schmooze	(Yiddish) To chat up
Shabbos	(Hebrew) The Sabbath (from Friday evening to Saturday evening)
Sheine	(Yiddish) Beautiful/Pretty
Sheitel	(Yiddish) Wig worn by married Orthodox Jewish women in accordance with the tradition of covering the hair as a sign of modesty
Shiksa	(Yiddish) A non-Jewish woman (often used pejoratively)
Shiur	(Hebrew) A Talmudic study session, usually led by a rabbi
Shivah	(Hebrew) The seven-day period of mourning after a close family member's death
Shmo	(Yiddish) A fool
Shmattah	(Yiddish) A rag
Shofar	(Hebrew) A ram's horn blown in a synagogue during services for Rosh Hashanah and Yom Kippur
Shul	(Yiddish) Synagogue
Shtupping	(Yiddish) Vulgar term for intercourse
Shvartze	(Yiddish) A black person. Often used pejoratively (see kaffir)
Shyster	(Yiddish) Unscrupulous person
Simcha	(Yiddish) A joyous celebration
Skinnering	(Afrikaans) Gossiping

Stompies	(Afrikaans) Cigarette butts
Tallis	(Hebrew) A prayer shawl, usually in white silk with fringes, worn over clothes
Tassies	Cheap wine
Toppie (old toppie)	(Afrikaans) Old man
Totsiens	(Afrikaans) Goodbye
Treif	(Yiddish) Non-kosher foods
Tuches	(Yiddish) Backside/Bottom/Buttocks
Tzimmis	(Yiddish) A sweet dish usually made with carrots, dried fruit and potatoes
Tzitzit	(Hebrew) The fringes at the corner of a prayer shawl usually worn by Orthodox Jewish men under their shirts
Ulpan	(Hebrew) School for the intensive study of Hebrew
Verkrampte	(Afrikaans) Politically conservative
Voetsek	(Afrikaans) Bugger off/Get lost
Windgat	(Afrikaans) Wind bag (pejorative) – usually someone who talks too much
Wits	University of the Witwatersrand
Yad Vashem	The large Holocaust museum in Jerusalem
Yarmulke	(Yiddish) A skullcap
Yeshiva	(Hebrew) A Jewish theological college
Yid/Yiddisher/Yidden	(Yiddish) Jewish people
Yok	(Yiddish) A non-Jewish man (pejorative)
Yom HaShoah	Holocaust Remembrance Day
Zaidah	(Yiddish) Grandfather/Grandpa/Gramps

Made in the USA
Coppell, TX
23 September 2021